SUCCUBUS ARISING

The door slid open. I heard the rain and wi   ide. I woke but couldn't move. My body   felt totally awake within it. I cou   ow and creaking.

At that moment   across the floor to lea   ened me first: mold and de   s mixed together. She was dressed   air like dirty straw, her limbs sturdy and mus   . I tried to scream but no sound emerged.

The hag smiled at me. She climbed on top of me and sat on my chest. She leaned over, her lips close to mine, and I knew she intended to steal my breath. I struggled with my paralysis.

"Get off the island," she hissed.

PRAISE FOR KIM WILKINS AND
THE AUTUMN CASTLE

"Strikes a tantalizing balance between pastoral and grotesque."
—*Publishers Weekly*

"Kim Wilkins is delightful and talented . . . Draws the reader into a world of welcome magic and dark imaginings."
—CHARLES DE LINT, author of *The Onion Girl*

"Exotic, vivid and believable . . . the perfect blend of sharp-edged realism and lyrically rendered folklore."
—LYNN FLEWELLING, author of
Hidden Warrior and the Nightrunner series

BOOKS BY KIM WILKINS

The Autumn Castle

Giants
of the
Frost

KIM WILKINS

WARNER BOOKS

NEW YORK   BOSTON

Copyright © 2006 by Kim Wilkins
Excerpt from *The Autumn Castle* copyright © 2006 by Kim Wilkins

Cover design by Don Puckey
Cover illustration by Shasti O'Leary Soudant
Book design by Giorgetta Bell McRee

Warner Books

Time Warner Book Group
1271 Avenue of the Americas
New York, NY 10020
Visit our Web site at www.twbookmark.com

Printed in the United States of America

First Paperback Printing: January 2006

10 9 8 7 6 5 4 3 2 1

Ian
Bróthir minn gerthi mér eyju.
Ek fyldi hana sögum.

Acknowledgments

This book provided some of the toughest research challenges I've yet had to face. I claim all errors, intentional and unintentional, as my own. However, I'd like to offer my sincerest thanks to the following people for their patience and expertise.

For assistance regarding climatology and meteorology, boreal forest flora and fauna, and general scientific information and logic, thanks to Hamish McGowan and Gerd Dowidheit from the University of Queensland, John Volder of Jan Mayen Station, Fiona Gray and Rob Thompson of the Bureau of Meteorology, Katherine Howell, Lynne Green and David Wilson.

For assistance with Old Norse language and literature and modern Norway and Norwegian language, thanks to Martin Duwell, Kári Gíslason, Stefanie Würth, Vidar Skrindo and Hanne Grønsund.

For island design, office space, and all assistance with boats and nautical knowledge, thanks to my brother Ian Wilkins.

For virtual horse-wrangling, thanks to Janine Haig.

For writerly support, thanks to Kate Morton, Louise Cusack, Traci Harding, Kate Forsyth, Paul Brandon, Drew Whitehead, Selwa Anthony, Faye Booth, Stephanie Smith and Jo Fletcher.

Thanks, too, to my family for the practical stuff, and for the not-so-quantifiable stuff: Mirko, Mum, Luka.

I

Almighty love takes the sons of men,
and makes of wise men fools.

—*Hávamál*

Prologue

[Asgard]

S he had returned, and Vidar knew this before he opened his eyes. Sleep swam away and the morning cold sucked at his nose and cheeks. His senses prickled. Halldisa was nearby. *Twice-born.* Most mortals came upon the earth, spent their lives, and ceased to exist forever after. But Vidar had been made a promise: Halla would be twice-born. All he had to do was wait.

Centuries of waiting.

And then this morning.

He rose and pulled on his cloak, cracked open the door and peered out. The deep slope of Gammaldal to the north-east hid the expanse of Sjáfjord. Mist hung low in the valley and the grass was jewelled with frost. Nobody in sight. No watching eyes to report back to his father, no waiting tongues to say, "I saw Vidar drawing runes in the seeing-water." The fjord would be cold, but the thought of Halla warmed his blood.

He stripped to the waist, waded into the shallows and waited—the water icy around his ribs—for the surface to still. He crossed his hands over his chest. Not a movement now, not a breath. He feared that the excited beat of his heart would make the water pulse and jump in harmony. But soon the surface became motionless.

Vidar lifted his hand. With a graceful movement, he traced a circle in the water. Steam rose where he drew. He waited, glancing all around him for watchful eyes, then focused and drew four runes in the circle. His breath crystallized on the morning air as he said her name: "Halldisa."

At first he could only see his own reflection, dark hair and dark eyes and the pale morning sky behind him. But then another face formed in the water and he recognized her instantly. Storm-eyed, snow-haired. Seeing her face robbed him of his breath. He drew another rune, and whispered, "Where are you?"

Danger, extreme danger. His heart chilled colder than the fjord. *Odin's Island.* He glanced to the east, toward the silver roof of his father's hall, which was hidden behind the miles of misty hills and wooded valleys Vidar had put between him and his family. Memories streamed through him: blood and fire and the helpless shrieks of mortal suffering. "There is no love, Vidar," his father had said. "There is only fate."

"Vidar!"

A woman's voice. His young bondmaid, Aud, had woken and found him missing. With a skilled hand he banished his seeing magic and turned to her, deliberately relaxed. "Good morning, Aud."

"What are you doing?" she asked, coming to the edge of the water.

"Catching fish."

Her smile said she didn't believe him.

He waded from the fjord, dripping and cold. "Come, Aud. You may draw me a hot bath and forget you saw me catching fish in Sjáfjord."

"I won't forget," she said, "but neither will I tell." She clearly relished being part of his secret.

He spoke no further and she walked beside him in her usual besotted silence. His mind turned the image of Halla over and over; desire warmed his veins, filled his fingers and swelled his heart. This time he would make her his.

This time he would protect her from the brutal rage of his father.

One

※ ※

[Midgard]

※

This is my story and it's a love story. Mad, really, as I'm a woman who at the slightest provocation has always cursed lovers for fools. I remember one evening, drunk out of my skull after splitting up with Adam, declaring loudly to all assembled at Embankment station that "Victoria Scott does not believe in love." And yet, not long after this declaration, not long after the messiest broken engagement in the history of messy broken engagements, this story commences.

This is my story. It's a love story and it goes like this.

I found myself on the supply boat *Jonsok* out of Ålesund, heading for Othinsey, an island at zero degrees forty minutes east, sixty-three degrees ten minutes north, or about two hundred nautical miles off the Norwegian coast. I was sick, sick, sick. The crew kept telling me to get up on deck for fresh air, but the fresh air was awash with rain and salt spray. Instead, I lay down, feeling nauseous, on a threadbare sofa in the aft cabin, listening to the hissing of a radio that baffled my every attempt to turn it off.

The ten-hour journey was made worse by the deep pit of misgivings that I mined while I should have been sleeping. Had I done the right thing breaking up with Adam? Should I have accepted so readily this traineeship at an isolated meteorological research station? Was it good sense to continue with my doctorate when academia had long since become dreary and stale for me? My mother had squawked a horrified "No!" on each count. But my mother, bless her heart, was still waiting on the big lottery win she insisted would solve all our problems. In the meantime, I had to try out some solutions of my own.

Eventually the waves gentled, the boat slowed and I knew we must be entering coastal waters. I ventured up the narrow metal stairs to the cold deck for my first glimpse of Othinsey.

We cruised through a passage between two enormous cliff faces into the still waters of Hvítahofud Fjord. I saw grey water and grey rock, dark green grass and trees, and painted red buildings with white windowsills. Those buildings made up Kirkja Station. Here, at the age of twenty-seven, I was about to commence my first job that didn't involve burning my fingers on a temperamental coffee machine. I was excited and terrified all at once, and felt a strong sense of . . . "destiny" is probably too loaded a word. Perhaps what I felt was a strong sense of being in the right place at the right time.

A tall, neat man with a close grey beard greeted me off the boat. "Good afternoon," he said, hand extended to help me onto the jetty. "I'm Magnus Olsen, the station commander. We spoke on the phone."

"Victoria Scott," I said. "Nice to meet you." I picked up my suitcase and turned, nearly running into a young man hurrying down the jetty. Magnus steadied me with his arm around my waist.

"Sorry," the young man said, indicating the *Jonsok*. "I'm eager to have something from the boat." He was about my age, rangy and sandy-haired, and attractive in a boyish way, and he spoke in the same faintly accented English as Magnus.

Magnus presented me for inspection. "Gunnar Holm, meet Victoria Scott. Gunnar's our IT man, and he's also in charge of your induction. He'll show you around the station tomorrow."

"Remind me to tell you about the ghosts," Gunnar said with a mischievous grin, hurrying onto the boat.

I smiled politely, supposing this was some kind of frighten-the-new-girl joke and wondering why Magnus still had his hand resting in the small of my back. We approached the assembled buildings of Kirkja Station, which all sat on a concrete slab abutting a dense pine forest on two sides. The fjord curved around the other two. The impression was one of civilization vainly making a stand against the deep waters and the ancient trees.

"Come on, Victoria. I'll introduce you to the others," Magnus said. "They're all at the mess hall having Wednesday afternoon drinks. It's one of our traditions."

I met all eight people at Kirkja that afternoon, and—sleep-deprived, bewildered—forgot their names as soon as they were spoken. I know them all now, of course, and it was Frida Blegen who made the biggest impression on me. Like me and Gunnar, she was in her twenties (everyone else was well past forty), and she had spiky hair, a swarthy complexion and eel-like lips. As Magnus stood there pointing out faces and assigning them names, I determined to try out some of my beginner's Norwegian. I said, "*Hyggelig å tre-ffe deg,*" which means something like "Nice to meet you." Frida snorted with laughter and I never spoke another word of Norwegian in my whole time on the island.

Finally, Magnus showed me to my cabin, one of nine laid out three-by-three behind the station. Mine was in the farthest corner to the northeast, crowded on two sides by the dark forest. I put down my suitcase at the front door.

"I assigned you this cabin as it's quieter here," Magnus explained, extracting the key from his pocket and unlocking the door. "In light of the sleeping problem you mentioned on your employee information form."

"Oh. Thanks for that." I'd had to fill out a four-page document about myself and had listed my chronic insomnia in the box headed "psychological disorders for which you have received treatment."

"The rec hall can get very rowdy at night." He opened the door and stood back to let me through, giving me six inches of distance from him for the first time since I'd arrived. "I'll leave you to it. You probably want to unpack and settle in."

I peered into the cabin. The words "chilly" and "dingy" sprang to mind. "Um . . . yes."

"I'll see you in the office at 8:00 A.M. sharp. It's downstairs in the admin building." He gave me a charming smile along with the key to the cabin. "I hope you'll like it here at Kirkja. Sleep well." With a wave of his hand, he left me alone.

The cabin had clearly been designed with scientists, not artists, in mind. Four perfectly square rooms, all of precisely equal size, stood left and right off a narrow hallway. Left, kitchen; right, lounge; left, bathroom; right, bedroom. There was a pleasing regularity about it. At least I wouldn't be awake at night shaving off imaginary percentages to make it even in my head. I dropped my suitcase on the dusty gingham bedspread.

The back door stood directly in line with the front door at the end of the hall. Outside, two moldy deck chairs sat on the slab.

Then the forest.

Spring rain fell lightly. I still wore my anorak, so I pulled up the hood and headed a little way into the trees. The smell was wonderful after the diesel and fish smells on the boat (just thinking of that brought back an echo of the nausea). I was about a hundred feet in when I realized I was counting footsteps. I stopped myself, took a breath and banished sums from my head. There was something familiar about this place and I wondered why. Had I been somewhere similar? In my head, I tracked back over places I'd visited and couldn't recall. The sense of familiarity was very deep, very strong, like a memory from childhood that won't be pinned down. Mum would know. Had we been on holiday near a forest? Given we were so poor we hardly ever left Lewisham, I couldn't imagine we had.

Two hundred and forty-eight, two hundred and forty-nine . . .

Damn it, I was still counting. I turned and made my way back to the cabin, subtracting a footstep each time from my total. I used fewer footsteps going back, probably because I was more confident about where I was going. I had eight left over.

Evening shadows crowded in and by the time I had unpacked and eaten the plastic-wrapped sandwich I had bought at Ålesund, I was exhausted: the result of four days of sleep troubled by new-life trepidation. I showered and snuggled under the tie-dyed bedspread.

It was nine o'clock. If I wanted to be at work at 8:00 A.M., I would have to wake up at seven, so I set the alarm on my watch. But maybe I needed to rise earlier, as I had to find the galley. Why hadn't I asked Magnus what time breakfast was available? Was there food in the cupboards in the kitchen here? Would I have to make my own breakfast? I obsessed about this for a while, realized it was now eleven o'clock and if I wanted eight hours' sleep I'd have to nod off *precisely then*, and of course that chased sleep away. So I calculated some more: most people really only needed seven hours' sleep so I had an hour to nod off, unless I decided to get up earlier. No, I wouldn't get up earlier, the galley couldn't be hard to find. And now it was after midnight, and I was still doing sums and trying to convince myself that six hours' sleep is all one really needs to feel refreshed and finally I gave up and got out of bed.

I set up my laptop on the coffee table in the lounge room and worked on writing up my thesis. Inside, the light was yellow and the bar heater warmed my toes. Outside, the forest waited, peaceful and cold in the rain; dense and dark and vaguely, vaguely familiar.

Any insomniac will tell you that they can nearly always sleep between 5:00 and 7:00 A.M., which is a pity as this is when most alarm clocks in the world go off. I'd been sleeping for just over an hour when a knock at the door of my cabin woke me. I resisted coming up; I willed the knock to go away. But my visitor knocked again and, with a groan, I pulled myself all the way to wakefulness. Checked my watch. Five minutes to seven.

Gunnar waited on the other side of the door. "Sorry," he said, when he saw how bleary I looked. "Magnus sent me. He forgot to tell you about breakfast."

It occurred to me that both my exchanges with Gunnar had commenced with him apologizing to me. "I had some trouble sleeping last night," I explained.

"Ah. Magnus told us you have insomnia."

"Not every night. Just when I'm tense. Would you like to come in?"

He slouched in, eyes averted from my blue-hippo pajamas. "Take your time. Get dressed and I'll show you around the station this morning."

I had a quick wash, threw on a skivvy and a pinafore, and applied some mascara and some lipstick. I had a phobia about my very pale hair, skin and eyes making me look washed-out. Silly, really, as Gunnar was by far the most eligible man on the island and he had already seen me in my pajamas after a bad night. My mother's fault: I'd have been far lower maintenance if her most-uttered phrase hadn't been, "Dress up nice in case there are boys there."

We stopped for breakfast in the galley, which was at the front of the rec hall, across a narrow walkway from the admin building. Toast and tea for me; disgusting pickled fish thingies for Gunnar. I almost couldn't eat watching him wolf them down. Maryanne, the cook-cum-cleaner, was flirting shamelessly with Magnus in an outrageous Manchester accent as they smoked together in the rec hall. We said hello, then Gunnar led me to the front of the admin building.

"Isn't Magnus married?" I said to Gunnar. "I saw a ring on his finger."

"Separated. He's on the prowl."

"Maryanne?"

"Anyone—but Maryanne is easy prey. I don't think he's really interested. I think he just likes to see the naked adoration in her eyes."

"How come your English is so good?"

"My father is English, and I lived with his family in Cambridge for two years." He indicated a large stone set into the ground. "Did you know that 'Kirkja' is Old Norse for church?"

"No."

"This is the foundation stone for an early-eleventh-century church that once stood on this site. It was discovered when the plans were being drawn up for the station. Historians excavated the area while the main building was being constructed behind it. There was a television program about it."

I indicated the three-meter-wide satellite dish mounted on the roof. "Tell me about the communications system."

Gunnar was just as happy to talk about technology as he was to talk about history. He took me around the whole station, showing me the water tank and desalination machine, which sat at the back of the station next to the water, and the generator shed and hydrogen chamber on the northern fence. An instrument enclosure, full of pluviographs and anonometers and celometers and a score of other gadgets, lay between the admin building and the cabins.

We entered the admin building via the back door, through a lino-floored storeroom and into a remarkably neat office. Magnus was at his desk, as was Carsten (Danish), the registered nurse who doubled as administration manager. Up a flight of spiraling metal stairs was the control room, where we found Frida, who was a maintenance engineer, and Alex (American) and Josef (Icelandic), who were both meteorologists. The other meteorologist, Gordon (English), had been on the night shift and was wisely in bed. The room was lined on all sides by desks, littered with stained coffee cups and half-finished paperwork, computers and other electronic devices. Both Alex and Josef were glued to a computer screen, complaining about a permanent echo on the radar. Gunnar took me out onto the observation deck. Rainy mist swallowed the forest and the other side of the island.

"There are raincoats in the storeroom," Gunnar said, noting my efforts to shrink back toward shelter.

"It's all right. It's only drizzle."

He raised his arm and I caught a whiff of his musty sweater. "It pays to take a walk out east through the forest. It's very quiet and beautiful and brings you to the beach on the other side in about forty-five minutes. The beach can be really cold if the winds change; sometimes they come straight off the Arctic, but the prevailing winds are westerlies and the cliffs protect us from them. The lake is nice too, though that's where the ghosts live."

"I'm not bothered by ghosts," I said, annoyed that he was continuing with the prank.

He smiled at me. "No? You don't believe in ghosts?"

"I don't believe in anything. And I don't scare easy. Save it for the next trainee."

The door opened behind us and Magnus stepped out. "Awful weather, isn't it?" he said.

"Sure is," I replied.

"We don't make it, we just forecast it," he said. "It's 8:00 A.M. Time to start work."

Gunnar backed away, apologetic hands in the air. "I'll leave you with Magnus. If you need anything, just let me know. I'm in the cabin directly in front of yours."

I spent the day doing little more than filling out forms.

Magnus was obsessive about administration. The last form he gave me was a questionnaire about meteorological instruments . . . well, he called it a questionnaire. To me it looked like one of those multiple-choice exams I'd left behind in my undergraduate years. It asked me to list the daily jobs in a weather station in their correct order.

"I don't know anything about the daily work," I said. "My degrees are in math and geophysics. I've never used any of the instruments. I have no idea what kind of reporting relationships are set up here."

Magnus smiled his charming smile. "Go on, just fill it out. See how you go. You might surprise yourself."

I got two items out of ten right. Magnus thought this was funny. I thought it was a unique way to embarrass me. By the end of the day, I'd had enough of him and everybody else. I stopped by the galley and asked Maryanne if I could take dinner back to my cabin, and I holed up there in my pajamas and got really, really homesick.

Someone knocked on the door around seven. I resisted the urge to shout, "Go away."

Gunnar again.

"Sorry," he said.

"Stop saying 'sorry' every time you see me."

He held out a bottle of red wine. "I'm really sorry. I need to explain something."

"Come in." I led him into the lounge room, a faded brown-and-grey room where I had the bar heater on high.

He sat in one of the armchairs while I found two glasses that looked like they had been jam jars in a previous life.

"So what do you need to explain?" I asked, sipping the wine.

"I wasn't trying to make fun of you with all the talk about the ghosts."

"No?"

"No. Seriously, no. You thought I was playing a trick on you? Like an initiation?"

"That's what I thought, yes."

"I'm so sorry, Victoria. I want you to feel welcome here. Magnus is the expert on embarrassing people."

"He's very good at it. And you can call me Vicky."

Gunnar laughed. "Really, Vicky, my intention wasn't to make you feel stupid or afraid."

"I'm neither," I said, too tersely.

"I know that."

"Then why mention the ghosts?"

"I'm really interested in history. Othinsey has a fascinating history and the ghosts are part of it. It's part of the story of the island."

"Do you believe in ghosts?"

He shrugged. "Who knows?"

I pulled my legs up onto the couch and made myself comfortable. "Go on, then. Tell me."

"This island was settled by Christians in the eleventh century. They built the church. One day a boatful of new settlers arrived to find everyone on the island dead. Slaughtered. Hanged with the intestines of the calves they'd brought, or burned, or pinned to trees with spears. As there was no sign of anyone having landed or left the island by boat, the story began that they were killed by vengeful spirits, sent by the old gods."

"And nobody tried to settle it again?"

"A few attempts were made. Nothing lasted. It's a long way from the mainland and too small to be self-sufficient.

Rumors persist of ghosts—strange noises, sightings down near the lake—which frighten the less rational away. The handful of scientists we have here don't care about those rumors. You don't believe in ghosts."

"I'm about the most skeptical person you'll ever meet. My mother is another story. Every week she visits a new psychic, who tells her she's going to win the lottery. She uses the same numbers every week—I know them by heart—and even though her psychic says they're the right numbers, they never come up. But . . ."

"She still goes back. I know. People need something to hope for."

"If she'd invested the psychics' fees and lottery ticket money into a mutual fund, she wouldn't be living upstairs at Mrs. Armitage's in Lewisham."

"What does your father think?"

"I don't have one. I mean, I suppose he's out there somewhere. My mum raised me alone, unless you count the three husbands who each left in under a year."

"It must have been very hard for her. No wonder she needs to believe she'll win the lottery." He refilled my glass.

"That's very generous of you." I smiled across at him, then wondered if the reason he was being so nice was because he thought he had a chance with me. I nearly groaned. A girl doesn't make the decision to move to a remote sea-bitten island lightly, and coming to Kirkja had seemed an excellent opportunity to avoid entanglements of the heart.

"Do you have a boyfriend back home?" he asked, confirming my suspicions.

"Um . . . I just broke off an engagement. It was messy."

"How messy?"

I sipped my wine: combined with extreme weariness, it

was sending my brain in circles. "He got another girl pregnant." Proud of myself for not saying, "He knocked up some tart."

"That's very messy."

"Yes, so I'm going to enjoy a few years of single life. Love is highly overrated."

"Do you think so? I think it's wonderful."

"It looks good in books and movies, I'll grant you that. But in real life it's just . . ." *Never quite enough, never really there, never living up to its promise.* "Let's change the topic."

Gunnar left at nine. I liked him; it would be good to have someone my own age around. I had the distinct feeling that after the wine and the conversation I would be able to sleep, and I was right. I drifted off soon after slipping into bed. Half-sleeping, half-awake, I heard noises outside in the forest. I thought about Gunnar's ghosts and smiled. Some people will believe anything.

TWO

O wing to a scheduling problem, I wound up working twelve days in a row. When Magnus realized the error (the vague and bumbling Carsten was at fault), he was both apologetic and full of bluster. "It's a good thing; you've learned so much; few people would get such a comprehensive induction." Then he gave me six days off.

Six days off on a tiny isolated island where I had one friend, and he was about to go on holiday leave. How dull.

Even so, I needed a break from working. Those first twelve days were a walking dream of new tasks, new words, new sounds and smells: the routine drudgery of observations and recordings; the dozens of objects whose names ended in "ometer"; the endless beeping of the computer system; the disinfectant Maryanne used in the staff toilet. All bookended by a confusion of sleepless nights. I had worked with three different meteorologists, and each one of them taught me the same tasks slightly differently, leaning conspiratorially close to say that "Alex does it wrong," or "Gordon always leaves the radar too quickly," or "Josef often forgets this part." If it hadn't been for Gunnar, who sought me out every lunch and dinner and talked to me like a normal human being, I would have lost my mind.

My first day off was Gunnar's last day on the island before he hopped on the supply boat back to Norway for his annual leave. It was one of the few clear skies since my arrival, so he suggested a walk across to the other side of the island. He came by my cabin late in the morning.

"Hi," he said. "I thought I'd give you a chance to sleep in."

"Sleep? What's sleep?" I asked, closing my cabin door behind me.

"You said you only get insomnia when you're anxious. You've got six days off." He pointed to the door. "You know you should lock that."

I fished out my key and did as he suggested. "I also get insomnia when I've *been* anxious. It takes me a few days to wind down. So, who's the thief? Is it Carsten? Frida?"

"Sorry?"

"You made me lock my door."

Gunnar laughed as we made our way into the forest. "Well, I'd say they're probably all trustworthy. But things occasionally go missing inexplicably. Magnus has a theory that thieves come over from the mainland, land at the beach, creep through the forest and steal things while we're all looking in the other direction."

"Do you think it's possible?"

He shrugged. "Perhaps. As I said, things do go missing. Since I've been here, we've lost an electric frying pan out of the galley and a DVD player from the rec hall."

I sidestepped a spider's web that glistened with the

remnants of dewfall. "It's a long way to come just to take an electric frying pan."

"Yes, it's a bit mysterious."

"My money's on Frida. She's got shifty eyes."

Gunnar gave me a bemused smile. "You don't like Frida?"

"She doesn't like me. Can't you tell?"

"She's unfriendly to most people. I think I've seen her smile once, and that was when Magnus tripped over his office chair and hit his head on the desk."

The track narrowed in front of us. Trees clustered close, gathering shadows into dark pools. The air was very still and the only sounds were the crack and pop of tiny branches falling or being crushed underfoot, of small animals moving and birds searching for food. We fell into single file, trudging along in silence for a long time. I found myself puffing and marveled at how unfit I was.

"Are we going the right way?" I asked eventually, when it seemed the landscape around me hadn't changed in twenty minutes.

"Yep. Don't worry."

"Is it possible to get lost on Othinsey Island?"

"I don't think so. Though it would be a good place to hide. And it's just called Othinsey, not Othinsey Island. The 'ey' means island."

I caught up with him and elbowed onto the track next to him. "So it's Othin's Island?"

"It's Old Norse. Odin's Island."

"Odin, like the god?"

"Yep."

I gave him a mischievous grin. "Does he live around here?"

Gunnar didn't bite. "No. I expect he lives in Asgard with the rest of his family."

I nearly tripped over a branch and Gunnar caught me, then politely let me go. I speculated on how many more seconds of body contact Magnus would have stolen, did a few calculations and deduced that Gunnar was ninety percent more polite than his boss. "So how come you know so much about Old Norse and gods and local legends?" I asked.

"I studied a little bit at university. I create games."

"Games?"

"For the PC."

"Like shoot-'em-ups?"

"No, role-playing games. Featuring mythological worlds." He dropped his head, embarrassed. "I know it's a little . . ."

"Nerdy?"

"Yes."

"It's fine. You're in good company. I'm obsessed with the weather. There's not much nerdier than that." I squeezed his arm. "So, you're going to make lots of money with these games?"

"It's an amateur interest at the moment. But, yes, one day, who knows?"

The trees opened out, letting in the sky. A petrel swept past overhead. I looked down the slope in front of me and saw a still, grey lake. More trees stood on the other side. "Oh, God. That's beautiful."

"Be careful down the slope."

I made my way down the rocky slope to the edge of the lake and sat on an outcrop. I could hear Gunnar behind me, collecting skimming stones. He crouched beside me and handed me a small, flat rock.

"I'm no good at this," I said, proving it by plopping the rock directly in the water.

Gunnar aimed and sent a rock skipping across the surface of the lake: one, two, three.

"Show-off," I said.

"I practice a lot. Not much else to do on Othinsey." He skimmed another, and another, and they skidded and fell until his hands were empty and I was sick of estimating trajectories and calculating averages. He sat next to me and the lake grew still. The water was dark green and murky.

"So why are you obsessed with the weather?" Gunnar asked.

"My friends back in London say it's because I'm so bossy. 'Vicky wants to control the elements.'"

"Is it?"

"No. Ever since I was a little girl, I've always sensed that there's something wonderful about weather. It's so commonplace and yet so mysterious."

"What do you mean?"

"Every year it leaves a trail of carnage behind it. People freeze to death, or die of heatstroke. Houses are flattened in storms, or pulled to pieces in tornadoes. As a species we can do almost anything, but we can't control the weather. We certainly can't guarantee accurate forecasts. We study it, we look for trends, we pretend to understand it and predict it. It's a force so much greater than us that we've had to learn to live with, kind of like living with a temperamental monster."

He smiled. "I've never thought about it much. I just listen to the weather forecast to see if I need to take a sweater."

"That's the mundane aspect of it." I cast my eyes back toward the station. "As I'm finding out. Forecasting is very monotonous work. It all seems a bit pointless."

"The shipping companies need us."

"I know."

"Why did you apply for this job?"

"I need the money, and it's a step in the right direction. I'd like to work in climatology or geophysics research one day." I sighed, stretching out my legs in front of me. "It's hard, isn't it? Being a grown-up. Getting a job. Realizing, once and for all, that your suspicion you were formed for greatness was misguided."

"You never know what's just around the corner. Your mother could win the lottery."

I smiled at him. "She could, I suppose." I indicated the tranquil lake. "Does anyone ever go swimming here? In the warmer months?"

"It's a bit treacherous. Hidden depths, lots of weed. Somebody drowned here once, back in the eighties. Besides, it never really gets that warm."

Behind us, in the trees, something thudded to the ground, then scrabbled in the undergrowth. I must have looked startled because Gunnar said, "Don't worry. Just one of the ghosts."

"Not funny. Really, what do you think it was? Are there animals on the island?"

"Sure. Weasels, squirrels, petrels, owls." He stood and helped me to my feet. "Come on, let's see the beach."

On the far side of the island, without the cliffs to protect us, the winds were cold and biting. The grey sand stretched away in both directions, waves pounding it mercilessly. I pulled up my hood. Gunnar's hair tangled and whipped around his face.

"See, this is why I don't believe Magnus's theory about thieves," he said, raising his voice to be heard above the waves. "Imagine trying to land a boat here."

"I expect there's a logical explanation. There always is."

"Do you want to know something else weird? You'll appreciate this. I discovered when I was committing some of the old logbooks to a database that items were often reported missing from the station after the aurora borealis was seen. In fact, since 1968, sixty percent of the items went missing within a week of an aurora storm."

I shrugged. "That's not enough to draw a conclusion from. Maybe the thief just takes advantage of everybody being preoccupied with the pretty lights. What's your theory?"

"I don't have a theory. I just find it interesting. Mysterious."

"Mysteries are just scientific facts that haven't been documented yet." I was already outlining a hypothesis about solar winds, transcranial magnetic stimulation and temporary insanity resulting in kleptomania.

Gunnar said, "You really are an incurable skeptic, aren't you?"

"The Queen of the Skeptics," I said with a royal wave.

"Life on Othinsey may very well dethrone you, your highness," he said, smiling.

"I doubt it."

He shrugged. "It's cold. Let's go back to the sheltered side of the island."

"Let's." I followed him into the trees and we made our way back to the station. Gunnar told me about his holiday plans—he was going to Amsterdam with some friends from Oslo—and I resigned myself to five days of thesis-writing before turning up to work again for more endless synoptic observations and data recordings. The near future seemed pointless, and I realized that if I hadn't caught Adam out, I would have been marrying him this coming weekend.

Gunnar sailed off on the *Jonsok* and I spent the rest of my long, long weekend decompressing in my cabin. A package from my mother came on the supply boat—I had phoned her on day two to ask for my bedspread and a few other things out of my bedroom—and I managed to make my new space a little more appealing. I spent one crazed, furtive morning writing a long letter to Adam about how glad I was that we weren't married, then tore it up before I was insane enough to send it. I worked on deciphering my stained field notes to write up my thesis and, best of all, I slept. I liked Othinsey a lot better when I wasn't witnessing it at 3:00 A.M.

My first day back at work commenced with the dullest staff meeting in recorded history. Magnus set the mood with an eye-wateringly long rundown about how important certain matters of administration were. I spent most of it counting the number of people in the room (seven—Gunnar was away and Maryanne didn't usually attend staff meetings); calculating the number of fingers and toes in the room (139—Carsten was missing the pinky off his left hand); and coming up with an average number of digits per person (19.857142 recurring). Then each staff member in turn had an opportunity to discuss problems they had faced in the last month. I began to draw spaceships in the corner of my notebook. By the time it was my turn to contribute, I had an entire starfleet capable of neutralizing humankind once and for all.

"I have nothing to add," I said. "I'm slowly grasping the basics of the work."

Magnus glanced at his diary. "Hmm. Well, by the end of the month we'll be relying on you to have more than the basics. You're on duty solo from Wednesday the twenty-eighth until the following Wednesday."

"Why's that?"

"The World Meteorology and Climatology Conference is on in Switzerland. All the other meteorologists are going. I have to attend as I'm receiving an award. Gunnar's been working on a temporary automatic data collection schedule, but you'll have to launch the balloons and do as many synoptic reports as you can during waking hours."

I wondered if Magnus had factored my insomnia into his plans. Based on his behavior so far, it wouldn't surprise me. "Do I have to get up every three hours?"

"No, no. Unless there's something unusual going on, like a storm. I know it's a lot to expect of you, but it's unavoidable. You don't have to keep regular hours. As long as the balloons go up and the Institute gets some figures from time to time. If you get into trouble, Frida and Carsten are here to help."

"No, we're not," Frida said, tapping her diary with her pen. "Remember? Carsten and I are going to my sister's wedding in Bergen."

How ghastly: Frida and Carsten were a couple. He was at least twice her age. Why hadn't Gunnar told me this juicy tidbit? Boys never understand the importance of gossip.

A frown crossed Magnus's brow. "Is that this month? I'm sorry, I forgot."

I worked it out before Magnus said it. With all the meteorologists away, Gunnar still on holidays, and Frida and

Carsten off the scene, that left Maryanne and me on the island alone for a week. I started devising ways to get rid of Maryanne too. The fantasy of having a whole island in the Norwegian Sea to myself had quickly taken grip in my mind: solitude, genuine solitude.

"I'll be fine," I said. "I won't get into any trouble. I look forward to the challenge." And the space. And the freedom.

"I'll need to speak to Maryanne," he said gruffly. "If she's not happy about running the station on such a low staff level, I'll have to stay."

"But you have to collect your award," I squeaked, my deserted island now replaced by squirming imaginings of being stuck alone with Magnus.

"We have a few weeks to work it out," he said. "Perhaps we can get a replacement meteorologist from the mainland."

"Just as long as you know that I'm quite happy to work here alone," I said.

"You've made that abundantly clear, Victoria. Now, on to the next agenda item. Formulation of best-practice benchmarks for the operational plan." Or at least I think that's what he said. I had glazed over before the end of the sentence.

I soon discovered that Kirkja Station had a lot of traditions that involved alcoholic drinks, brought over from Norway by the *Jonsok*. They included (but certainly weren't limited to) Wednesday afternoon drinks, Friday evening drinks, Saturday afternoon drinks, and post-staff-meeting drinks. All this was paid for by the social club, which skimmed money from everyone's wages to raise funds. Norway was a nation with, possibly, the most expensive alcohol in the world. When I opened my first pay slip and saw how much the social club was taking out, I decided that I would have to ensure I got my money's worth.

And so, while it's never wise to get drunk around your boss, I found myself plastered in Magnus's cabin, with Frida, Carsten and Magnus himself. Alex, Josef and Gordon had long since called it a night.

Magnus's cabin was as neat and ordered as he was. On the way back from his spotless bathroom, I found a photograph in a frame on his bookcase. Two children, perhaps around nine years old, smiled out at me.

"Are these your children, Magnus?" I asked.

"Yes. Matthias and Nina. They're twins."

I plopped back down into an armchair. "Do they live with your wife?"

"My ex-wife, yes," he replied.

"One of his ex-wives," Carsten added with a grin. "All the men here have at least one ex-wife. That's why they've all run away to a deserted island."

"Except Gunnar," Frida said quickly.

"Of course. Gunnar's single." Magnus gave me a knowing smile, and I realized that everyone had picked Gunnar and me as a potential couple.

"I've run away, too," I said. "I've given up on love."

"People say that but they never mean it," Carsten said, taking off his glasses and rubbing them on his sleeve. Frida patted his hand affectionately.

"I mean it. This past weekend, if I hadn't wised up sooner, I would have become Mrs. Adam Butler." I sounded bitter, damn me.

"A broken engagement? That's what you're running away from?" Frida asked with a curl of her eel-like lips. I swear she looked delighted to hear of my misfortune.

"Yes."

"I'm sorry," said Magnus.

"It's the second one," I confessed, wondering why I was confessing it. "It was my second broken engagement."

"Really?" Carsten said. "So either you're very clever because you break up with them before it goes too far, or . . ."

"Or she picks the wrong men to start with," Frida said helpfully.

I wished it were that simple. I honestly loved Adam, just as I loved my childhood sweetheart, Patrick, before him. I simply didn't love them enough. If I told you that I split with Adam because he knocked up another girl, that's only half the story. It doesn't account for how unloved by me he felt, how cold I was with him, how endlessly disappointed I was in his imperfections and how obvious that disappointment was to him.

"I just can't do it," I said, emphasizing each word with my glass, nearly spilling my wine. "I can't do love."

The conversation went elsewhere, fortunately. I already felt sobriety edging into the haze and waving a finger because I'd flashed my emotional underwear. But if I'd kept talking, I would have said something like, "There is something missing from love. There is something empty about love. Love should be stellar and lunar and pull your breath from your body and make your teeth ache and your nerves sing, but I have not felt that. I have only felt disappointment. And I am absolutely certain there should be more."

I was off duty the next afternoon, and remained in the rec hall after lunch. I had a sheaf of papers, which represented what I had written so far of my thesis, and I spread them out on one of the big wooden tables, preparing to organize them into chapters. I was deeply involved in this task when I heard pots and pans banging in the adjoining galley. I ignored the noise for a few minutes, but it grew louder and more violent.

I left my papers and peered around the doorway.

"Maryanne?"

She was crouching at a cupboard, pulling out pots and throwing them toward the sink with a crash. She looked up with an irritated expression, but when she saw me her eyebrows shot up, and she said, "Oh, Vicky. You're not going to let him do it, are you?"

"What are you doing? What are you talking about?"

She stood up. Her frizzy blond hair was yanked high into a ponytail tied with a pale pink ribbon. "I'm cleaning out the cupboards. I always do in the first week of the month." She looked at the frying pan in her hand, then flung it into the sink.

"Why are you doing it so . . . vigorously?"

"I've just had an argument with Magnus. He wants to leave us alone here for a week! Just two defenseless women!"

"Defenseless against what?"

"There are dangers, Vicky. I suppose he didn't tell you that."

"What dangers?" Gunnar had spoken about thieves coming onto the island. I hadn't believed it, but Maryanne was round-eyed and trembling at the idea of being left alone.

Maryanne's voice dropped to a conspiratorial whisper. "Haven't you heard the noises?"

"No."

"You must have. In the night. When you can't sleep."

"No."

"From the forest." She turned her eyes meaningfully in that direction, then met my gaze again. "There are noises in the forest."

"Sure. Birds, animals—"

"No, no. Vicky, this island is haunted."

I was so relieved I almost laughed. She hadn't been imagining hooded intruders with glinting knives; she had been imagining spectres with rattling chains.

"Oh. I see," I said.

"You have to tell Magnus you won't do it. He doesn't have to go to the conference. He's duty bound to stay here. It's the award—he wants to get up there on the podium and accept it."

I guessed how fervently Magnus was playing that fantasy out in his head, and I smiled. Perhaps I could get this entire island to myself after all. "Maryanne, I'm sure if there's only a skeleton staff we don't need a cook."

"Pardon?"

"Instead of making Magnus stay, why don't *you* go? I'll be fine by myself."

"But Vicky, this island is not safe for—"

"I'm not afraid of ghosts," I said. "Look, I'll talk to Magnus. I'll get you the week off. You can go home to Manchester, or you can go shopping in Oslo. I'll offer to stay here alone."

Maryanne shook her head sadly. "You think I'm mad, don't you? You think you know for certain that there are no ghosts on this island."

"I don't think you're mad. But I do know for certain that there are no ghosts on this island."

"For certain? Some people are so bloody arrogant." She turned abruptly and went back to clearing out the cupboards. *Crash, bang.*

*   *   *

By dusk, I had convinced Magnus to let Maryanne have the week off. It was almost too easy. He had grown blustery and said that, no, he would stay, it was his duty as station commander and he couldn't leave a trainee to run the station. I reminded him that I wasn't just a trainee, I was highly qualified, levelheaded, nearly thirty years old. I reassured him that I had memorized the lockdown procedure, our last line of defense on an island hours from police assistance. "And Magnus," I said, "who will accept your award if you're not there? Alex?" Alex was the second-most-senior meteorologist, a newly minted American with a loud voice and big white teeth. Magnus clearly despised him.

"I'll consider it," he had said. Twenty minutes later he was at my cabin door. "I think it would be a good opportunity for you, Victoria. There are more remote postings than Othinsey out there, and my brief was to expose you to a range of experiences you can bring to bear in your future career."

His justifications were unnecessary. I was delighted beyond description. In three weeks, I'd have the whole island to myself.

That afternoon the weather turned foul.

The wind changed direction and howled harsh and flat from the northeast through the forest and over the station. I'd heard of pines "whispering" in the wind, but the ones outside my cabin were screeching. It was a cruel sound, reminding me that Mother Nature had teeth and claws.

The wild weather continued day after day. The others at the station weren't bothered by it, they were used to the extremes the Norwegian Sea had to offer. But my nerves were jangled by the relentless howling and the way the wind jumped down my throat every time I ventured outside. I slept poorly. By the fifth day, I was so tired that I dozed off around 8:00 P.M., then continued falling deeper and deeper under the soft dark layers until I was in that subterranean pocket of slumber from which the old and the sick never return.

Then I woke suddenly. A noise had roused me. A cold finger of air in the room. I peered into the darkness, could see the window frame standing ajar. I rose. My senses were addled. The floorboards were cold under my feet. My eyes were heavy. I reached for the window to close it, when a hiss sounded from close outside. I paused. Listened again.

"Psssst." Like someone trying to get my attention, just below the windowsill.

Outside, the world was night grey. My vision tunneled; murky shadows formed at the periphery. I leaned out. The wind whipped at my face, brought tears to my eyes. I thought I could see, about four feet away on the ground, a pale grey shape made of slender birch twigs. I focused on it, my eyes trying to make sense of it. Had a branch blown off a tree in the same gust that had pushed my window open? I stepped back to close the window, when the shape moved. At first it seemed it was shifting under the wind's momentum, but then it kept moving, pulling itself up to its feet. Quick shivers of horror ran over my skin; it was the feeling of spotting a stick insect where you thought there was only a stick, magnified a thousandfold. Black, shiny eyes stared at me under a wild thatch of spiky hair. I screamed once and slammed the window shut, but not before I had heard the thing say, "Don't swim in the lake. The draugr will get you."

I collected myself quickly. I was dreaming, I was muddled. I had imagined it. I pressed my nose against the glass,

looking for the pale grey shape so that I could reorganize it
in my head, make it look like the broken branch it really
was. There was no pale grey shape, there was no spiky-
haired creature, there were just the trees moving in the wind,
outside, in the gloom.

I pressed my hand against my heart and laughed. I
climbed back into bed but didn't return to my deep sleep. I
amused myself by imagining what Maryanne would make
of my story, and vowed to be more careful about closing the
latch on the window properly.

But, in my mind, deep and locked away, I knew I *had*
closed it properly.

Three

Every Wednesday, the supply boat brought mail. Magnus delivered to my cabin an envelope with my mother's handwriting on it, and a postcard from my friend Samantha, who was on holiday in Italy. I read the postcard and stuck it in the corner of my mirror, then picked open the letter from Mum. I was curious. I had telephoned her twice already, and she wasn't the kind of woman who ordinarily sat down and wrote letters.

Dear Vicky,

I'm writing this down because I know if I tried to tell you on the phone you wouldn't listen. I went to see my new psychic, Bathsheba, this morning. She told me something very disturbing. Right in the middle of the reading, she closed her eyes and gasped, then she said, "Whose name starts with V?" Of course, I said, "That's my daughter, Victoria." Then she said, "There are dark psychic forces gathering around Victoria."

Vicky, I know what you're thinking, and I know

you want to throw this letter in the rubbish, but consider it, darling. How did she know about somebody whose name starts with V? There are twenty-six letters, and V is not that common. I asked her a lot more questions that she couldn't answer, but she did say I should tell you to come home. I trust Bathsheba, she's very good at what she does. Please come home. I'm so worried about you.

Love, Mum

I didn't know whether I was more amused or annoyed that my mother trusted somebody named Bathsheba. What Mum had failed to clarify was whether or not she was wearing the little enamel "V" around her neck that Aunty Clementine had bought her when I was born. I put the letter aside, wondering if Bathsheba had given her another useless batch of lottery numbers or advised her that she would meet the love of her life in June. I'm sure that at least two of my mother's failed marriages were encouraged by psychics.

I loved my mum, of course, but she had made such a mess of her life. She was born into disadvantage and stayed there. I had watched her ramble unsuspectingly from failure to failure—men, jobs, diets—always complaining about a lack of money, brains or luck, but never realizing that what she really lacked was the ability to manage her own life. I was different. I wanted to escape where I came from, from the welfare rolls, from the overcrowded schools, from having the phone cut off every second month. When I took the job at Kirkja, I was running from it so hard that the momentum kept me awake at night. I didn't want to be swallowed alive by circumstance. I didn't want to be like Mum, spending so much time predicting what fate had in store for her that it hadn't occurred to her that her future was for herself to make.

There are dark psychic forces gathering around Victoria.

Mum wanted me home, and she would say anything to get me there. I didn't know if it was because she missed me or because she felt that my successes proved her choices in life wrong, but she had elected to use precisely the worst method of persuasion. As I had told Gunnar, I didn't scare easy.

Not back then, anyway. That was all still ahead of me.

I showed up at the control room for my first solo shift that evening. The late shift was eight until four, hours that I was already intimately acquainted with from my sleepless nights. Alex handed over to me, and I spent the first few hours going through my list of tasks, launching the balloon, filling the blanks in the database. After 1:00 A.M., I had less to occupy me. I turned off the bright fluorescent lights so that the space was only lit by the glow of three computer screens. The room was punctuated all around with floor-to-ceiling windows. Outside the sky was cloudy, stained by the inky black of treetops. I had a training manual to read, but I put it aside to sit on the long couch near the staircase, lying back and enjoying the solitude. I lay there a long time, letting my mind drift. Every ten seconds, the transmitter sounded a gentle beep. The heating whirred softly. The printer hummed. Dark and still.

I didn't notice that my eyelids had fallen closed.

The sound of my breathing. The door from the observation deck opening wide. A cool breeze on my skin. Struggling to sit up, to look around. Paralyzed in my own body. A hot rush of fear. There was someone in the room.

Brrring.

I sat up with a start. The phone. I reached for it, glancing around. No, the door was closed. I was still alone.

"Hello?"

"Vicky? It's Gunnar."

I checked the clock above me. "Gunnar, it's two in the morning."

"It's three in Amsterdam," he said cheerily. "I just got back to the hotel. I remembered you were working your first night shift tonight, so I thought I'd call and see how it's going."

I could hear other male voices in the background, calling out to Gunnar in Norwegian. I didn't know what they were saying, but their voices betrayed that juvenile tone peculiar to men in small groups who suspect one of their number is trying to score. That and the fact that Gunnar had bothered to remember my first night shift told me that he was still sweet on me.

"It's going fine, thank you."

"You sounded anxious when you picked up the phone."

"I'd dozed off. I was having a bad dream."

"Oh? The one about the old woman who comes in and sits on your chest?"

"I . . . no. I dreamed that someone had opened the door to the observation deck—"

"That's her. The hag."

"Gunnar, is this more of your supernatural shite?"

He chuckled. "No. Alex and Josef have both dreamed of her while dozing on the night shift. They thought it was spooky until Josef did some research and found out it was a very common sleep disorder, especially at that time and under those circumstances."

Common sleep disorders. That's what I liked to hear. Perhaps my encounter with the bundle of twigs that talked was explainable in this way too. "Tell me more."

"It's called isolated sleep paralysis, occurs most often at the onset of sleep, and is usually accompanied by hypnagogic hallucinations of a presence in the room."

"Isolated sleep paralysis."

"I like the other name. The hag."

"How about imagining you see someone outside your window with twigs for hair and he offers you advice? Is that a common sleep disorder?"

"No, haven't heard of that one."

Damn. "You would have laughed your head off, Gunnar. I screamed like a girl."

"You are a girl."

"A *little* girl."

"What did he say?"

"Who?"

"The thing with twigs for hair."

"Oh. Something about not swimming in the lake because of the draugr, whatever the hell that is."

A brief silence on the line. Then Gunnar's voice, cautious. "Really?"

"Yes, really. Why?"

His voice returned to normal. "When you knock off, go to my cabin. There's a book on my desk about mythological creatures. You'll find it interesting reading."

"Why? What's a draugr?" I'd assumed it was a nonsense word that my addled brain had invented.

Noisy voices broke out behind him. "You'll see. I've got to go, we're heading back out."

"At 3:00 A.M.?"

"It's *Amsterdam.* My key's in the dead pot plant at the back door of the cabin."

"Gunnar, just tell me what—"

"Gotta go. Bye."

The phone clicked. The room was growing cold, so I turned up the heating. I filled the rest of my shift and changed over with Gordon at 4:00 A.M.

First I went back to my own cabin to shower and put my pajamas on. I was fooling myself that going to Gunnar's cabin and finding that book was not so important to me, that I didn't really care what a draugr was or where I'd picked up the word—because I'd clearly picked it up from somewhere, some movie or book or conversation. But as dawn broke and I still wasn't asleep, I decided that I simply *had to know.* I pulled my anorak on over my pajamas and left my cabin. Gunnar's back door was about ten yards from my front door, screened by the six-foot-high wooden lattices that stood between all the cabins in a miserable bid to provide privacy. I found my way around the lattice and to the dead pot plant he had spoken of. The key was hidden inside. I opened his back door and let myself in.

Gunnar's cabin had the same faint musty scent as his clothes. Probably because his clothes were strewn all over the floor of his bedroom, bathroom and lounge room. I was astonished at how messy he was. My mother always said that men, left on their own, will eventually revert to savagery. I found his computer set up at a desk in a corner of the lounge room. The walls around it were decorated with sketches—not particularly good ones—of Viking warriors and mythic beasts. A fake sword was hung on the wall, and a photograph was pinned to the corkboard: Gunnar and some male friends, dressed in costume. Long tunics, pants with leather straps crisscrossed around the ankles, spears and shields. I felt dimly embarrassed for him, though not sure why. His desk was overflowing with papers and dirty cups and glasses. I found the book he had mentioned, cleared a space on the sofa, and looked up "draugr."

> **draugr** (*plural:* draugar) The undead spirit of a drowning victim, often a fisherman, usually residing in a body of water. The draugr is bloated and discolored with contusions, his eyes shine faintly and he is often covered with algae and weeds. His goal is to drown others so that he may have them for company. A draugr can only be destroyed by cutting off his head.

I read it a few times, turning the problem over in my mind. Where had I heard this before? I had no recollection of reading any Scandinavian folklore. Perhaps I had learned it in school, when we were told about the old gods and the days of the week, which were named for them.

I returned the book, put back the key, and went to my own cabin. The sky was streaked with pink clouds and I needed to sleep.

After a week of night shifts, Magnus considered me sufficiently trained in meteorology for the moment, and pulled me off forecasting to assist him with his climatology research. This was far more stimulating work, and his research about carbon sequestration in boreal forest climates was related to my own work for my thesis.

One morning, a few days before they were all due to

leave for the meteorology conference, he came to collect me to help him set up some recording instruments in the forest.

"Good morning, Victoria. Did you sleep well?" he asked, as I locked my cabin door and pocketed the key.

"Yes, thanks. I think I'm still catching up from the night shifts."

"Ah, yes. It can be difficult for your body to return to its natural rhythm. Here." He handed me a rattling plastic box with a lid. It was heavy and he carried nothing. "Follow me."

He led me into the trees for a few silent minutes. As Kirkja receded, he called to me over his shoulder, "What do you think of Maryanne?"

"Maryanne? She's nice enough. She makes a wicked shepherd's pie."

"But do you think she's pretty?"

How utterly baffling. "Um . . ."

He fell back so we were walking side by side. His expression was boyish. "Do you think she'd be a good match for a man like me?"

I didn't know whether to be appalled or embarrassed. His frankness was almost charming, but the fact that he had waited until he was alone with me to ask was undeniably creepy. "I don't know how to answer that," I said, squirming, hoping he would leave it at that.

"I think she likes me," he said confidently. "What do you think?"

I considered the ravenous look in Maryanne's eyes every time she spoke with Magnus. "Um . . . maybe."

Rain started to fall and he pulled his hood up. My hands were full, so I couldn't do the same.

"I don't think we'd be good together, though," he continued. "I'm really a man who needs someone smarter. That was the problem with both my ex-wives. They were pretty enough, but not clever enough."

I didn't point out that they were clever enough, in the end, to become ex-wives. I remained silent and hoped that it would encourage him to do the same.

"There's a large clearing with a big anvil-shaped rock that I've marked out for an instrument field," he said. "We'll be stopping there."

We trudged through the forest. The rain lightened to drizzle. Magnus broke a shoelace and stopped to fix it. I told him I'd meet him at the site, rather than wait with him and chance another uncomfortable conversation. I had just arrived at the clearing and was setting down the box when he ran up, panting, behind me.

"Did Gunnar bring you here?" he asked.

"Sorry?"

"I didn't tell you where the clearing was."

I must have stared at him for a full ten seconds without speaking.

"Victoria? Is everything all right?"

"Yes," I said. "Gunnar brought me here." This was entirely untrue, but it was all I could say because I couldn't otherwise explain how I had found the place without Magnus's help.

As we set up the instruments, I rewound the journey in my head. Magnus had described a clearing, an anvil-shaped rock. I had been preoccupied with his creepiness. But if I concentrated hard, I could remember knowing where to go the instant he described it. So how had I known? Gunnar had certainly not brought me here. We were at least half a mile south of the route Gunnar had shown me to the beach.

I stood up for a moment and looked around. Sensations

washed over me: familiarity, fear, longing. Dizziness rushed down my body. I heard Magnus's voice. A moment later, he caught me under my elbow and lowered me to the ground.

"Put your head between your knees," he was saying.

I did as he instructed and the blood throbbed in my temples, my thoughts sharpened and became clear again.

"Are you feeling better?" Magnus asked.

"Ah . . . yes. Thank you."

"Did you eat this morning?"

"No."

"Make sure you always eat something before you come out to do fieldwork."

"Yes, I will in future."

He crouched on the forest floor next to me, watching me closely. "Your color's coming back, but I think you should go to your cabin and rest. Carsten should have scheduled you another day to recover from those late shifts. It can be hard on the system at the beginning."

I nodded, but didn't venture to say anything. I had an overwhelming urge to cry.

"Here, let me show you something. It will cheer you up," Magnus said with his boyish smile. He opened his palm and a dirty fragment of metal sat on it.

"What is it?" I asked.

"I found it just now while making a hole for a transpiration sensor. It's a piece of the past."

"I don't know what you mean." An inexplicable feeling of dread stole over me as I considered the object.

"Forged iron doesn't just show up spontaneously in forests, Victoria. This is part of something left here by previous residents, maybe a thousand years ago." He considered the fragment carefully. "It might be a pot or a piece of jewelry."

It's not a pot; it's not jewelry. I said nothing, watching Magnus, wondering what bizarre mental illness had gripped me.

"I'll keep it for Gunnar." He slipped it into the pocket of his anorak and stood, reaching down to help me up. "He collects old bits of rubbish like this."

"I'm fine," I said, as he put his arm around my waist.

"No, let me take you back to your cabin."

We left the forest behind. I had read that the feeling of *déjà vu* was caused by a misfiring in the part of the brain responsible for recognition, causing a sensation of memory that was not genuine. I wondered if the sudden change my life had taken, accompanied by sleep deprivation and anxiety, had caused a similar misfiring in my brain. I had never been there before. It felt astonishingly familiar, but I had never been there before. How had I found the clearing? Simple. Magnus had been tending in that direction; I simply kept heading southeast and the clearing was there.

And the cold fear I felt looking at Magnus's "piece of the past"? Some kind of projected fear, which produced an uncanny certainty that I knew what that metal fragment was. A piece of a murderer's axe.

On the Tuesday before the island became my own, I had difficulty falling asleep. I dutifully climbed into bed at nine o'clock and closed my eyes, relaxed my body and tried to clear my mind. But my concentration flickered from topic to topic, the way a dirty CD skips over snatches of music. I breathed deeply, but the sound of my own breath irritated me. My body felt awkward no matter which position I lay in.

The empty hours of the night were upon me before I drifted off. Consciousness receded down sleep's dim thoroughfares. Dark blue enveloped me. A chill wind touched my skin; somewhere a pale blue light. Inky shadows surrounded me.

I started; I was outside my cabin window, looking into the forest. Confused, I turned to the window, only to see my own blond hair spread across the pillow inside, my own body breathing deep and low under the covers. My heart jumped into my throat and bright fear hissed along my veins. I turned back to the trees. The wind was harsh in the treetops, bending them and making them groan in their hard, flat voices. Overhead, a quarter moon pierced the dark. Slivers of streaming cloud made the light from the moon flutter and dim. I was cold and afraid. Branches stood out like bony fingers against the moon-washed sky. A skittering noise emerged from among the dark trees. I turned to prise open the window to my cabin and climb back into my body, but my fingers skidded over the painted sill as though I were made of vapor.

"Victoria."

I didn't want to turn and see who was talking to me in that rasping, childlike voice. "Victoria, I'm only trying to help."

I shot a glance over my shoulder and yelped. The twig creature. He was dressed in rags, his hair stood up above his pointed face, pale and rough like a collection of old birch twigs. He reached out a hand to me and his fingers appeared long and sharp in the sickly moonlight. He stood only a few feet from me, wary, swaying rhythmically.

"I'm sorry to come into your dream," he said, "but I want to help you."

"What are you?"

"My name is Skripi. I'm a wight, sent from Asgard. I know my appearance frightens you, but I have a kind heart. You must be careful. The others on the island don't have kind hearts."

"The others?"

"The draugr, the hag." He took a step toward me and I screamed, turned back to the window and hammered on the pane. This time there was a sound.

An instant later I woke up in my bed, whole. A thumping had roused me. I sat up with a start and my eyes flicked to the window. Was that a glimpse of my ghostlike self? Or just a shadow cast by a branch in the moonlight?

I breathed, letting my body relax. It had simply been a nightmare. And what a nightmare. My pajamas were damp with sweat. I tried to settle under the covers once more, but the moist patch under my back grew cold and uncomfortable. I got out of bed and turned on a light, chasing shadows away. My sheets, on close inspection, were soaked. I quickly stripped off my pajamas and put on dry ones, and pulled the sheets off the bed. How could I have sweated so much on a cold night? Outside, shivery blue light fluttered in the trees, and a chill ran over me. I wrapped myself up in my bedspread and went to the lounge room, turned on the heater and lay down on the sofa.

I dozed, I didn't sleep: too afraid of nightmares. When the first smudges of dawn crept into the sky, I rose and pulled on my anorak, and headed for Gunnar's cabin.

The book on mythology lay where I had left it. I looked up "Skripi" but didn't find it. Relief. Just a nonsense word that my brain had conjured. I moved to set the book down, glimpsing another one in the pile. A dictionary of Old

Norse. My hand picked it up, even though my brain advised otherwise. I flicked through, singing the alphabet song in my head . . . *Q, R, S*—

Skripi. It was there. An Old Norse word meaning "phantom" or "horror."

I had never heard a word of Old Norse in my life, I knew that. I also knew I would find a rationalization, but it was too far from my reach as I prepared myself for a week of solitude. I didn't like lurking in this uncertain space of superstition; it made me feel as though I were falling through clouds.

Later that day, as the *Jonsok* cruised out of Hvítahofud Fjord, I thought about how fervently I had pressed Magnus for this opportunity to be alone.

The forest behind me beckoned like a dim memory of something unpleasant, and being alone on Othinsey didn't seem such a good idea at all.

Four

[Asgard]

As the trees grew closer and the open spaces of Gammaldal disappeared behind him, Vidar realized he was being followed.

At first he had thought it just the sounds of birds catching worms in the undergrowth. But now the light, almost-inaudible footsteps had become rhythmic, too much like the gait of a hunter.

He paused, listened.

Whatever it was, it didn't want him to know it was there. Vidar shivered. The sun was obscured by the branches above him and the afternoon was deepening toward evening. These woods, like all the woods in Asgard, were home to half-magical wights and spirits. Most would do him no harm, but he had crossed a brook, and wherever there was water, there was danger of a draugr. Perhaps one had journeyed downstream from the northern parts, those treacherous icy waters where many had drowned.

Or perhaps it was a wolf. Unusual in the mild south of Asgard on the well-used paths of travel and trade, but a lone hunting animal might have skulked its way out of the wild deeps in search of food.

Vidar turned and waited, balancing his weight on his feet, utterly silent. He pulled an arrow from his quiver and, without a sound, positioned it on his hunting bow. He strained to hear. The footfalls had quieted. His ears rang softly. The rustle and thud again, hushed but close. He blew a strand of dark hair out of his eyes. The muscles in his arms tensed as he drew the string, poised to shoot the instant his pursuer moved from cover.

A figure stole from the trees, Vidar's fingers uncurled, realizing almost too late that it was friend, not foe. He tilted the bow down.

"Aud!"

The arrow hissed through the air, grazing her thigh.

She called out and fell to her knees, her hand pressed into her skin.

Vidar dropped his bow and hurried to her. Her dark hair was loose and hung over her shoulders, shoes shoved into the pockets of the apron she wore, and her skirts were hoisted to her thighs and tied at her hips, revealing her long pale legs.

"It's nothing," she said, setting her teeth. Blood oozed between her fingers.

"You're bleeding," he replied. He reached for his hunting knife and cut off a length of material from the bottom of his tunic.

She seemed to grow embarrassed about her bare legs, pushing her skirts down. "They make such a noise trailing in the bushes," she muttered.

"Let me see." He forced her fingers aside to inspect the

wound. It was only a graze, but he felt sick at the thought that he might have injured her worse, or killed her.

"What are you doing out here?" he asked, expert fingers binding the wound tightly. He already knew the answer; since the day she had discovered him in the seeing-water, she had been increasingly curious about where he went and what he did.

Aud wouldn't meet his gaze. "Searching for wild rosemary. For lamb stew."

"Stay closer to home next time," he said, testing the knot and standing up. "Are you well? Do you feel faint?"

"I'm perfectly well." She quickly arranged her skirts. "I'm sorry, Vidar."

He went to slide his hunting knife back into his belt, dislodging the pouch he wore around his hips. The contents spilled to the ground: a drinking flask, a whetstone for his knife, and a half-burned Midgard book.

Aud's fingers closed around the book before he could snatch it up. "What's this?"

"Nothing," he said, taking it from her gently but firmly. "An old piece of rubbish from my father's hall."

"It's a book, isn't it?"

"From Midgard," he admitted. A book written in English, Halla's language. He had heard a few words, muffled by the water in Sjáfjord. Years ago he had known the language well; learning the many tongues of Midgard had filled his waiting centuries. But he needed to be fluent. All he had was this one book, saved from the fire at his last visit to Valaskjálf.

"Loki has dozens of those," she said, pulling herself to her feet and testing her weight on her injured leg. "See? It doesn't hurt at all."

"When did you see Loki's books?"

"Last time we were there together. When we went to find that saddle he stole. He has a whole shelf of them, not all burned like that one. I could go to fetch some for you."

Vidar rubbed his chin in thought, his whiskers scratching the callused skin of his palm. Books would be useful, but Loki was unpredictable. His cousin, who lived halfway to Odin's hall, was both part of the Aesir family and a volatile outsider. Vidar couldn't foretell which precarious course his plans might take if he renewed contact with Loki.

"Why are you so interested in Midgard?" Aud said, leaning forward to slip her shoes on. A late glimmer of sun caught her pale cheek and her skin looked very soft.

"It's full of beauty," he said, thinking of Halla.

"It's full of mortals," she countered. "They're exhausting. They move too fast and worry too much."

"They only have short lives to fill." Vidar was achingly aware of how short.

"Do you want to go there?"

"I've been there." He frowned. "A long time ago now."

"And did you like it?"

"Yes."

She shook her head as she straightened. "I don't want to go there. I don't think it's so special."

Her dismissiveness irritated him, as though she were maligning Halla herself. "Are you not interested in anywhere other than where you are, Aud?"

Her dark eyes flicked downward and he immediately regretted his words.

"I'm sorry," he said, gently touching her hand. "My mouth moved before my mind."

Aud was already turning away. "I've troubled you long enough. I'll head home."

He watched her go, guilt sour in his throat. Aud was a princess of the Vanir family, longtime rivals of his own family. She had been sentenced to one thousand years of servitude to the Aesir for a crime she had committed in her own land of Vanaheim. Her high birth was complemented by her seidhr, the women's magic she had been forbidden from using while in service.

For one who had fallen so low, Aud was unshakeable in her acceptance of her lot. Vidar had met her five years ago, on a rare visit to Valaskjálf, where she had just commenced her service in Odin's hall. His father was working her to exhaustion, inventing disgusting tasks to humiliate her, and encouraging the other men to make veiled sexual threats. Stone-faced, she had endured it all. Vidar had taken pity on her and asked his father if he could take her into service. Odin had many servants, Vidar had none, so he agreed. The usual argument had ensued.

"Why must you live so far away in such poor conditions? When will you return to Valaskjálf and live with the rest of us?" Odin had demanded.

"I prefer my simple life. I'm happy living at Gammaldal," Vidar replied. He couldn't live with his cruel, decadent family. He couldn't live in the company of the terrifying bully who was his father. He couldn't live with the million shining objects, the rich meals and the endless revelry. He had packed up Aud and taken her away. Was that the last time he had spoken with Odin? Five years was not such a long time. If he were fortunate, Odin wouldn't summon him again for another fifty.

It had taken Aud three weeks before she relaxed in

Vidar's company, before she finally understood that his gentle treatment of her was not the setup for a cruel joke. He never asked what crime she committed, but she had made mention of leaving behind an infant son: Vidar didn't probe too deeply. It was already obvious that she had fallen in love with him, and he had no desire to encourage a mutual intimacy. His heart belonged elsewhere—on the other side of the mists and colored lights of Bifrost.

Birds fluttered past overhead, the dappled sunlight warm on their wings. Vidar slid the Midgard book back into his pouch and tried a sentence in English. "Halla, do you remember me?" But of course her name would no longer be Halla. He would have to return to the seeing-water to discover her new name. And he wasn't allowed to ask her outright if she remembered him. The conditions had been quite specific: she would return to Midgard, but he was not to remind her of their shared past until she had fallen in love with him again, and if she didn't fall in love with him, then he had no business interfering in her life.

And to woo her, he needed her language.

Vidar ran after Aud, calling her name. He caught her on the near side of the stream.

"Vidar? Is something wrong?" she said as he approached.

"Are you well enough to walk?"

"As you see."

"I need you to go to Loki for me."

Aud nodded, eager to please.

"I need you to borrow Midgard books, in English. Every one he has."

"Of course. I'll go immediately."

"Take care. Go easy on your leg."

She smiled. "I'm perfectly fine, I'll enjoy the walk."

Vidar watched her disappear into the woods, banishing a momentary twinge of guilt. She didn't limp, the wound had been very shallow. He stretched out on the grass and looked up. The sky was washed clean after a week of rain. He felt young, not like a man who had lived more than a thousand years. The light and jolt of love had lain dormant within him for centuries. He'd shaped it into a dull, aching thing to be buried deep and best not remembered. Now she was back he could allow himself to feel it once more. The fantasies unfolded, the memories washed through him. With the aid of Loki's books, Vidar would remember her language in a week or two. Then he could start planning the next step: his return to Midgard.

Through the forest, where only random shafts of light penetrated the gloom, past the steep black cliffs and still fjords, Aud made her way to Loki's house. The last time she had journeyed this way she had been with Vidar, snuggled against his back on Arvak, caught up in such a swirl of longing and sadness that she barely registered the route. The heat of Vidar's body through his soft woollen shirt, the warm tickle of his hair whipped into her face, the addictive rhythm of his heartbeat against her cheek. She remembered that Loki's house lay to the east after the open fields, where the trees began to close again, and she eventually spied the roof. Loki's house was easily three times as big as Vidar's, but barely a tenth the size of Valaskjálf. It huddled among the crowded trees, whose trunks and branches were overgrown with dark moss. The leaves of many autumns were layered atop the roof and mist hung and swirled low around it. Vines—some dark, some sickly pale—crawled over Loki's house as though it were something organic, something that had grown out of the ground long ago, ancient and elemental. He had no fields of barley or animals for food and clothing as Vidar did. Instead, Loki was a regular visitor at Odin's hall, borrowing some things and stealing others to support his solitary existence. Aud fought through the overhanging branches down the path to the door.

"Loki?" she said, pushing the door open.

Aud found herself standing in a large room; a fire burned on the hearthstones in the center. All around, on every wall up to the ceiling, were overflowing shelves. Midgard things. Books, toys, strange appliances, decorative objects, junk metal, pots and mirrors. She approached a shelf and reached out for a mirror decorated in silver and pearls. It was beautiful. She traced the design with her finger.

"That's mine!"

Aud jumped at the roar from behind her and dropped the mirror, which shattered on the floor. Loki stood near the door, biting his lip with amusement.

"I'm so sorry," she said, crouching to retrieve the fragments.

"Seven years of bad luck. That's what the Midgard mortals say when you break a mirror."

"Seven years isn't such a long time." She handed the pieces to him. "Here."

"I liked this mirror. I'm very disappointed to have lost it." Aud watched him examine the pieces. Loki was a handsome man, with gleaming black hair, unusually light grey eyes and long pale hands. He was tall and thin, and always dressed in fine, dyed clothes. He was wearing a circle of gold around his head.

"I'm very sorry," Aud said again. "You gave me such a fright—"

"Don't blame me!" he shouted, raising his eyebrows in shock. "You shouldn't have picked it up in the first place."

"I—"

"You'll work it off, of course. Vidar can spare you. A day a week until the end of the year."

"Of course."

He bent to the floor and swept his fingers over the stone, checking for missed fragments. "Why are you here, Aud? Does Vidar want something? It's been a long time since I heard from him. All the wenches at Valaskjálf ask about him."

"He wants books," she replied. "Midgard books to learn English."

"English? He already knows English." His fingers left the floor now and crept up her foot, closing around her ankle. His hands were icy.

"Perhaps he has forgotten it," she said, taking a step back. His hand slipped off.

"You have good ankles, Aud," he said, looking up at her. "I'd like to put one either side of my neck." He lunged forward and she stepped back farther, sending him sprawling onto the floor. He laughed loudly.

"I prefer them where they are."

"Ah, well." He climbed to his feet, dusting himself off. "You've been spoiled by Vidar. If you had stayed at Valaskjálf, they all would have had you by now." He moved close, leaned down to whisper into her ear: "Though I can tell you wouldn't mind if Vidar wanted to feel your ankles." His breath was hot, his voice laden with snide inference.

"Loki, I've come for Midgard books. In English."

"You think that Vidar is a kind man, don't you? You think

him gentle and ténder and you imagine him touching you gently and tenderly."

"The books, Loki."

"But I have seen him awash in the blood of his victims. He is of the Aesir, Aud. We are a cruel family."

This revelation pressed her heart. It couldn't be true of Vidar. He despised his family. He only ever spoke softly and moved quietly. "I don't believe you."

"Our feud with your family goes back centuries," he said lightly, turning from her and searching his shelves. "I've no doubt that Vidar slaughtered a few of your cousins."

"He is only ever kind and patient with me."

"Perhaps one day I'll tell you more about him. About what he was like before he left Valaskjálf and became a re-formed man. Here . . ." He turned around, holding four books in his hands. "These should be enough for him."

"Thank you." She took the books and tucked them under her arm.

"Now, you can do a favor for me. Find out why he wants to learn English again."

"Perhaps he—"

"No, no. No *perhaps*. Find out for certain. If you find out, I'll let you go. You won't have to return weekly."

"I'll see," she said. Even if she did know what Vidar in-tended, she would never tell Loki. She would hold the secret inside, sweet and aching, allowing it to tie Vidar to her. She could endure Loki's cruel humor, his sudden rages and his advances if it meant staying faithful to Vidar. His secrets were as precious as her own, and she had many.

Loki strode ahead of her, opened the door and peered out. "The afternoon grows dark, Aud. You had better stay tonight."

"I have plenty of time to return," she said, though dark clouds blotted the last of the sun and the trees in the distance were dim and forbidding.

"I can make you up a soft bed next to the fire. I could keep you warm myself."

"No, I—"

"Foolish girl," he said gruffly. "I'll take you back on Heror."

"I can find my own way home."

"No, I need to talk to Vidar. We'll arrange the terms of your service to me. Come." He captured her arm in his long, cool fingers and pulled her outside. "Besides, it's been far too long since I saw my cousin."

Vidar worked on the shutter with one eye on the storm. Grey clouds had started gathering shortly before dusk, and now they built up high and thick over the sea, swirling impatiently toward land. He tightened the last hinge and tested it to make sure it was secure. In the distance he could hear beating hooves. Aud was returning, Loki with her. He closed the shutter and it slipped snugly into its lintel. Behind him, the hoofbeats slowed and came to a stop. He turned.

"That's good work, Vidar," Loki said, his tone both mischievous and disdainful. "I have shutters that need fixing too." Comfortable atop his gleaming black stallion, he was dressed in a dark red coat, a gold circlet keeping his long black hair in place. Aud, tiny next to Loki's long frame, clutched a stack of books against her.

Vidar lifted Aud to the ground. "Thank you for returning Aud to me."

"There's a storm approaching. Can I stay?"

Vidar checked the clouds again. They drew close; the

wind chilled and rain spat down. He couldn't consign his guest to the wild weather. "Yes, of course. Take Heror to the stable and I'll stoke the fire."

Loki rode off as Vidar ushered Aud inside. The firelight bathed the dark wooden pillars and beams in warm amber, chasing shadows into the alcoves.

"I'm sorry," she said, making a taper to light the candles. "He insisted on bringing me."

"I'm glad he did. You would have been caught in the storm." A rumble of thunder shook the shutters.

"But now he'll stay the night and you don't like him."

"Nor do I dislike him," Vidar said, carefully placing two fresh logs on the fire. "I just don't trust him."

She offered him the four books. "This is all he would give me. I'll have to go back."

"No, these are enough."

"You don't understand. I have to go back because—"

Loki threw open the door. "What's for dinner?"

"Welcome, cousin," Vidar said, taking Loki in a brief hug. "Sit with me. Aud will prepare us a meal." He led Loki to the bench nearest the fire.

Loki fingered the carvings around the pillar beside him. "Beautiful work, Vidar. Your own?"

"Of course." Vidar had hewn and carved every inch of wood in this house of his own construction. He had thatched the roof, laid the hearthstones, hung every door and shutter. Then there were the fences, the stable, the chicken coop. His father had said such menial work brought shame on the Aesir. "Eternity is a long time to fill, Loki," Vidar said. "It's wearisome to be idle."

"I agree."

Aud brought them two cups of mead. Rain beat heavily

on the roof, but inside was warm with the smell of woodsmoke and wax.

"Have you seen your father lately?" Loki asked.

"Not in five years. You?"

"I visit from time to time. I'm not always welcome."

"Because you steal things."

"I *borrow* things. I intend to return them all. Eventually."

"How is he?" Vidar asked.

"The passing of time eases neither his arrogance nor his folly."

Vidar smiled. "But is he well?"

"Oh, they're all well. Your brother is well." Thunder sounded outside and Loki pointed upward. "All the drunken sods in Valhalla will be cowering, thinking it's him—Thor, the great god of thunder."

"A sad fool with a hammer."

Loki laughed loudly. "You can't tell them, Vidar. They still think they're gods. Nobody worships them anymore, their great hall grows emptier every year. I can't remember the last time Odin was sober enough to raise a battle with Vanaheim. Yet their self-deception continues."

Vidar sipped his mead. He preferred not to think of his family. Aud was in and out of the cook-room, her hair tied in a knot at the nape of her neck.

Loki followed his gaze. "Your bondmaid broke something that belonged to me today," he said.

"I'm very sorry."

"She can work it off. One day a week until the end of the year."

"I'll give you until winter."

"It was an object very precious to me."

"Did you steal it?"

Loki assumed a mock-indignant expression. "There's that word again."

"Until winter, Loki. It's a long way to travel between our two homes. I don't want her making the journey in snow-storms." Loki was within his rights to demand some payment from Aud. Vidar just hoped it wouldn't mean weekly visits from his cousin.

"Until winter, then," Loki conceded.

Vidar waited until Aud had left the room. "And you are not to force her to lie with you."

"I've never forced anyone to lie with me. They eventually come willingly. *She* will." He hooked a thumb toward the cook-room. "I'd wager Heror on it."

Vidar watched Aud as she held the door open with her hip. With her slender wrists and white skin, she looked very young and vulnerable. "Be kind to her, Loki."

"Ah, here's dinner."

Aud approached with a tray. She handed them each a bowl of soup and a chunk of bread, then moved to sit across from them.

"What's this?" Loki asked. "Your bondmaid eats with you?"

"It's only the two of us," Vidar said gruffly. "And you know she's a princess of the Vanir."

"She's a *bondmaid*, Vidar. Have some dignity. She should eat with the horses."

"I'll go," Aud said, picking up her bowl.

"No, you can stay," Vidar said.

"I need to discuss something very sensitive with you, Vidar," Loki said, shaking his head. "Make her go."

Vidar smiled at Aud apologetically.

"I'll take my food to my room," she said.

"Thank you, Aud."

Aud quietly took herself away.

"She has her own room? She doesn't sleep with you?"

"She's not mine to sleep with."

"You're too kind. You know the Vanir wouldn't be as kind to you."

"I know." The Aesir and Vanir were locked in a perpetual blood feud. There were periodic stretches of truce and hot flashes of extreme violence. The resentments ran deeper than measure. "What did you want to discuss with me?"

Loki gestured to the Midgard books stacked beside them on the table. "Why?"

"I'm learning the language." Vidar broke off a piece of bread.

"You already learned the language."

"I want to learn it better."

"Why?"

"Because it's an interesting language."

"Why?"

Vidar smiled. "Because it's a whore which allows any new word in, and because it has conquered nearly all of Midgard."

"You're not thinking of going, are you?" Loki's pale eyes narrowed. "Not after the mess you got yourself in last time?"

"I have no intention of going to Midgard," Vidar said.

"You're lying." Loki put aside his soup.

Vidar shook his head. "I'm not lying."

"Lying, lying, *lying*," Loki said with a wild laugh, leaning forward so his elbows rested on the table. "I can tell. You're going to Midgard."

"I'm not going to Midgard."

"You can't do it alone. You'll need me to help you."

"Loki, if I were going to Midgard, I could manage to get there myself."

Loki smiled and tapped his fingers on the table. "You don't even know, do you? Odin put out an order shortly after you moved here." Loki straightened and puffed up his chest, putting on an uncanny impersonation of Odin's booming, slurring voice. "'If anyone sees Vidar near Bifrost, I want to be told *immediately*.'"

A cold arrow shot into Vidar's heart.

Loki waved his finger. "Aha! I can see it in your face. You didn't know that. Heimdall will see you, he'll ask questions. He'll *interfere*." Heimdall was the guardian of the bridge between Asgard and Midgard. If he focused, he could hear a blade of grass moving twenty miles away.

"I'm not going to Midgard," Vidar said evenly.

"I can help you."

Vidar didn't reply. He concentrated on eating his soup.

"I know how to get past Heimdall. I can help you get to Midgard."

Vidar sat back, brushing crumbs from his hands. "You waste your breath, Loki."

Loki turned his attention to his meal, a knowing smile on his lips. The rain pounded outside and the fire crackled in the hearth. The last thing Vidar needed was to be forced into confidence with his unpredictable cousin. And yet, he had to cross Bifrost unnoticed. Halla was over on the other side and he needed to see her, to speak to her. Knowing she was nearby and being separated from her was torture.

But her name wasn't Halla. Vidar had returned to the seeing-water that afternoon while Aud was away. He had spent nearly an hour gazing, watching her, until the water grew so cold he feared it would make his skin freeze.

Halla was a modern woman now, a scientist who had just arrived at the outpost on Odin's Island. She wore her hair cut blunt to her chin, and her clothes clung to her figure and her eyes were painted dark. She was both a new woman and the same woman. And her name was Victoria.

Five

Early-morning shadows fluttered across the path as Aud made her way to Loki's on horseback. The air was dewy and cool. She had left Vidar sitting by the fire with his Midgard books. Firelight glimmered in his dark hair. Where she had hoped to see some sign of sadness at her absence, she saw instead a distracted frown.

"Where are you going?" he had said.

"To Loki. Remember?"

"Ah, yes. Take Arvak. I don't want Loki bringing you home again." Then he had returned to his book.

Why had he become so obsessed with the Midgard books? Did he intend to go there? When she questioned him, he said he had no plans to leave Gammaldal and gave that half smile he always gave her. As though he wanted to smile at her kindly, but was afraid such a smile would bend her heart too firmly toward him.

Too late for that kind of caution.

The first rays of sunshine emerged over the horizon, glittering on frosted leaves. Aud turned Arvak off the path and down the slope to Loki's house. It sat very still and quiet in the gloomy shadows of the trees. She dismounted and set Arvak to wander nearby in the morning sun that bathed the road. Opening the door, she called out, "Loki?"

No answer. Had he forgotten she was coming? She glanced around at the shelves, remembered last time and touched nothing. Dust lay on every surface. She wondered if she should just start working. She grabbed a log from the pile and fed it to the fire.

"Aud? Is that you?" His voice came from behind the doorway at the end of the hall.

"Yes, I'm just getting the fire started."

"Don't touch anything."

"I just—"

"Come here."

Aud went to the door and pushed it open. She found Loki lying among blankets on the floor. His shoulders were bare and his black hair was loose.

"You woke me," he said.

"I'm sorry. I thought I should come early."

"I don't mind that you woke me," he said, smiling slowly, "but Aud, you mustn't touch anything in my house unless I expressly ask you to."

"Yes, Loki."

"It may seem like a mess to you, but to me everything is perfectly in order."

"I understand. You need only let me know what you want me to do."

He threw back his blankets to rise, and Aud saw that he was naked. She quickly turned her back while he dressed.

"What does Vidar make you do?"

"I clean and cook. I spin and weave. I grind the barley and milk the cow."

"Hm. I don't care much for any of those jobs. What else? How do you spend your days with Vidar?"

A smile touched her lips. "We are companions for each other," she said.

"Companions?" He stood beside her now. A quick glance told her he was dressed. "Is that really so?"

Aud thought about his question. Vidar spoke little, shared nothing of himself, asked her no questions about her life. He was kind, he was warm and often funny, but none of the intimacy that would translate to companionship was apparent. Her heart drooped.

"Ah, your face says it all." Loki touched her shoulder. "Come, Aud. You can be *my* companion. Let us sit by the fire and you can tell me stories."

A cold squally rainstorm blew in that morning as Aud recounted to Loki some of the histories of her ancestors. Stubby candles sputtered in the alcoves between the pillars and the room filled with smoke. From time to time, Loki would declare he was bored with the facts, and made her retell a battle story as a love story, an adventure as a domestic comedy. Laughing, she would comply, enjoying inventing more and more outrageous plots and casting the less-loved members of her family in them.

"Now you tell one," she said, her voice exhausted after hours of continuous use.

He waved a long finger. "No, no. *You* are the servant."

She bit down her pride. "Of course."

"There's a story you haven't told me," Loki said. "How did you come to be in Asgard?"

"I was sentenced to a thousand years—"

"Yes, I know that. But why? What terrible crime did you commit?"

A cold ache stole over Aud's heart. "No crime," she whispered.

"You must have done something awful to receive such a punishment. Who ordered you out? Was it your father?"

She shook her head. "I wish not to speak of it."

"You must speak of it. You are in my service for the day and must do as I say."

In the five years she had lived in Asgard, she had never revealed her story to anyone. Although she had longed to unburden her sad heart to Vidar, he, ever gentle with her feelings, had never asked. She didn't want to tell Loki, who might make fun or shrug coldly. But she was in his service.

His pale grey eyes were fixed on her face. "Oh, I *long* to hear this story," he said. "You look so unhappy, it must surely be a beautiful tragedy."

"It's real," she snapped, then softer, "It's not just a story. It's my life."

He sat back. She thought he looked chastened. "Tell me, then," he said.

"I was sentenced by the Norns. You know of them?"

"Those ridiculous hags? Of course."

"When I came to womanhood, I was chosen as a student of the seidhr and sent to wander in the roots of the World Tree as an initiation. You have no doubt been to the World Tree, Loki. You know that a man can wander for years and never see another soul. And yet, on the first day I entered the tree, I happened upon the abode of the Norns."

Loki's body flexed forward, eagerness in every muscle. "You know where they live?"

She shook her head. "I will come to that. Because the

Norns are the guardians of fate, they decided that my finding them was an act of fate, and chose me as their intermediary. I was to visit them regularly with news of the world above ground, bring them gifts, spend time with them as a companion. And so it continued for seven years.

"In my youth, in my thoughtlessness, I took a lover from the elven lands. He returned immediately to Alfheim, but I bore his son. Helgi." His name stopped up her throat and tears pricked her eyes.

"You have a child?"

She nodded, pressing her lips together. "Yes," she said softly. "I have a son, his name is Helgi."

"Go on," Loki said, "I'm fascinated."

"My father was enraged about my birthing a half-elven child, so I took myself away from court and lived simply on an old apple farm that belonged to my family. I raised Helgi alone, with very few cares. In time, my father relented and invited me home, but I was stubborn and I loved the intimacy of the two of us. I played with Helgi, I told him stories and sang him songs. He was a bright, loving boy, with soft plump arms and trusting eyes . . ." Aud took a deep, shuddering breath. She could almost taste his skin on her lips and the unending sadness rolled over her like a wave. "But one day, on his third birthday, it all changed. Everything changed."

The fire crackled and popped and the smoke stung her eyes. Loki sat very still, watching her. She didn't want to lay her heart so bare to such an unsympathetic audience, but the story had gathered its own momentum; the words spilled out of her.

"I wanted to collect some apples for breakfast. Helgi was sleeping when I left. He looked so peaceful that, rather than wake him, I chose to leave him there. I intended to dash to the orchard and return within minutes. But I found one of our goats wounded and caught in a rope trap I'd hung for foxes. She was panicked and made it impossible to unpick the knots. We relied on the goats for our milk and cheese, so I persisted, finally setting her free and gathering the apples. I dashed home.

"By this time, Helgi had been alone for nearly half an hour. I hoped he was still sleeping, but a hundred feet from the cottage I knew my hopes were dashed. I could hear him crying . . . wailing like he hadn't wailed since he was a tiny baby.

"I ran to the house, dropping the apples, and found him next to my bed, sitting on the floor and sobbing. I scooped him up to comfort him, and soon his sobs turned to hiccups and he said to me, 'Mama, you were gone for so long.'

"'Shh, shh,' I said. 'I'm sorry, I'm sorry.'

"'It's my birthday, Mama. It's not nice to be so unhappy on my birthday,' he said.

"'I know, my precious, I know. What special treat would prove how sorry I am?'

"He looked up at me. His face was red and tear-stained, but he managed a smile. 'Could we ride on Steypr?'

"Steypr was one of my father's horses. I had been granted her when I left court. She was a mighty beast and I was afraid of riding her. I would certainly never let Helgi ride her, but he adored her. He spent hours sitting astride a fallen log by the fence and pretending it was Steypr. I said, 'No, Helgi, you know Steypr is too big and too strong to be ridden by such a little boy.'

"He sobbed again, so hard that his little body shook in my arms, and wailed, 'But I *am* big. I am three years old!'

"I felt so guilty for leaving him alone on the morning of his birthday that I conceded."

Loki leaned forward, his hands pressed together between his knees. "You regret this."

"Oh, yes." Her voice was little more than a whisper, choked by tears.

Long seconds passed, and Loki waited with a patient smile.

"Go on," he said at last. "He fell, didn't he?"

"I thought it would do no harm if I propped him on Steypr's back, held the reins myself, and led him round in a circle. But Helgi was too excited. He giggled and shouted and squealed, and grabbed her mane and yanked. Steypr reared, the reins pulled from my hands so violently that the flesh tore away with them, and she galloped straight to the fence. Helgi screamed. I called out to him to hold tight. Steypr looked like she would take the jump, but balked. Helgi flew from her back and hit the ground with such a thud . . . like all the love in the world falling to the bottom of a deep pit." Tears spilled onto her cheeks and she palmed them away.

"Was he dead?"

Aud shook her head. "He breathed, but barely. In the scant minutes it took to get him to his bed, he grew purple and swollen and I knew he would die." Her voice broke and she fought to steady it. "I sat by his side and held his hand and sobbed. He was unaware of my presence, already vanishing down that foggy passageway even we cannot understand. Immortality, true immortality, is only for those who take extreme care." She drew a long breath, bringing her lungs once more under her control. "My child was everything to me: he was my spirit, my heart. I could not sit there and do nothing. I knew where the Norns lived, the vendors of fate. This time when I left the house, left his sad limp body behind, I was not afraid of Helgi waking while I was gone. It seemed certain he would never wake again."

Aud paused and glanced up at Loki, who gazed at her without speaking. She needed to rein in this tale; it became dangerous to reveal too much detail to her audience. "I journeyed to the World Tree. Helgi's fate was just appearing on Verda's loom. I made a deal with her: in exchange for reweaving Helgi's death into life, she sent me here to Asgard for a thousand years."

"In punishment?" Loki interjected. "She was angry that you dared to use your association with them for personal gain?"

Aud nodded. "I don't regret it. I was very lucky to know them. I was lucky to be able to save my son's life. Verda cut me a piece of her thread and handed it to me. It glowed with bright colors. I was told that when I left the World Tree, I could turn west toward Vanaheim and Helgi would die, or east toward my new fate in Asgard and Helgi would live. I made my decision, the thread turned black and I have not seen nor held my son in my arms since that day. He grows up happily in the good care of my family." Aud dropped her head and pressed her palms against each other.

"And the Norns?" Loki asked.

"They moved so I wouldn't find them again. They no longer trusted me." She glanced up from the fire to see his face, trying to read his expression. "Has my story amused you?"

Loki rose and pulled her to her feet, clasping her hands in his. "I'm not a monster, Aud," he said, "I'm genuinely moved. Look at you, you aren't fit for more work today. Perhaps you should return to Vidar."

She was surprised by his generosity. "I . . . thank you."

"Vidar doesn't know, does he? About Helgi?"

"No. He hasn't asked."

"Perhaps you aren't as close as you think you are," Loki said, a cruel edge touching his voice. "Perhaps you should rely upon me as a friend instead of him."

"Vidar is a good friend to me," she said, but was aware of how weak the protest sounded.

"Do you know he plans to go to Midgard?"

"He says he has no such plans."

"I can tell. Lies lurk like dim fireflies in the eyes of their tellers. Have you any idea why he wants to go?"

Aud thought about the seeing-water, but shook her head. "No."

"And now *you* lie. You have some inkling, don't you?"

"No. No, I don't. I don't know anything."

"Are you protecting some secret of his?"

"No."

Loki leaned in close, his grip on her hands tightening. "Your loyalty is misplaced. He's not what he appears to be, Aud. Believe me. He has a cruel streak—"

"He has always been good and kind to me," Aud interjected. "I don't like to hear bad things said of him."

Loki released her hands. "And now all my pity has drained away. You should have accepted my kindness while it was offered. Now you can spend the rest of the day scrubbing pots. But when you do return to Gammaldal, take a message for Vidar. 'Only Loki can get past Heimdall.'"

Aud found the menial work less complicated than the storytelling. As she worked she thought about Loki's assertion that Vidar was not all he seemed. When she considered the huge omissions she had made from her own story, she supposed nobody was as they seemed. Aud knew where the Norns lived still. But they held something very dear to her to ensure she never spoke of it.

Only Loki can get past Heimdall.

All through the long night, this message—offered solemnly and softly by Aud on her return—bound Vidar to wakefulness. Was it true? The question turned in his mind as a scrap of seaweed twists and dances in an ocean wave. Heimdall was a giant-killer and the most battle-hardened of the Aesir. His senses were keen, his loyalty to Odin keener. There was little chance of crossing the bridge unnoticed. Others could come and go to Midgard as they pleased. Loki went regularly, and was amassing a treasure trove of Midgard objects. Odin cared nothing for Loki's journeying, because Loki had never threatened to unravel the strands of fate that bound the Aesir. Vidar had. He had fallen in love with a mortal woman.

Vidar turned under his blanket and watched the dying glow of the fire. Outside, a rain squall beat on the roof and shutters. The occasional drip popped and hissed on the dim embers. Secrecy was the key.

And yet he must ask for Loki's help, a man who dealt in trickery and deception, in theft and blackmail, whose loyalties were as slippery and skittish as fish.

Vidar acknowledged also a connection with Loki. Both of them were outsiders to the debauched and violent insanity of Valaskjálf; both of them despised the folk who shared their blood. Could their mutual abhorrence for their family bind them together in confidence?

The rain passed as Vidar lay awake, tracing the patterns on the carved roof beams with his eyes. Softly, the sound of Aud muttering in her sleep became audible. Aud lay just beyond the door. Why couldn't he fall in love with her? She clearly loved him. She was beautiful and accomplished and noble, and many times he had caught a glimpse of her white arm, or the curve of her breast, and the ancient and ever-supple machinations of desire stirred in him.

But desire was nothing without passion, without love. He still loved Halla, he would *always* love Halla. In some long-extinguished moment his soul and hers had brushed against each other, creating a friction that gathered into a spark, a flame, a mighty star. It was primal and eternal. He closed his eyes. His fingertips longed to touch her lips, his mouth longed to find the soft flesh at her wrists and elbows. *Victoria.* Could any misgivings about Loki really keep him away?

He sat up and threw off the blanket, found his clothes and shoes. Dawn was scarcely an hour away. He let himself out of the house and headed for the stables to saddle his horse. Arvak's dark flanks glistened in the half-light as Vidar led him outside. Rain had blown in again, the sky stained with night and clouds.

"Vidar? Where are you going?" Aud stood at the door, her hair loose, her expression sleepy.

"I'm going to see Loki."

Realization spread across her face. "He'll be asleep," she warned. "You should wait a few hours."

"I'll wake him up." Without a backward glance, Vidar mounted and spurred Arvak toward the east, toward Loki and the pale sunlight struggling through clouds.

Six

Every time Aud approached Vidar to ask for a day to herself, he always agreed. "Of course, Aud," he would say, dark eyes crinkling at the corners. "Take your time, do as you please." And yet, she always felt uneasy about asking. Was it because, secretly, she wanted him to protest her absence? Was every request for time away from him laden with hope that he might reveal some trace of affection in his answer?

Sometimes she returned in the early hours of the following morning, long after he had gone to sleep. On those occasions he would wake, ask if she was well and safe, then return to his slumber. He never asked where she had been. Was he too respectful of her privacy to ask or too indifferent to her actions to care?

Vidar had returned from Loki's late in the morning. He had never been more attractive, with a wild gleam in his dark eyes, a flush of color high on his cheeks. Clearly, he had decided to go to Midgard and to ask Loki for assistance. She longed to know what attracted him to the mortal world. His restlessness had started around the time she had seen him drawing runes in the magical water of Sjáfjord. He had seen something there, something that beckoned him compellingly enough to put his trust in Loki.

Now she watched Vidar from behind her door. He sat by the fire, carving a small piece of wood. His expert hands were concentrated on the task, but his eyes told another story. He was daydreaming. She watched his fingers move, the tendons in his wrists, and a swelling of tenderness and desire for him caught her breath.

"Aud, I can feel your eyes on me," he said, not looking up. "Is something wrong?"

"No, no." She stepped out of her room and hovered uncertainly near him. "I had hoped for a day to myself. To walk . . ." She gestured toward the west.

He turned from his work and smiled at her. "Of course, Aud. Take your time. Gather your thoughts."

Aud slipped on her shoes and pinned on her cloak. She hesitated near the door to the cool outside and glanced back. He had returned his attention to his carving. She could see now what it was: a bird, curved over itself to grasp its own claws in its beak. Beautiful work, lovingly rendered. Was it a gift for her? A flutter of excitement stole over her. He looked up again, saw her gaze and hid the carving under his sleeve. "Go on. Enjoy your day."

"Do you never wonder, Vidar, where I go?"

With a patient sigh, Vidar put his work aside and turned to her. "Aud, I have given you every reason in the past few years to trust me. You've been sentenced into my service, but I feel no need to belittle you, to mistreat you, or interfere in your affairs. I am happy for you to take a day for yourself and I don't mind how you spend it."

Aud moved forward and knelt before him. "Yes, yes. You're always kind and respectful. But do you not *wonder* where I go and what I do?" She wanted to ask, "Do you not think of me when I am away?"

"You head west," Vidar said, his dark eyes growing soft. "I have seen you. You head toward Vanaheim." He stood, drawing her to her feet. "Go, Aud. I will enjoy the solitude."

He led her toward the door and ushered her into the cold bright morning and on her way.

So he thought she went to Vanaheim. He knew she was forbidden to return to her own land, so perhaps he imagined she lingered pitifully on the border. She trudged up the slope. He was partially right in that her destination was the border of Asgard and Vanaheim, but not so that she might gaze longingly at her homeland. Her destination was the World Tree. In truth, if Vidar did ask about her destination, she would have to lie. The Norns had been very particular about secrecy.

Last night's rain had cleared, the sky rinsed to pale blue. The World Tree was a three-hour trek west from Gammal-dal, across the plains and through the thick pines, then winding up farther and farther into the drenched mountain passes and across the plateau of grey volcanic rock where only hardy tufts of yellow grass grew.

In time, she could see it, an ancient sentinel rising from the next valley. A vast ash tree, half a mile high, with twisted black branches that sent sinister, whispering shadows to the west into Vanaheim, her own home; to the east into Asgard; to the north into the islands of Jotunheim and the realms of the dead; to the south into the elven lands where Helgi's father lived. The tree's leafless boughs bent to the wind, and its labyrinthine roots snaked in and out of the earth as though injecting it with poison. Aud took a breath on the grassy verge, then set her foot upon the first of the three hundred and thirty-three wide stone steps that led down to the base of the tree. How she despised each of those steps on her return, ascending relentlessly, until her heart pumped so hard it pressed her ribs.

She descended in silent contemplation. The Norns expected her to return to them two or three times in a season bringing news and stories and gifts from the outside world. In her apron she had a collection of flowers she had dried, some river stones she had polished and a hair clasp she had carved under Vidar's tutelage. Above her, the giant branches swayed, dimming the sunlight to eerie shadows. The tree was ancient and monstrous, stubborn and eternal. Between two of the enormous black roots, she spied the tiny opening and entered the tree, leaving the pale sky behind her.

Aud knew the dark underground maze by feel. Her eyes adjusted to the absence of light, but there was little to see. Twisting passages weaved amongst the roots, the earth and stone and plant matter. No passage was a consistent height or width: some narrowed so tight that Aud had to turn sideways to fit, some so low that she had to walk bent until her back ached. Aud could not estimate how long the journey took to the abode of the Norns; each time it seemed longer, the return shorter. But, winding through the dim passages, she never once faltered on her route. It was burned into her mind like memories of ill times.

Eventually, a faint glimmer of light greeted her eyes. She moved silently up the tunnel and peered around the vast arc of a tree root into the warm grotto that the Norns called home.

The room was dim, lit only by the glimmering threads

with which they spun and wove. They were identical triplets. Aud could only distinguish between them by the tasks they performed. Closest to the door was Skuld, who, with a distaff clamped between her knees, pulled thread from the ground and spun it. Next was Verda, who picked up Skuld's threads and wove them onto a loom. Farthest away was Urd, who untied the cloth at the crossbeam of Verda's loom, unraveled it and cast the thread, hand over hand, into the gloom beyond their cave. Aud didn't know where the thread came from nor where it went after they had finished with it. It belonged to the World Tree and was as black as the maze around it, unless one of the Norns touched it, when it became dazzlingly rainbow-bright. In the thread were the fates of all men; Skuld worked the future, Verda the present, and Urd the past.

"Look, look, it's Aud," Verda said, glancing up with a smile. Her hands kept flying over the thread, supernaturally fast and nimble. All of them had pale white fingers, which seemed to be jointed in every direction.

"Aud, what have you brought us?" called Urd, dropping her thread.

"Always too quick to drop your work, sister," said Skuld, running a thread expertly between her fingers. Aud had once held a length of their thread in her own fingers. She couldn't read it as they could, but she had tried to separate it into strands, only to find that the strands separated into more strands and so on into vanishing infinity.

Urd shuffled to a corner and found the stump of a deformed candle. She lit it and approached Aud. "What do you have for us?" she asked.

The other two were there a moment later, their pale red hair glistening in the candlelight, their blinking blue eyes focused on her. Once, they must have been great beauties, with broad cheeks and almond eyes and full lips. Now they were shriveled by age and made pallid by confinement underground. Pleasure came vicariously, through reading the threads of other people's fates.

Aud held out the gifts she had brought them. "Here, sisters, some treasures from the outside world for you."

"Ooh, treasures," Urd cried.

"I'll have that."

"No, me!"

As their wormlike fingers picked at Aud's hands, they squabbled over the flowers and stones and nearly came to blows over the hair clasp. Eventually they sorted out what belonged to whom, and Urd and Skuld settled back to work. Verda, the Norn with whom Aud had made her bargain five years earlier, smiled at her in the dim light. "I suppose you want your treat now?"

"Yes, I do," Aud said. Whenever this moment approached, a deep longing like an ocean current possessed her.

"Here, then," Verda said, reaching into her pocket for a round brooch of rock crystal set in silver. It had once belonged to Aud. "Here's your boy."

Aud reached for the brooch greedily and gazed into it. Out of cloudy shadows, a vision formed. Helgi. He bent over a puddle with a toy boat. Her breath twisted up in her breast; she had to remind herself to exhale. He couldn't hear her, but she said his name anyway. "Helgi. My dear Helgi."

After Aud's bargain with the Norns, Verda had enchanted the brooch so that Helgi would always be visible within, then withheld it so that Aud would never tell where they lived. The Norns protected their privacy with good reason.

Armies of people from Asgard and Vanaheim would be on their doorstep in a second, asking them to change this or that about their lives. The Norns' work would be slowed, time would begin to lose its shape, fate would begin to fall apart.

Aud devoured Helgi with hungry eyes: his honeyed skin and his long lashes and the curve of his cheek. She longed to touch him, to hold him. But he would be a man before she could be with him again. In their first year apart, whenever she had held the brooch to gaze at Helgi, she would find him crying for her. In her sister's arms, he asked over and over, "Where is Mama? When will she return?" His questions and his tears abraded her heart, but as seasons passed, a greater pain transpired. It became clear that he had forgotten her.

"He is so beautiful," Aud said. "Look how strong and tall he grows."

"He is a handsome boy, more like you than his father, I think."

"I can barely remember what his father looked like," Aud replied. "Though Helgi has his fair hair."

"It will grow darker," Skuld called. Aud didn't know if this were a grandmotherly assertion or if Skuld had seen it with her fingers on the thread.

Aud continued to gaze, despising each blink which robbed her of an instant. Finally, Verda reached for the brooch. "That's all for now," she said. "Tell us stories of outside, and you may see it next time you return."

"Please, a little longer," Aud begged. "It may be hard to get away again. Vidar already loses me once a week to Loki and—"

Urd shrieked and threw her hands in the air. "Loki? No, no, not Loki."

The other sisters clucked in a frightened chorus: "You know Loki? You see him?"

"I see him weekly," Aud said, wondering what the fuss was about. "I spend a day with him telling him stories—"

"Stories!" Verda's white hand grabbed Aud's wrist, her pale eyelashes blinking rapidly. "You don't tell him stories about *us*, do you?"

"I . . ." Aud considered the version of events she had related to Loki. "I told him about Helgi, yes."

"No! We're done for!"

"He'll find us! Whatever shall we do?"

"Please, sisters, please," Aud said, her hands held palm up in front of her. "Don't worry. He doesn't know I see you. I haven't given him a single clue to where you live."

"He's too crafty, too cunning," Urd said. "He'll take a tiny hint and work it out from there."

"No, no, I promise you."

Slowly, after repeated reassurances, the Norns began to calm. Finally, Aud asked them, "Why are you so afraid of Loki?"

They exchanged worried glances.

"We owe him," Urd said.

"What for?"

"Never you mind."

"If he finds us," Skuld said, "he'll expect payment."

"You know, Aud, that we don't change fate for just anyone," Verda said. "We did it for you because we like you and because you were prepared to bend your neck to the punishment."

"To restore the balance," Urd added.

"Because we don't conceive fate, we only make it manifest in the world," Skuld said, indicating the threads all over the floor. "The threads of fate are mysterious and eternal."

"But Loki . . ." Urd began.

Skuld took over the story. "We owe Loki a favor. Whatever he asks us, we have to grant. The consequences could be dire. He could ask us to unpick the past and make him the king of Valaskjálf. He could ask us to respin the future so that Ragnarok comes early. He could interfere in the lives of too many. He has no sense of right or wrong."

"He must never find us," Verda whispered, trembling at the thought. "Never."

"You must be so careful."

"Don't you tell a soul where we live."

"I'll break your brooch!" Verda threatened. "You won't see your little boy for a thousand years."

"We shan't tell you a thing about him."

"Beware of us, Aud."

Aud shook her head. "I won't tell anyone. You know I won't. I've never betrayed your trust. And don't I bring you pretty things from the world outside?"

Verda touched the carved hair clasp, which she had pinned at the back of her neck. "Yes, that's true."

"Perhaps we shouldn't worry," Urd said.

Skuld fixed Aud with a snake's glare. "She'll give us no reason to worry."

Aud reached out. "Verda. May I see Helgi once more before I go?"

"No," snapped Verda, returning to her loom. "You've upset us all with your talk of Loki."

"Go home," Urd said, resuming her work. The bright thread flew from the loom to the floor. The candle guttered and dimmed.

"Come back with more presents," Skuld said. "I'd like a hair clasp too."

"And me," said Urd.

"I'll bring them as soon as I can." She looked longingly at Verda, but the brooch was not forthcoming. She tried to burn the image of Helgi into her mind, knowing it was all the comfort she would have until her return. In the meantime, she would cherish the ache of his absence.

As Aud returned home through the dark passages, up the steep steps and across the passes and plains to Gammaldal, she considered the images of Helgi in her mind's eye. He looked well, he looked happy. She had done the right thing. He was alive, even if he was beyond the circle of her arms. The memory of his accident haunted her with sickening regrets. If only she hadn't let him ride Steypr. *If only, if only, if only.* By the time they met again, she would be a stranger to him, where once she had been the center of his bright world. Her heart was as leaden as the sky before a week of rain. *If only.*

From the top of the slope of Gammaldal she spotted a figure in the water of Sjáfjord. Vidar. She paused to watch him and felt a warm morsel of consolation. What a blessing that he had taken her in. His kindness had eased her first few years in Asgard, calmed her desperate unhappiness, taught her that good still existed in the world. Slowly, slowly, her heart had expanded again after the shock of losing Helgi and she had fallen unexpectedly in love.

Aud lifted her hand to wave and call out to Vidar, but then she noticed he was drawing runes. He was using seeing magic again.

This has something to do with Midgard.

Aud crept closer. Vidar would not be expecting her; she

usually returned after dark. She found the shelter of a thicket of trees and watched him. He was stripped to the waist. Aud felt an unruly flutter of desire at seeing the long strands of his hair stuck to his wet shoulders. Her fingers could too easily imagine how it would feel to brush that hair away; her lips could too easily imagine the warm salty taste of his skin. The water wrapped around his lean, hard ribs as eagerly as her eyes. His body blocked the vision in the water, but she didn't dare move any nearer. Then, just as she thought that the reasons for Vidar's journey would remain a mystery, he shifted his weight to the left and Aud saw into the water.

A woman.

The barb of jealousy was as cold as it was swift. He would risk a journey across Bifrost for a Midgard woman? He would enter into confidence with Loki for a Midgard woman?

Vidar banished the vision and turned. In the unguarded instant before he saw Aud, she recognized on his face all the signs of love: longing, desire, tenderness. She realized her hands had balled into fists.

"Aud? he said, straightening his shoulders. "How long have you been there?"

She opened her mouth to lie, to say she had just arrived, to convince him she had seen nothing. Instead, she said, "Who is she?"

Vidar's face grew ashen. He hastened out of the water. She turned to walk away from him. He grasped her shoulders with dripping hands.

"Aud, no. You mustn't tell. You mustn't."

She shrugged him off. "I have nobody to tell."

He seized her again, more roughly, and turned her to face him.

"Don't tell Loki," he said urgently.

Did he think her loyalty so easily swayed? The insult stung her. "Of course I won't tell him."

"This can't get back to my father. The consequences would be . . ." Such a look of vulnerability crossed his face that she wanted to hold him and kiss his fears away. But he did not dream of kissing her. He was in love with somebody else.

"Who is she?"

"I won't speak of it again." He released her and strode toward the house. "Come inside. We'll make some supper and forget what has passed here. Forget what you have seen."

Aud followed him home. Pale streaks of sunset glimmered over the sea and jealousy coiled in her stomach like a poisonous snake.

Seven

Vidar and Loki arrived at Valaskjálf in the last dark wedge of night. On the distant horizon, pale light resolved. The horses' breath was silver fog in the gloom.

"We'll leave Arvak and Heror here," Loki said, dismounting and giving Heror a pat on the flank. "The rest of the way we'll go on foot."

Vidar did as he was told and followed Loki through the dark woods. "I don't like being so close to my father, Loki," Vidar said as they tracked through the trees. "Are you going to explain why we're here?"

Loki had been delighted and eager to help Vidar with his secret crossing to Midgard, but had refused so far to explain a single detail of his plan. Vidar, so long used to being self-sufficient, found this profoundly unnerving. A step into the beyond with only a vague idea of what lay below.

"It's simple. Heimdall watches Bifrost at night."

"Yes." The bridge in and out of Asgard was only open during the hours of darkness.

"And Heimdall has exquisitely sensitive hearing . . . so

that he can protect us from enemies who might try to steal in."

"Yes."

"Then how do you suppose Heimdall sleeps? For he must sleep."

Vidar shook his head, perplexed. "I'd never thought of it."

"He must sleep during the day, when the light is brightest and the world is busiest. How can he manage even a moment's rest when he can hear a fish's tail in the river?"

"I don't know."

Loki smiled in the dark. "Aha! So you see, I am worth the trouble. I already know more than you do. Heimdall can only sleep under a cloak specially woven to block out all sights and sounds. It was made for him by the sea giant, Eistla. I know all this because Eistla admires no man more than she admires me." Loki smiled vainly.

Vidar finally understood Loki's plan. "So, if we steal his cloak I can wear it across Bifrost and he'll neither see nor hear me."

"Almost right, cousin," Loki said. "If we steal his cloak, we'll wake him up and you'll have to answer to Odin. But Eistla told me something that not even Heimdall knows. The cloak is magical. If we steal a single thread, we can spin enough to weave a cloak for you and for Arvak if you like."

Vidar touched his finger to his lips. "Quiet now. Heimdall will be on his way home soon. We want him to think we are animals in the forest, not conspirators waiting to prey upon him."

They paused at the hem of the wood. The early light swelled, the first glimmer caught the silver roof of Odin's hall. The vast black building with its hunched spine was silent, but seabirds called to the morning overhead. Dew shivered on the still fields of flax and barley, the dawnlight was white and cold.

Loki elbowed Vidar and gestured toward the east. A shadow approached. Vidar shrank behind a tree and watched. Heimdall returning from Bifrost. He walked nearly the full length of the hall before finding a door and letting himself in. Minutes dragged by. A dim light peered through a crack in a shutter at the end of the hall, then was extinguished. Vidar waited, his heart squeezed tight.

Finally, he touched Loki's shoulder. "Come, Loki," he said quietly. "He must be asleep by now."

Loki followed him out of cover of the wood, and said, "Perhaps on the way, you'll explain why you want to go to Midgard?"

Vidar fell silent, his lips pressed tight together. Protests and arguments were dangerous. Loki would pick over his words, the silent inflections of his hands and eyes, and make uncannily clever guesses.

"No?" Loki asked. "You won't explain? I'll find out eventually. You'll let something slip."

"Believe what you will."

They approached the western end of the hall. Loki dropped his voice to a whisper. "Vidar, you look nervous. Are you really so afraid of your father?"

Afraid of his father? Afraid of the monster in his stained furs and dazzling jewels; one eye baleful, the other just an empty socket. Afraid of that black space, that void in Odin's skull, which had sent men mad? The rumors about it were many: to look into Odin's eye socket was to look into eternity reeling away, into one's darkest, most secret fears, into the combined nightmares of every religion's underworld. Or afraid of Odin's dangerous delusions, his drunken logic, his deafening anger?

The sick misgivings Vidar had about Odin were more than just fear. Vidar was Odin's son; they were formed of the same flesh and fiber. Vidar feared the part of himself that resembled his father. Somewhere, under the layers, that sinister miasma of ruthless cruelty could be waiting to spiral up like an ocean storm.

"I'd simply prefer never to have to deal with him again," Vidar muttered.

"Eventually, you'll be pulled into the family," Loki said. "You know that."

"That's not necessarily true."

"You're fooling yourself. Your fate is with them. One way or another, they'll draw you back; they're inescapable."

"I don't wish to discuss it."

Loki pointed to a door at the far west end of the building. "Heimdall's door. It's bolted from inside of course. Heimdall sleeps so soundly with his cape on that he worries thieves might visit him unnoticed." He gave Vidar a wicked grin. "Thieves like you and me."

"How do we get in, then?"

Loki pulled a piece of dark rock from his pouch. "Once again, I'm indispensable," he said. "Really, Vidar, what would you have done without me?"

Vidar had to smile. "I don't know, Loki. I just hope the cost is not more than I can afford."

"I'm offended, cousin," Loki said, sounding not at all offended. "I'm helping you because we are two of the same, you and I. We are outsiders." Loki admired the rock in the dawn half-light. "This I stole from a fire giant named Muspel." He weighed it in his left hand. "It has special properties. It draws metal to it. So if I place it just behind the bolts and pull it across . . ." Loki pressed the rock against the door, pulled slowly. With a satisfying *snick* the bolts slid out of place.

Vidar realized he was holding his breath.

Loki slowly pushed at the door. It squeaked. He stood back. "Go on, Vidar," he said, "after you."

Vidar slipped through the doorway, his eyes searching the room. It was dim and small with a low roof. The fire spat halfheartedly in the hearth. Heimdall was nowhere to be seen.

"There," said Loki, indicating a lump of shadows near the hearth. Vidar peered closer, spied Heimdall's toes. The cloak he wore sucked up light, smudging itself into the dark.

"You know he's snoring like a forest fire under there," Loki said. "We just can't hear it because of the cloak."

Vidar set his teeth; Loki was talking so loudly. "I know Heimdall can't hear us," he said, "but what about . . . others?"

Loki sighed. "Vidar, you have lost your taste for danger. What have you been doing out at Gammaldal the last thousand years? Weaving dresses and singing love songs?"

Vidar didn't respond. He crouched next to Heimdall, peering at the cloak. "I think I spy a loose thread," he said.

"Well, pull it," Loki said. He was circling the walls slowly, picking up jewelry and carvings and examining them.

Vidar tentatively seized the loose thread. At that moment Heimdall stirred in his sleep, startling Vidar off-balance. He tipped over, nearly plunging his hands into the fire.

Loki laughed gloriously from a corner of the room. "Oh,

well done, Vidar," he said, slipping a carved whalebone into the front of his tunic. "That's the Aesir spirit."

Vidar ignored him, reached forward and this time got hold of the thread. He pulled. It eased out. Other threads caught behind it and bunched up. With his spare hand he held them flat. Soon, he had a thread the width of the cloak.

"I have it," he said, standing and winding it around his wrist. "We should go."

Loki's tunic was bulging with stolen goods. "Yes, we should. But careful now. The sun is up, and you know Odin likes his early-morning walks."

Vidar pulled open the door and ushered Loki out. The sun had crested the horizon now, a searing white glow. As Loki closed the door behind them, Vidar caught sight of a dark shape on the periphery of his vision. He turned with a gasp. In the distance, the hulking figure of his father. A thousand years compressed into a moment and Vidar remembered the broken body of his murdered lover. His breath stopped and he flattened himself against the wall. Loki instinctively did the same.

"What is it?" Loki asked, his pale eyes wide.

"Odin." His blood rushed like a hot wave through his fingers and toes.

Loki leaned carefully forward. "All is well, cousin," he said. "He heads toward the east. He hasn't seen us."

Vidar's heart slowed. "You're certain?"

"Yes. But we must be silent and quick." Loki indicated the woods with a tilt of his head. "As soon as we see him disappear over the rise, we should run."

Vidar chanced a glance toward the east. The dark figure moved slowly into the sun. Vidar could see Odin's back; if Odin turned even a fraction to his right he might catch sight of them. Vidar felt vulnerable and exposed, and longed for the cover of the trees.

"Wait," Loki said, his arm extended in front of Vidar's chest.

Odin approached the summit of the slope, then disappeared over the top of it.

"Now," Vidar hissed.

They sprinted for the woods. Vidar half expected that his father's booming voice would call "Vidar?" and freeze the blood in his veins.

But, miraculously, they plunged into the trees without notice.

Loki's eyes were wild. "What an adventure, eh, Vidar?"

"Let's just find our horses and leave," Vidar said, "and may the next time I see Valaskjálf be a hundred years hence."

Aud was working on carving another hair clasp for the Norns. Without Vidar's expert help, the design was out of proportion and the curves hard and chunky. Hoofbeats outside had her springing to her feet and throwing open the door.

Not Vidar. Loki on his black stallion, his long hair tied behind him, his pale hands on the reins, his lean body erect in the saddle. He turned to smile at her and she felt herself smile back.

"Hello, Aud," he said. "I have a gift for you."

"Vidar's not here," Aud said. He had disappeared before she was awake, all part of his new secrecy.

"Vidar's just a minute behind me," Loki said, dismounting and letting Heror roam off. "We've been making preparations for his trip to Midgard. We raced home from

Valaskjálf." He advanced and touched her hair conspiratorially. "Well, I did. Last I heard he was calling out behind me,
'Loki, it's not a race.'"

Aud scanned the trees in the distance. So Vidar was going
to Midgard. Her heart felt bruised. How long did he intend
to be gone? How did he intend to spend his time with that
woman?

"What's wrong, Aud?" Loki said, studying her face
closely. "You look positively desolate."

Aud checked herself. She couldn't allow a single hint of
Vidar's secret to be displayed to Loki. "I will miss him if he
goes to Midgard."

"You may come to stay with me if you want company,"
Loki said. "Here, a gift for you." He pulled out of the front
of his tunic a pair of moonstone brooches joined by a golden
chain.

"I can't accept it," she said, though her fingers itched to
take it. So pretty.

"I insist."

"I heard you tell Vidar I was just a bondmaid and if he
had dignity he would make me eat in the stables."

"That was before I came to know you." His pale eyes
were fixed on hers. "Before I came to like you."

Then Vidar broke from the trees on Arvak, and Aud
gladly took a step back from Loki.

Loki turned to Vidar, laughing. "I won, cousin."

Vidar drew his eyebrows together, irritated. "It wasn't a
race."

"Yes it was, and I won." Loki waited for Vidar to dismount. "Vidar, tell Aud she may accept this gift from me."

Vidar looked at the brooches. "Aud, if you want the gift,
you may take it, but don't wear it at Valaskjálf in case some-

body recognizes it and wants it back. Now, come inside. I have an important task for you."

Aud felt a thrill of excitement followed by a sick flicker of unhappiness. She loved to be able to help Vidar with an important task, but realized it must have something to do with the Midgard woman.

"Vidar, I have invited Aud to stay with me while you are away," Loki said as they moved toward the house.

"She'll stay here at Gammaldal," Vidar said, without turning around.

Loki gave Aud a conspiratorial glance. "What if she *wants* to stay with me?"

"Aud? Do you want to go to Loki's while I am away?"

"No," she said, and Loki narrowed his eyes with contempt.

"Very well, it's settled. You'll stay here except for your weekly visits." Vidar paused by the fire and Aud joined him. Loki hovered near the door.

"How long will you be gone?" Aud asked, trying to keep the helplessness from her voice.

"I do not know," Vidar said softly, meeting her gaze. "I'm sorry, Aud. But I hope to find you here on my return, and I hope that my home will remain in good order and that you will be well and happy."

His tender voice made her heart turn over. He was so dear and so perfect, and yet his tenderness was not born of any special love for her. She wanted to cry and rage against this Midgard woman, but Loki lurked nearby and, besides, it wasn't her place to say anything. "I will take good care of your home," she said solemnly.

He pushed up his sleeve and she could see that he had a brown thread wound tightly around his wrist, pressed into the scars he wore there. He unwound the thread and handed it to her. "I need you to weave me a cloak, and one for Arvak too."

Aud was puzzled. "From this?"

Loki stepped in. "The thread is enchanted," he said. "Let me show you. Fetch your spindle."

She did as he asked, presenting it for his inspection.

"Wind it on," Loki said, "you'll see."

Aud wound the strand of thread around the spindle and dropped the whorl. It spun and kept spinning, more thread magically winding out from the end that she held. She laughed, delighted by the magic. She had been forbidden the practice of Vanir magic while in service and missed the unexpected charms of enchantment.

Vidar touched her shoulder earnestly. "I need the cloak as soon as you can make it. It must cover me from head to toe, and Arvak the same. Can you manage it?"

"Of course," she said. "I won't let you down."

Despite her misgivings, she spun and wove all through the next week. She set up the loom by the fire and worked until her arms ached from lifting and pushing the heddle rod and batten. The material it made was curiously dark, as though it absorbed and stored shadows between its threads. Then there were fittings, adjustments, sewing and finishing. From first light to the last gutter of the candle she worked, hating herself for infusing so much care into it.

Finally the task was done and Vidar stood before her by the door. Arvak was saddled and cloaked nearby in the evening gloom. He was almost invisible. If she hadn't known he was standing there, she might not have seen him at all. Vidar pinned the cloak around his shoulders and smiled at her. She noticed that his hands trembled with excitement.

"Be careful," she said.

"I will."

"Be careful of your heart," she blurted out before she thought better of it.

He didn't respond. He glanced over his shoulder. "You must go to Loki tomorrow, as arranged."

"I know."

"But only for one day a week. Do not let him bully you. I need you here at Gammaldal. I'll come back . . . eventually."

"Yes, of course." She noticed the carved wooden bird tied at his waist. Even though she had guessed long ago that it wasn't for her, to see confirmation that it was a love token for someone else made her feel empty and lost.

He pulled up his hood and moved toward Arvak. "Good-bye, Aud."

"Good-bye, Vidar." And then he had disappeared, a dark shape among shadows, heading for Midgard.

A curious falling sensation gripped Vidar in the black woods. The cloak blended so perfectly with the dark that the familiar boundaries of his body disappeared, leaving him off-balance. He couldn't hear Arvak's feet, though the rhythm of hoofbeats drove up through Vidar's body. His heart kept a rhythm with them: *forward, forward.* His thoughts swirled and bubbled like waves trapped in a rock pool. What if the new Halla, Victoria, was different? What if she were vastly changed and all that Vidar loved about her— her spirit, her fierce intellect, her wit, her tenderness—had not been reincarnated along with her pale skin and liquid eyes?

Forward, forward.

He had no choice. If he were to go on breathing, he had to be with her again. In her presence, he found serenity and self-acceptance. He could escape his fate and be Vidar the man, not Vidar the son of Odin: cruel, heartless, brutal, Aesir.

The road forked in front of him. To the north, Valaskjálf. To the south, Bifrost. Both stood on mighty cliffs over the ocean. Vidar had often stood, as a boy, giddy with excited fear, looking down at the raging water that stretched as far as his eyes could see. Far and deep and deep and far, full of sea giants and snake-limbed creatures and wonders beyond the dreaming even of the immortals. The grand, thrilling mystery of the endless sea. He could hear it now, its relentless beat and draw. Tonight he would ride off that cliff into the dark. The lights of Bifrost were only visible when a traveler stepped onto it. A tumble of vaporous colors, invisible to those behind, leading in more and more gentle arcs and slopes to other worlds. Vidar knew the routes, as all Aesir did.

East to Odin's Island. To Midgard. To Victoria.

Vidar slowed as the trees thinned. He came to a stop on the edge of the wood, leaned forward and patted Arvak's cheek through the cloak. Only the horse's eyes were visible, gleaming in the dark. "Are you ready for an adventure, old friend?" Vidar said. "No matter what, you must go forward. You've been here before, don't be afraid." The cloak swallowed his voice, but the words were not for Arvak anyway. The reassurance was for himself.

Vidar settled himself upright. Ahead of him, on the edge

of the cliff, were two mighty stone sentinels a quarter of a mile apart, marking either side of Bifrost. The white stone was carved and painted, and glowed faintly in the dark. Between these, carrying a lantern and dressed in a grey cloak, Heimdall paced as Vidar watched. Heimdall moved from one end to the other and back again, his face thrown into strange shadows by the dark and the flickering lantern flame. Vidar edged forward slowly. He aimed for the north pillar. He wanted to time it so that Heimdall was at the farthest distance before he turned. He couldn't risk a flash of Arvak's eyes or hooves catching Heimdall's attention. He waited in the dark.

Heimdall moved up slowly, back slowly: two times, three, four. An hour had passed and Arvak grew restless beneath him. Heimdall turned again. Vidar counted seconds, counted Heimdall's footsteps. His heart picked up its speed. The cold sea wind threatened to whip his cloak from his face.

Almost . . . almost . . . Now.

Vidar urged Arvak forward, rode him hard down the slope. Heimdall was nearly at the other pillar, where he would turn. Vidar urged Arvak on. Now he could see the cliff edge, the raging sea miles below, the huge dark leap of nothing that he had to take. If Arvak balked, it would all be over.

"Go, Arvak," he muttered, "forward, forward."

The pillar loomed close, its grotesque carvings in strange relief among the shadows. The giant leap ahead of him. Arvak didn't slow.

The ground fell out from beneath them. Vidar's heart leaped into his throat, his stomach filled with air.

And then Arvak's hooves struck the bridge and the lights

roared into life. Greens and yellows and blues all around them; rainbow colors sparking and spitting where the horse trod. Down and down in slow undulations. A rush of excitement gripped Vidar's chest. He spurred Arvak forward, faster and faster, leaving Asgard behind him in a trail of invisible stars.

Eight

[Midgard]

Rain fell.

When the supply vessel had disappeared from view, it was only a light drizzle, the clouds streaked through with pale blue, seeming nonchalantly to say, "Oh, sure . . . it will become fine." But as the day wore on and I busied myself with my tasks, the sky grew darker and darker, the rain heavier and heavier. By three o'clock, it was driving like nails onto the roof of my cabin and thrumming through the pine trees. From my window, it appeared as though the whole of Kirkja Station had been drowned and now lay abandoned underwater, an unexotic Atlantis.

The heavy cloud cover meant daylight dwindled early. The anxiety I felt about darkness approaching was entirely new for me. Even as a child I hadn't been afraid of the dark. Now I appreciated daylight for its ability to drive shadows out of corners. A rationalizing commentary ran through my head all day: *there is a logical explanation, there is a logical explanation, there is . . .* Science was daylight for me, and I needed it to rescue me from that murky twilight of superstition inhabited by people like my mother and Maryanne.

I took comfort in mundane tasks and kept my mind off last night's experience. Who could measure the depths of the unconscious, really? It might be entirely possible for a word I heard long ago to have lodged there and worked its way loose during a stressful time. I had periods of calm during the day, where I almost enjoyed my coveted solitude. But the darker it grew, the itchier my stomach got. I was supposed to be doing three-hourly synoptic observations, but I decided that I would just fudge those results tomorrow and hunkered down in my cabin, working on my thesis to keep me distracted.

The eleven o'clock balloon launch, however, was unfudgeable. I decided that I didn't want to end up astral traveling in the forest again, I didn't want to meet up with Skripi the stick-boy again, and I didn't want to dream one more word out of Gunnar's nerdy book collection. Although it was far from comfortable, I was going to camp out in the control room. I rolled up my pillow in my quilt, pulled on my anorak and made a mad dash through the rain and the dark to the station.

The door thudded behind me. The quiet was soothing after the howling wind and driving rain outside. I dropped my things and went straight through to the storeroom to make up the balloon. Another mad dash to the hydrogen chamber and back completely soaked my hair. I hung up my raincoat and slipped out of my wet shoes, then took my pillow and quilt upstairs to the control room. I launched the balloon from the remote launch mechanism and fixed the radar on it, then mucked about with a few other tasks. Finally, I decided I'd made myself exhausted enough to sleep.

I closed the sliding door to the observation deck, but at first I didn't turn out the light. Electricity was almost as good as daylight for keeping ghosts at bay, but even with my eyes closed it was too bright to sleep properly, so I bravely made the room dark (except for the comforting light of the computer screens) and settled down. My hair smelled damp and I wondered if I'd catch a cold or if that was just an old wives' tale. My anxiety was abating, sleep approached, I slipped under.

The door slid open. I heard the rain and wind outside. I woke but found I couldn't move. A dark presence stole into the room. Terror compressed my lungs. Then I remembered Gunnar's explanation: isolated sleep paralysis. That was all it was.

I tried to pull myself all the way to wakefulness. Even though I had the scientific explanation lodged in my mind, the fear still ran over me in hot waves. My hands felt as though they were made of cement, electric stars spangled behind my eyes. My body was stiff, unmoveable, and I felt totally awake within it. The dark presence lingered nearby.

It's just isolated sleep paralysis.

The rain thundered down. I strained against my body. The presence drew closer. I could hear breathing, shallow and creaking. What horror was in the room with me?

It's just a dream. Gunnar told me about it. He called it the hag.

At that precise moment she appeared, on all fours, crawling across the carpet to lean over me. Her foul stench reached me first: mold and decay and female smells mixed together. She was dressed in rags, her hair like dirty straw, her limbs sturdy and muscular. I tried to scream but no sound emerged. I prayed for the phone to ring, for something to drive this nightmare away. In my head I began a mantra: *you're not real, you're not real, you're not real.*

The hag smiled at me, almost as if she understood my thoughts. She climbed on top of me and sat on my chest. The wind sucked out of me and I heard myself gasp. She leaned over, her lips close to mine, and I knew she intended to steal my breath. I struggled with my paralysis.

"Get off the island," she hissed.

My jaws were clamped hard against each other as I tried to thrash my head from side to side. A huge scream was gathering in my chest, if only I could free my body to let it out . . .

Beep, beep, beep.

The sound liberated me. She was gone and I could move again. I sat up and screamed, even though I could tell that I was alone, that the door to the observation deck was closed and it had all been a dream, a perfectly common sleep syndrome.

Thank God for the thirty-minute timer, reminding me of my regular data entry chores. I had forgotten about it. The ensuing tasks drove the recent horror from my mind. The lights were on, there was business to attend to. The shock passed, or perhaps it just burrowed deep under layers of common sense. Of course it was just a bad dream. I was bone-achingly tired, but I wouldn't sleep again. I sat, my head propped on my palm, until morning came. Then I made my way back to my own cabin, hoping daytime sleep would be more restful. As I stripped off in the bathroom to change into my pajamas, I saw them.

Two wide bruises on my ribs, right where the hag had placed her knees.

* * *

I had long since made a solemn vow never to phone my mother for advice, for help, to share confidences or to ask opinions. Any such conversations usually ended in frustration: we might as well have been speaking different languages. All her answers were laden with New Age platitudes. "Vicky, why can't you learn to trust the universe?" "Focus on white light for guidance." "If your chakras were in better alignment, you wouldn't get into these messes." I would become infuriated with her vagueness and try harder and harder to pin her down to a concise, clear answer. She wasn't capable of producing one, grew defensive, then came the eye-rolling, exasperated groans, even shouting sometimes, and a conviction on my part that some mix-up had taken place at the hospital on the day I was born.

Yet here I was, in the control room, still in my pajamas, dialing Mum's number back home in Lewisham.

The phone rang seven times. Mum thought it was good luck to let the phone ring seven times. "Hello?"

"Mum?"

"Vicky! Are you all right?" She sounded panic-stricken, which didn't reassure me at all.

"Yes, yes, I'm all right. Why wouldn't I be all right?"

"Oh, Vicky, Bathsheba's warning has been weighing on my mind. Weighing on my mind like a brick. Are you coming home?"

Despite my fears, I grew irritated. "No, I'm not coming home."

"You can't fight against your path, Vicky. One day you'll have to get on it."

"How do you know I'm not already on my 'path'?" I asked.

"Because it feels all wrong and Bathsheba was very

specific. A person with a name beginning with V is in danger from otherworldly forces."

I didn't point out that Bathsheba's prophecy was far from *specific,* and reminded myself that I had initiated this phone call and had better get on with asking her what I had to ask her, as much as it pained me to do so.

"Mum, I've been sleeping poorly, having terrible nightmares. In all the reading you've done, have you ever come across what it means to dream of being outside your body? Or trapped in your body?"

"Oh, Vicky!" I swear she sounded delighted. "That's it. That's what Bathsheba was talking about."

"I think they're just nightmares—"

"I'm going to see her tomorrow. I'll ask her about it. I'll take one of your old scarves, something with your psychic vibration on it." My mother always said "something" as though it were spelled "sumfink." This, along with her other mispronunciations, irritated me beyond measure. Mostly because I knew that under the veneer of my self-modified elocution, those same mispronunciations lurked.

"Psychic vibration?"

"I'll have to tell her what you've been dreaming about," she said. "Wait while I get a pen . . ."

I heard the phone drop on the sideboard and cursed under my breath. What the hell was I doing, going to my mother for advice? Disturbed sleep was nothing new to me, especially after such a monumental life change. The bruises could have been caused by any instantly forgotten bump . . . perhaps the dream had been generated in response to them, not the other way around. I nearly hung up while she was away, as a moment of extreme clarity cut through the fuzz and fear of the last two nights. I had encouraged my (quite

possibly clinically insane) mother to solicit advice from a
(quite clearly fraudulent) psychic named Bathsheba.
Bathsheba!

"Are you there, Vicky?"

"Yes," I replied mournfully.

"I must say, I'm very happy that you've finally come
round to my way of thinking."

"Mum, I—"

"Now tell me about the nightmares. What happens?"

I sighed, knew I was in too far by then to pull back. "A
hag. She comes and sits on my chest and tries to steal my
breath."

"Oh, Vicky, I wish you would come home."

"And a stick-man in the forest tells me he won't hurt me."

"Ah, a nature figure. See, Vicky, it's all so clear. You're
too far off your path."

"How do you know what my path is?"

"I know you're not on it. Chronic insomnia is a clear sign
that you're out of alignment with the universe."

I bit my tongue. I had asked for this.

"You'll get back on it eventually, I'm sure," Mum said in
a reassuring tone. "I'll ask Bathsheba for advice. In the
meantime, you need some sort of ward against evil spirits."

"Where am I going to get a ward against evil spirits?" It
was almost impossible for me to form the sentence with my
mouth, like trying to speak Spanish for the first time.

"I'll find out. Call me tomorrow night, I'll tell you what
Bathsheba has to say. Now, Vicky, I want you to think hard
about your future, about where the universe really wants you
to be."

"Can you be more specific?"

Mum made that familiar snorting noise she employed to

show me her disdain for anything specific, rational or scientific. "Don't fight fate, Vicky, it's dangerous."

"Thanks, Mum," I said through gritted teeth. "I'll call you."

Dealing with my mother's mad extremes of superstition had helped. It made me feel more like myself, more able to dismiss what had happened there so far and plan to get some sleep. I got through the morning balloon launch and retired to my cabin. The rain had begun to ease, but the wind had grown stronger, howling through the trees and battering the windows. I got into bed. I closed my eyes. I couldn't sleep. My mind was a Grand Prix racetrack, my thoughts were Formula One cars zooming around and around: Mum, the hag, Skripi, Gunnar, Magnus, synoptic observations, hydrogen chamber, radar, Mum, the hag, Skripi . . .

I got up.

Sleep, or rather the getting-to-sleep aspect of it, had always been a miserable torture to me. Rather than endure the torture, I preferred to be active, to fill my waking time, and so it was that I spent my day wandering around a sodden haunted island in pajamas with blue hippos on them and a muddy anorak. Wretched, overtired, anxious, confused.

Night fell. The wind intensified, the rain dwindled. I launched the last balloon, then went back to my cabin and climbed into bed. I closed my eyes. I couldn't sleep. This time it wasn't thoughts keeping me awake. I had no trouble dropping into that state of happy confusion that meant my brain was shutting down. But two steps down the hallway to sleep and I startled myself awake, my stomach twitching, my feet jerking away from an imaginary missed stair. Over and over I dozed, startled, dozed, startled. The wind raged. The panes were rattling, the door thudding softly in the jamb. I burrowed under the covers and tried not to try too hard to sleep.

That's when I heard it.

A knock. At the door of my cabin. Three sharp raps.

I sat up, pulling my covers up to my chin, and held my breath.

I must be mistaken, there's nobody else on the island, there can be nobody knocking, it must be something blowing against the door.

Eventually my bursting lungs reminded me to breathe. No further knocking. Just the sounds of the wind. I dropped my head into my hands and moaned. I wanted more than anything to be home, near my mum, in my lumpy old bed, sleeping and sleeping and sleeping. My eyeballs felt as though they had been sandpapered and my brain didn't fit right in my skull. My neck ached, my back ached, my soul ached. The urge to put my weary head somewhere soft and succumb to oblivion was so strong it made me want to weep. And yet, sleep was just beyond my reach, behind a veil of half-formed fears and intensifying hysteria. Gradually, night receded, the wind calmed itself, and I drew my curtain and peered out at the day. Everything was dull grey. I couldn't tell left from right.

Only one solution remained for me. I had to sleep somewhere that wasn't my cabin or the control room. I had to sleep in Gunnar's bed. I stumbled to the door and warily opened it, remembering the knocking I thought I heard the previous night, and peered outside into the grainy daylight. I was utterly alone. Of course. I closed my cabin door behind me and, as I took a step, I saw something odd sitting at the foot of an old pot plant, just beside the lattice. I crouched to look.

It was an intricately woven bed of tiny twigs about the size of a small paperback, with a black skimming stone perched in the center. I recoiled from it, the weird mix of plant matter and crude workmanship. The stone had a symbol scratched on it, like a Y with an extra tine, like a three-fingered stick hand held up in a stop gesture. I glanced around again. Was it possible this had been here all along and I'd never noticed it before?

Of course it's not possible.

Perhaps I had just blithely walked past it every morning because I'd never been concerned about ghostly strangers knocking on my door before. Ever. In my life.

I needed to speak to Gunnar. I needed to call Magnus and tell him I wasn't coping on my own and he had to come back immediately. I kicked over the ugly bed of twigs, sending the stone skittering along the cement and into the dirt. I headed straight for the control room and phoned Magnus's cell phone. After four rings it connected to a machine, a disembodied Norwegian Magnus. I presumed he was asking me to leave a name and number, so I said, "Magnus, it's Victoria. Could you please call me as soon as you get this?" Then I hung up and started looking around for a directory of staff phone numbers. I had no idea where Gunnar was staying in Amsterdam, but his parents might. I flicked through the directory, found Gunnar's name, and a number under the heading "Next of Kin." I dialed, praying his English father would answer.

"*Hei, det er hos Holm.*" A woman's voice. Damn.

"Um . . . do you speak English?"

"Who is this?"

"Ah, sorry. My name is Victoria Scott, I'm a friend of Gunnar's, stuck here on Othinsey—"

"Oh, Victoria, Gunnar has spoken of you. I'm Eva Holm, Gunnar's mother."

"Nice to meet you. I mean—"

"Gunnar isn't here."

"I know, he's in Amsterdam."

"Actually, he's on his way back here. I'm expecting him home tomorrow."

"Tomorrow?" That was one more long sleepless night away. I almost sobbed.

"Is everything all right?"

"I need to speak to him. Can you ask him to call me?"

"I certainly can. You sound anxious, my dear."

"I haven't been sleeping very well," I said, trying to make my voice calm and measured.

"Gunnar said you suffered insomnia."

What was Gunnar doing telling his mum all this stuff about me? I was irritated with him, realized it was because I was tired, then became conscious that I hadn't spoken for five seconds.

"Victoria?"

"Um, yeah. I'm alone on the island and I haven't been sleeping well, and if Gunnar could just call me and put my mind at rest about a problem I'm having with . . . the equipment, it would be really good."

"Certainly, I'll pass on the message."

"Thanks. Good-bye."

"Good-bye, dear. I hope you get some sleep soon."

I hung up, annoyed that I hadn't spoken to either of the people I so sorely needed to speak to. I checked the clock and decided to catch up on work before the morning balloon launch, hoping that Magnus would return my call. No luck. At a quarter past twelve I let myself wearily into Gunnar's cabin. The rain had cleared, the wind had blown away the cloud. I could see miles of clean sky above me and the air was still. I shut it all out and walked determinedly past all Gunnar's books (I didn't want to find that scratchy symbol inside one of them and learn it was a supernatural kiss of death) and climbed into his bed.

All around was the smell of him, warm and faintly musty. Reassuring. I closed my eyes. I disappeared—blissfully, finally—into sleep.

When I woke it was dark. But not quite dark. Gunnar's curtains were open, allowing some reflected light from the station. His cabin wasn't as sheltered by the forest as mine. I checked my watch. I had been asleep for six hours. I predicted I could easily sleep another six, or sixteen. I got up and almost closed the curtain when something caught my eye.

Filling the sky above the trees, a curtain of fluttering rainbow lights.

"Oh, my God!" I gasped. Aurora. I had never seen it before and I pressed my hands and face against the window to gaze at it. Soft undulations of pale orange and green fluttered gently from one end of the sky to the other. My first urge was to rush outside and look at it properly. The old Victoria would have, the one who scoffed at irrational fears. But I was too afraid, because Gunnar had sown that seed in my head . . . aurora storms coinciding with thieves on the island. It made absolutely no logical sense at all, but I couldn't bring myself to go outside. In fact, I went to both the back door and the front door to check they were locked.

Though I wasn't entirely certain what fearful strangeness I was so carefully locking out.

Nine

Thanks to Gunnar's cabin, its musty warmth and saggy bed, I finally caught up on all my lost sleep. As my tiredness abated and my mind cleared, the hysteria of the past forty-eight hours came to seem less and less justified. I still wasn't completely comfortable—I kept my head down and dashed to the admin building when I had a task to perform, and hurried back just as quickly—but I began to reassure myself that rational explanations were probably lurking around there somewhere. Perhaps the knocking on my door was an effect of the wind; the stone carving a lost possession that fell out of the sodden pot plant; the horrid nightmares a combination of suggestibility (Gunnar and his ghost stories) and stress (because sleep is *always* my anxiety barometer).

Refreshed and no longer tired at the impolite hour of 3:00 A.M., I sat at Gunnar's desk and booted up his computer. It was networked with the control room and I spent an hour entering some of my fudged figures. Then the siren call of the Internet, that purveyor of unsubstantiated knowledge, seduced me. I found myself looking for sites about isolated sleep paralysis, or the hag. There was plenty written about her. All of it, every single page I found, comforted the sufferer that it was a common sleep disturbance, that evil spirits probably didn't exist and that, no matter how real it felt, it *absolutely was not real*.

Reassured, I explored further. Information about psychosomatic wounds was plentiful, mostly in relation to stigmata, where people bleed from their palms in imitation of the wounds of Christ. A couple of dull rib cage bruises were barely worth a raised eyebrow in comparison to that. I kept surfing, flicking from page to page, pleased to be on the mild end of the insanity continuum.

Finally, I searched for anything about odd stone carvings. I hit a site all about runes, the alphabet of carved letters that the Vikings used. I now surmised, remembering Gunnar's Viking fetish, that the stone I had found belonged to him. Pictures of the various letters of the alphabet loaded in front of me. Finally, the rune on the stone popped up: *Eolh*, a rune for protection from evil spirits. I leaned back in the chair and yawned. My mother would be pleased; she had told me to find myself some kind of ward and one had turned up. Then I frowned, remembering that I had kicked the stone off the cement slab. Was I going to crawl around on my hands and knees, scrabbling in the dirt for it?

I guessed that depended on how much more frightened I became, alone on Othinsey.

No matter what imagined bogey lurked outside ready to spring forward and eat my brains, the balloons had to go up—twice a day, twelve hours apart, eleven o'clock Greenwich Mean Time—as they did all over the planet. This necessitated my being over at the hydrogen chamber, then the control room for about an hour. By Sunday morning, I was growing bolder, facing the outside world as though it didn't frighten me. I was out on the observation deck, getting a fix on the balloon with the radar, when the phone started ringing. I finished what I was doing, then raced to scoop it up.

"Hello?"

"Victoria, it's Magnus. What's the matter?"

"Pardon?"

"You sounded frantic on the answering machine." He chuckled. "I knew if I left you alone for long enough you'd revert to a frightened girl. All that bravado—"

"I'm not frightened and I wasn't frantic," I said, anger heating up my voice. "I just wanted to ask you about the instruments at the research site. We've had a lot of rain. Do you need me to check on them?" It was the best excuse I could conjure on short notice. It made me squirm with shame that Magnus believed, even for an instant, that I'd succumbed to superstition and hysteria like Maryanne.

"Actually, Victoria, that's a wonderful idea. You can take a set of readings for me."

"Fine. I'll do that." Damn me for a fool.

"The folder for the readings is on my desk. It has a blue spine."

"Consider it done." Alone in the forest. I needed to *think* before I opened my mouth.

"Are you sure you're not frightened out there in the Norwegian Sea?" He was teasing now. "The ghosts not bothering you?"

"No, I'm fine," I said tersely.

"I'm glad to hear it. I look forward to seeing you on Wednesday. Good-bye for now."

"Bye."

I replaced the phone in the cradle and checked the balloon's progress on the computer. I was annoyed. Not just by Magnus's ill-natured teasing, but by the realization that they would all be back on Wednesday and I hadn't had any fun alone on the island. Rather, it had been a torture, ruined by sleep deprivation and hysteria. I drummed my fingers on the table. The phone rang again. I assumed it was Magnus with more mockery.

"Hello, Vicky?"

"Oh, Gunnar."

"You sound surprised. You did ask me to call."

"Yeah, yeah I did." I had called everybody, hadn't I? Gunnar, Magnus, my mother. God, *my mother*. "Thanks for calling back. How was Amsterdam?"

"Great. Mor said you sounded anxious when you phoned."

I dropped my head on the desk. "Yeah, I was a little panicked. I've hardly slept at all, and weird things have been happening since I've been alone."

"Really?"

"I had that nightmare . . . the hag."

"It's isolated sleep—"

"Yes, yes, I know. But I had two huge bruises on my ribs afterward."

"Are they still there?"

I sat up and pulled up my pajama top. "Um . . . no."

"You could have imagined them."

"I didn't, Gunnar."

"Anything else?"

"Thursday night, somebody knocked on my door. The next morning, I found a rune stone outside."

"How do you know what a rune stone is?" he said.

"I looked it up. *Eolh*."

"Protection. Well, that's a good thing."

"But where did it come from? I was hoping it was yours."

"No, not mine. But Nils, who used to live in your cabin, he was interested in historical reenactment, like I am. He probably left it behind and you never noticed it before. And as for the knocking, you said you were low on sleep. You could have—"

"I know, I could have imagined it. What if I didn't, Gunnar? What if I'm not alone on the island?"

Gunnar chuckled. "Didn't I tell you that Othinsey would challenge even the most hardened skeptic? Don't worry. You're alone, Vicky."

"How can you be so sure? What about thieves? And I saw the aurora . . ."

"Let's think straight. First, you don't fear anything supernatural, do you? Really? You told me when we first met that you don't believe in ghosts."

I thought about the hag and the bruises: scary, but probably explainable. "No. No, of course not."

"Second, could there really be somebody else on the island?"

"That's what I'm afraid of."

"It's not possible. You would have seen or heard them if they'd come up the fjord, and I don't believe they could land on the beach."

"Couldn't they?"

"When you get off the phone from me, I want you to walk through the forest and over to the beach. Have another good look at it. There's no way somebody could land there in a small vessel."

"What about a large vessel?"

"They'd have to leave it where they landed, so if there's a boat there, at least you'd know for sure there's someone about. Then you can call Magnus and go into lockdown."

"With the hag."

"It's just a dream, Vicky. You know that."

He was right, I did know. For the first time since everyone had left, I felt like I might be able to return to myself. Rational, fearless Victoria. "Thank you, Gunnar," I said. "Thank you for letting me be so . . . vulnerable. And thank you for not teasing me about all this."

"You're welcome. I can't imagine how lonely you must be."

"I don't know if I'm lonely, I'm just—"

"You can call me anytime, Vicky. Even in the middle of the night. I'll be here until Tuesday morning, then I'm heading up to Ålesund to catch the *Jonsok.*"

"It'll be nice to see you." It was true, and I didn't care if it gave him faint romantic hope. "I'm going to do just what you said. I've got to check on Magnus's instruments, then I'll go out to the beach. An act of boldness will be therapeutic."

In this renewed spirit of self-assuredness, I moved out of Gunnar's cabin, decided that my pajamas were becoming a little grubby, and changed to day clothes. In my jeans and black turtleneck, with my anorak tied about my waist, I gathered Magnus's folder and a pen from his desk and headed out into the mild, clear day with a sense of purpose.

As I left behind the concrete, civilized space of Kirkja and moved into the forest, with that mild, clear sky obscured by dark trees, my sense of purpose faltered. The haunting familiarity returned to me. I bent my mind toward remembering what trigger linked my memories to this place, but the

search pulled me so far back that it felt like I was falling out
of time. I concentrated instead on counting my footfalls,
making them rhythmic. An acute awareness of my own vulnerability seized me. I was alone, on an island, in the middle of nowhere. Completely defenseless wasn't a feeling I
was used to. I usually felt capable and robust. But there, in
the deep forest on Othinsey, it seemed I was so transparent
and flimsy that a gust of wind could knock me over. Was this
at the root of my recent hysteria? I had thought being left
alone would be thrilling. Was Magnus right? Had the solitude caused me to revert, in some primitive biological way,
to a frightened girl?

I banished the thoughts and kept counting, dividing footsteps and spaces, making rudimentary calculations that
meant nothing. Twenty minutes later I arrived at Magnus's
instrument enclosure. The big, anvil-shaped rock jutted out
of the ground like a crooked tooth. I leaned back on it and
looked up at the sky. A black feeling swooped down on me.
Something bad happened here. I shook my head, straightened up and glanced around. Nothing bad was happening. It
was a soft spring day. I could hear the ocean in the distance
and I was surrounded by cool green colors, fresh air and the
scent of pine needles. Weak sunshine formed a pillar down
into the clearing.

Magnus had marked the transpiration monitors in the soil
with small red flags on posts. I flipped open the folder and
found his pen inside. With a squirm of guilt, I realized it was
one of those expensive Mont Blanc pens, probably worth a
small fortune. I held it very tight, afraid to lose it, as I went
from one red flag to the next, taking readings and writing
them down. My handwriting looked childish and loopy next
to Magnus's neat, spare marks. Concentrating on the work

helped me to relax. I found a spot in the sunshine and sat down, flicking through Magnus's folder and notes. Most were in Norwegian. It was growing warm, so I rolled up my sleeves. As I did so, I glanced up and saw a dark shape moving among the trees in the distance. My heart started; I leaped up. Was it just a trick of the light? I strained my eyes, but could see nothing more than shifting shadows. I listened into the distance, but could only hear the sea and the wind.

This was becoming tiresome.

Gunnar was right. I needed to go out to the beach and see with my own eyes that I was alone. I packed up and headed away from the clearing, following my ears to the beach, hoping the wind off the Norwegian Sea would blow away the fog of silly fears.

As the trees thinned out, the wind pulled my hair into tangles. The ocean roared, the beach was flat and grey. I pulled on my anorak and walked right to the edge of the waves, where they sucked and crashed on the sand. I cast my eye along the beach to the north and the south. It was empty, vast and empty. Where the sand ended, rocks took over: nobody could land a boat on rocks. Watching the wild water, I doubted anybody could bring a boat anywhere near this beach. I felt relief; it was abundantly clear that no thieves and brigands had arrived on the island.

I really was alone. Not just on Othinsey, but in the vast incomprehensible space of existence. I was born alone in my skin and knew I would die that way too. It was so awful and tragic that I wanted to cry. What use were scientific explanations? They were great for chasing away imagined spectres, but provided no comfort in a sudden moment of mortal dread. Not a scintilla of proof existed that a spirit inhabited the body of man: when we die, we die.

I turned my back on the sea and began the return trek to Kirkja.

At ten-thirty on Sunday night, I dutifully left my warm cabin and went to the cold lino-floored storeroom to assemble a weather balloon, then out into the crisp darkness to load it into the hydrogen chamber. As it filled, I did a quick check on all the equipment, did a visibility check and worked out the angle of the wind (it was a very still night), then launched the balloon and fixed it with the radar. By then, these tasks were becoming so familiar that I could do them without thought, and yet I concentrated on them very hard. Thinking about what I was doing kept me from falling down the neurotic rabbit holes in my head. I fussed around a bit longer in the control room, then left just after midnight (that made it Monday, it happened on a Monday) and went downstairs to lock up.

My hand was falling away from the door, the keys returning to my pocket, my breath fogging in the still night air, a chill on my cheeks, a warm fulfillable desire to return to my cabin, the smell of pine and faraway sea, a susurration in the treetops. I seem to remember holding my breath, or perhaps that's one of those false memories, perhaps I am holding my breath now.

I heard a sound. I turned. The dark figure of a man stood directly before me, tall and broad, his face in shadow. My heart leaped into my throat and I opened my mouth to scream.

He grabbed my wrist and said, "Please, please, don't scream. I couldn't bear to hear it."

Ten

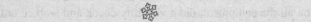

I screamed anyway. Not the bloodcurdling scream you might hear in a horror film; more a cross between a shout of shock and a moan of helpless terror. Here was the nightmare made manifest, the stranger on the island that I'd been trying to convince myself was not real. I tried to wrench away but he had me firmly by the wrist. My heart and lungs were bursting and a million scenarios played out in my head in an instant.

Then he took a step forward and the light from the station fell across his face. And everything changed.

"You're . . ." I opened my mouth to say his name, but I didn't know it. Though I was sure I must. He seemed so very familiar to me.

"I'm sorry that I frightened you."

He released my wrist and I took a step back, knowing I should run, knowing I should lock myself in the station and call Magnus. I stood before him, breath held, and merely stared. He was overwhelmingly attractive. Dark brown hair swept away from his broad forehead and fell in waves to his shoulders. His eyes were almost black, wide-set and feline; he wore an untidy goatee. His height and breadth made him appear very masculine, but his movements were agile and lithe, his hands pale and long. His physique betrayed both an athlete and artist, both power and patience. An ancient and unutterable longing drew up through me, gathering me like a needle and thread gathers silk.

"Who are you?" I asked.

"My name is Vidar," he said, his voice faintly accented like Magnus's and Gunnar's. "Don't run away. I promise I won't hurt you."

"I know," I said.

He smiled, and the keen stab of familiarity stole my breath again. I knew that I had never met this man, but some long-buried spark in my heart ignited in response to him as though he were deeply significant to me.

"I'm glad you know," he said, relieved.

"How did you get here?"

"To Othinsey? I have been here for a number of days. I can't reveal how I came to be here, I'm sorry."

His reluctance to explain made me suspicious. Had he stowed away on the *Jonsok* and been hiding in the forest? Gunnar had said it would be a good place to hide. Perhaps he was running from the law.

"Are you in some kind of trouble?"

"Don't ask me any more, I can't explain further. I know it's difficult to trust me when I say so little, but you must trust me."

I smiled. "At least you're not a ghost."

"No, not a ghost." There was no return smile; his eyes were fixed on my face and he struggled with some inner distress. "Your name is . . . ?"

"Victoria."

"Victoria," he said. "That's a pretty name."

"Thanks." I noticed, for the first time, the clothes he was wearing beneath his cloak. A brown tunic to his thighs and trousers with leather straps crisscrossed up to his knees, similar to the costume Gunnar was wearing in the photo over his desk. "Are you a friend of Gunnar's?"

"I don't know anyone named Gunnar."

"Your clothes—"

"Are muddy and cold," he said. "Could you help me, Victoria?"

I took him to Gunnar's cabin. I couldn't think what else to do. Leaving him outside in the dark while I fetched him clothes did not occur to me, though obviously it would have been more prudent. Yet I had no sense of vulnerability or of a threat to my safety. So I took him to Gunnar's cabin because I thought some of Gunnar's clothes might fit him—he said he had slipped in the mud near the lake—and I wanted to see him in a better light.

"Would you like a warm shower?" I asked as I led him in through Gunnar's back door.

"A shower?"

I indicated the bathroom. "Through there. I'll find you some clothes."

I went to Gunnar's bedroom and in his drawers found a pair of dark track pants and a crumpled white shirt that looked larger than the others. Vidar was about Gunnar's height, but not so skinny. I emerged from the bedroom to see Vidar standing in the bathroom, considering the shower with a confused expression.

"Oh, it's a strange one," I said, walking in and handing

him the clothes. My fingers brushed his wrist; his skin was very warm. "Here, you have to wind this dial up to the right temperature, then . . . pull this tap." Warm water sprayed from the showerhead. "There. When you're done, push the tap in and turn the dial back to zero."

His gaze went from the tap, to the clothes in his hand, to me. He looked bewildered and, in this better light, tired. Dark circles shaded his eyes.

"Are you all right?" I said.

"Yes, yes," he answered quickly. "I'll go in the shower."

"Fine. Towel there, soap there. I'll wait in the lounge room." I left him, closing the door behind me. I collapsed into Gunnar's sofa with a groan. What was I doing? Would I be kind to any homicidal lunatic in need as long as he was handsome? But that wasn't fair. Vidar wasn't a homicidal lunatic. I don't know how I knew that for certain, but I *was* certain. Oh, doubtless he was in some kind of trouble. Why else would he hide on an island in the middle of nowhere? But I was more intrigued by him than I was frightened. There was something vulnerable about him—something unsure about his eyes, something hesitant about his lips before he spoke—in spite of his obvious physical strength. I rubbed my wrist where he'd held it. My most violent struggle hadn't been enough to break his grip.

I went to the window, pushed the sash up and leaned out to breathe in the deep, still air. Far off in the forest a rustle and a thud echoed among the trees. I wasn't afraid of it, as I would have been just hours before. I had met the bogey—not some supernatural monster, just a man.

I heard the shower turn off and held my breath. Delicious images formed in my mind: the plane of his bare back, the hard curve of his shoulder . . . I shook my head to dispel them. My attraction to Vidar was completely puzzling: he was far from my type. Patrick and Adam had both been clean-cut, well dressed, aspirational. The kind of men who paid for manicures.

A minute later Vidar stood in the lounge room, dressed in Gunnar's clothes, his hair damp.

"They fit then?" I said, standing up to greet him.

"Just." He smiled at me. "I've imposed too much on you. I should go."

"Go? Go where? Stay a while, talk to me." A stern voice, much like my mother's, echoed in my mind, telling me not to sound so desperate.

He brushed his damp hair from his face. "Could I?"

"Of course, sit down. Would you like something to eat? You must be hungry."

"I brought supplies with me. I've eaten already." He sat in the armchair opposite me, glancing around the room.

"A glass of wine, then," I suggested brightly, hoping that Gunnar's supply had not been polished off.

"Wine? No," he said slowly, "no thank you, Victoria." He gazed at me for a few moments, then said, "Why are you being so kind to me?"

"Because you . . . because I . . ." Words simply would not spring to my tongue. Then he broke the gaze and his eyes turned to the window and I could speak again. "You seem so familiar to me," I said softly.

"Do I?" he said, his gaze far away.

"I know we haven't met, but—"

"Perhaps I remind you of somebody. Your brother or your father."

"I have neither."

"An old friend."

"We haven't met, have we?"

He turned to me. "You know the answer to that."

A silent moment grew between us. It felt like the moment before a roller coaster dips over a curve. I laughed to break the tension. "I guess I do. Sorry if it sounded like a pickup line."

He looked puzzled, and I realized that perhaps his English wasn't as good as Magnus's or Gunnar's. I apologized again, but he didn't hear me.

"What do you do here, Victoria?"

"I'm a scientist. I watch the weather." I drew my legs up under me on the sofa. "And you? What do you do?"

He tilted his head to one side and pressed his lips together thoughtfully. Finally, he said, "I'm a woodworker."

"Ah. And what are you doing on Othinsey?"

"I can't tell you." He leaned forward and lowered his eyes. "I'm so sorry, Victoria, but I can't tell you."

"You're in trouble, aren't you?"

"You could say that."

I shivered. "Have you done something bad?"

"Some would consider it bad. I don't. You wouldn't."

"Are you sure?" I said softly.

"I have committed no crime," he said. His eyes were intense, almost desperate. "But I have broken a rule."

"Now I'm even more confused."

He waved a hand, dismissive suddenly, all intensity evaporating. "You are very kind, Victoria, but I should return to my camp and dry out my clothes by the fire."

"Your camp?"

He gestured toward the window. "In the forest."

"But it's cold out there. You could sleep in—" My tongue was galloping along without the assistance of my brain. I paused. I thought. I couldn't offer him Gunnar's bed. I still didn't know if he was Othinsey's resident thief and it wasn't fair on Gunnar to leave Vidar alone with all his computer equipment and CDs. I couldn't offer for him to stay in my cabin because, despite my recent behavior, I wasn't a complete fool; supplying a fugitive with warm clothes was one thing, going to sleep while locked in a small space with him was another altogether.

"Victoria?"

I remembered the storeroom. An internal door locked it off from the rest of the admin building. "You could sleep in the storeroom," I said.

Vidar needed a little persuasion. Although the night was mild and clear, I assured him that the rain clouds around Othinsey blew in at an instant's notice. I fetched him blankets, pillows and a quilt from the linen store at the back of the rec hall, locked everything that I could, and made up a bed for him in the storeroom. I glanced around, assessing the risk of him stealing anything from there. Weather balloons, cleaning supplies, spare parts of obsolete equipment, old record books growing mildew, Magnus's blue folder. Good luck to him if he thought anything there had any market value.

"I won't take anything," he said, guessing that I was counting with my eyes. "I'm not a thief."

"I'm sure you're not," I said quickly.

He smiled at me gently. "Thank you, Victoria. You're a good person. I hope that one day I can repay you."

I hesitated at the door. "No repayment necessary. I just hope you sleep well."

"I'm certain to," he said, his gaze lingering for a moment. "Good night."

"Good night."

I closed the door behind me and hurried back to my cabin. I predicted a sleepless night: my thoughts were moving like wildfire, my heart burst with guilt and excitement. And yet, safely locked in my cabin and tucked in my warm bed, I thought of Vidar and a sense of peace and happiness stole over me. Nothing else troubled me. Until morning.

I took a little more care choosing my clothes in the morning. I pulled on a warm dress, and even scraped on some makeup for the first time in nearly a week. I trembled as I locked up my cabin: my knees felt rubbery and my heart was in my mouth. I didn't know if it was fear or desire, but the two together were a potent combination and I felt faintly sick, as though I'd drunk too much coffee and stayed up all night.

I made my way over to the admin building. The smell of ocean bristled on the air. I opened the back door to the storeroom and peered in.

It was empty.

A tumble of realizations: Vidar had left and he had taken Gunnar's clothes and the linen I had loaned him. Magnus's blue folder was open on the bench and . . . *that's right, oh my God* . . . his Mont Blanc pen was missing.

I tried the door through to the station, but of course it was locked. I ran out the way I'd come and quickly scanned around. I glanced toward the forest. He was in there, no doubt. Hiding. All at once, I guessed his plan: a ring of thieves dropped him off on the island and picked him up later with the swag. I raced over to the rec hall to see if he'd broken in to steal the television. It was still locked, but I let myself in, checked around (nothing missing) and went through to the galley (nothing missing, but the chicken breast I'd left out to thaw two days ago was getting stinky).

"Well, I hope your trip was worth the damn pen," I muttered as I headed back to the admin building. I was keenly irritated with myself. What kind of an idiot would trust him? As I sat down at the desk in the control room, a darker thought occurred to me. Was I safe with him on the island? I had been so enamored of him that I might have overlooked crucial signals. Perhaps he intended far worse than just stealing expensive pens.

I put my head on the desk. My breathing echoed loudly in my ears. My intuition told me that he wouldn't hurt me, but since when had I believed in intuition, let alone listened to it?

The phone rang, jerking me back to reality.

"Hello?"

"Ah, Victoria, I hoped I'd find you there."

"Oh. Hi, Magnus." I felt guilty and ashamed all at once; it made my face hot.

"I'm back in Oslo, meeting the others at Ålesund tomorrow. We're going to have drinks, we'll miss you."

Ah, life used to be so uncomplicated. Drinks with the staff. I sighed.

Magnus chuckled. "Don't worry, we'll have drinks when we arrive back on Wednesday too. How is everything there?"

I opened my mouth to say what I should have: *There's a strange man on the island and he stole your gold pen and I'm locking down immediately.* Instead, I said, "Everything's fine. Nothing to report."

"Good girl. You're doing a fine job, Victoria."

"Um . . . thanks," I said. "I appreciate your saying so."

"I'm giving credit where it's due, Victoria. You're a smart girl, a capable girl. All in all, I think I displayed very good judgment in hiring you," he said, without a trace of humor. "Now, I need to ask you something important."

I grabbed a pen and a piece of paper. "Go ahead."

"Do you think it's a bad thing for a boss to become romantic with a member of his staff?"

Words failed me. "I'm sorry?" I managed to choke out.

His loud laugh in the receiver spiked my ear. "Don't worry, Victoria, I'm not asking you out. It's Maryanne."

"Maryanne?"

"We met yesterday for lunch at Bygdøy, and took a romantic walk along the beach. She kissed me."

I realized I should gather together some kind of bluster and tell him off for being unctuous, but it seemed impolite to do so after I'd just lapped up his praise. "Magnus, I'm not sure that I'm the right person to ask about this," I said.

"Victoria, you're a woman, and I'd value a woman's opinion."

"Well, I . . . if she's . . . I mean . . ." I trailed off into silence, wondering why I was embarrassed when clearly he should be. I tapped my pen violently on the desk.

"Young people have it so easy." Magnus sighed. "You and Gunnar, you're at the age when you can think about love and talk about love and nobody shrinks from you. Nobody finds it distasteful."

"What's that? Me and Gunnar?"

He sniggered. "Victoria, it's obvious to all of us that there's something between you . . . some spark."

"No, no. We're just friends."

"Gunnar doesn't see it that way," he said, channeling the

spirit of a naughty schoolboy. "He told me that—Oh, that's right, he asked me not to mention it."

I kept my mouth shut. I didn't want to know what Gunnar had said about me.

"Anyway, I was saying," Magnus continued, "that romance is not reserved for the young. Do you know how old I am, Victoria?"

I was guessing somewhere around his mid-creepies. "No."

"I'm fifty-one," he declared in a revelatory tone. *Voilà!*

I realized this was my cue to express astonishment. "Oh," I said.

"I know I don't look it, I like to take care of myself, keep myself trim. But I'm not a young man anymore and I want to grab romance with both hands."

"Then perhaps you should pursue Maryanne," I said, hoping this would be an end of it.

"But I don't know if she's right for me."

"Then perhaps you shouldn't. Magnus, I have some bad news for you." The only way to change the subject.

"Bad news?"

"Your Mont Blanc pen. I took it out to the instrument field and now I can't find it. I think I dropped it out there."

"What! Oh, Victoria, what were you thinking, taking it out in the forest?"

"It was with the folder. I didn't realize until I was out there. I'm really sorry."

"That pen was worth a fortune. It was a collector's edition! A Meisterstuck!"

"I know, I know. I'm sorry."

"Can you go out and look for it?"

"I'll try."

He had forgotten about Maryanne and romance for the over fifties, and babbled some instructions about meaningless tasks I was to perform until he returned, a penance I'm sure. I jotted them down and thankfully hung up the phone.

I leaned back in my chair, feeling strangely deflated. The thrill of fear (negative though it had been) was gone. Vidar wasn't a romantic hero, just a common thief, my boss was a jerk and the island would be inhabited again in just two days. My own company weighed on me; I was bored with the endless monologue of numbers and rationalizations in my head.

Most of all, I felt let down by Vidar. I realized this was ridiculous. I didn't know him, but he had asked me to trust him and I had, and now I would probably never see him again.

And I wanted to see him. I wanted that very badly indeed.

Eleven

I had eaten nothing but bread and cheese in my room for the last few days so I went to the galley for lunch, determined to cook myself something with vegetables in it, lest I succumb to scurvy. I made a stir-fry and took it to the rec hall to eat. The big empty space echoed with the sound of my chopsticks and plate.

Footsteps near the door. I looked up. Vidar. He stood there in Gunnar's clothes, lit from behind by the bright outside, wordless, motionless. A surge of fear. Why had he returned? I jumped out of my seat.

"Victoria?" he said at last, and a puzzled expression crossed his face. "Is something wrong?"

"Magnus's pen," I blurted out.

"Who?"

"I won't call the police if you just leave now." Yes, and just how long would it take for the police to respond to that particular emergency call?

"The police?"

"You took Magnus's pen," I said, angry now.

He felt in the pocket of Gunnar's track pants. "This pen?" He approached, his hands spread out in front of him. "Why does it frighten you so? You're trembling."

I snatched the pen from his hand. "Because I didn't know you were a liar and a thief, and I wonder what else you might be."

"No, no, Victoria. I didn't steal the pen. I didn't know it was valuable. I borrowed it to draw you a map, you see?" He unfolded a piece of paper and handed it to me. "I wasn't comfortable in the storeroom, so I headed back to my camp. I drew a map so you would know where to find me if you needed me, if I could repay you somehow for your kindness."

I glanced from his face to the map and back again. Sleepless shadows were smudged beneath his eyes.

"You must believe me, Victoria," he said softly. "I'm not a liar and I'm not a thief."

"Then explain what the hell you're doing here," I said, guarding my voice, my body, my heart. And when he opened his mouth to refuse, I said, "Don't tell me you can't, that's bollocks. I'm nobody special. I've no friends in high places to repeat it to, and you assured me you haven't broken the law, so what does it matter if you tell me?"

He dropped his head. "I'm sorry. Victoria. Perhaps one day very soon you'll understand, but I—"

"Just tell me who you're hiding from," I said.

Vidar pushed up his sleeves and held his elbows, the gesture of an eight-year-old boy. I noted a long scar on his left forearm, a knotwork tattoo around his right wrist. "My father," he whispered. "He must not find out where I am."

"Your father? You're afraid of your father?"

In an instant he had pulled himself up tall. "No, of course

I'm not. Not for myself. I'm afraid of what he might do to . . . to those I love." He ran a hand through his long hair. "He's a very powerful man."

Suspicions formed. Who was his father? Head of a multinational corporation? A billionaire playboy? Didn't Norway have a royal family? I had met men like Vidar before: despite a background of privilege, they wanted to escape their families, their fates. I could understand that.

"He sounds like a nasty piece of work," I said.

Vidar found this turn of phrase amusing. He smiled guardedly. "He is."

"He'd actually hurt people you love to punish you?"

"He would." Somber now, Vidar's gaze darted away from mine. "He already has."

"Just for the hell of it?"

"No. For very powerful reasons."

"What did he do?"

He slid his hands in his pockets and shook his head. "You wouldn't believe me if I told you."

I realized my lunch was going cold. "Do you want something to eat?" I said. "There's more in the pan."

"I would, yes," he said hesitantly. "I've eaten nothing but bread and cheese for days."

"Me too," I said. "Wait here."

When I returned with a plate for him, he was sitting at the end of the table, diagonally across from my seat. He picked up the chopsticks I offered him and eyed them carefully.

"Oh, sorry," I said. "You've never used chopsticks?"

"No."

"I'll get you a knife and fork."

"A spoon, please," he called after me.

I settled at the table with him once more and watched him

eat with a spoon, figuring this was how Scandinavian royalty must eat their rice.

He glanced up, spoon halfway to his mouth. "Why have you been eating bread and cheese?"

"It's your fault actually."

"My fault?"

"Well, not entirely. I'm here alone, you see. Ordinarily there are eight other people here, but the World Meteorology Conference is on in Switzerland and I volunteered to run the station alone. I've been hiding, frightened, in my cabin. I've been hearing noises—probably you—in the forest, outside. And having terrible dreams and weird feelings."

"I couldn't have caused your terrible dreams or weird feelings," he said.

"No, no, I suppose not. I'm an insomniac, you see. I sleep very poorly a lot of the time, and when I get tired perhaps I imagine things."

He didn't meet my eye and focused on his food. "What things? What dreams have you had?"

"The hag," I said. "Though I know it's not real, it felt very real."

He put his spoon down carefully and steepled his hands under his chin, gazing at me. "Go on, tell me of this hag."

"I was paralyzed, and she came in and sat on my chest. I knew, somehow, that she intended to steal my breath." The unnatural fear rippled over me again, even though it was daylight and I was no longer alone. Gooseflesh shivered along the backs of my arms. "And then there was Skripi," I said, forcing brightness into my voice. "The stick-man who warned me about the draugr."

"A draugr is a thing to be feared," he conceded.

"You don't believe in it, do you?"

"I believe that legends arise from often-told tales, and that perhaps in each fable there lurks a shadow of honest experience. And if that is so, then it pays to be cautious—especially where a draugr is concerned." The barest hint of a smile touched his lips, but I couldn't tell how serious he was. "Tell me again of your dream of the stick-man. You called him Skripi?"

"He met me in the forest . . . I mean . . . it sounds crazy." I laughed nervously. What kind of impression was I making? "Of course, it was a dream and dreams are often crazy. He said he wouldn't hurt me, and he said his name was Skripi, which I found out is Old Norse for—"

"Phantom. Yes, I know."

"*You* know, but how could *I* know? Why would I dream a word in a language I'd never heard?"

He shrugged and returned to his food. "Perhaps it wasn't a dream."

"Ha ha. Funny. Anyway, now I know what some of the strange noises and shadows in the forest were, I don't feel so bad about this place." I toyed with a cold piece of carrot on my plate. "Now I'm not alone."

Vidar finished his food and stood up. I felt a keen sense of disappointment that he was leaving. "You're going?"

"I've taken up too much of your time. You have work to do."

I thought about all the data that I had to enter to catch up on the hysterical hours when I'd hid in Gunnar's cabin, not to mention the meaningless tasks Magnus had dictated to me over the phone. Vidar was right. "Yes, I have."

He pushed the map over the table toward me. "This is where I am camped. If you would like to visit . . . otherwise, I'll leave you be."

I looked at the map. His camp was a mile northwest of the instrument field.

"I thank you, Victoria," he said, touching my shoulder gently. "I thank you for your kindness and for trusting me. Good-bye."

"Bye." I watched him leave, savoring the fantasy of visiting him that night. Foolish, maybe. Perhaps he was luring me into a trap. I didn't entertain that thought for more than a half second. I felt safe with him, I knew he was gentle and honest and good, and I was certain that nothing ill could come of me following his path into the forest after work to find him.

I suppose that the end of any path is rarely visible at the beginning.

Dusk closed in and stars began to sparkle, and the barest breeze quivered in the trees. The faraway beat of the ocean hissed and shushed, and I locked up the station and headed to the galley. I heated some soup and poured it into a Thermos, and tucked the Thermos with two cups and four recently defrosted bread rolls into a plastic bag to take with me.

Just twenty-four hours ago the idea of heading off into the forest alone at night would have been unthinkable. Now I relished the thrill of my isolation in the soft darkness, the kiss of the breeze, the gleam of the lonely stars. My stomach fluttered with the sweet tension between promise and delay, and an ache of desire shimmered across my body, making my skin vulnerable to sensation. As I found my way through the trees, the dark weighing all around me and the tree branches like the frozen arms of some primitive nightmare creature, my mind tripped up over and over again. This was surreal. Who was I and what was I doing? During that walk through the ancient and gloomy passages of the forest, I realized something about myself. My obsession with divisible figures and regular shapes and logical explanations had forever kept me from taking even one step into the unknown. Why a ragged stranger with black eyes and a soft voice should lure me into that mystery was incomprehensible to my conscious mind, but in the hidden alcoves of my thoughts and my body, it made some sort of inexpressible sense.

The reflected glow of a fire caught my eye and I headed toward it. Vidar sat with his back to me, but I could tell from a tensing of his shoulders that he knew I was there.

"You came," he said, without turning around.

"I brought you food." I walked to the fireside. The linen I had given him the previous night had been layered on the forest floor to make a soft place to sit. I settled next to the fire and pulled out the Thermos and cups. "Pumpkin soup. I hope you like it."

"I'm sure I will."

I ventured a glance at him as I poured the soup. He was more ragged than before, his hair unbrushed and stubble growing on his cheeks, Gunnar's shirt stained with mud or charcoal or both. I tried to assess what age he might be: definitely older than me, perhaps in his midthirties. He met my eyes briefly, then leaned forward to throw a handful of twigs on the fire.

"The fire's nice and warm," I said, handing him a cup of soup and a roll.

"I find I can't sleep without one, even in summer," he said. "I'm so used to the sound of it, that quiet crack and pop. It's the sound of still moments in tranquil places."

"Is that why you couldn't sleep in the storeroom?"

He tore off some bread and dunked it in his soup. "Yes. There were a lot of sounds."

I shrugged out of my anorak. "Oh, sorry. There's equipment in the building. It's always beeping or buzzing to remind you to do something."

We ate in silence for a few minutes. He still hadn't smiled at me, or even looked at me for more than a few seconds, but I detected no coldness in his reception of me. I was not made uncomfortable by his reticence, as would ordinarily be the case. Whatever it was about him that made him so familiar to me, also made me content to sit with him in silence. As though the preliminaries to our sharing company had already been processed.

Finally, he dusted crumbs from his fingers, and said to me, "Why are you here?"

"Here with you? Or here on the island?"

"Both. Either." He smiled. "Start with the island."

"I'm here as a trainee. I'm helping on a climatology study."

"No, no. I didn't ask *what* are you doing here. I asked *why* are you here. Why, not what."

I pushed a strand of hair off my face. "I'm running away from my mother," I said, and laughed nervously. "Although I've never thought of it like that before."

"Why are you running away from your mother?"

"Because I'm afraid of becoming like her."

He dipped his head in a nod. "Then we understand each other perfectly well."

"You're afraid of becoming like your father?"

"Oh, yes."

"I bet he's not as bad as my mother."

"I bet he is," Vidar replied quickly, with a laugh. "Still, there's no value in competing." He stood and held out his hand to me. "Come, let's walk in the forest a little way."

I could feel myself beam. He helped me up, and I felt the reluctant withdrawal of his fingers from mine. I followed him away from the campsite into the cold pools of night that waited between the trees.

I'd forgotten my anorak and tensed my shoulders against the chill. "This forest has always felt strangely familiar to me," I said. "It's weird."

"Perhaps it is familiar to you," he replied. "Perhaps you have been here before."

"No, I'd remember."

"Before *you*," he said. "Before Victoria."

This had never occurred to me. It was the kind of idea my mother would come up with. "You mean like reincarnation? Do you believe in reincarnation?"

"I don't know. Do you?"

"No. I don't believe in anything."

"Nothing at all?"

"Nothing I can't experience with my own five senses. Nothing like God, or ghosts, or mind reading, or reincarnation."

"What if you experienced one of those things with your own five senses?" he asked. "What if you saw God, or felt the touch of a ghost, or read somebody's mind?"

"It's never happened."

"But if it did."

A soft breeze caressed my face as I considered this. I tasted salt faintly.

"Then I'd reevaluate," I replied. Strangely, I wasn't irritated with him for pushing this point, nor was I disappointed that he hadn't sided with my skepticism.

"I don't think you would reconsider," he said.

"Why do you think that?"

"Because I think you've already experienced something with your senses that is inexplicable, and you still hold that you believe in nothing."

A frost of fear stole over my skin. "What do you mean?"

"Skripi," he said.

"Oh, that."

"Did he look as though his hair was made of twigs?" he asked, breaking off a twig to hold in front of me. "Were his hands and fingers pointed and pale? Were his eyes the oily black of a forest creature's?"

"Yes," I managed to gasp. "How did you know?"

"He's a forest wight, I imagine," Vidar said. "I know the lore of these parts. Forest wights are common in the local tales."

I snapped my fingers. "That explains it. I must have seen something on television or in a book, perhaps when I was a child. If it's a common tale, I'm more likely to have heard of it. And heard his name." I was very satisfied with myself for reaching this conclusion, and it took me a few moments to realize that Vidar had been trying to prove quite a different point. "Sorry," I said, "but I'm a fundamentalist atheist."

"Never mind," he said, not sounding troubled in the least.

We weaved through the dark trees, among the shadows, surrounded by the smell of pine needles and salt. Occasionally my arm would brush his, raising electricity. The cold sky above was indifferent to us, the last two souls for miles and miles.

"You believe in supernatural things then?" I asked.

"I have seen many strange things."

"Like what?"

"They're all tales for another time. You answered only one-half of my question earlier. Why are you here? Here with me?"

The question caught me off my guard and I lost my footing, stumbled, then quickly righted myself.

"Are you all right?" he asked, his hand under my elbow. We had come to a stop, facing each other in the shadowy forest. I looked up at him, he looked down at me. The breeze lifted his hair, and his eyes glittered in the dark. "Victoria?"

"Yes, I'm fine," I said, finding my tongue. "I'm here because you intrigue me."

"I do?"

"Yes. It's completely out of character for me . . . I should warn you of that, so you don't think I'm something I'm not."

"I know you well enough," he said, so softly the murmur of the wind in the treetops almost drowned it out.

A magical feeling stole over me, a feeling of anything being possible. I thought he was going to kiss me, but he stepped back gently, his fingers lingering, then grazing my elbow. I shivered.

"You're cold," he said. "We'll head back to the fire."

"I don't mind," I said, but he was already leading the way. I walked next to him in silence and we passed the instrument field. Magnus's red flags were invisible in the dark. The anvil-shaped rock was ghostly among the shadows. The conviction that something bad had happened there walked my spine once more.

"We're doing research in here," I said, signaling around.

"In here?" There was a frown in his voice.

"To be honest, the place gives me a bad feeling."

"Perhaps it's a bad place."

"Remember? Fundamentalist atheist?" I said dismissively.

"Of course." Vidar was laughing as we moved on. "I'm sure it's a perfectly ordinary clearing in a perfectly ordinary forest on a perfectly ordinary island."

"Everything's perfectly ordinary once you look at it closely," I said, jolted by how sad that was. At the moment Vidar seemed like a romantic hero, but I expected that any prolonged contact with him would eventually reveal all his ordinariness. "Except the weather," I added softly.

"Ah, the weather. You know, once people believed that the gods controlled the elements."

"And that the earth was flat, and that hysteria was caused by a woman's womb moving about the body."

"You mean it's not?" I caught a glimpse of his smile.

I laughed. "No. And I should know, because of the hysteria I worked myself into the last few days." The glow of the fire was visible again. I felt anxious and disappointed. I wanted him to kiss me, but he hadn't taken advantage of the perfect moment. Did that mean he didn't want to kiss me? "Vidar," I said, "how long are you staying on the island?"

"I can't say."

"I think I know how you got here," I ventured, thinking of my theory that somebody had dropped him off over at the beach.

"You don't," he said. "I can't answer any more questions."

"You're being so enigmatic," I teased.

He turned to me, the fire lit his face. His eyes were intense, his mouth firm. "I'm not doing it to entertain myself,

Victoria. I really can't tell you, not without risking . . . everything."

The rebuke had been gentle, but still stung. "I'm sorry." I scooped up my anorak. "I should go."

"Victoria, don't be angry with me," he said, and his voice was imbued with sorrow and tenderness and it reminded me of something . . . something wonderful and just out of grasp of my memory. He picked up the Thermos and cups and handed them to me. "But you should go. You should get some sleep."

"Not likely. I've got to send a balloon up at eleven." I checked my watch. I didn't want to go back to my cabin and sit there longing for him. "Let me stay until then."

He motioned that I should sit down. "Certainly, I'd be delighted if you stayed. You can tell me all about your mother."

So I shared with him some of my favorite Beverly Scott stories, and it was nice to sit and talk and laugh by the firelight. But it was odd, too, because the conversation was so one-sided. I didn't dare ask him to repay me in stories about his troubled relationship with his father, and as I became more and more open to him, he became even more mysterious by contrast.

Finally, it came time for me to go. I tried not to look reluctant as I packed up my things. I still hoped he might kiss me. I had that fluttery first-date feeling. But he busied himself with the fire as I hovered uncertainly nearby, waiting for him to say good night.

"Good night, Victoria," he said at last, glancing up from the fire. A strand of hair fell over his eyes.

"Come by for lunch again tomorrow," I said. "I'll cook for you."

"I can't. It wouldn't be right."

"I won't tell anyone."

"I don't feel comfortable over at the station," he said. "I'm sorry. But you have the map, you know where I am camped. If you wish to see me again . . . I'll leave it to you to find me."

"I'll find you," I said quietly.

He gave no indication he had heard. "Good night, Victoria."

"Good night."

All of my work the following day was impossibly mundane, devised by insipid morons for profoundly unexciting purposes. Despite his avowals, I still held out hope that Vidar might turn up at the rec hall for lunch. He didn't. Time dragged. Clouds blew in and I worried about rain ruining my plans to sit by his fireside and be brave enough to kiss him.

No rain fell, twilight came. This time he was lying beside the fire, staring up at the sky. "I heard you coming," he said. "You'd never make a good hunter."

"I've never wanted to be one."

He pulled himself up and grabbed my hand. "Come," he said.

"Where? I brought dinner."

"We'll have it later. Leave it here." He smiled, and his bright mood was a contrast to the previous night's intensity. "Come, I'll show you how to be as silent as a hunter."

I was swept up in his enthusiasm and let him lead me beyond the firelight into the dark forest.

"First," he said, "you have to balance your body on your feet. Your weight can't be any greater on one part than another."

"Like ballet," I said, remembering lessons I took as a child.

"Your feet have to be as sensitive as your hands," he said. "If you were feeling around on the forest floor with your fingers, you'd be able to avoid loose rocks that click, or sticks that might crack."

"Should I take my shoes off?"

"No, because you need your feet to be protected if you run."

"Then how . . . ?"

"It's practice. Go on, take a step and don't put any weight on your foot until you've felt the ground beneath you."

I did what he said, and a stick broke with a loud *pop*.

"Oops," I said.

"And if you do make a noise, you have to disguise it." He crouched and grabbed a rock the size of a fist and sent it skittering along the ground. It sounded exactly like the footsteps of an animal running away.

"That's amazing."

"I'll show you."

For the next half hour Vidar had me practice silent steps and animal impersonations. I'd never been the outdoorsy type, so I was surprised by how much fun we had. The dark and shadows made it thrilling; Vidar was by turns patient and playful. Finally, he stretched his arms over his head in a tired gesture.

"Practice it when you can," he said. "You'll become good at it very quickly. You're graceful."

I felt a rush of pleasure. It was perhaps the only spoken confirmation I had from him that he might be attracted to me. "I will," I said, "but I don't think I'd ever hunt. I prefer my meat already dead. It takes the guilt out of it."

He smiled. "It's useful for hiding as well as hunting," he said. "Now, stand here a moment. Let me show you how quiet I can be."

I laughed. "Why?"

"Because I want to show you. Because it's something I'm proud of." He squared up my shoulders, and said, "Stand here, and close your eyes."

I did as he asked and waited for him to leave. I didn't sense him move, so after about ten seconds I opened my eyes.

He was gone.

"Vidar?" I called, still amused but also a little disturbed. I strained my ears, but could only hear the sounds of the forest, the breeze and the sea in the distance. I turned to look around me. Was that him over to my left, a shadow among shadows? I felt very alone, deserted in an empty place. I peered into the gloom, toward the movement I thought might be him. "Vidar? Is that you?"

A hand grasped my right shoulder and I shrieked before I could check myself.

"Sorry," he said gently, "I didn't mean to frighten you."

I laughed loudly. "God, I nearly wet myself." I instantly regretted saying that, but he was laughing too and it was a lovely sound, warm and humble.

He backed off and gestured toward his campsite. "It grows cold," he said.

We returned to the fireside to eat, then he sat cross-legged while I lay on my side on the folded quilt. The flames were hot and bright; I felt mellow and besotted. That ache of desire had returned, the space between us grew magnetized. We were silent for a few moments, considering each other in the firelight.

"How much longer will you be alone here?" he asked.

"Until tomorrow," I said.

"Tomorrow?"

"The *Jonsok* comes back. The rest of the staff will be on it. Don't worry," I said, "I won't tell them about you."

"I'm not worried. Not about that."

More silence. I locked my gaze on his and was certain that I saw in his black eyes the echo of my own desire. I rose and started across the space between us.

He dropped his gaze and said, gently, "Victoria, it grows late."

"But I—"

"You should go."

This was hellishly embarrassing. I hovered in the seasick space between him and where I should have remained. "Yes," I said meekly, "it's late and you're right. I should get back for the . . . balloon . . ."

"Good night," he said. His voice was infinitely tender, giving me pause.

"Good night," I said, making myself busy packing up the Thermos and cups. "I'll see you soon."

"Good night," he repeated, and he seemed forlorn and uncertain and even afraid to be alone. "Good night, Victoria."

I went back to my cabin, my face hot with embarrassment and my mind in a turmoil of incomprehension. I had misread him somehow. I had failed to understand some nuance in his words or actions. I had been *certain* that he was falling for me, but I was wrong. Or was I? Perhaps he was married, or engaged to somebody back home. Perhaps that's what he was running from. And now he had met me and wanted me instead and . . .

I checked myself. I would ask him the next day. No mat-

ter how embarrassing it proved to be, I would ask him what
barrier existed for us, because I *knew* that he felt as I did.

So, the following morning, I psyched myself up, rehearsed a speech, put on a little too much mascara. I wound
my way through the woods toward his campsite, tense and
uncertain. I found his fire, extinguished now. I found the
linen I had loaned him, folded neatly. I found Gunnar's
clothes, washed and hung over a tree branch to dry.

My heart fell all the way to the forest floor.

I crouched to pick up the linen. A wooden carving lay on
top, about as big as my hand. It looked like one of those
Viking carvings, a bird curled over on itself to grasp its feet
in its beak. Vidar had said he was a woodworker and I wondered if he had carved this himself, for me. Nobody had ever
made me anything.

I noticed a black smudge on my finger and looked closely
at the carving. Around the edge, written in charcoal, was one
word.

"Good-bye."

Twelve

A quarter of an hour before the *Jonsok* was due to arrive, I pulled on warm clothes and wheeled the pallet down to the jetty to wait. I sat on the rough wood and breathed the clear air. The water of Hvítahofud Fjord was very still and very dark and very deep, like the calm eye of a stern parent. The sky was the color of slate, and periodically a gust of wind and a shower of drops would buffet me. I pulled up my hood and curled my fingers into my gloves and watched the space between the two tall cliffs where the supply boat would eventually appear.

It was just as well that Vidar was gone, I told myself. It was a good thing, because hadn't I come here, to this remote place, to escape from matters of the heart? Wasn't the whole idea to give myself some breathing space after the twin disasters of Patrick and Adam? In daylight, grey though it was, memories of Vidar grew mysterious. His black eyes and his soft voice in the dark; his refusal to speak of himself; the odd clothes he had been wearing when we first met. He was too enigmatic, simmering with secrets and contradictions and tensions. I needed none of it. I wanted none of it.

Despite all this rationalizing, I had never ached like this for someone before. It was all-consuming and it hurt all over my rib cage, made me want to cry and close my eyes and think of nothing but him, but I couldn't succumb to those feelings because I wasn't a teenager anymore. I was a grown woman with two degrees and boundless common sense and many responsibilities. So I sat in the cold and waited for company, for conversations and jokes and bottles of wine to take my mind off the strangest week of my life.

It was with an odd mix of relief and disappointment that I finally spied the boat in the distance, a white dot against grey sea. As it motored up to the jetty, I calculated its lateness as a percentage of the total journey and wondered why I hadn't done a single sum while in Vidar's company. I climbed to my feet and stretched. Gunnar was on the deck, waving to me. I waved back, forcing a smile. The boat docked and the sailors tied it off and brought down the gangplank. They loaded our supplies onto the pallet. Maryanne charged down the gangplank in a huff. Magnus rolled his eyes at me and made no movement to catch up to her. I figured their new romance had foundered. Magnus turned and called belowdecks, and two children—a boy and a girl—came up, all agog and dressed in warm coats.

"Victoria, meet Matthias and Nina," Magnus said, introducing them one at a time.

"Hi, nice to meet you," I said, offering what I thought was a child-friendly smile.

"They're a bit wary of speaking English," Magnus told me, when the children had worn speechless blank expressions for longer than was comfortable. "They're here for a week, hopefully to improve their English if you wouldn't mind helping them."

"Um . . . I suppose not," I said, and thought about saying my one much-practiced Norwegian phrase, but changed my mind when I spied Frida.

"Magnus, I found your pen."

"Mmm, good."

Magnus said something to the children and they ran off down the jetty shouting to each other, Magnus trailing them. Carsten and Frida got off together and I noticed a shiny new ring on her engagement finger. Josef, Gordon and Alex were arguing with one of the sailors over his rough handling of a carton of "expensive Swiss brandy." Gunnar ambled down the gangplank and I thought he might give me a hug so I turned my shoulder and pretended I was watching Maryanne run away from Magnus and his children.

"All is not well," I said.

"They had a fight when we were boarding at Ålesund. It's been a long ten hours." He touched my shoulder lightly. "How are you?"

I shook my head. "I'm . . . I can't even describe it. I suppose I'm all right. It's been a very strange week."

"Magnus got into a lot of trouble for leaving you here alone."

"He did? He said nothing to me on the phone."

"He wouldn't. He would think it a sign of weakness." He indicated his suitcase. "I'm going to unpack and have a coffee back in my cabin. Want to join me?"

"Yes, that would be nice."

I was very relaxed in Gunnar's company and the day brightened. If Gunnar saw signs that I had spent a few nights cowering under his bedclothes or that anything had been borrowed, he made no mention of it. Instead we drank coffee while he unpacked, and he told me about how many stoned English tourists wandered the streets of Amsterdam, and how his best friend had announced he was getting married, and how he'd thought himself mortally sick after a particularly long night of varied drinking. I listened, and I laughed in the right places, and he cheered me up with his reassuring ordinariness. I offered him help with cleaning up his cabin, and as we picked clothes up and washed coffee cups and dusted furniture, he finally said to me, "So, I didn't hear from you again after our last phone call. I assume you decided you weren't being stalked?"

I laughed and shook my head. "Turns out I was perfectly safe."

"No more weird happenings? Visitations from ghostly creatures?"

"No. And don't make fun."

"I'm not making fun," he said with a mischievous twinkle in his eye. "I'm serious. It must have been the protection rune. Once you had that—"

"I didn't keep it," I said dismissively.

"No? Where is it?"

"I kicked it off the slab."

He dropped his cleaning rag and grabbed my hand. "Come on, let's go find it."

"Gunnar—"

"Come on, just for fun."

I followed him out his back door and around the lattice to my cabin. Following his lead, I dropped to my hands and knees in the dirt of the forest's edge and started hunting through dead pine needles and tough undergrowth.

"Is this just a way of putting off tidying your cabin?" I asked.

"Maybe. But if a ward falls into your hands, you should

keep it. You never know when you'll be alone on an island with the bogeyman."

"Stop teasing," I replied. "It was hard for me to call and be so weak."

"I'm not teasing you." He sat back and smiled at me. "Victoria, we're mates, aren't we?"

I lifted my head and blew a strand of hair out of my eyes and thought about how I hadn't mentioned Vidar to him. "Yeah, of course."

"So let me be your mate."

"All right, all right, I'm being overly sensitive, I know," I said, "but you've got to understand my history. My mother is completely mental and I don't want to be the same. You can tease me about anything else, just not that."

"But you know you're nothing like your mum. You know you're not mental."

I thought about the past week: the hysteria, the mania, the imprudence. "Umm . . ."

"There it is!" Gunnar leaped forward, then stood up, holding out the ward.

"You found it, great," I said, feeling oddly relieved.

He inspected it. "Oh, Vicky, this one's incredible."

"Why?"

"See this hole?"

"I guess that's for stringing it on a chain."

"Yes, but it's not man-made. A man-made hole would break the magic. It's worn through, probably by water." His pinky finger indicated the smooth, fine edges of the hole. "It's the luckiest charm there is."

"In what way?"

"Wards found in water are lucky, wards with an eye are doubly lucky, wards with a protection rune scratched on them are luckier still." Gunnar's fist closed over the stone and he shoved it, nonchalantly, in his pocket. "Well, if you don't want it . . ."

I opened my mouth to protest, but stopped myself. It was all superstitious nonsense after all. "Keep it," I said. "I don't need it."

I picked up my mail from the station. I had a letter from Samantha with photos of a new boyfriend she had met in Florence, a confirmation of my remote study status from my university and, of course, a letter from my mother.

Dear Vicky,

I know why you didn't phone me back, and I know you are afraid of what's happening to you and how it makes you feel. I took an old scarf of yours to Bathsheba for a reading. There is good news and bad news. I'll start with the bad.

Bathsheba says you are in way over your head, especially as your skepticism has left you unprotected. There are wild elementals loose around you, and they are interested in you and malevolent. The good news is that there is a helpful spirit looking out for you. You should trust this spirit.

The other good news is that Bathsheba says you have definitely already met the man you are going to marry and spend the rest of your life with.

Please, please, please be careful, and phone me very soon!

Love, Mum

*   *   *

I put the letter aside with a roll of my eyes. Well, maybe Bathsheba was right and Vidar was The One, though I wasn't sure if the dates matched up. And anyway, nobody who called herself Bathsheba should be trusted for any kind of advice, much less the psychic variety. I lay back on my bed to daydream about Vidar.

I hadn't got far when there was a knock at the door. Magnus stood there, and about three feet behind him were his children, wide-eyed and tight-lipped.

"Ah, Victoria. I wonder if I might ask you a favor?"

"Certainly." I was worried. Magnus had applied his most charming smile.

"I know you've been working seven days in a row, and I know I promised you four days off when we returned, and . . . I was rather hoping that Maryanne could watch the children this afternoon, but she's busier than I'd anticipated and I'm sure you can appreciate I've got a lot of paperwork to get through after being away for so long—"

"You want me to look after your children?" Insult upon insult.

The tone of my voice gave him pause. "Just for an afternoon. You could help them practice their English."

Matthias said something in Norwegian to Nina, who giggled. Magnus turned to give them a stern look.

"I don't know anything about looking after kids," I whispered, leaning forward so the children couldn't hear me. "What if I break one?"

Magnus shook his head. "These two are indestructible. Just take them to the rec hall and make them some afternoon tea, and speak to them in English." He sensed I might be ready to yield. "Please, Victoria. You'd help me out of a tight spot."

I was annoyed. I was a scientist, not a babysitter. However, Magnus was my boss and I was stuck on a remote island with him, so it would probably pay to keep him happy. "Certainly," I said.

"Thank you so much," he said in a voice that sounded so sincere it must have been faked. "Matthias, Nina, you stay with Victoria this afternoon and you speak only English."

They watched him go with mournful eyes while I fetched my coat. I locked up behind me, and said, "Come on."

Outside smelled like pine needles and the salty sea. I took a deep breath. "How long are you staying?" I asked as they shuffled behind me to the rec hall.

Matthias and Nina exchanged glances, looked at me and shrugged. Perhaps their English wasn't that good after all.

"How old are you?" I tried, very slowly.

Nina gave me an innocent smile and shook her head.

"Right, let's just get some afternoon tea," I muttered. I led them into the rec hall and sat them down. "Wait here," I said, pointing at the chairs.

Matthias nodded. He said something to Nina in Norwegian and she giggled.

Maryanne was in the kitchen, sharpening her knives.

"Hi, Maryanne," I said lightly, shouldering open the door to the cold room. I emerged a minute later with chocolate cookies and milk.

She peered at me with flinty eyes. "What are you doing?" she asked.

"Making afternoon tea for Magnus's children."

Maryanne snorted. I think it was meant to be a bitter laugh. "Oh, he's passed them on to you, has he?"

I poured two glasses of milk and arranged the cookies on a plate. "He said you were busy."

"Busy! That has nothing to do with it. I refused, point-blank, to look after those little shits again. They come four times a year, and he can't stand them, so he dumps them on me. I told him on the boat, I'm not looking after them this time. He can ask somebody else." Her knife sharpening reached a frenzied speed. I took a step back. "He's too afraid of Frida to ask her, and God forbid that he should ask a man, so look who's next on his wish list, the pretty new trainee. Well, enjoy yourself with the nasty beasts, Vicky."

I took a couple of seconds to process this diatribe. "Did you and Magnus have a fight?"

"He's a bloody pig."

"What did he do?"

Maryanne dropped her head and examined the knife blade. "I'd rather not talk about it."

To my horror, she began to cry. I put a hand on her arm. "I have to go, Maryanne, but if you need somebody to talk to . . ."

"No, no, I'm fine."

I backed away slowly with the kids' afternoon tea on a tray. When I entered the rec hall, they were sitting exactly where I'd left them. I set the tray on the table and they helped themselves, giggling and talking to each other in Norwegian, and giving me sly looks. I decided to try one more time with the most basic English sentence I could think of: "How are you today, Matthias and Nina?"

More giggles. Then Matthias, in perfect English, said, "Our father is your boss. He tells you what to do."

I swallowed the retort I wanted to spit at him. "Oh, so you *do* speak English well."

"Naturally," Nina said, reaching for another chocolate cookie.

"So why didn't you answer my questions before?"

"Because they were stupid questions," Matthias said.

Nina, impersonating my pained pronunciation with mortifying precision, said, "How long are you staying? How old are you?"

I set my teeth and forced a smile. "How about this then. What is the mean distance between two random points in a unit square?" And when they didn't answer, "That shut you up, didn't it? Now, eat your cookies."

More Norwegian dialogue passed between them. I'm sure most of it was insults aimed at me but I didn't mind. They were only kids after all. Magnus was the one who should have known better.

A staff meeting and drinking session had been organized for after dinner that evening, presumably when Matthias and Nina were watching videos in Magnus's cabin and no longer in need of English lessons. I sat in the rec hall with Josef and Alex to wait for the others. The station was so different now there were people around. The spaces seemed warmer, better insulated against the weather outside; the buildings seemed safe and sturdy, rather than abandoned shapes being reclaimed by the forest. While this was a good thing—it put my recent brush with gullibility firmly behind me—it also saddened me. The loss of Vidar was tied up with the loss of the haunted feeling. He had been strange, he had been part of the forest and the bare night sky. All the ordinariness around me underscored his absence.

Magnus bustled in last, apologizing and blaming his lateness on getting the children settled.

"Now, this meeting will be neither long nor boring," he

promised, then in the next hour and twelve minutes set about breaking that promise.

At eight-thirty, just as Maryanne was bringing out a bottle of scotch and nine glasses, Magnus held up his hands, and said, "Wait, wait, one last agenda item."

The collective groan was inaudible but palpable.

Magnus smiled. "Trust me, this one is interesting. I was talking to some of the other station commanders in Bern, and they all have social club events that go beyond getting drunk every Wednesday night. Would you like to hear?"

Glances passed around the room. Gunnar said, "Go on."

"I propose a monthly social event, for which we all pay a nominal sum from our wages, to go toward funding our Christmas party. So it acts as a fund-raising event as well as a team-building experience. Now we should probably discuss this at length because—"

"That sounds great, Magnus," I said quickly.

"A wonderful idea," Carsten said. "I'll vote for that."

"Me too, me too," Frida said. "No need to discuss it."

"Good," said Magnus, pleased with himself. "Any ideas for our first social event? Considering that we are stuck on an island in the middle of the Norwegian Sea."

"How about a picnic?" Gunnar said. "The days are getting milder."

"In the clearing," Frida suggested.

"No, by the lake," Josef said.

"Ah, the lake," Magnus said. "Good idea."

So the picnic at the lake was set for the coming weekend, various tasks were assigned, a levy was agreed upon, and we finally started drinking the scotch.

And long after everybody else finished drinking, I was still going. My need to decompress was greater than my determination to behave prudently. I simply didn't want to go to bed. I didn't want to close my eyes on the day that I lost Vidar and have the next day be an ordinary day. I wanted the world to be wild and thrilling and, that night, alcohol was the nearest shortcut to hand. Gunnar, who had overindulged on his holiday, was the first to bed, followed by Gordon going off to the night shift, followed by Alex and Josef, whom I was starting to suspect were lovers, followed by Frida and Carsten—who still hadn't officially announced their engagement—which left Magnus, Maryanne and me in the rec hall with Maryanne's Cat Stevens CD on repeat-play.

I bobbed my head along with the music and made occasional comments about the night being young and asking who was up for a seventies folk music drinking game, before it became clear that Magnus and Maryanne were probably waiting for me to leave so that they could sort out their differences. I didn't want to stop drinking, nor be alone, nor do anything so mundane as go to bed, but the glances passing between them were laden and, come to think of it, hadn't Maryanne said four times in the past half hour that I looked very, very tired.

"Right," I said, pushing my chair back, "I'm off to bed."

"Good night," Maryanne said forcefully.

"I'll see you in the—" My parting sentence was cut short by my chair becoming entangled between my ankles, sending me sprawling across the floor. The shock of the fall was greater than the pain that shot up my wrist as I tried to save myself. I was drunk. I started crying.

"Hey, it's all right." Magnus was already crouching next to me, helping me up. He put his arm around my shoulders and gave me a squeeze. "Don't cry."

"I'm not," I cried.

Magnus was solicitous and soothing as he helped me to my feet. "Are you hurt?"

"I'm not crying because I fell," I blurted.

"Shh, shh, it doesn't matter." Now Magnus enclosed me in a hug and stroked my hair. I sobbed into his shoulder, hating myself for it and knowing I'd regret it.

I heard the sound of a chair scraping back and looked up to see Maryanne glowering at Magnus and me.

"I'll give you two some privacy, shall I?"

I stepped out of Magnus's embrace and brushed my hair off my face. "Don't be silly, Maryanne, it's not—"

"Good night to both of you," she declared, striding toward the door and seizing her coat.

"Maryanne!" Magnus called, going after her. He grabbed her arm; but she twisted out of his grasp and ran, slamming the door behind her. Magnus considered the door for a few moments, then turned and walked back toward me.

"Um, sorry," I said.

"It's not your fault. Maryanne has a jealous streak."

"Jealous?"

"We're trying to work things out but she thinks that you and I . . ."

I tried not to shudder too openly. "What?"

"I talk about you a lot," he confessed, then smiled.

I crossed my arms over my chest, feeling horribly vulnerable. Cat Stevens played on.

"Don't worry," he continued. "She's insecure. Before you came along, she was the most attractive woman on the island. I've reassured her that there's nothing going on between us, she just doesn't believe me."

"Oh. Well. I'm sorry anyway. I'd better . . ." I indicated vainly in the direction of the door.

"Wait, Vicky," he said. "I've just got to ask."

"What?" I squeaked.

"There isn't any chance, is there?"

"Chance for . . . ?"

"For something between us. Perhaps we could have dinner one night in my cabin, a date."

"No," I blurted, before good sense told me to let him down gently. "No, no, no."

"I see," he said. "I'm sorry I brought it up." And then he left the room, calling over his shoulder, "Make sure you lock up."

I mentally assessed the evening. I'd drunk too much. I'd fallen over. I'd cried on my boss, who then came on to me. What a stellar performance.

I gave Magnus a few minutes to disappear from sight, then pulled on my anorak and locked up the rec hall. My breath made fog in the dark. I knew that if I went to bed I would simply lie there until dawn, replaying the disastrous events in my head, all the more horrifying in contrast to the past two evenings spent in the quiet woods with Vidar. The ache of desire squeezed my lungs. I pocketed my keys and headed into the trees.

I walked for ten minutes, in no particular direction, with no particular hope that Vidar was still there. He'd said *goodbye*. Not *see you tonight*. Whoever had dropped him off over at the beach had picked him up again, and he was gone.

I sighed and sagged against a tree. The dark and the cold clung to me, the treetops moved softly. A chill rose up my spine and it sobered me a little. I headed back to the station, arms wrapped tightly around myself. Desolation washed over me. He was gone and, crazy though it seemed, I knew that my last chance of finding love had slipped through my fingers along with Vidar.

Thirteen

I predicted I wouldn't sleep, so I set myself up on the sofa with a book and a cup of instant cocoa. I turned the pages and scanned the words, but none of them made it from my eyes to my brain. I was very drunk and Vidar consumed my thoughts—memories of Vidar, fantasies of Vidar. The melancholy saturated me.

I was nodding off when a tap on the window jolted me awake.

Vidar! It had to be.

I went to the window and lifted the sash, peered into the dark. I could see nothing, but I could hear footsteps retreating into the forest.

I hesitated. What if it wasn't Vidar? What if it was . . . ?

What, Vicky? One of the monsters you swear you don't believe in?

It must have been Vidar, on the island still, letting me know to follow him into the forest. I checked my watch—3:00 A.M. He wouldn't risk waking one of the others, hanging around near their cabins. I grabbed my anorak, threw open the cabin door, took two steps out, then my courage ran through my fingers like fine sand.

I didn't want to go out there into the forest.

"Damn you, Victoria Scott," I muttered. "You won't be intimidated by imagined bogeys."

Despite the lingering fear that curled in my stomach, I strode off the slab and into the forest, listening for footsteps. Branches and twigs swayed and bent around me, their ancient shapes made grotesque by the dappled light from the station behind me. I waited until I was far enough away from the cabins to call out, "Vidar? Where are you?"

Footsteps to my left. I turned, poised and listening.

"Vidar?"

I knew he could be perfectly silent if he wanted to be, so I scanned in a circle. My field of vision kept moving when I had stopped and I steadied myself against a tree. The weary fug of alcohol and sleep was hard to shake.

"Vidar?" I said again. If Vidar wasn't answering, perhaps it wasn't Vidar at all. I hunched inside my anorak and shuddered. Time to head back to the cabin. This had been a bad idea.

I turned. And shrieked.

Skripi stood there, his oily eyes blinking at me in the gloom, his spiky hair and fingers made grey by starlight.

"Vidar is gone," he said.

It must be a dream. "Wake up, wake up," I said to myself, pinching the skin on my wrist hard. It hurt. I didn't wake up.

"You are awake," he said. "Don't be afraid."

"Wake up!" I screamed, backing away.

"Listen to me, I want to help."

I remembered my mother's letter, something about a good spirit. If this was a dream, I should probably listen. I swayed uncertainly. The dark forest was surreal, my ears were ringing.

"You lost the ward. You have to get it back. I can't get another one. I found it in the draugr's lair. He saw me, he tried to kill me. You have to get *eolh* back. I can't make another, the draugr is watching me."

"I am going insane," I said.

"Vidar is gone. He can't protect you."

"Where has he gone?"

Skripi pointed to the sky. "On his horse."

"Oh . . . that's reassuring. Because I know that horses can't fly, so you must be talking nonsense, which would mean that I'm dreaming."

"You must find the ward. It's yours and you might need it." He backed away from me with his hands in front of him, the long spiky fingers stretched out. "I'll go. I don't mean to frighten you."

He disappeared into the shadows and I stood, rooted to the spot, waiting to wake up.

"I'm drunk. I'm dreaming. I'm going insane," I said. I couldn't move my feet, a whirlwind of panic was eddying up my rib cage, my breath was trapped in my lungs, and then . . .

A hazy cloud descended and I lost track of sights and sounds and time . . .

And I woke up in my bed.

"Oh, thank God," I gasped. The dawnlight glowed behind my curtain. "Thank God, thank God." I leaned my head in my hands and sobbed with relief. I wasn't going mad after all, it was just a peculiarly vivid dream fueled by too much scotch and too many wild emotions. The fact that I didn't remember putting myself to bed was a little creepy, but not anything to fret over . . . memories were soft, and hard spirits often obliterated them.

My wrist hurt from my fall in the rec hall and I noticed for the first time a gash across my palm. I must have cut it on the back of the chair I pulled over with me. I rose and washed it, smoothed a bandage over it, then went to the window to draw the curtain. The forest looked back. Fear stole over me; if I didn't know better, I would have declared it haunted and never set foot in it again. I touched the cold glass of the window and sighed, wishing very deeply that I hadn't let Gunnar take my good luck charm. Skripi was right: it was mine and I might need it.

At 9:00 A.M. I was amazed to find Magnus at my door with Matthias and Nina.

"Um, hi," I said, squirming inside with the uncomfortable memories of the previous night.

Without even a blink that would acknowledge he felt the same way, Magnus smiled, and said, "Good morning, Victoria. Matthias and Nina insisted that I bring them over to see you this morning."

I glanced at the twins. Nina screwed up her face at me. "Did they?" I said.

"They've grown very fond of you, and I can see you feel the same way. Perhaps you'd spend a little time with them this morning, and—"

"Magnus, if I'm going to look after your kids, I at least want time off in lieu," I said.

"Done," he said, clearly relieved he didn't have to lie, charm and wheedle anymore. "I promised you four days off in a row, you can have five after the weekend."

"It's a deal. Come on, you two. I'll teach you how to play poker." I ushered them inside.

Magnus caught my arm and drew me conspiratorially close. I tensed, thinking he might repeat his offer of a date, but instead he whispered, "I'm paying you now, so don't let them out of your sight."

"I won't."

"Last night while we were in our meeting, Matthias made a climbing rope out of my ties. A number of them are ruined."

I hid a smirk. "I see. I'll watch them closely."

Nina grew bored with card games very quickly and spent her time playing in my makeup case and wardrobe. Matthias was a born cardsharper and cleaned me out of matchsticks before lunch.

"Come on," I said, packing up my deck. "I'll take you over to the rec hall for lunch."

"I'm hungry," Nina declared, rubbing her eyes and smearing mascara down her cheeks.

"I'm not hungry at all," Matthias said. "I don't want to go to the rack hall."

"It's the *rec* hall," I said. "Short for *recreation*. And you have to have lunch, so come on."

"I want to play cards some more!" he shouted.

I handed them their coats. "Well, I want to eat, and we're all stuck together." I gestured them out the door. "Come on."

Nina proudly strutted ahead of me with her unevenly made-up face. Matthias slouched out the door and whined something to Nina in Norwegian. She shook her head.

"Do you want a sandwich or one of Maryanne's vegetable pies?" I asked.

"I said I'm *not hungry!*" Matthias turned and ran, astonishingly fast, into the forest.

"Damn it!"

"Is that swearing?" Nina asked. "I want to learn English swearing."

"Nina, can you go to the rec hall and wait for me? Tell Maryanne we're having pies for lunch."

"I don't want pies. Teach me a swear word."

"No. Now go to the rec hall and wait for me." I dashed into the forest after Matthias. I'd already lost sight of him, but could hear his footsteps ahead of me. Then they slowed, slid about and stopped. I panicked. What if he'd fallen and knocked himself out?

"Matthias? Matthias, are you all right?"

I slipped through the trees as quickly as I could, then stopped, panting, looking around. "Matthias?"

No answer. I was certain his footsteps had stopped nearby. I peered closely between the trees and a wash of sensation overwhelmed me . . .

Last night you were here. Running panicked through the trees, away from Skripi . . .

But that had been a dream. I'd woken up in bed . . .

No, you were here.

I spotted a narrow branch, broken, and a memory crushed down on me. Running in the dark, putting out my hand to stop the branch hitting my face, the flash of pain across my palm as it cut me.

I looked at the bandage on my hand, frozen with fear.

"HA!" Matthias jumped out from behind a tree, scaring the wits out of me.

I shrieked, then when I saw it was just a rotten kid, I pressed my hand over my heart and taught him every English swear word I knew. He ran away from me again, this time in the direction of the station, but I was through with running. I headed out of the forest at my own pace. I felt helpless and afraid, but mostly I felt angry. I'd thought all this nonsense was over, that I'd managed to make it all rational. I didn't want to feel helpless and afraid, but how could I feel otherwise when I could no longer reliably distinguish dreams from reality?

Magnus took the kids over to the beach to collect seashells that afternoon, and I decided to abandon my pride and ask Gunnar for my protection ward. This plan was foiled in the first twenty seconds when Gunnar opened the door, grinned at me, and said, "Let me guess. You've finally abdicated as Queen of the Skeptics and you want your lucky charm back."

"Of course not. What makes you say that?"

"I heard you scream in the forest."

My heart jolted. "Last night?"

"No, today. Around lunchtime."

"Oh. Yes. Matthias gave me a fright."

"Hm. I think it's just a ward against evil spirits, not small naughty boys." He ushered me in.

"If only," I said, sitting at his kitchen table. "Make me coffee?"

"Of course. You look tired."

I dropped my forehead on the table. "Those kids are driving me nuts."

"Then tell Magnus you won't look after them."

"He's paying me in days off." I lifted my head to watch him make coffee.

"Don't tell Maryanne. She always does it as a favor."

"Why would anybody want children? They're hideous beasts."

"Matthias and Nina are. Yours wouldn't be," he said, pointing a spoon at me emphatically.

"How do you know that?"

"Because your kids won't have a psychotic shrew for a mother and Magnus for a father."

I laughed. "Don't speak too soon. I'm already psychotic, and Magnus has already asked me for a date."

Gunnar dropped into the chair opposite me in shock. "He didn't!"

I waved my hand. "I don't want to talk about it."

"What did you say?"

"No, of course!" I exclaimed quickly. "I was drunk. He was drunk. And this morning he's acting like nothing happened."

"Maybe he's forgotten. If he was drunk—"

"I hope so. But Magnus is so shameless it wouldn't surprise me if he remembered everything and just intended to carry on as usual."

"So did you scream when he asked you?"

"Sorry?"

"When I said I'd heard you scream, you thought I meant last night."

"Oh, that. No, I didn't scream at Magnus. I had a nightmare around three. I dreamed I was in the forest and when you said you'd heard a scream from out there, I thought . . ."

He was smiling at me again. "You thought? What?"

"Nothing." I slapped the table. "Where's my bloody coffee?"

Gunnar laughed. "I think I have some information that might interest you."

"If it's about ghosts—"

"No," he said, returning to the bench to pour the coffee, "it's about the weather."

"Go on."

A coffee cup in each hand, he shrugged a shoulder toward his computer desk. "Come over here. I'll show you."

He booted up his computer as I slipped into the chair beside his and sipped my coffee.

"I've been entering all the old paper records into the database," he explained as the soft blue glow of the screen lit his face. "Magnus wanted me to pay particular attention to unusual weather events, for his research work. So I've been scanning the records for storm reports, heavy snow, long rain periods . . . and I got all the way back to day one." He punched a few keys, and the screen filled with text. He tapped the screen. "Here, seventeenth of June 1964. The grand opening of Kirkja Station, attended by all of eight people, the first staff members. Temperature at 11:00 A.M. was twenty-two degrees. Sky was cloudless, humidity low. And here . . ." He clicked and the next screen came up. "Same date, 3:00 P.M. They report a snowstorm."

"Yes, but it's obviously a mistake," I said. "You double-checked?"

"I did."

"Their mistake then. They wrote it on the wrong day."

He clicked an icon in the corner and a box appeared. "In some instances I added comments from the journals. 'We were outside enjoying a few celebratory drinks at lunchtime when the temperature began to drop and clouds blew in. Soon after, snow began to fall and by afternoon it was heavy, accompanied by thunder and lightning. We're all baffled.'"

"Interesting," I said. "Did they manage to explain it?"

"I don't know. There's nothing else about it in the record books."

"The weather does odd things," I said. "Raining frogs—"

"There are two instances of raining frogs in here," he said, "but I'm not interested in that. I don't even think the snowstorm was particularly odd in itself. It's the other stuff I've read that makes it intriguing."

"What other stuff?"

He reached across his desk and began plowing through an .overflowing in-tray. Something clunked out of a pile of papers. He scooped it up and handed it to me. "Oh, did I show you this? Magnus found it in the forest."

It was the shard of metal that I'd thought was part of an axe blade. It was cold in my palm. I felt no conviction about what it was this time. It was just an unidentifiable piece of anything.

Gunnar had seized a set of photocopies and shook them in front of me. "Remember I told you about the first settlement here? In the eleventh century? It was a Christian settlement and the Christians loved to keep records. There were a few records left behind on Kirkja, and they're now in a museum in Bergen. This is a copy of a modern translation of the Latin. It's very boring, mostly. But look at this . . ." He pointed to a sentence.

"I can't read Norwegian," I reminded him dryly.

"It says: 'On the day the foundation stone was laid for our new church, the warm summer morning gave way to a mighty storm and deep snowfall.'"

"Wow," I said. "Amazing coincidence."

"Just a coincidence?"

"What else would it be?"

"I don't know," Gunnar said. "I *like* not knowing. I like to wonder. Don't you?"

I shook my head.

"There's more," he said.

"Go on."

He shuffled the pages. "Here, at the end. The last entry. Before the . . . before whatever happened to them. 'This morning is cool and clear, the first signs of winter.'" Gunnar's finger scanned down the page. "This is all boring nonsense about the Bible. And then, here: 'The late morning grows hot. The children paddle naked in the water. I have never experienced such a heat, even in the middle of summer. The fires of hell itself could not be warmer.'" He flipped the page over. "And here: 'The peculiar weather continues and many of our number grow superstitious. At dusk, the heat drained suddenly and sharply, and across the whole island stole a great frost. The trees are white, the lake has frozen over and the ground is covered in crystals. If I had not seen it with my own eyes, I would never believe it. It is now dark and there are fearsome sounds in the forest. A cruel wind gathers force and we all huddle inside by the fire in fear of what may happen next.'"

As Gunnar read aloud I found myself holding my breath. There was something so familiar about the tale. Imagined impressions flashed across my mind: desperate faces in the firelight, the weight of their fear. The piece of metal in my palm was growing warm. I dropped it on Gunnar's desk, finding that it repelled me. "What happened next?" I said.

"Don't know. That was the last entry. It's great, isn't it? A real mystery. And all that stuff about the weather, it makes you think."

I gathered my wits. "You said it was written hundreds of

years ago. It would be impossible to confirm if it were authentic or not. Or perhaps one of the translators has played with the language to make it more dramatic. You know, in light of the history of the island."

"I suppose so," Gunnar said, putting the pages aside. "Is it not possible for a frost to come on the afternoon of a very hot day?"

I shook my head. "Not here in the midlatitudes. In the Arctic, a change in air mass can mean katabatic winds and a sharp temperature drop. But certainly not how it's described there."

Gunnar smiled. "Are you trying to convince me, or yourself?"

"What do you mean?"

Gunnar waved his hand. "It doesn't matter. Let's go over to the rec hall. I promised Maryanne I'd help her with sandwiches for tomorrow's picnic."

Gunnar reached over to turn off his computer and I saw the ward on a chain around his neck, under his shirt. If I caved in and asked for it, he would think he had won. He was obviously goading me, telling me mysterious stories. I preferred to be the old Vicky, who was scared of nothing.

As Gunnar locked the cabin door behind us, I glanced up toward the trees. For a second, another image laid itself over the forest in my mind's eye: ice hanging from branches, hoarfrost all over the ground, a strange creaking almost silence. The image troubled me. As though I had really seen it, once, somewhere.

As though it might have really happened.

Despite drizzle the evening before, Kirkja predicted a mild, clear day for our picnic and we were right. Shortly after the morning balloon launch, we all traipsed into the forest carrying blankets and baskets of food. Matthias and Nina ran ahead and ran back, calling in excited voices. The forest didn't feel strange and haunted under these circumstances. I was looking forward to our day out. Night and solitude brought the yearning back. Being around other people helped me forget about Vidar for a few relaxed hours.

The area directly around the lake was muddy, but we found a grassy verge at the edge of the trees on the eastern side of the water and spread out our blankets. I lay on my back and looked at the sky through branches, and listened to the sounds of the picnic being unpacked, of plates and glasses being handed about, of conversations and laughter.

Gunnar crouched down on my blanket. "Vicky, why are you the only one not doing anything?" he asked.

"I am doing something. I'm watching Magnus's kids." I turned my head, saw they were still shouting to each other as they ran round the lake, and turned back. "See?"

He settled next to me. "So you're still babysitting?"

I sat up and said, mock-cheerfully, "Magnus says I'm the best babysitter he's ever employed and he wishes he could take me home to Oslo one day."

"I think you'll have some competition from Maryanne." He pointed to Magnus and Maryanne, head to head, talking quietly.

"That's progress," I said.

"I saw him leaving her cabin first thing this morning."

"Do you think they . . . ?"

"I'm fairly sure."

I screwed up my nose. "Yuck."

"It's like a social experiment, this place," Gunnar said, folding his long hands around his knees. "Eventually they all pair off. Frida and Carsten. Magnus and Maryanne. You know that Alex and Josef . . . ?"

"I guessed."

"So that leaves me a choice between Gordon or you," he said.

"Gordon's a safer bet," I said lightly.

"You have better teeth."

I laughed. Gordon had big protuberant teeth, with a gap between them wide enough to sail the *Jonsok* through. "But really," I said, "teeth or no teeth, I'm not—"

"I know, Vicky. It was only a joke," he said quickly.

I felt uncomfortable, but tried to pretend I wasn't. "I know," I said.

"Victoria!" This was Magnus, calling from a hundred feet away where he and Maryanne had started a bottle of champagne. "Can you tell the children to be careful not to slip in the water?"

I looked around and spotted the kids on the far side of the lake, faking a sword fight with branches. I got up and walked around the lake toward them. They saw me coming and ran away.

"Hey!" I called. "Be careful you don't slip into the water."

Matthias turned and brandished his sword. "I want to go swimming."

"Well, you can't. It's dangerous."

"I'm the best swimmer in my school. Far said I could go swimming."

"No he didn't. Now behave or I'll make you come and sit with me and Gunnar."

He turned to run after Nina with his sword held high, but I noticed he put three more feet between himself and the

muddy edge of the water. I returned to the picnic site to see
Maryanne looking at me smugly. Gunnar and Josef had
pulled all the picnic blankets into a communal square, and
champagne and sandwiches were served. Carsten and Frida
made an official engagement announcement and the two
sips of champagne I took as a toast were my limit for the
day. After Wednesday night's debacle, I was easing off on
the social club's alcohol. Magnus clearly had a different
agenda, and he and Maryanne both became Saturday-
afternoon tipsy and exchanged desiring looks for the entire
picnic. Nobody was more embarrassed than Mägnus's children, who dealt with it by taking a plate of sandwiches and
a flask of orange juice to the far side of the lake for a private
picnic.

At around four, the warmth of the afternoon gave way to
the first chill of approaching evening. Magnus buttonholed
me while I was patrolling for plastic wrap that had blown
into the edge of the forest.

"Will you watch the children?" he slurred.

"I'm watching them," I said distractedly, glancing over
my shoulder.

"For the rest of the day," he added. "Maryanne and I
are . . . heading back to her cabin."

I was glad my back was turned to him. The look of horror on my face was best kept a secret. "Fine."

I gathered rubbish and, when I turned around, Magnus
and Maryanne were scurrying off like American teenagers at
a frat party—she was giggling, his hand was firmly attached
to her bum—and everyone else at the picnic looked away
politely. We gave them a half hour lead, then started saying
how late it was getting and it was probably time to head
back.

We had packed up and were twenty feet into the trees when Matthias pulled my arm, and said, "Vicky, I've left my sword back at the lake."

"Can't you find another?" I asked. "It was only a stick."

He shook his head.

"Go on, be quick," I said, waving him off. Nina ran away with him. I walked another hundred feet in conversation with Gunnar when I realized that I should probably not be so casual in my responsibilities to Magnus's children.

"Actually, Gunnar, I'd better wait for the kids."

"See you back at the station," he said, and disappeared into the trees.

I was halfway back to the lake when I heard Nina scream. My heart jumped. I ran.

"Matthias! Matthias!" she shrieked. "Far! Far! *Help!*"

I broke through the trees. Nina stood helpless and sobbing in the mud.

"Nina, where's Matthias?"

She shrieked at me in Norwegian and pointed to the water. A stream of bubbles about fifteen feet out.

"I'll go in after him," I said, throwing off my coat and shoes. "You run that way and call loudly for Gunnar."

She tore off, screaming Gunnar's name while I splashed into the cold lake . . .

A draugr is a thing to be feared.

. . . and swam toward Matthias.

Under the surface the water was grey-green and murky. Below me all was black, choked with weed and cloudy shapes. I spotted a pale flailing arm and headed in that direction, scooped up Matthias and broke the surface with him.

"Are you all right?" I gasped.

He spat out a mouthful of water and began to cry, pushed at me angrily and swam toward land. I guessed he was all right.

Something brushed my ankle. A weed or . . .

With a rush of bubbles I was yanked under. I opened my mouth to scream and swallowed the lake. I was spinning, something had me around the thighs. I struggled away. Had I been caught in a float of weed? I felt around near my legs and was horrified to feel fingers brush my own.

They pulled me down farther. The water was icy. My throat was raw and I was running out of breath. My lungs felt hard, blocked. My brain was bursting its bounds.

Out of the murky green darkness, a face loomed in front of me, a nightmare of weed and veins and algae. It was the last thing I saw before I blacked out.

The next face I saw was Gunnar's, close and hot.

Then more blackness.

Voices shouting. Being carried.

Carsten's voice above them all, shouting orders.

Carsten?

Our nurse, that's right. I've been saved.

"Am I alive?" I mumbled, and my throat felt as though it had been lacerated.

Relieved laughter. Being pushed and pulled, and a warm towel gathered around me. I opened my eyes. I was sitting in a chair in the sick bay, a linoleum-floored room which saw most of its use in storing our alcohol. Carsten leaned over me and smiled. "Welcome back."

Gunnar stood anxiously in the corner. I touched my wet hair. Memories swung toward me and I shuddered. "What happened?"

"As far as we can figure, you went in after Matthias and then got tangled up in some weed," Carsten said.

"I saw a face under the water," I said, "just as I was blacking out. A nightmare—"

"I'm sure that's not unusual in those circumstances."

"You're fine now," Gunnar said. "Nina called me and I pulled you out."

I smiled. "Did you save my life, Gunnar Holm?"

"Would that be all right if I had? Or would that contravene our 'just mates' rule?"

"No, that's all right."

"And the whole kiss-of-life thing?"

"I don't remember it, so it's like it never happened." I laughed and it hurt my lungs, so I stopped.

"You were very brave to go in after Matthias," Gunnar said. "He might have died in pursuit of his sea monster."

"Sea monster?"

"He told Magnus that's why he went in the water."

I closed my eyes and even that hurt.

"Are you all right?" Carsten asked.

"I thought drowning was supposed to be a nice peaceful death," I said.

"Not at all," he replied emphatically. "Filling your lungs with liquid is very painful. Gunnar, could you tell Magnus what happened."

Carsten listened to my lungs and checked my eyes, gave me some painkillers and told me to go to my cabin, have a warm shower and get into bed.

"I'll come over in an hour to check on you," he said, giving me a fatherly pat on the shoulder, "but I think you'll be fine once you've had a rest."

I did as he said, and as I was climbing into my bed I noticed something on the bedside table.

The ward. Gunnar had left it there. I picked it up and clutched it in my palm. Did he leave it without saying a word because he thought I really needed it and was afraid to ask for it? He was probably right on both counts.

I dangled it in front of me and it spun slowly on its chain. Matthias, despite being a good swimmer, had gone into the lake and been pulled under. I had gone in and been pulled under. Gunnar had come after me and he'd been fine. Anything to do with a certain good luck charm?

Images from the last weeks crowded my imagination: sticks and weeds, night grey, lake-gloom, matter neither animal nor vegetable, sick moonbeams and nausea in my heart valves. If I lay still and thought hard enough, I might be able to pin all these horrors down, but my lungs ached and I wondered what was more important, thinking or breathing.

I opened the clasp and fastened the ward around my neck. I decided I liked breathing.

Fourteen

[Asgard]

The house at Gammaldal was silent and still as Vidar reined Arvak in. A thin streak of smoke curled from the chimney, but Aud did not emerge to greet him.

"Aud?" he called, dismounting. He removed saddle and bridle and set Arvak free to walk about, then looked inside the house. The remains of a fire; the quiet darkness; the smell of old cooking. No Aud.

He scanned outside. What day was it? Perhaps she was with Loki. Vidar cursed as he led Arvak to the stable to feed and water him. Vidar didn't want to be alone. He needed company and conversation to break the obsessive circle of his thoughts.

It had seemed so simple before he met Victoria. In his imagination, they would meet, fall in love, then together they would hide from his family, just for a lifetime. And yet, when he finally saw her again, reality weighed heavily on his heart. Had he really forgotten how fine her skin was, so pale he could see the blue veins at her wrist? Had he forgotten the lightness of her voice, the narrow circumference of her waist, the softness of her cheek? She was so vulnerable, so *mortal*. His whole time in Midgard he'd longed to hold her, to crush her body against his and burn his lips on the heat of her skin. In her presence, a longing so acute had gripped him that his whole body would have trembled had he not forced it to be still. But when the moment arrived for him to declare his feelings, he had become acutely aware of the possibility that he might attract to her a danger she was not equipped to battle.

Vidar left Arvak in the stable, but couldn't bear to return to the house, to sit quiet and cautious indoors when such a passion of indecision clouded his mind. He crossed the wide flat fields and found himself walking up and down the muddy beach in the early light.

Nearly a thousand years he had waited. On each day of each week of those years, he had thought about Halla with longing and tenderness, knowing eventually she would return. He had yearned for that day so violently that sometimes he feared it would injure him. How could he turn his back on her now?

It was simply that the obstacle that stood between him and Victoria was so great. His father. A beast—foul, brutal and malevolent. Not happy unless everyone around him was intimidated. Damn him. Vidar set his teeth. Sometimes the shadows of a fantasy taunted him. In his fantasy he went to Valaskjálf at night, burst into the cavernous hall, and killed all of them: his detestable father, his preening brothers, the hard-faced women they surrounded themselves with . . . But before the fantasy could spawn the kind of detail that would make it addictive and poisonous, he suppressed it.

Vidar stopped, crouched on the beach and watched the waves for a long time, no closer to knowing what to do next.

The sun behind him cast his shadow on the mud, as it rose over Valaskjálf many, many miles away.

Aud had arrived at Loki's house to find he wasn't home. She stoked the fire and sat beside it, deciding she would wait one hour, then return to Gammaldal. Vidar had been gone for a week and the cottage was empty and forlorn without him, but returning was better than sitting among the towering shelves of dusty objects Loki had collected. Time crawled and she wished she'd brought some mending. She didn't dare touch any of Loki's things in case she broke something and found herself bound into his service two days a week.

She wondered when Vidar would return. The longer he was away, the more likely it was that this Midgard woman returned his affection and kept him permanently from his home. She had hoped, bitterly and deep in her chest, that the Midgard woman would be indifferent to Vidar, sending him back to Aud broken and in need of comfort; although she couldn't imagine that any woman could be indifferent to Vidar. What aspect of his great beauty or tender heart could be found wanting?

The door slammed inward and Loki stood there, outlined by daylight. It gave Aud a start.

"Did I frighten you?" he said, laughing.

"No. Did you forget I was coming?"

"No. I remembered." He slid inside and closed the door behind him, plunging his features into shadow. "I've been out hunting."

"Hunting?"

He produced a posy of yellow flowers. "Hunting wild-flowers. For you."

Aud smiled in spite of herself. Warily, she took the flowers. "Thank you, Loki."

He crouched in front of her. "You see, I'm not so bad. I'm sweet and tender."

She laughed. "They aren't the first two words that spring to mind when I think of you."

"What are the first two words, then?" he asked, leaning so close she could feel his breath on her hands.

"Thief" and "liar." "Master and servant," she said, refusing to be flustered by his proximity or the hot little kisses he laid upon her fingers.

"Oh, come," he said, taking her hand, "we are more than that."

"Loki, I have very strict orders from Vidar. I'm to serve you. What would you have me do today?"

He rose and began hunting through the objects crowded on a shelf on the other side of the room. "Vidar tells me you are a fine weaver and seamstress. Is that right?"

Aud flushed with pleasure. "Did he really say that?"

"Oh, yes," Loki assured her. A shining silver pot fell and hit him on the head. He cursed and proceeded more carefully.

"When I came to Gammaldal, he had two tunics and two breeches, both plain wool, both poorly woven and sewn by himself," she confided, giggling at the memory. "I found madder and lichen, dyed some wool and spun it fine, then wove and sewed him new clothes. The old ones I threw on the fire." Aud patted the apron she wore with her sewing tools in it. "It was very satisfying."

"I suppose you used an Aesir loom, though," he said over his shoulder. "Big, heavy, rough."

Aud frowned, puzzled. "Yes. Why do you ask?"

He turned. He had dislodged from the shelf a lightweight carved loom of maple, which he presented to her.

Her fingers traced the carvings. "These are Vanir runes," she said.

"It's Vanir work," he replied. "I found it on my last trip to Valaskjálf. I was looking for honey and this was tucked away in the back of the cook-room. Probably spoils of war, dusty and long since forgotten."

A sad-happy feeling tingled up her fingers and into her heart. Something from home.

"Do you want me to weave a cloak for you?" she asked.

"No. I have many fine clothes." He rose and took the seat next to hers at the fire, stretching languidly. "It's a present. Do what you want with it."

"Then what am I to do for you today?"

"You were a witch princess in Vanaheim, weren't you?"

Aud savored the appellation. Before she'd left her own country, she had been developing a sense of how powerful she might one day become. The family's seidhr magic was strong in her, and to have Loki acknowledge it filled her with pride. "I am," she said. "Though a hobbled witch princess in Asgard."

"Can you make me an elf-shot to use against Thor?"

"I'm forbidden from using magic except in service to the Aesir," she replied.

"It would be in service to me."

"Yes, but it would be against your own family. I wouldn't risk contravening the terms of my service."

He pouted. "All right, then. Tell me stories."

"More stories? I don't have any. I've told them all." Even the animal fables she'd used to tell Helgi.

"Make something up. Be inventive."

She shook her head. "I can't, Loki. I'm not a storyteller. I'm—"

"But I *command* you." Loki's pale eyes narrowed. "You must do as I say. You have very strict orders from Vidar." He pronounced Vidar's name in a whispery, feminine voice.

"Very well," she said, "I'll make something up."

As the morning progressed, Loki laughed ill-naturedly at every attempt she made to invent a story. Finally, she could stand it no longer and stopped midsentence to say, "Loki, you mock me so much that I cannot concentrate."

"Petulant girl," he said, "you are in my service and I may treat you as I please. I'm kinder to you than those oafs at Valaskjálf, aren't I?"

She bit her lip and nodded. "Yes, I suppose."

"You've been spoiled by Vidar. You aren't a princess here in Asgard. You are lower than the lowliest worm."

Aud dropped her eyes, her chin set against the outburst that wanted to break free. He was right, Vidar had spoiled her. She had taken the punishment with a willing heart— anything to preserve Helgi's life—and now she allowed herself to be upset by Loki's teasing. She was too proud. And Loki was too sly. He seemed to know her vulnerabilities instinctively and prodded them like a curious child prods the breast of a dying bird.

"Aud?"

She looked up to find him, bafflingly, smiling at her. "Yes, Loki?"

"You are a worm, aren't you?"

She tried laughing with him. "Yes. Yes, I am."

"Good, now that we have established that, let's have more stories."

"No, Loki. Let me do something else, I beg you. Let me climb to your highest shelf and clear down the cobwebs."

"What fun would that be for me?" he asked.

"Then *you* tell a story. You have so many. You have lived so long and been involved in dozens of famous adventures."

"Hmm," he said, stroking his bare chin in a theatrical impression of consideration. "Should a master grant a servant's wish?"

"Oh, come," she said, repeating his own words from earlier, "we are more than that."

This amused him. Laughter peeled out of him so loudly that Aud found herself laughing too.

"Very well," he said finally. "Which story would you like to hear?"

"Any story."

"Would you like to know how I fell out with the Norns?"

"Yes, I would.-I had wondered—"

"Had you? Then you knew I fell out with them?"

Aud felt her heart start. Had she revealed too much? Was everything threatened by a few careless words? "I had heard tell along with many other stories about you," she said smoothly.

If Loki suspected anything, he gave no indication. "It's a fine story, Aud. You'll like it. It happened a few centuries ago. Have you ever seen a giant, Aud?"

She shook her head.

"Oh, they aren't so fearsome as they sound. Most of them are only seven feet tall, and half of them are women and not frightening at all. But fate says that they will be enemies to the Aesir at Ragnarok, and for that, Odin has them trapped at Jotunheim. They aren't clever or cunning, so they rarely try to escape. And if they do, there is only one route out:

Utgard Bay. They hate water, and Odin often sends his spying ravens over to watch. Yet, occasionally, one slips through. So it was, on this occasion, that Aurgrímnir overcame his fear of drowning and arrived on the shores near the World Tree.

"Now, Aurgrímnir was just under eight feet tall, brawny and ugly, and very, very shortsighted. He climbed directly up into the World Tree to use it as a lookout. He was so rough and reckless that the tree shook and the Norns, all the way in the roots, believed it was an earthquake. They ran to the nearest opening and Urd peered out. Aurgrímnir slid down the tree to grab her. Skuld and Verda ran back inside, doubtlessly shrieking, while Aurgrímnir dragged Urd to a cave on the bay.

"By the time Skuld had worked up the courage to go after her sister, Aurgrímnir had fallen in love with Urd.

"'Let my sister go, brute!' she demanded.

"He squinted at her and smiled. 'Another beautiful maiden!' he declared, and lunged at her. She slipped his grasp by inches and ran as fast as she could back to the safety of the World Tree.

"Poor Skuld and Verda! Without Urd to unpick the cloth, the loom stayed full, no new fates could be spun and woven. Before long, they knew that time would begin to slow down. They were desperate for a solution. Verda ran all the way to Valaskjálf for an audience with Odin. She burst into the great hall, calling, 'Oh, oh, a giant has stolen away my sister!'

"I happened to be there on a visit, borrowing a few necessities. Before she found Odin, she found me. She was in such a lather, all flushed and trembling. 'Verda,' I said, taking her aside into the shadows of a recess, 'you seem troubled.'

"'I must find Odin,' she spluttered. 'A giant has fallen in love with Urd and kidnapped her, and now detains her in a cave on the shores of the bay. Odin must rescue her.'

"'Tch,' I said, 'Odin neither can nor will rescue her. He's afraid of giants and cares little for your troubles.'

"'But he must rescue her, or time will slow down, fate will become jammed.'

"'He will merely tell you and Skuld to work harder. You will have to unpick as well as weave.'

"A look of horror crossed her face. 'No, no.'

"'You know, Verda, I'm not busy, nor am I afraid of giants.'"

Aud laughed. "Surely she didn't accept your offer."

"Of course she did. She was desperate. I *love* desperate people, Aud. They reveal secrets, they grant wishes without prudence, they shed their dignity with delightful haste. I grabbed a few important objects and, within minutes, I had her on Heror's back with me, heading all the way across Asgard to Utgard Bay.

"When we arrived I spoke to Skuld and got her version of the story, then told them both to wait at the World Tree for me. I had brought with me women's clothes and a wig of tawny horsehair. I dressed as one of the Norns and headed for the cave."

Aud gasped with amused surprise. "You dressed as a woman?"

"Yes, and a fine-looking woman at that." He rubbed his chin. "I've never grown a single hair on this chin, my face is as smooth as any wench's. On the way, I pushed apples down my dress to fill it properly, then I stood outside the cave on the grey shore of the bay. Seagulls cried overhead, riding the wind. I checked that I had everything I needed and began to sing in a woman's voice. *Oh, love has passed me by, I must forever remain alone . . .*"

Aud was astonished at how much his voice sounded like a woman's. "That's incredible."

"I'm teeming with hidden talents, Aud," he said with a slow smile. "I can reveal them at any time."

"Go on," she said. "What did the giant do?"

"I watched the cave from the corner of my eye, dancing to express my sorrow." Loki leaped to his feet and imitated a sinuous, effeminate dance. Aud burst into loud laughter.

"I saw his face peering out, watching me. I turned and smiled." He continued to mime the events, smiling girlishly. "He charged out and grabbed me around the waist and took me to his cave." Loki sat down again, leaning forward. "Urd cowered in a dark alcove. She looked at me, astonished. I cried out, 'Sister!' to alert her to my ruse. She was so frightened, though, that she didn't speak a word the whole time.

"The giant put me down near the fire he had built. Fish bones scattered the sandy cave floor and the whole place stank of sweat and old seafood. He peered at me very closely, and said, 'Are you one of her sisters?'

"'Yes,' I replied, smiling beguilingly at him, 'but you may only have one of us. I mean to say, you can only have me. Urd is miserable and heartless and her legs are harder to prise apart than the jaws of Fenrir the wolf. Let her go, and let me be your bride.'

"The giant glanced from me to Urd and back again. 'I'll have you both!' he declared, and started chasing me around the cave.

"'No, no!' I cried, running from him. 'For I will not share

you with my sister. Turn her out and I will gladly surrender myself to you.'

"Once again he stopped and studied me and Urd in turn. Then, chest puffing up decisively, he said to Urd, 'Go, then. I'll have your sister instead.'

"Urd took a few seconds to understand what was happening. I gestured toward the opening of the cave. 'Go,' I said, 'leave me alone with my prince.'

"All trembling elbows and knees, she hurried to her feet and scurried out. 'Good-bye, sister,' I called from the entrance, watching to see that she disappeared far enough into the distance to be safe. When I turned, Aurgrímnir had lustful, blinking eyes fixed on me.

"'Come, my darling,' he said. 'Let me undress you.'

"'No, no . . . let me undress you,' I replied, lunging toward him and untying his breeches. I had them down around his ankles in a second. I pushed him onto his backside and stood before him, teasing him by lifting my hem to my ankles, my calves, my knees, my thighs . . . then I paused.

"'Keep going,' he rasped.

"'Are you sure?' I said.

"He nodded vigorously. I lifted my skirt completely and revealed . . .'"

Aud doubled over with laughter.

"Aurgrímnir was not expecting what I revealed," Loki finished. "You remember he was shortsighted. He had to lean closer to peer at it, to make sure he was really seeing it. I whipped the two apples from my dress and pitched one into each of his eyes. And then, while he startled backward, I pulled off my wig and wrapped the long strands around his throat to strangle him."

"Did you kill him?" Aud asked.

Loki shook his head sadly. "No. Some fools from Valaskjálf had alerted Odin to what had passed between Verda and me that morning. He sent Thor, with his big yellow beard and that ridiculous hammer, and he burst in upon us just as the giant's face was turning blue. He stopped me, bullied the giant into the bay, and demanded that he swim all the way back to Jotunheim and never return, under threat of extinction.

"But worst of all, Thor turned to me after the giant had swum away, and said, 'I have sent the Norns back inside the World Tree.'

"'What?' I cried. 'But they made a bargain with me! They are in my debt.'

"'It is a debt my father does not wish you to collect.' Then he climbed back on his horse and rode off, leaving me flat-chested in my pretty dress on the shores of Utgard Bay.

"I returned to the World Tree, of course, and wandered inside for the rest of the day. I was aware that centuries could pass without my ever finding the Norns, so I headed home before dark, gnashing my teeth at how unfair it all was. So, Aud, that's my story."

"It's a very entertaining one," Aud said. "I like to imagine you in a dress."

"Do you?" he asked slyly. "Perhaps I can put one on for you."

She dismissed his comment with a wave of her hand. "And you've never been tempted to go back and find the Norns? To extract your payment?"

He leaned his elbow on his knee, rested his face in his palm and tapped his cheek with his long fingers. "No, no. That would be a waste of my time. Eventually somebody will tell me where they are."

Aud smiled, careful not to let the faintest shadow of her thoughts color her eyes. "What would you ask of the Norns in payment?"

Loki gestured around him expansively. "Oh, I could think of a hundred things. It would depend on what presses me as being the most important when I find them. Something wicked, perhaps. Something that would annoy everybody." He stretched and yawned. "I'm tired of talking. Another story from you, Aud?"

"Loki, I have no more stories."

"Next week, then. Think of some. I'll let you clear those cobwebs now, if you like."

"It would certainly be less tiring," Aud said, grateful for a break from his unpredictable company.

"Can I look up your skirt while you're doing it?" he asked.

"No."

He shrugged. "That's a shame," he said. "I'll fetch you a ladder."

That afternoon, as Aud trudged over the slope with her new loom and Vidar's house came into view, she noticed smoke from the chimney. Her pulse quickened. He was home! She hurried her steps, arriving at the door flushed and breathless.

"Vidar!" she called, dropping her loom by the door.

"In here," he replied.

She followed his voice to her room, nursing a half-formed fantasy of finding him there amongst her blankets, ready to tell her he had found the Midgard woman wanting, that it was Aud he desired all along. It was the shutter on her window that had attracted his attention—he was tightening the frame.

"Aud, I'm surprised you haven't been freezing at night with the wind howling through this gap," he said.

"I didn't think it my place to complain," she answered. Her eyes drank him in greedily while he wasn't looking. His skillful hands, his long dark hair, his lean muscular back.

"Of course you can complain if you're cold or uncomfortable." He turned and offered her half a smile. It was immediately apparent that some keen sadness troubled him. He looked drawn, his eyes were empty.

"Did all . . . did all go well in Midgard?" she ventured.

He sighed and glanced away. "No. Not really."

Aud felt hope lift through her chest. Had the Midgard woman rejected him? She tried to keep her relief out of her voice. "I'm sorry to hear that. Why don't you come and sit by the fire. I'll make you a meal and, if you like, you can tell me what happened."

Vidar tested the shutter again. "I suppose I should eat," he muttered.

Aud rushed about making fish soup and lighting the candles in their metal brackets, while Vidar concentrated on carving a small piece of wood by the fire. He barely looked at her throughout his meal, and would have returned directly to his carving after they had finished eating had she not said, "Vidar, perhaps you would feel better if you talked about what happened on Midgard?"

Instead of the indifferent refusal she was expecting, he said, "Perhaps . . ." Then his gaze returned to the fire and he drew his brows together.

Aud ached. If only his sadness and yearning were for her instead of this plain mortal woman. "I can listen well enough, Vidar," she said, "if you'd care to speak."

He was silent a few moments. Outside, the wind was soft

in the trees, the shush of the sea rhythmic behind it. The cabin was filled with the smell of smoke and the herbs Aud had used in the soup. Without meeting her eyes, Vidar spoke softly and slowly: "Aud, if you loved someone as much as the sun loves the moon, would anything keep you apart?"

Unexpectedly, tears sprang to her eyes as a wordless, primal yearning pressed on her heart. A quick intake of breath prevented the sob.

"I'm sorry, Aud," Vidar said, touching her shoulder gently. "I didn't mean to upset you. How callous of me to forget you're so far from home and the ones you love."

"Far from my son," she said, the words trembling. "So far that he no longer seems real."

"You've never told me about him, Aud."

"You've never asked."

He smiled at her, so tenderly and warmly that her heart caught in her throat. In all the long years she had been living with him, he had never been so openly warm. It astonished her more than it delighted her. Her blood pounded.

"I'm asking now," he said. "I can listen well, too, Aud, if you'd care to speak."

And so she unlocked the story again and found more relief in revealing it to Vidar than to Loki. As the story drew to the point where she should end it, she saw in Vidar's eyes a well of raw pity. She suddenly felt vulnerable and annoyed. For the Midgard woman, he had the love of the sun for the moon; for Aud, just pity. Vidar already imagined that her long days off were spent standing at the border of Vanaheim and pining for home. Now he must see her even more as a weak, pathetic creature. Was it not loss of dignity enough that she—witch princess of the Vanir—must be reduced to servitude? No wonder he didn't love her. She had hidden her spirit, her pow. . . e she could check herself, she began to speak too freely.

"Vidar," she said, leaning closer, conspiratorially. "I still see the Norns."

His eyes widened. "You do?"

Her pulse fluttered in her throat. She should stop. Immediately. Before it went any further, before she revealed too much. "That is where I go," she said, "on days when you are kind enough to allow me time for myself. I go to the World Tree, and there, in exchange for news about the outside world, they reveal my son to me in an enchanted crystal." She sat back, immediately regretful. "Please never tell another soul. If I should lead somebody to them . . ."

"Of course, Aud," he said quickly. There had been a subtle change in his voice. Instead of speaking to her as one might speak to a child, he spoke to her firmly and warmly. She had revealed too much, but it had worked in her favor.

"Thank you for listening to my tale," she said, brushing her hair off her shoulders and stretching her hands out to the fire. "I feel better for telling somebody."

Neither spoke for long minutes. The wind howled over the chimney and the fire sputtered. At length, Aud grew impatient for him to offer her a secret in payment. "You've been so kind to me, Vidar, but I can be more than a servant to you," she said. "I can be your companion. We can be friends for each other."

Almost imperceptibly, he leaned back. She cursed herself for going too far, but she couldn't let him go now.

"As for the answer to your other question," she continued quickly, trying to keep her tone light, "no matter how much the sun loves the moon, they are separated by miles and miles of stars. They are fixed and cannot reach each other.

And they must accept that and get on, as I do. As anyone must when love is made impossible."

He stood and stretched his arms over his head, as though he hadn't heard her. "I need a moment in the fresh air. The smoke stings my eyes."

"I'll wait here by the fire," she said.

"No, no. Go to bed. I might look in on Arvak. That stable door sounded loose." He pulled on a heavy cloak and left.

His sudden coldness made her stomach tie in knots.

"Fine," she whispered angrily. "Sleep with the horse."

Fifteen

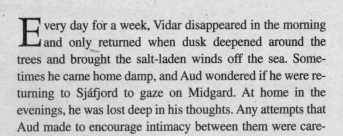

Every day for a week, Vidar disappeared in the morning and only returned when dusk deepened around the trees and brought the salt-laden winds off the sea. Sometimes he came home damp, and Aud wondered if he were returning to Sjáfjord to gaze on Midgard. At home in the evenings, he was lost deep in his thoughts. Any attempts that Aud made to encourage intimacy between them were carefully blocked by Vidar. Aud, sick at heart, felt him slip further and further from her confidence, and was helpless to change the situation.

One bright morning, about an hour after Vidar had left, Aud was collecting firewood from the pile by the stables when she heard hoofbeats approaching from the woods. She looked around to see Loki burst from the trees on Heror. He was dressed all in black, his hair loose and flowing, a silver circlet around his forehead and an ornate box brooch fastening his cloak. With her arms full of firewood, she moved toward the house to greet him.

"Good morning," she said, curious.

He jumped off Heror and loosened the bridle, smiling at her over his shoulder. "Greetings, Aud. You look well."

"Thank you."

"Is Vidar about? I need to talk to him."

"No, he's out."

"Where?"

"I don't know."

Loki narrowed his eyes. "You don't know?"

Aud shook her head. "He didn't say. I didn't ask."

"Ah, disappointing. I rather felt like some company today." Loki surveyed the area around them. "Perhaps I'll go to look for him."

Aud grew concerned. What if Vidar stood in Sjáfjord, unsuspecting? If Loki found him and learned of his secret . . . what then? Did she really care if others learned of Vidar's love for this Midgard woman, especially if their disapproval stopped him seeing her?

"Which direction did he go, Aud?" Loki was asking.

She gathered herself and shook her head. "I don't know," she said. "I'm sorry." Vidar had trusted her not to tell and she intended to be worthy of that trust.

Loki fixed his gaze to the northwest, toward the seeing-water. "Perhaps I'll head over the slope to—"

"If you want company, I'll gladly provide it," she said quickly, dropping the wood and dusting her hands.

"I've no intention of sitting by the fire on such a beautiful day," he said.

"Then let us walk, in the woods."

"Walk? Wouldn't you like to ride with me?"

"I couldn't keep up."

"No," he said, grasping her elbow gently. "*With* me. On

Heror." He whistled loudly and Heror turned and walked toward them.

A shiver of fear frosted her skin. She was uncomfortable on horseback—preferred her feet on the ground—let alone a fast, powerful beast like Heror with Loki at the reins. "I'm not sure . . ."

"Didn't you say you'd keep me company? Come."

"Must we go very fast?"

Loki laughed his wild laugh. "Of course we must!" With swift grace, he mounted Heror, then put his hand down for her. "Come, Aud. Don't be frightened. You may trust me."

Trust Loki? Aud almost laughed. She wondered if Vidar would appreciate her actions when she told him this evening. "Very well," she said. She tied her skirts around her hips and, reaching up, allowed Loki to help her onto Heror's back.

"Hold on tight," Loki said, slapping her thigh playfully. Aud needed no prompting. She locked her arms about his waist, her hands tight over his hollow stomach. No warmth emanated from his body. His black hair caught against her lips and cheek. She screwed her eyes tight.

Heror needed little encouragement from Loki. Almost as soon as they were settled, he sped off like lightning. Aud cracked open one eye to see where they were going, but hurriedly closed it when the branches of the wood loomed close enough to terrify her and the shadows between the trees flew past like wild ghosts. She tightened her grip on Loki's ribs, wishing they were not so narrow and cool. From time to time, she could feel his body shake with mad laughter. Their journey, while it probably only lasted twenty minutes, seemed interminable as she willed him and willed him to slow down. Finally, she felt Loki pull on Heror's reins. The horse slowed to a walk, and she ventured to open her eyes.

They had left the woods and were entering a sunlit field of waving grass, daisies and orange hawkweed. Heror stopped, they dismounted and Loki sent the horse off to cool down. Aud's legs were shaking too much to stand so she sank into the grass, feeling the warm sunshine fill her hair.

Loki sat next to her and began idly to pick daisies. "Did you enjoy our ride, Aud?"

"No," she answered, taking a deep breath and stilling her trembling hands.

"I'll try harder on the way home," he said, reaching over to twine a daisy in her hair. "Why did you want to come with me, Aud? I suspect you wanted to keep me from finding Vidar."

"I've been lonely and I have been trapped in the house," she said, "and fresh air, sunshine and company are appealing to me."

"Why have you been lonely?" His hand came to rest on her knee.

"Vidar has spent a lot of time away from home," she said dismissively.

"He has been to Midgard again?"

"No. He goes out in the morning, and returns in the evening with little to say to me." She realized her voice sounded bitter.

"What do you think he does all day?"

Aud regretted opening this line of conversation. As always, Loki was sifting her words for secrets. "I really don't know," she said plainly. "I sometimes wonder if he simply wants to be away from me."

"Why would he want that?"

"Because he knows I love him, and he'd sooner avoid me than reject me." Aud sounded so pitiful that she had to laugh at herself.

Loki reached up to wind another daisy into her hair; she plucked a flower from the ground and did the same to him. For a few minutes, as they decorated each other with flowers, she felt like a child. Loki and the sunshine and the bright field seemed so simple.

"You know, Aud," he said, "Vidar isn't worthy of such devotion from you."

"He is," she said. "I know he shares no intimacies with me, and I know he feels no special love for me, but he is kind and patient and cares for my comfort." She dropped her hands in her lap. Speaking of Vidar's indifference to her made it more real, and she experienced it as an ache of emptiness all across her body. "He is a good man," she said softly.

Loki tilted his head to the side and touched her cheek with his cool fingers. "You are a good woman," he said. "You are very beautiful to me, Aud. Could you not offer your affections to someone who will be more tender with them?"

Aud brushed his hand from her face. "I am your servant," she said bitterly.

"No. Not today. Save that for tomorrow. Today we are Vanir and Aesir, together in a sunny field. History says we should kiss each other or kill each other." Loki smiled and leaned forward, gently grasping her chin. "Hold still now. I won't kill you."

His lips pressed against hers, cool and smooth. For a moment she held her breath, tensed against him, but his arms encircled her waist and pulled her close, and it had been so long—*so long*—since anyone had held her. She sighed against his mouth, his kiss deepened and he lowered her to the grass. His hands tangled in her hair, his lips tickled her ears and throat and returned again and again to her mouth.

Aud opened her eyes and saw the bright sun watching them. She wondered where Vidar was, what he was doing. Loki's hand closed over her breast.

"Stop," she said.

Loki lifted himself off her, his eyebrows drawn together. "Stop?"

"Please," she said. "I don't want to. I'm sorry."

His eyes were furious. "A woman in service should be careful not to start what she doesn't intend to finish."

"I'm sorry. Please don't force me."

This seemed to anger him more. He sat up and brushed his hair over his shoulder. A daisy fell to the ground. "Force you? Aud, I would never *force* anyone. Besides, you'd tell Vidar and he's bigger than I and he's a brute."

"He's not a brute."

Loki sniffed dismissively. "You are very, very young." He stood and held out a hand to help her to her feet. "I'll take you home, and tomorrow I'll have invented a task more disgusting than anything you ever had to deal with at Valaskjálf."

Aud felt empty and bereft, guilty and angry, all at once. He took her home at a much more civilized pace and she was glad to see the house at Gammaldal appear as they broke from the woods. A second later she spotted Vidar, returning from the northwest, clearly damp. And Loki had seen him too.

"Isn't that your master?" he asked over his shoulder.

"Yes." What was he doing home so early?

"He's wet. Any idea why?"

"No."

"Then you're stupid. Anyone can see he's come from Sjáfjord. He's been using seeing magic." Loki spurred his horse forward. "Ho, cousin!"

Aud saw Vidar look up, anxiety troubling his brow. He waited wordlessly as they approached, then helped Aud down from Heror's back.

"You're damp, Vidar," Loki said.

"I've been swimming. It's a hot morning."

"That it is," Loki said, his face revealing his skepticism.

"Why are you here?" Vidar asked.

"I thought to see you, but your bondmaid spirited me away. But now we've returned and I need to ask if you took anything from Heimdall's chamber the night we went to steal a thread from his cloak."

Vidar looked puzzled. "No. Just the thread."

Aud pulled close to Vidar. "You gave me a pair of brooches, Loki," she said.

"I'll need them back," Loki said to her. "Fetch them for me."

"Why?" Aud asked.

"I don't need to explain myself to you. Just fetch them," Loki said.

Vidar nodded, smiling at her kindly. "Go on, Aud."

Aud raced inside and found the brooches in a carved wooden box amongst other of her trinkets. She dreaded what Loki might say about her once alone with Vidar. Would he brag about their kiss? From the door of the house, she could see Loki laughing as he told Vidar a story. Vidar didn't share in his amusement. He quieted as she approached.

"Here," she said, offering Loki the brooches.

Loki snatched them from her fingers and turned his horse around. "I will see you tomorrow, Aud. Arrive before dawn, I'll have a lot of work for you. Good-bye, Vidar."

"Good-bye, cousin," Vidar said.

Loki sped off. Aud ventured to ask Vidar, "Did he say anything about me?"

"You? No."

She felt relieved.

"But I have trouble," he continued. "When Loki and I went to steal a thread from Heimdall's cloak, Loki stole some treasures from his chamber."

"And?"

"And Heimdall noticed them missing, took Valaskjálf apart looking for them, then finally deduced what had happened. Loki must return them."

"That isn't trouble for you, though, is it?"

They turned and headed back to the house. "Who knows what Loki will tell Heimdall?" Vidar said. "What if he reveals that I was there? Why we came to Valaskjálf in the first place?"

Aud offered him a smile. "You trusted him when you let him take you there. I suppose you must continue to trust him."

Vidar gave her a sidelong glance. "You trust him," he said firmly. "I can see that."

Aud was puzzled. "How do you see that?"

He kept his eyes in front of him now, avoiding her face. "You have flowers in your hair; he has flowers in his hair."

She stopped, reaching for her hair and brushing out the daisies. He kept walking.

"No, Vidar, it's not as it seems. We aren't close, I don't

trust Loki," she called after him, running to catch up. "But he draws me into his confidence sometimes and I—"

Vidar paused, and turned to face her. His eyes were very intense, dark. She couldn't remember him ever looking at her with such naked feeling, and it both thrilled her and frightened her. "I warn you, it will be at your peril if you tell him about Victoria."

Her temper flared. "You insult me with your mistrust," she said shortly.

A second passed, two, three. The friction had heated the space between them.

"Leave me be, Aud," he said curtly. "I'm going to change into some dry clothes."

A breeze off the sea swirled past, lifting her hair and sending a few last petals diving to the ground. Aud watched Vidar go, but didn't follow. So she had a name, this Midgard woman. *Victoria.* She said the name out loud. It was bitter on her tongue.

Vidar had spent too much time wandering in the last few weeks. Wandering about in his own mind, imagining and reimagining himself with Victoria, then chastising himself for putting her in danger; wandering about in the fields and on the water's edge, spending so long in the seeing-water gazing at her that his hands wrinkled and his skin froze; wandering about the farm at Gammaldal, repairing things that didn't need repairing, tending to needs that the chickens didn't have, carving presents for Victoria that he didn't know he would ever offer her.

Then the morning's exchange with Aud, when he had accidentally released Victoria's name, had brought him out of his reverie and back into the world. Aud knew about Victoria, Aud spent long hours with Loki, and Loki was curious about Vidar's trip to Midgard. If somehow the secret slipped from one tongue to the next, and made its way into the ear of Odin, then matters would be out of his hands.

He regretted speaking harshly to Aud. He regretted every occasion when a spark of temper overrode his good sense, but love and fear, the two mightiest of passions, had driven him to it.

Though in the back of his mind another voice suggested that perhaps an emotion less grand had also played a part. Seeing Aud and Loki return together, both flushed and decorated with flowers, had caused a twinge of jealousy. Over the last five years, he had discouraged Aud's fantasies that they were lover and beloved, yet he had been blind to a different relationship developing between them: owner and possession. Aud was his. Vidar knew she was in love with him; he knew he didn't love her. But she was his. He was ashamed of such possessiveness; it was petty, cruel, arrogant, everything he despised about the Aesir. The only way Vidar knew he could make peace with his feelings was to apologize to Aud.

Vidar returned to the house at dusk. The fire was not stoked and Aud was not waiting. He threw some wood on the fire and searched the other rooms. They were empty. He opened the back door and looked out. Right at the bottom of the barley field he saw her dark hair. He made his way down the corridors of green shoots. She turned.

"Aud, are you hiding from me?"

"No. I was . . . thinking."

"May I sit by you?"

"You may do as you please. I'm your servant."

"May I sit by you as your friend, Aud?"

"You didn't speak to me as a friend this morning."

"I know," he said gently, crouching on the cool grass next to her. "I want to apologize. Let me sit by you. I do trust you, Aud. I have to explain myself to you."

"You don't have to."

"I would like to explain myself. I would like to make peace with you because I leave soon to visit my mother." He needed good counsel and, although the way was treacherous, he'd decided to make a journey to Jotunheim.

She shifted and patted the ground beside her. He settled in the offered space, his legs stretched out in front of him. The sea beat its quiet rhythm, black shadow-birds arrowed across the dull pink sky.

"Go on," she said.

"I can't tell you everything. Not because I don't trust you, just because it's not in my nature to tell everything."

"I understand."

"I am in love. You're clever. You've deduced this much."

"Yes."

"Her name is Victoria, she lives in Midgard, she doesn't know what I am. She wouldn't believe me if I told her."

"Why her, Vidar?" she said, her brows drawing down so that she looked like a petulant child. "Why a Midgard woman?"

"She's special."

"How can you know this? How can you know somebody from seeing her reflection in a pond? Is she so beautiful?"

Vidar chose his words carefully. "I *know* her, Aud. I've known her for a long time."

"Before I came into your service?"

"Yes, before that. Long before that."

Disappointment flashed across Aud's face before she

dropped her head and her long hair hid her face from view. "I see."

"Aud, I know that .... I know how you feel about me."

She didn't reply.

"Under any other circumstances—" he began.

"Don't, Vidar." She gave him a pained smile. "Leave me a little dignity."

"I would preserve your dignity at all costs, Aud," he said softly. "That's why you're here at Gammaldal and not servicing those oafs at Valaskjálf." He nearly warned her about Loki, how Loki had bragged that Aud would eventually succumb to him, but decided against the warning in case they were already lovers.

"You've been so good to me," she said. "I owe you so much. That's why I couldn't bear that you thought, even for a moment, that I wasn't a safe keep for your secret."

"I'm truly sorry." He slumped forward. "So much is at stake."

"Is that so?"

Vidar nodded. "You know my family, Aud. You know Odin. Is there anything he wouldn't do were he angry?"

"But why would he be angry?" she asked hesitantly. "Others cross to Midgard, take lovers, have their fun and return."

Vidar said nothing, letting his silence speak for him.

"Oh," she said. "They return."

He dropped his head, felt the weary yearning weigh him down. A salty breeze licked over him and he shivered. "I've already told more than I intended to tell."

"You love her so much," she said sadly. "As the sun loves the moon. That's what you said when you first came back."

Vidar stood and stretched his arms over his head, feeling

the subtle release along the length of his spine. "Shall we go up to the house and eat, Aud? Can I cook for you, in recompense?"

Aud didn't respond. She was staring at the deepening sky, a troubled expression on her forehead.

"Aud?"

She turned to him, and said quickly, "If Odin found out, Victoria would be in danger?"

"Yes," Vidar said, his heart picking up. She sounded so serious.

"Does she know this?"

"Of course not."

"Then, Vidar, how is she to protect herself?"

Vidar paused, his mind blank. Aud was right. It would be too late for Victoria if Odin found out—even if Vidar never saw her again, it would be too late. If Odin knew she had returned, he would want her dead. So should he go back and warn her, help her protect herself? Or should he stay away and deflect any further suspicion?

"Vidar?"

"She can't," he said, his stomach hollowing out with fear. "She can't protect herself."

The sky was still inky when Aud crept to the door to leave for Loki's. Vidar woke, said foggily, "Take Arvak," and went back to sleep.

Arvak greeted her in the stable; the warm straw smell contrasted with the salty, rime-frosted air outside. She saddled him up and made her way to Loki's. She wondered what task he had dreamed up to punish her for rejecting him. At Valaskjálf, Thor had once made her clean out the dog kennels with her bare hands, transporting all the flyblown dung to a heap by the door. Later, when he had come to inspect her work, he had pushed her in the heap and laughed until tears ran down his cheeks. She doubted Loki would be able to better that.

As he had demanded, she arrived at Loki's before dawn. Aud was puzzled to see him waiting in front of his house, fully dressed, on Heror's back.

"About time, Aud."

"I didn't think you'd be awake."

"We're going on an expedition. We need to get away early. I'm glad you brought your own horse." He guided Heror's nose toward the east. "Come on."

"Where are we going?" she asked, following him, bewildered.

"That depends on how soon we get there. Do you want to go to Valaskjálf?"

Valaskjálf? Was he going to put her in service with her old masters for the day? "No, no I don't."

"Then we'll have to be quick. We'll have to catch Heimdall before he leaves Bifrost."

"We're going to see Heimdall?"

"To take him these things I borrowed." He patted a satchel over his shoulder. "I thought you'd enjoy the journey. Now come on." He kicked Heror and the horse leaped forward and galloped into the forest.

Aud took a deep breath, urged Arvak on and held tight.

Loki didn't match the mad pace he had set the last time, and for that she was thankful. Arvak, too, was more surefooted than Heror. They rode on through the forest, out past volcanic cliffs where water gushed into darkly glittering fjords, through a misty valley, then back into trees. The first glow of dawn had begun to bleed into the clouds when they approached a fork in the road. Loki pulled Heror up sharply and waited for Aud to catch up.

"Heimdall should still be down at Bifrost," he said. "We'll head to the south."

"I'll follow you. I don't know the way."

He set a relaxed canter. Aud caught up and rode next to him. "We don't have to go to Valaskjálf?"

"No."

She looked to the north and could just make out the black curve of the hall, a hunched and sleeping dragon in the half-light. "Good." Straggling yellow grass lined the cliff in front of them and sea-blasted trees marked the edge of the track. "I thought you said you would prepare a demeaning task for me," she ventured. "Is that still to be on our return?"

He shook his head and smiled. "No. I couldn't stay angry with you, Aud." He rolled his pale eyes. "You know I don't have a cruel bone in my body."

They advanced over a rise and the road sloped away sharply. In the distance, pale dawnlight awash around them, were two giant, gleaming stones.

"Is that—?"

"Bifrost. Impressive, isn't it? And see that dark figure standing at the north pillar? That's Heimdall, he knows we're coming. By now, I presume, he's focused in on our conversation." He smiled, then without raising his voice, said, "Am I right, old man? If I am, lift your hand and wave to us."

The dark figure ahead lifted his hand and Loki laughed. "Have you met Heimdall?" he asked Aud.

"Yes," she said, wary of saying anything else. She had once caught Heimdall spying on her from behind a post while she bathed, his hand firmly jammed down the front of his breeches.

"I'll be quick," Loki said. "Then we can take our time heading back. Perhaps see some more of the coast?"

"I'm at your command," she said, wondering why she felt a happy thrill at the idea of being out all day and not cooped up doing chores and telling stories by Loki's fire.

"Where are my things?" Heimdall called as they drew closer.

"I have them here," Loki said. "I only ever borrowed them. I always intended to return them."

They slid to a halt beside the north pillar. It towered over them. The patterns carved and painted on it had an odd crudeness, with uneven lines, unsophisticated angles. It put Aud in mind of a time before this world, of relics from an ancient past. She knew that the Aesir had once lived like gods; mighty primal beings that evolved in the void of being, terrifying to behold. Time reeled backward from her and the weight of her thousand years of service pressed on her lungs.

"Borrowed?" Heimdall spluttered. He wore a thick, grizzled beard that made him seem old. "Then why slip into my room while I was sleeping?"

"In case you refused me," Loki said, as though it were perfectly obvious.

Heimdall looked at Aud. "What are you doing with him?" he asked. "Are you his whore or his servant?"

"Servant," she said, a little too proudly.

"Then Vidar is all alone?" Heimdall asked. "For I see you have his horse as well?"

"Vidar is—"

Loki cut in. "Aud lives with me now, as does Arvak."

"Odin will want news of Vidar," Heimdall said.

"I know none," Loki said. "I don't see him as he never leaves Gammaldal."

Heimdall lowered his bushy eyebrows. "My possessions, Loki."

Loki handed him the satchel. Heimdall squinted inside and hitched it over his shoulder.

"Next time," Heimdall said, "come announced."

"I might not come again," Loki said dismissively.

"Even better."

They watched him trudge away toward Valaskjálf, then Loki turned his horse south. "An adventure, Aud?"

"Not too fast," she said.

"I'm in a good mood today," he replied, "so, yes. This way."

He led them past Bifrost's south pillar and along the cliff's edge for a few miles. Aud couldn't take her eyes off the dark ocean, no islands to check its savage currents. So wide and open, the very edge of the universe and beyond it nothing. The air was icy and Loki found a rocky path that wound down from the cliff top to the broad pale beach. Nothing like the narrow strip of coarse grey sand and the wide mudflats near Gammaldal.

"Down here," he said, then spurred Heror and galloped away.

Aud took the path more cautiously, but as soon as Arvak's hooves hit the sand, he pulled at the reins and she had no choice but to let the horse set the pace. His hooves sank into the sand and she could feel the strong muscles in his legs working. She clung to him as they flew along the beach, her hair streamed behind her, cold air bit her nose and lips. She felt exhilarated, cleansed. Her heart pumped and she managed to forget, at least for a little while, all about Vidar.

Loki had slowed ahead of her. He was dismounting when she caught up.

"Here's a sheltered place we can sit a while," he said. "Let Arvak run off with Heror. They'll return soon enough."

Aud followed his lead, letting Arvak free to roam. Loki had found a shallow cave, protected from the cold wind. She picked her way over salty rock pools and settled near him, gazing out at the sea. The sun had burst through the clouds on the horizon and sent glittering streaks across the water.

"Did you note how I protected Vidar from Heimdall's questions?" Loki said, his pale eyes fixed on her.

"I did. I'm sure he'll appreciate it."

"You see? I can be as loyal and thoughtful and caring as your Vidar."

"He's not *my* Vidar," she muttered.

"Poor, sad Aud," Loki said, an edge of cruelty touching his voice. "Unlucky in love."

She didn't answer. How had she managed to find herself, once again, out alone with Loki, enjoying herself one moment, recoiling from him the next?

"Tell Vidar to come and see me," Loki said, leaning back against the rock wall, his hands folded behind his head. "Tomorrow, maybe."

"He's going away tomorrow."

"Back to Midgard?"

"To see his mother."

Loki sat forward eagerly and Aud was afraid she had revealed too much.

"His mother?" Loki asked.

"Maybe he didn't say that."

"Oh, Aud, don't worry. You haven't given away a secret. I'm just surprised. You know who his mother is, don't you?"

Aud shook her head sadly. "I know so little about him. As you've pointed out."

"Let me tell you then, girl. His mother's name is Gríd. She's a giant."

Aud was speechless a few moments. Then she said, "Vidar's mother is a giant?"

"Yes, that's why he's so strong. Don't you know, Odin has a taste for the big girls. He's taken at least a dozen as lovers."

"Then Vidar has to go across to Jotunheim?" Aud felt a twinge of fear. The way was marked by treacherous currents, wolf-infested marshes and evil magic in the woods.

"I expect so. But don't worry, Aud, he's more than just a mild-tempered woodworker. He's very strong, and wily, and few could stand against him in battle."

"I know that. Or at least, I always suspected it." She hesitated, thinking of the stories of the Aesir from before her time, and the ruined drunkards they appeared to be now. "How long has Vidar lived?"

"More than a thousand years," Loki said. "I can't remember his birth. He's much younger than I, though I think I've aged better. He was born during the Aesir's days of glory when men in Midgard worshipped us as gods. Vidar grew into the fiercest of warriors. He had a sword, Hjarta-bítr, which was the most feared blade in Vanaheim. A cup of his own Aesir blood had been forged into the iron, so it would never rust, nor split, nor grow dull. It glowed a faint red even in the dark. I saw Vidar so often covered in gore and battle dust that I barely recognized him clean."

Aud drew down her eyebrows. "Do you tell me this to frighten me?"

"I tell you this because it's true." Loki smiled, spiteful humor lighting his eyes. "You can't stand to know of his brutal blood, can you? You must believe him all womanish and compassionate. Aud, you weren't even born in our days of glory. How could you know him better than I do?"

"How can it be true? How could he be brutal and yet so tender now? Has his blood changed? That's not possible."

"A man can try to change. He can remove himself from temptations and influences, lock himself up in a house with only an exiled Vanir princess for company and divert his energy into his farm and his building projects. But he'll always be terrified that his blood will one day betray him."

Aud shook her head. "I still don't believe you. I've met the Aesir and they are nothing like him. I can't imagine anything that would change them so radically as you say Vidar has been changed."

"Can't you? Can't you really?"

Aud frowned in puzzlement. "No."

Loki's voice dropped almost to a whisper. He leaned close. "How about love?"

"If he loved somebody enough to leave his family, then where is that somebody now?" she asked. "Why doesn't she share his home?"

"Odin murdered her."

Thoughts and feelings traversed her. She must not let Loki read any of them. "Tell me, then," she said. "I'll admit I don't know him, hardly at all. You must tell me."

Loki tilted his head to the side, his gaze drawing far out to sea. "Oh, I don't know if I will. It all happened so long ago."

"Please tell me. He loved someone? Who was she?"

"No, no. I won't burden you with those old stories."

Aud huffed in exasperation. "Loki, I'll go mad if you don't tell me."

"I'll tell you, if you let me kiss you afterward."

She would have laughed if she hadn't been so desperate to hear about Vidar's love. "I suppose so. I've let you kiss me once already."

Loki smiled slowly. "Do you believe in Ragnarok, Aud? Do you believe in the end of our world?"

She shrugged. "We have all been waiting for thousands and thousands of years for it to happen. Sometimes I wonder if it's just a tale told to frighten children."

"Odin believes in Ragnarok. All those at Valaskjálf believe it will come."

"Of course, because they still believe the stories told about them in Midgard. They still believe they are gods."

"Vidar has a part to play at Ragnarok, according to the stories. Odin will be swallowed whole by the giant wolf, Fenrir. Vidar will save him so that he may rule over the new world." Loki held up a long index finger. "Vidar is indispensable to his father, so Odin kept him close at hand. Then Vidar met a girl. A Midgard woman."

A tingle of surprise. So Vidar had loved a Midgard woman before?

"As for what he saw in this woman, you'd have to ask him yourself. Vidar bragged to everyone at Valaskjálf, 'She is irreplaceable, she is always and forever all I will ever love.' He said he'd leave Asgard and be with her. So Odin took his dogs to Midgard and hunted her like a deer."

Aud shook her head. "But that's awful."

"There's more. The best part. Vidar was enraged when he

found out. He went directly to his father's chamber, Hjarta-bítr drawn. The sky grew black and the beams of Valaskjálf quaked. Would he murder his own father?" Loki shook his head and adopted a feminine voice, "Oh no. He was too frightened."

"Odin is a fearsome man," said Aud.

"Instead," Loki continued, "he killed all Odin's servants."

"What?"

"Petty, isn't it? Too afraid to break down the door to his father's chamber, he went on a murderous rampage and slaughtered every servant—woman and man—who waited on Odin. Had you been in Odin's service at the time, Aud, he would have killed you."

"I don't believe it."

"He left their butchered bodies lying about outside Odin's door and disappeared. It is said that Odin stepped out of his chamber and laughed at the scene before him."

Aud shook her head, completely disbelieving. "Come now, that isn't true. Vidar wouldn't hurt innocent folk."

"I'm telling you, Aud, he would and he did. He is not as he appears." Loki shrugged. "Anyway, Vidar disappeared for a long time. Odin grew frantic, but Vidar eventually resurfaced at Gammaldal. He never returned to live at Valaskjálf, too ashamed, or too afraid . . . Who knows?"

Aud struggled to process everything that he had told her. She couldn't believe that Vidar was capable of such brutality and cowardice and was certain that Loki was bending the truth. But what about this mortal woman? *She is irreplaceable, she is always and forever all I will ever love.* Then how could he have already fallen for another?

Unless she wasn't *another.* Vidar's words returned to her: he had known Victoria since long before he knew Aud.

"I see I've given you something to think about, Aud," Loki said, pulling himself to his feet. "Ask him yourself about why he left Valaskjálf. Though I suppose he may lie."

"He lives apart from his family for the same reasons you do," Aud asserted. "Because they are heartless, petty, selfish and proud, and he despises their company."

Loki helped her to her feet. "That's only half of the truth. It's because they are heartless, petty, selfish and proud," he said, "and Vidar *knows* he's one of them."

Aud shook sand from her skirt. "I suppose I must let you kiss me now. As payment."

Loki's eyes went out to sea, squinting against the bright sun. "No. I'm not particularly interested in kisses just now. Let's head back." He strode down to the sand to whistle for Heror, leaving Aud in the shadow of the cave.

Sixteen

Vidar arrived at the World Tree in the middle of the morning, when the sun was warmest and brightest. He had set his hopes on a fine day for his journey and had not been disappointed. At the top of the ridge, he set Arvak to wander and stood for a few moments, surveying the scene spread before him: the mountains of Alfheim, the wide, grass plains of Vanaheim. The outlands of Jotunheim waited across Utgard Bay, grey clouds lowering over their volcanic peaks and plains. His mother, Gríd, lived on the southern tip of Jotunheim—over the water, through the woods, in a wild green valley. A full day's journey from his own home at Gammaldal. Beyond Jotunheim, north and farther north, were the misty lands of the dead. Few went there and returned. He had. Centuries ago . . . A frost slithered over his skin. He shrugged it off.

"Arvak, I'll return tomorrow, around the same time," he called. Arvak was already heading toward a field of long, waving grass. Vidar took his breath between his teeth and headed down the steep rock steps. A high breeze found the branches of the World Tree and transformed into a low moan. He walked briskly across the valley and around the tree's massive girth in half an hour, then down farther and farther, and out toward the honeycombed cliff faces that watched Jotunheim across the water.

Vidar stopped and surveyed the bay. Even though the day was warm and a light sweat was forming under his shirt, he dreaded the water. Cold dark undertows pulled any warmth from the surface. He gingerly waded in to his waist, then dived outward. The shock of cold seized him and for a moment he couldn't move his limbs. Then he took his first breath and began to swim.

Swimming so many miles was tiring, even for an immortal man with giant's blood like him, and the only way to keep his stroke even and strong was to concentrate. To banish all the thoughts that vied for his attention: Victoria, Aud, Loki, Odin. He pushed them out of his mind and focused on his muscles and joints moving, the rhythm of the water and his breathing. The water was grey and flat around him, salty on his lips. For a long time he saw nothing except sea as he plowed forward.

Vidar found the solitary nature of his journey energizing. His intention when he left Valaskjálf had been to live alone, contemplative, silent. Aud had come and chased away his solitude. Though he was grateful for her company, it sometimes seemed he couldn't retreat far enough inside his own shell.

Three-quarters of the way to the other side, a dark shape passed over the sun above him. He didn't look up. *Just a petrel.* Then another dark shape. He chanced a glance upward.

Hugin and Munin, Odin's spies. Two mighty ravens, vast

black wings spread to catch the warm updrafts that kept them hovering above him.

Vidar rationalized his alarm. Though Odin wouldn't be happy that he visited Gríd, it was no crime. He rolled onto his back in the water and called to them, "Tell my father I send my best to him!"

One of the ravens cawed as they both turned on their wings and swept off, two black shadows in the perfect blue sky. Vidar took a moment paddling on his back to regain his energy. The sun shone on his face, making water drops on his eyelashes explode in rainbow colors. Then he turned and continued. His arms and shoulders burned with exhaustion, his lungs cramped, but he kept moving.

The shores of the bay eventually drew closer, and he finally heaved himself ashore. He found a patch of rough grass to lie on and catch his breath while the sun dried his clothes and hair. His fingers were white and wrinkled from nearly two hours in the water. When he sat up and cast his eye back over the bay, he felt daunted; tomorrow, he would have to swim all the way back.

"Don't think about tomorrow," he said, stretching his arms over his head. He glanced around. The grassy slope led up into a tangle of trees and bushes: the woods, infested with wolves. He would have to travel silently.

When the strength returned to his limbs, he stood and trudged up the slope. The dark trees were very close together, shutting out all but a few strangled sunbeams. Vidar moved quietly amongst the shadows, careful to keep narrow branches from whipping into his face. The ground beneath his feet was uneven with roots and rocks, and the lack of sunshine caused his barely dry clothes to chill on his body. From time to time he heard the slithering of an animal's body—to the left, to the right—among the quiet trees. He tried not to let it trouble him, keeping his eyes ahead, watching for twigs and rocks that might sing and draw notice to his passage. The trees drew closer together, the grass higher, the rocks were stacked more precariously. It took all his concentration to pass through the trees without making a sound. He could smell smoke nearby and knew he was near the home of the troll-wife Jarnvidja, who bred the wolves that inhabited the fens and hunted in the wood. Her home was at the point farthest from civilization, where rough country transformed to godless wilderness.

The slithering noise again. Vidar stopped, surveyed the area carefully. He could see nothing. He closed his eyes and opened his ears. Nothing. Nothing.

There!

He spun, eyes snapping open. A streak of pale grey between trees in the distance. Nothing again, a ghost disappearing.

The snarl from behind him shocked his heart. He turned; but before he could see the wolf, she was on top of him, bringing him crashing down onto the rocky ground. Immediately she went for his throat. He struggled, a rock beneath his head gave way, he dropped out of her jaws and they snapped shut empty, spattering saliva over his face. He skidded backward, she snapped again, got his tunic. It ripped as he rolled, a rock stabbed his stomach. She got a loose grip on his leg but he kicked her off and scrambled to his feet, blood trickling into his shoe.

Vidar glanced around, counting them. Five. They formed a circle. He reached for his hunting knife. Which was the alpha? If he could distinguish the wolf that led the pack and kill her, then he had a chance the others would retreat. A half second passed and the first wolf closed in again. He caught her around the middle and rolled with her onto the forest floor, his knife plunging into her chest. The others were on top of him now. Blood splashed his face and he didn't know if it was his or the wolf's. The dim realization that this was going very badly crossed his mind, then he remembered: none of these wolves was the alpha. They were bred by Jarnvidja. Only she could call them off.

"Jarnvidja!" he shouted through a mouthful of fur and sour blood.

In reply, a cry from among the trees. A howl, but made with a woman's vocal cords. The wolves instantly shrank back, and he sat up, threw the dead beast off him and waited.

"I thought I smelled Aesir." The disembodied voice was thick with disgust.

Vidar glanced around, trying to track her voice. "Call off your wolves, Jarnvidja. I pass through on the way to see Gríd. I mean you no harm."

"Aesirs always mean harm," she said. Her voice echoed from all sides. She was hiding herself well. "You've killed one of my children."

Vidar glanced at the dead wolf. "You would have done the same to protect your own life. Let me go."

"And you will go straight to your mother's?"

"Yes."

A few seconds of silence ensued. Movement among the trees. Another wolf loped forward, a broad black ribbon clenched in her jaws.

"My daughter has something for you," Jarnvidja called. "Take it from her."

Vidar stood as the wolf approached. He took the ribbon from her and looked at it, puzzled.

"What do you want me to do with this?"

"Blindfold yourself. You may proceed in and out of these woods only with a blindfold."

"How am I to see where I am going?"

Jarnvidja snorted, a primitive laugh. "You are Aesir. You think yourself a race of gods. You'll find your way."

"I don't like your terms," he said.

"There isn't a choice, Vidar. Either you wear the blindfold or you die at the hands of my children. Twelve more wait at my side, upon my orders."

"What guarantee do I have that your wolves won't attack me anyway, when I am blindfolded?"

"You have my word," she said, in a mock-girlish voice.

"Your word?"

"Be brave, Vidar. Life is a journey in the darkness."

Vidar considered the ribbon. Resigned, he tied it around his eyes. All in front of him was black.

Another cry from the woods, half woman, half wolf. He heard the wolves retreat. Tentatively, he moved forward, taking his weight on his injured leg. Pain shot up into his hip. He limped a few paces, hands in front of him cautiously.

Cold, crooked fingers closed over his wrist. "Take care that you wear your blindfold on your return journey," Jarnvidja said. Her breath smelled like stale meat and spittle. "Should you dare to venture back this way without it, my girls will have no mercy for you."

"I understand," Vidar said solemnly. "But, Jarnvidja, I have passed this way before without troubling you—"

"I needn't explain myself to you," she snapped, releasing his arm. Her footsteps retreated and he divined that he was alone in the woods.

One foot in front of the other, carefully as he could, he made his way to Gríd.

The blindfold slowed him down and it was an hour before he perceived that the light was changing, the trees parting. He didn't dare remove the black ribbon just yet though. Only when full sun touched his face was he clear of danger. He untied the knot and slipped off the ribbon.

Vidar had arrived in a sun-drenched field of flowers. His mother stood a hundred feet away, a sheaf of flowers in her arms, watching curiously as he emerged from the woods.

"Vidar?"

"Gríd." He smiled.

She rushed toward him, dropping her flowers, and enclosed him in a hug. Gríd was nearly a foot taller than Vidar, and broad and muscular as most giants were, but she was a beauty, with hair the color of midnight and emerald eyes. She was old too, extremely old, centuries older even than Odin, although ageing had been kind to her, and she looked not more than ten years older than Vidar himself.

"I can't believe it's you!" she said, covering his face in excited kisses. "It's been so long."

He wound the black ribbon around his wrist so he wouldn't forget it on his return tomorrow. "Jarnvidja made me wear this," he explained, as Gríd put her arm around his waist and led him from the field of flowers.

Gríd clicked her tongue. "Insanity closes in on her. I'll tell you something so long as you never tell your father."

"You know I tell him nothing."

"Jarnvidja is tired of waiting for Ragnarok. She's breeding a wolf; Mánagarm, with teeth and claws deadly to the Aesir—wilier than Loki, more vicious than Thor. She blindfolded you so you could see nothing that might give away her secret." Gríd chuckled. "She'd be cross if she knew I'd told you, wouldn't she?"

Vidar dismissed it. "I have nobody to reveal her secret to. I'm Aesir in name only."

"I'm glad to hear the feud continues," Gríd said with a slow smile. "You were always more like my family than his." They crested a green hill, dotted with pines and grey rock. Before them, in the valley, was Gríd's home, a small round hut that resembled an upturned bird nest. "Come inside. You're limping. Let me look at that wound."

Inside, he sat by the fire while Gríd cleaned and dressed the wolf bite. He gazed around him. The house was made of clay and twigs, and the inside walls were lined with birds' wings. Mostly the dull whites and greys of seabirds, but an occasional flash of blue or red glowed among the soft feathers and delicate pinions. The sun shone dim through the walls.

"There," she said, sitting back on her heels. She smiled up at him and patted his knee. "You're hard to kill. It's in your blood."

"Sometimes I wish I had mortal blood, Gríd."

"Oh, don't say such a thing." She stood and gave him a playful clip on the ear. "How would I live if you had to die?"

Vidar waited for Gríd to settle on the stool next to his. "Mother, she's back."

Gríd's eyes widened. "The mortal girl?"

Vidar nodded.

"Ah, I see."

"She's on Odin's Island, just the other side of the rainbow bridge. I don't know what to do. I've come to you for advice."

Gríd smiled. "A woman's life divides into thirds, Vidar. First, she must find a mate. Next, she must raise her children. Last, she must be wise. What would you have me say to you, Vidar?"

"Something wise."

"Odin will kill her the moment he finds out about her."

Vidar felt his heart sink. Of course he had known it, but a small hope had remained that Gríd might speak of Odin as a reasonable man. "You're sure?"

"You're not? Vidar, he grows worse, not better. He can't see that Asgard is a civilization in decline. The trade routes are overgrown, their weapons grow rusty, the last few souls rattle around in Valhalla longing for a second death, a permanent one. Odin clings to the old stories as a drowning cat clings to the arm of its rescuer. He has been promised Ragnarok, a great cataclysm, then a new world. He can only survive the cataclysm if you are there to save him from Fenrir's jaws. Odin won't let you go, Vidar. No farther than Gammaldal."

Vidar hung his head, helplessness overwhelming him.

"I know you love her, Vidar . . ."

"I've loved her for centuries," he said, his voice husky.

"But for her own safety, you shouldn't make contact."

He looked up and smiled ruefully. "Too late, mother."

Gríd shook her head. "Vidar, what are you telling me?"

"I've been to see her already. She doesn't know who I am. Or who she is."

Gríd hitched a deep sigh. "Vidar, you are Aesir, you are made of a different substance to her. If you have so much as touched her, she bears your mark. Odin may sense her."

"Sense her?"

"Don't underestimate your father just because you think

he's a fool. Certainly, he may never turn his attention to Midgard. He's immersed in his drunken moment. But what if he does, Vidar?"

"He can't know for sure unless he looks in the water at Sjáfjord. I'd know if he came so close to my home. I could stop him."

"Odin wouldn't bother himself with traveling to Gammaldal, Vidar. He possesses his own supply of seeing-water. I filled a crystal bottle for him myself, he keeps it in his chamber. He need only pour a little in a bowl."

Vidar buried his face in his hands. "I didn't know that."

"She must be warned to leave Odin's Island, go somewhere Odin will never find her, to the other side of the world."

"She won't believe me. She doesn't believe anything. And there were conditions—I can't tell her anything until she's fallen in love with me."

Gríd leaned forward and grasped his hand. "Oh, Vidar. What a mess."

He met her eyes. "What should I do?"

"You'll have to go to her. You'll have to woo her. And then you'll have to leave her."

A crushing weight pressed on his chest. "How can I leave her, Gríd? I have waited and waited and waited. She is everything. Life without her is too long and too pointless." His words caught on a helpless sob and he bit his lip to prevent it escaping.

"I'm sorry, my love. That is my advice to you. You are safe, Odin won't harm you. But he will harm her, and gladly."

"Why did you ever love him, mother?"

The question took her by surprise. Her eyes welled with

tears, quickly blinked back. "We don't choose whom we love, Vidar. The heart is a fool. Besides, had I not loved Odin, I wouldn't have you to love now." Gríd brightened, offered him a smile. "Perhaps you could override your foolish heart and fall in love with someone else?"

Vidar thought of Aud. "There's nobody else. There never will be."

"Forever is a long time. Take heart," she said. "Now, you must be hungry. Let me make you something to eat."

She bustled about preparing a meal, and Vidar waited by the fire a few moments. *Go to her, woo her, leave her.*

The first two he could manage, but the last seemed all but impossible.

Late-afternoon sunbeams were reflecting off the sea when Vidar approached Gammaldal on his return the next day. Arvak was the first to sense something wrong; he whickered and pulled against the reins.

"What is it, Arvak?" Vidar asked, bending down to pat the horse's neck. He paused a moment, looking around. He could see his house and the outbuildings between the fields, smoke curling from his chimney . . .

Then he saw movement behind the stables. Arvak had smelled her already: Tanngrísnir, Thor's horse. She was a beast, a monstrous creature who could transform to a goat or a boar to be eaten for a feast, then regrow from the bones overnight, a fraction more stupid and malignant each time. And she was riderless, which meant that his half brother was inside, with Aud.

"I know you don't like her, old friend," Vidar said, spurring Arvak forward, "but I can't leave Aud alone with Thor. Come on."

Arvak was at first reluctant, but soon picked up his speed, sensing the urgency in his master's voice. Vidar's back and neck tensed, as he braced himself against the exchange to come. He allowed Arvak to wander rather than leaving him at the stable with Tanngrísnir. Vidar's body was weary from travel, and he felt sweaty and grimy. He had hoped this evening would yield a hot bath and one of Aud's best rabbit stews. Nothing so complicated as dealing with his family.

Vidar pushed the door open. Thor sat on a bench, his red-blond hair and beard reflecting gold in the firelight. He gave Vidar a crooked smile, spat on the fire, and said, "Hello, weakling."

"Where's Aud?"

Thor indicated with his head. "Hiding from me. She looks well. You have been treating her too kindly. She's Vanir scum, show some family pride."

"My family are nothing to be proud of," Vidar responded.

In a flash, Thor had pulled out a knife and thrust it into the pillar beside Vidar. Its handle quivered. "I'll stick it in you next time you say a word against the Aesir," Thor muttered, his mouth curling into a sneer.

"Why are you here?"

"Odin sent me. He saw you swimming the bay."

"You mean his two pigeons saw me."

"The ravens' eyes are his eyes. You went to Jotunheim, didn't you? To see the whore?"

"If you mean my mother, yes, that's where I went."

Thor pulled his knife out of the pillar. "Odin wants to see you."

Vidar felt his heart pull up. "Why?"

"You're to come to Valaskjálf with me."

Vidar shook his head. "I'm not going anywhere with you. Arvak won't travel with Tanngrísnir."

"Then Arvak's a soft-cat just like his master. Odin was insistent. You're to come to Valaskjálf with me. He has questions to ask you."

"Tell Odin I'll come in three days. I've just returned from Jotunheim and I'm tired."

Thor narrowed his eyes. "You'll come tomorrow."

"Or the day after."

"Don't bend my temper too far, Vidar."

The two of them locked eyes for a few moments, then Thor looked away. "I'll tell Odin you're coming the day after tomorrow. In the morning." Thor heaved himself up from the table, cast a glance toward Aud's door. "Bring her with you, if you like. I'll entertain her."

"Aud stays here, she's mine to command. Odin gave her to me."

Thor leaned close, his beery breath in Vidar's face. "Tell me you've pricked her, brother. Give me something to be proud of."

"Are you leaving?"

His brother laughed, collected his cloak and sword belt. "Yes, I'm leaving. I'm afraid if I stay any longer my balls will shrivel up like yours." He moved for the door. "Day after tomorrow, Vidar."

"I'll be there."

A moment later the door had closed behind him and his footsteps retreated toward the stables. Vidar held his breath until he heard hoofbeats thundering off up the slope. He sank onto the bench and put his head in his hands. What did Odin want? Vidar was glad to have a few days to think things through. In all likelihood, Odin would want to speak to him about his mother. But Gríd's warnings had stirred fear in him: he had touched Victoria, he had marked her. Odin might have already sensed her. Maybe he intended to confine Vidar and cross to Midgard and . . .

Vidar shook his head, took a deep breath. He was tired, he was overwrought. There were two nights yet before he had to confront his father. In the meantime, he should look in on Aud.

"Aud?" he said, cracking her door open. "You can come out. He's gone."

Aud looked up from her sewing and Vidar saw the bruise covering her right cheek.

"Oh, Aud." Vidar moved into the room and knelt beside her. "Did Thor do this?"

"When I wouldn't tell him when you would return." She touched the bruise carefully and winced. "It's very tender."

Vidar tucked her hair behind her ear and examined the mark. "What a brave soul he is, beating a bondmaid." He stood and held out his hand. "Come out by the fire. How long was he here?"

"He arrived this morning at first light." She took his hand, not meeting his eye. "What did he want?"

Vidar tasted the anxiety again. "I've been summoned to Valaskjálf. To see my father."

"Are you going?"

"If I don't go, he'll come here." Vidar sighed. "I have no choice. He's inescapable."

Seventeen

As Aud made her way through the winding passages in the base of the World Tree, she tried to unravel the sense of sadness and dread she was feeling. It wasn't unusual to feel gloomy and anxious on her way to see the Norns, but normally the negative feelings were tempered by her excitement about seeing Helgi.

Today, the excitement hadn't caught her.

She ducked a spider's web. A cold breeze from somewhere deep under the earth caressed her hair and face as a dying lover might. She shuddered and pushed on. Last time she had watched him in the crystal, Helgi had been laughing and playing with Aud's aunt, Thuridh. He had looked happy; he had put his arm around Thuridh's waist and cuddled her savagely, as a small boy might cuddle his mother. Maybe this memory was the cause of her melancholy. Aud, his real mother, dreaded seeing how little her son missed her, how fiercely he had bonded with someone else.

Dim light beckoned around the bend ahead. Aud was a few bare yards away from the Norns' alcove, but she stopped a moment, leaning against the wall. Her lip quivered and sudden tears sprang to her eyes. This was not the life she had dreamed for herself: separated from her child, in love with a man indifferent to her, creeping around this gravelike labyrinth with an ache in her heart deep enough to crack a mountain to pieces.

She took a breath and pulled herself together. Her heart had to be stronger than any mountain. One day, centuries hence, she would finally see Helgi again. He would be grown, a stranger to her. But he would want to meet her and learn what kind of a woman his mother was. Aud had to be worthy of that meeting: a woman of integrity and wits, not a ruin.

Verda's laugh echoed down the passage and Aud looked up. She could hear them chattering softly amongst themselves, and wondered at their lives, whether they had ever longed for a fate of their own. She took to the path once more, rounding the corner a moment later.

"Good day, sisters," she said, imbuing her voice with a shred of cheer.

"Aud! Did you bring me a hair clasp?" Urd said, dropping her thread and approaching.

"I did. I brought one each for you and Skuld. I had to carve them without Vidar's help, so . . ." She pulled the two wooden clasps out of her bag and offered them as explanation.

Urd shrank back almost imperceptibly. "Oh."

"Which one do you want?" Aud whispered, leaning forward and indicating the one with the less crooked carving.

Urd snatched it up. "I'll have this one. Skuld, there's another for you. It's not as pretty as mine." She shuffled into the back of the alcove and lit a candle.

Skuld was winding thread onto her distaff. "Put it aside, I'll look later." She raised her head and squinted at Aud. "How are you, Aud?"

"I'm well."

"Have you seen or spoken to Loki?"

"I have both seen and spoken to Loki. I haven't told him anything about you."

"Good. That's as it should be," said Verda, tying a knot and dropping her work. "Sit with us. Tell us about outside. How is Vidar?"

"He's well. He's been to see his mother this week, and Thor came to pay us a visit."

Much giggling followed this statement and the high color in Urd's cheeks told Aud that Thor was a favorite of hers.

"How did you receive that blow to your face?" Verda said.

Aud touched her bruised cheek. "I fell over," she said. If all Urd had was imaginings of Thor, it wasn't for Aud to spoil them.

They drew her out about Thor and Vidar, but she kept as quiet as possible about Loki, in case they grew afraid and refused to show her Helgi.

"Sisters," she said, when they had their fill of gossip, "is it true that Vidar is fated to save his father at Ragnarok?"

"Yes, yes," Skuld clucked. "He's very important to the Aesir."

"No wonder Odin worries about him so much," Verda added.

"Vidar loved somebody once, a mortal woman . . ."

Urd indicated the threads all over the floor. "It's in the past," she said.

"Is there anyone for him to love in the future?" Aud asked.

"Aud!" Skuld snapped. "You aren't asking us to tell the secrets of the future?"

"Or the present?" Verda added.

"You know you are forbidden."

"And you know we won't tell."

"Imagine the trouble we'd have if everybody knew everybody else's business."

Aud held up her hands. "I'm sorry. But you know I love him."

"He doesn't love you," Verda said decisively.

"Don't you ask us to make him love you," Urd said. "We won't make another deal with you, Aud."

Skuld was kinder. "The future is planned but not fixed, Aud. Fate is being made in every moment. It's more mysterious than even we can find words for. Take heart. Anything could happen."

Verda gave Skuld a cautionary glance. "Thank you, sister, that is enough." She felt in her apron and pulled out the crystal brooch. "Aud? You want to see your boy?"

"Yes," Aud said, reaching for the brooch. "Thank you, Verda."

"Take your time," she said, smoothing Aud's hair kindly. "We have much work to do."

Aud settled at their feet in the dim alcove and gazed at the brooch. He was sleeping. What sight was more divine than the face of her sleeping child? She examined him closely. He had changed since last viewing. His cheeks were not so plump, his hair grew tawnier. Over the last year she had grown to realize that he wasn't a tiny child anymore, not the little boy she had cuddled in her arms that last day at the apple farm. Still a boy, yes, but a scant five or six years from his change into manhood. Aud felt the world slipping through her fingers. It was already too late. What point was there in nourishing herself on fantasies of an eventual reunion with him? Helgi, her dear tiny child, was already gone. Perhaps it would have been better to let him die that day five years earlier and go on grieving for him in her own land, a free woman.

But no, she hadn't saved Helgi for herself. She had saved him precisely so he could grow from boy to man, so he could fall in love and have children of his own one day.

She gazed at the brooch for a long time, admitting that there were no pleasant feelings associated with watching him. Had it always been so? Perhaps, but seeing him was worth the pain, knowing he was safe and happy. He slept for a while, then Thuridh came and they moved outside to plant some herbs. He ran about with his arms spread, pretending to be a bird. Aud's father, Mímir, emerged from the hall and Helgi called out to him. Mímir took Helgi in a rough embrace. A bondmaid brought them a meal, which they ate on the sunny grass. After, Mímir gave Helgi a wooden sword and play-fought with him, always letting the small boy win. Aud watched it all, longing and longing to be amongst them.

Eventually Verda reached down and touched her shoulder. "Aud, it grows late."

Aud shook herself out of her reverie. Hours had passed. She would be making her way home in the dark. "Of course," she said, handing Verda the brooch. "Thank you, Verda."

"You seem unhappy today," Skuld said, eyes narrowed.

"I am happy enough," Aud replied. "What good does it do to be unhappy with fate?"

* * *

It was past midnight when Aud returned to Gammaldal, and she was surprised to see Vidar still awake.

"Vidar?" she said, closing out the cold night behind her. "You are up late."

He was carving, something small and fine. He put it aside and rose. "Come and sit by the fire, Aud. I've a favor to ask you."

She shrugged off her cloak. Even though her blood was warm from the long walk, her face and hands were icy. "I don't think you need to ask me for favors, Vidar. You can tell me to do whatever you want. I'm your servant." She followed him to the fire and sat.

He brought her a cup of ale, waited a few moments until she was settled, then said, "This goes beyond household duties."

"So did everything your family ever asked me to do at Valaskjálf." She gulped down the liquid, caught her breath.

"You know I'm not like them."

"Go on, then. Ask me."

"In good time. First, how was your day? Did you see your son?"

The walk had cleared the leaden sadness from her body. His question dragged it back. "Yes, I did. He looks well, but . . ."

"But?"

"I miss him," she finished on a whisper.

Vidar let a few seconds pass in silence. The candle in the alcove above her sputtered and died. Then he said, "Aud, you must comfort yourself in knowing that you made it possible for him to live."

"I try." She shook her head—it was dangerous to think too much about the gulf between her situation and what might have been. "I'm often happier when it's far from my mind," she said. "Tell me about this favor."

He took her hands in his, a solemn expression crossing his face. She tried to still her heart.

"You won't like it. But it's very important, Aud."

"Go on," she said.

"I have to go to Valaskjálf tomorrow, to see my father. I don't know what he wants, but I'm afraid that . . ." He couldn't finish the sentence, cast his eyes down.

"You're afraid he knows about Victoria?"

"Yes. It's a very small chance, but one I must take seriously." His eyes were almost black in the firelit room, intense and focused on her. "I can't let him find her," he said. "She's so precious to me."

Aud didn't reveal how much his words hurt her. "How can I help you?" she asked.

"I'm suspicious of my father. My concern is that he calls me to Valaskjálf under false pretences, that he'll trap me somehow, stop me from seeing her, and when I can't help her, he'll . . . He'll do something terrible."

She felt a wave of tenderness for him. "Is that what happened last time?"

His eyebrows drew down. "How do you know about last time?"

"Loki told me. I guessed that Victoria is the same woman."

"I can't tell you anything, Aud. Every twist in this story is secret. I'm sorry."

She smiled brightly. "You needn't apologize to me. I'm your bondmaid, remember?"

"Aud, you're my friend," he said simply.

"Ah," she said, "your friend." It was more affection than

he had ever shown her, and yet it gave her no comfort. She wondered if this sudden offer of friendship was calculated to bend her to his will, then cursed herself for seeing plots in the actions of a desperate man. "Go on, Vidar, I'm sorry. Explain to me what you want me to do."

Vidar sat back and took a deep breath. He reached down for the carving he had been working on and held it in front of him. "If I don't return tomorrow evening, I want you to go to Midgard. I'll leave you my special cloak so Heimdall won't see you at Bifrost. I want you to find Victoria and tell her that she must leave Odin's Island and go as far away as she can. She won't believe you at first, but you have to convince her . . . do whatever it takes." He handed Aud the carving. "Give her this," he said, his voice soft, "and tell her I love her."

Aud looked down at the carving, an intricate pattern of a wolf among leaves. It was exquisite. Her breath caught in her throat and she couldn't speak for a moment.

"Aud, will you do this for me?"

She raised her head and met his eyes. She wanted to cry, to rage at him, to fling the carving into the fire, to demand if he had given even a second's consideration to what might happen to her if he didn't return.

"I will," she said hesitantly.

"Are you sure? You seem doubtful."

She shook her head and said more firmly, "No, no doubt. I'll do it. But I predict you'll come home tomorrow night. Odin will just want to ask about Gríd."

"I hope you're right." Vidar stood. The intensity and intimacy evaporated. "Good night, Aud. I'll speak to you again in the morning."

She understood she was being dismissed. She took the carving with her and retired to her room.

Aud lay for a long time without sleeping, snuggled under the layers of blankets. She could hear Vidar beyond her room, still awake, pacing. Silently, she went to the door and opened it a crack. His back was turned to her, his hands were folded on his head as he stood by the fire and rocked back and forth on his heels. She returned to her bed and reached under her pillow for the carving. In the pale reflected firelight she admired it, wished until it hurt that he had made it for her.

Vidar woke with a start, a sense of urgency like a handful of sand in his belly. What was wrong?

Light from the crack under the shutter. *Oh, no.* He had slept too late. He leaped to his feet and opened the door to peer outside. The sun was just an hour short of midday. He had been expected hours ago.

There wasn't time to think. He pulled on his cloak and shoes and hammered on Aud's door. Why hadn't she woken him earlier?

Her bleary face at the doorway told him she had slept no better.

"Vidar?"

"I'm late. I have to leave. Immediately."

"Take care."

"You remember what I asked you last night?"

Irritation crossed her brow. "Of course."

He took her hand in his. Her skin was very soft. "Thank you, Aud. A million times, thank you." He released her and turned. "I have to go."

She didn't respond as he hurried from the house.

Although Vidar was feeling rushed and half-asleep, Arvak was in fine form and thundered down the path to Valaskjálf without protest. Clouds crossed the sky a quarter of a mile from home, and the rain started shortly after. He wondered if Odin were responsible; one of his customary ways to show his displeasure was to fiddle with the weather. It was the last of his great powers, the one that had him mistaken for a god in their glorious years. Now those powers were all fading, as though the very stories that mortal men told had provided the energy to drive them.

The rain intensified, and soon Vidar was wet right through to his skin. As he drew closer to the coast, the winds strengthened, chilling his damp clothes to ice. He pushed his wet hair out of his eyes as Arvak carried him out of the ring of forest, and he saw Valaskjálf. No sun shone off the silver tiles of the roof, and the gloomy sky seemed to blend with the dark perimeters of the building. The stables were at the rear, away from the ocean wind. Vidar hurriedly handed Arvak over to a stableboy, attempted to straighten his sopping clothes and strode up the path.

Two massive carved doors, inlaid with silver, opened into the long hall. Vidar stood a moment, allowing his eyes to adjust to the dark smoky interior. Stepping across the threshold felt like stepping into the belly of a whale: dark and cavernous and swollen, the smell of sea and blood. Lanterns lined the walls, illuminating the spaces between the beautifully carved beams that held up the roof. Every alcove was filled with lush treasures: carved chests, silverwork, thick furs and richly dyed cloth, and jewel-encrusted weapons. All plundered in battles on Midgard hundreds of years ago and all covered in dust. Vidar's eyes were drawn upward to the ceiling. The silver tiles gleamed dully in the firelight. Odin's longship, black wood decorated with crystal and moonstone, was suspended from the roof beams by ropes. Two huge fires warmed the space, one at each end of the hall.

The long tables and benches were empty, but a group of servants gathered around a cauldron and spit at one end of the hall, hanging a deer's carcass over the fire. Behind the fire, through a heavy wooden door, was Odin's chamber. In the other direction the hall narrowed off to a long corridor. It led down into the private rooms of his uncles, aunts, cousins and brothers, where they were sleeping off the previous night's excesses.

A young bondmaid approached him. All the servants at Valaskjálf were mortals who had longed for immortality, which Odin had granted to them in return for their service. Although, like his family, they aged slowly and had the potential to live forever, misery had driven a number of them to suicide. It wasn't unusual to find a body hanging from Odin's longship, or see a fish-nibbled corpse wash up on the beach below the cliffs. This woman's face was pale and hollow, illustrating that eternal servitude was not better than death.

"Vidar?" she said.

"I'm here to see my father," he replied.

"Sit down by the fire. I'll tell him you're here." She shuffled up the hall and through the doors. Vidar found a bench near the fire and leaned his shivering body as close to the flames as was safe. The maid returned.

"He says he'll see you soon," she said. "I'll get you a hot drink."

"Can you find me some dry clothes?" he asked.

Her eyes wouldn't meet his. "Odin said I'm not to fetch you anything but a hot drink until he sees you."

Vidar sighed. "I see. Yes, I'll have a cup of spiced wine." This was typical of Odin, who liked to assert his power in small annoyances. Vidar pulled off his sopping shirt and hung it over a table, and slid onto the floor to be closer to the fire. His drink arrived, the deer roasted, servants came and went, his clothes began to dry.

Still, Odin didn't come.

Finally, the heavy door creaked. Vidar looked up, told himself not to hold his breath. His pulse quickened.

Not Odin. Vidar's half brother, Vali, stepped out.

"Vali? Where's Odin?" he called, annoyed.

Vali closed the door behind him and approached. "Why are you sitting here half-naked?"

"My clothes are wet and skin dries faster."

Vali was very similar to Vidar in appearance because his mother was Gríd's sister, but Vali's hair and eyes were lighter, his beard fuller and wilder. They had once been very close, but the events with Halla had made them enemies. Now Vidar saw his brother as a strange ghost of himself, the person he might have been had he stayed here among his family.

"Could I have a blanket?" Vidar asked.

"Odin will be here soon," Vali said. "You can wait and ask him."

"Vali, this is ridiculous. I'm cold."

"Endure it like a man, not a prissy virgin," Vali said, sitting next to him.

"Do you know why Odin wants to see me?" Vidar asked, hoping his voice gave away none of his fear for Victoria.

"I've no idea."

"He hasn't said anything to you?"

Vali smiled, revealing a gap of three missing teeth. "Guilty conscience?"

"No."

"Perhaps he just misses you, Vidar. You're his favorite son."

"I'm certainly not," Vidar answered gruffly.

"You know you are, we all know you are. He would have eaten anybody else who behaved as you have, ingrate."

Vidar said nothing more. He felt his shirt. It was semidry so he slipped it back on.

Vali rose and slapped Vidar's shoulder playfully, maybe hatefully. "I'll see if he's ready for you yet."

Vidar watched him disappear behind the grim wooden door. The servants bustled about, doors opened and closed, footsteps shuffled here and there, Thor strode through the hall on his way out, sneering at Vidar and calling him a gelding as he passed. An hour passed, two. But Odin didn't come.

Vidar started to worry. What if Odin weren't here? What if he was already on his way to Midgard? But no, he would have to wait for nightfall. Unless he'd left the night before?

Vidar paced. The young bondmaid offered him a reassuring smile.

"Is Odin really in there?" he asked her.

Her puzzlement was evident. "Of course."

Vidar kept pacing. The last place in the world he wanted to be was there at Valaskjálf, cold and damp, waiting endlessly for his father to appear. He knew by then that this was a game, that the rain had been sent to soak him, that the long delay was calculated to unsettle him and remind him that, no matter how far from his family he lived, he could still be made subject to Odin's power.

A loud clunk echoed through the hall. Vidar spun round as the door opened, irritated with himself that his heart had picked up its rhythm once more.

Vali stood there again.

"Where is he?" Vidar demanded, striding toward him. "I'm cold and I'm hungry and I'm tired and . . ." He paused. He sounded petulant. Of course, Odin's whole plan was to have him cold and hungry and tired.

"I'm sorry, brother," Vali said in a low voice, a cruel smile on his lips. "Our father is not feeling well. He has asked me to pass on a message to you and send you home."

"What message?"

"Odin would prefer it if you didn't visit your mother."

The relief was like warm honey in his blood. "This is about Gríd?" Thank all the stars and the moon it had nothing to do with Victoria.

"Odin says that the giants have been exiled to Jotunheim for wise reasons, and your crossing the bay to see her makes Odin look less wise."

"You can tell my father," Vidar said, trying to keep his voice even, "that I have no immediate plans to see my mother again. Now may I go?"

"Of course." Vali opened his arms expansively. "Vidar, you are always free to go. We are your family, not your jailers."

Vidar collected his damp cloak. "Thank you."

"Odin says you're welcome to visit at any time."

Vidar was already halfway out the door. The drizzle intensified to rain almost immediately.

"Do you have any message to pass on to your father?" Vali asked.

Vidar paused in the doorway, looking back inside the gloomy hall with all its gleaming riches. "No."

"Good-bye, then."

With relief, Vidar closed the door behind him and headed for the stables. The sea roared in the distance, the cold harsh smell of seaweed and salt heavy in the air. Victoria was safe for the time being, but he had to get across to her very soon.

Eighteen

W hen Vidar returned from Valaskjálf safely, Aud noticed that he slipped back inside his shell, as though he wanted to compensate for having shared too much of himself. He spent the next two days outside in the fields and the mild nights concentrating on his carvings by the fire. Every attempt Aud made to draw him out resulted in a polite smile, a shrug or a gentle protest that he had nothing to say on the matter. Each night, as she slid into bed, she felt more and more isolated. From Vidar, from her family, from her home. From everyone.

In the years since she had left Vanaheim behind, she had sustained herself on imaginings that Vidar would eventually come to love her. Now that possibility had been erased, she couldn't bear the long days, the empty nights.

On the third day, Vidar woke cheerful and came inside early. Aud was struggling to fix the heddle rod on her loom, which she had dropped and cracked the previous day.

"Do you need some help with that?" he said, peering over her shoulder.

She glanced up, cautiously hopeful that it might mean he would spend some time with her. "I do," she said. "I've glued it back together, but the rod won't fit into its seat."

He leaned over and began fiddling with the beam. "My mother once got so angry with Odin that she snapped her loom over his head," he said with a laugh. "I had to make her a new one."

"What did Odin do?"

"He sent her into exile in Jotunheim."

"Oh. I'm sorry." While he wasn't looking at her, she gazed at the muscle clenched in his jaw, the curl of his eyelashes. An ache of longing swelled inside her.

"There," he said as the rod snapped back into place.

"Thank you."

"I'm going to warm up some wine. Do you want some?"

"Yes, please." She tied threads onto her loom, her fingers worked as she watched Vidar. "You're not going out again this afternoon?"

"I've finished for now," he said. "The chickens seem happy with their new roof. No leaks."

"You are in a fine mood," she ventured. "Is fixing a roof so restorative?"

Vidar laughed. "Hard work is its own reward."

She kept working, and a few moments later Vidar handed her a cup of wine. She put aside her loom and sipped the drink.

"What are you making?" he asked.

"A light cloak for the summer. My last one has fallen apart."

"Make me one too," he said.

"Gladly."

"I'm going away tonight."

Aud snapped to attention. "Tonight? Where?" But she knew where, and she also knew why Vidar was in such a good mood.

"Midgard." He pressed his lips together, a clear sign that he was about to stop answering her questions.

"Is that safe? For her?" Her heart beat a little faster and she could feel a blush start in her throat. She knew she shouldn't ask.

"I'm going to warn her," he said. "It may take some time. If anyone from my family should come looking for me, tell them I've gone off to Alfheim to meet an old friend."

Aud wouldn't meet his eye. "Certainly."

"I'm sorry, Aud. I don't like to make you lie for me."

"Lying to your family is a pleasure," she said, thinking of Thor. "I just hope that they don't decide to vent their frustration at your absence on me."

Vidar raised his eyebrows. "Aud, I hadn't even thought of it. Will you be safe here by yourself?"

Hadn't even thought of it. "I'm sure I'll be fine."

"You can go to Loki if you'd feel safer."

"Safer with Loki?" she snorted.

"Safer than with Thor," Vidar said.

Aud shook her head. "I'm certain I'll be fine. Why is it, Vidar, that it's you, alone of your family, that I can trust not to hurt me?" Although he had, really. His indifference caused her more pain than Thor's blow.

He shrugged, the tight-lipped expression returning. "I'm not like them," he said.

"I know." She thought of the story Loki had told her. "Were you ever like them?" she asked, keeping her voice low and her eyes averted.

A long silence followed. She looked up. Vidar was staring into the fire, expressionless.

"Vidar?"

"I cannot deny my blood," he said on a breath, "but I was made anew when I met Halldisa."

"Halldisa?"

"Victoria."

So she had two names to hate her by. "Loki said that—"

Vidar turned to her, his brow dark with anger. He looked so fierce that Aud could imagine him as the cruel warrior Loki had warned her about. "Loki knows *nothing* about me," he said, pressing his index finger into her shoulder.

"I'm sorry, I . . ." She trailed off. He wasn't listening to her anyway. He had walked away and was rummaging in the corner for his pack and cloak.

"Vidar?"

"It grows dark outside. I'm heading off for Bifrost."

"I didn't mean to anger you."

Vidar looked up and offered her a sympathetic expression. "I am pleased to have you in my service," he said, slowly, as one might speak to a child, "but there are questions I will never answer for you because they are questions you should never have asked." He returned and stood above her. "Try to understand. You're young."

Anger and indignation washed over her. Here he was, offering her pity again. She, a princess of the Vanir!

"I don't care for your secrets, Vidar," she answered, rising and flinging her cup away from her. It clattered to the floor. "I have enough of my own to entertain me." She stormed off, slamming her door behind her. She threw herself onto her bed and buried her hot face in the blankets. The horrible injustice of her situation seized her around the ribs with an iron grip, pushing her breath from her lungs.

For a long time she lay there, a few hot tears squeezing from her eyes. Finally, she heard the sound of hoofbeats and knew that Vidar had left. She sat up and peered behind the shutter. The sun was setting, but clouds blocked the light. She was so keenly *lonely*, and had no idea how long it would be before she saw Vidar again.

An itch in her hands, a prickle in her lungs.

What on earth am I thinking?

She grabbed her cloak and went to the door.

What on earth am I doing?

Aud set off into the twilight, heading for Loki's house.

Night had sent its long cool fingers across the land by the time Aud neared the hollow where Loki lived. A faint light glimmered under the shutter, the only bright spot in a landscape of grey shadows. She tried not to think about Vidar, whether he had reached Bifrost, whether he held his beloved in his arms already. Head down, she kept moving.

Paused at the path to Loki's door.

This was ridiculous. Surely, Loki cared nothing for her loneliness. Much of the time she could scarcely tell whether he liked her or loathed her.

The door opened.

"Well, Aud," Loki said. He was backlit by the fire. The soft-sharp smell of smoke was rich in the air. "Are you coming in?"

"How did you—?"

"I heard footsteps, I took a peek under the shutter." He hugged himself and shivered theatrically. "Come on, then. It's cold out here."

She hesitated.

"Come on, girl. I don't mind you coming. I'd like the company." He turned his back to her and went inside.

Aud took a breath and held it. Released it slowly. One foot in front of the other, she made her way through the overhanging branches to his house.

"Where's Vidar?" Loki asked as she closed the door behind her.

"I don't know where he is," she said carefully, following him to the fireside.

Loki smiled. The flames painted his skin with amber. "Of course you don't. You don't know anything at all. Do you even know why you're here?"

"I . . . I . . ."

Loki wrung his hands and adopted a high girlish voice. "I . . . I . . ."

All the anger and loneliness burst inside her. "I'm here because I don't know what else to do," she sobbed.

Loki's face instantly softened. He pulled her toward him and enclosed her in a hug. "I know why you're here," he said.

She sobbed against his chest. A small rational part of her, far outside herself, watched her and condemned her foolishness. "It's not fair," she cried. "It's not fair."

"No, it's not, Aud."

Aud clung to him and vented her tears, relishing the contact with another body, even if it was Loki, cool as a statue. "I love him," she said through her tears.

"I don't know why."

"He's good and kind and—"

"I can't tell you how sick I am of hearing that rubbish," Loki said, pushing her away. "Look at you. You're a tear-stained mess. What man who cared for you would leave you in such a state? He hasn't the slightest consideration for you. I'll grant you he doesn't beat you and insult you like those rock-heads at Valaskjálf, but he has frozen you with his indifference. All you want is for him to recognize that you have a warm, beating heart; all you want is for him to acknowledge that what you care about *matters*. But he doesn't." Loki leaned close, smiling mischievously. "Aud, he cares more about his horse than about you."

She felt her face crumple again as a hiccuping sob wrenched at her throat. Willingly, she put her arms out for Loki to hold her. He pressed her against him, his fingers idling with the knot of her scarf at the nape of her neck.

"Ah, there," he said softly. "Have a good cry, girl. You'll feel happy again soon."

"I'm so far away from happy," she whispered, bringing her tears under control. Her pulse was jumping under his cold fingers. "Farther than the most distant stars."

He bent his head to kiss her cheek, and his lips ran down across her chin and found a warm curve at her throat. "Then accept your unhappiness and live a life of selfish, meaningless pleasures."

A slow tide of desire was making its way up her body, starting in her toes, flooding into her stomach and fingertips. "Is that what you do?"

"I'm not unhappy." He stood back and shed his shirt, led one of her hands to his smooth chest. He was no warmer than moonbeams. She traced her fingertips across his skin and shivered.

"Let us find a warm place to lie," he said, stepping away from her.

"I won't lie with you."

"Yes, you will," he said without a backward glance. He gathered an armful of skins and spread them on the floor next to the fire, then sat down. "Come," he said, offering her the space next to him.

Aud felt like a marionette, poised in space by an idle string.

"Come, Aud. It's nothing. It's just sharing a few body parts. It will feel nice, then we'll have something to eat."

How she ached, then, for Vidar, for lovemaking that wasn't *nothing*. She sighed. "I might as well," she said.

"You flatter me with your ardor," Loki replied, biting back a laugh.

Aud went to him. He undressed her and laid her gently on her back. She closed her eyes.

"No, no," he said. "Keep them open. I don't want you pretending I'm *him*."

Aud was glad for the fire, because her lover was skilled but cold. She gave herself over to sensation, let her body lead the way instead of her troubled mind, and when the selfish, meaningless pleasure had ended, she was glad for Loki's company.

"Do you think dogs and horses and birds enjoy that as much as we do?" he asked, pulling a bearskin up over their intertwined bodies.

"I'd never thought of it," Aud replied, snuggling her head into his chest. "I don't suppose they do."

He kissed the top of her head. "You are beautiful, Aud. Vidar is a fool not to return your love."

She smiled even though he couldn't see it. "Thank you."

"Where is he really?" Loki asked. "He's in Midgard again, isn't he?"

Aud thought about the carefree, excited Vidar she had

seen that afternoon. All that joy for somebody else. "Promise you'll never tell."

"Of course not."

Aud sat up, her pulse jumping guiltily. "He's in Midgard," she said, and it felt good to say it. "You're right, that's where he is."

Loki narrowed his eyes, looking at her closely. "You know what he's doing there, don't you?"

Aud bit her lip. She'd waded out too far. The current was tugging at her legs.

"No, Aud, don't back out now," Loki said, reaching out to stroke her hair.

She tried to flinch away, but his grip on her hair tightened.

"I don't know," she said. "Let go of my hair."

Loki allowed her hair to run through his fingers, but he grasped her wrist. "You are all open to me, Aud," he said, and, for the first time this evening, the familiar cruel glint lit his eyes. "Mind and body, I see it all."

With her spare hand, she pulled the blanket up to cover her breasts.

"Too late for that," he said. "You confirmed for me that Vidar is in Midgard and now I *know* everything."

"What do you mean?"

"If you are so lonely that you come to me for comfort, then Vidar has finally broken your heart. You have abandoned any hope that he'll return your feelings. So you must think he's in love with someone else."

She sat silent, gazing at him, her face flushed.

"As he has gone to Midgard, I assume that his lover lives there. And as he had not been to Midgard for a thousand years before I helped him with Heimdall's cloak, he can't have met anybody new. It's her, isn't it? The missionary's niece? She's back, somehow."

"I don't know what you're talking about," she said.

Loki slapped his thigh in triumph. "I'm right! I never would have thought of it. You look sick with dread, Aud. Is it really so bad that I know?"

She felt vulnerable, naked in every sense. "Don't you tell a soul," she managed.

"It's desperate, isn't it?" he said. "Odin mustn't find out."

"Vidar would kill you."

"I've no doubt about that, Aud, but I won't tell anyone. I have no reason to hurt Vidar. He never troubles me. He never stands in my way." He turned to find his clothes and pull them on. "I'm curious, though. Aren't you?"

"About what?"

"About the woman. About why he feels so strongly for her."

"Love has neither eyes nor good sense, I suppose," she said grudgingly.

"I'd like to see her," he said. "I'd like to meet her." Then he burst into loud laughter. "Perhaps I'll drop in for a visit."

Aud grabbed his shoulder and turned him toward her. "No," she said, "Vidar will find out. He'll know that I told you, he'll never forgive me, he'll hate me."

"Ah, well. We can't have that," he said, shifting his weight onto his side to lie next to her. "I'll try to restrain myself."

The pain of guilt and regret swirled in her stomach. Vidar had been right not to trust her.

"I wish I hadn't come here tonight," she said.

"I'm glad you did. Aren't you a little bit glad?" He dropped a kiss on her collarbone.

She smiled ruefully. "Maybe a little bit," she said.

"All your secrets are safe with me, Aud," he said, gently twining a strand of her hair around her throat, then letting it free. "Just so long as we remain friends, you have nothing at all to worry about."

II

Wanton woman, you have awakened
the grim wrath of the gods.

—*For Scírnis*

II

Nineteen

[Midgard]

Carsten ordered five days of rest, and at first that seemed like it would never be enough. I was absolutely flattened. I felt sore and afraid. I wanted to go home very badly and if it hadn't been for the hope that Vidar might return, I probably would have. My world had been twisted on its axis and I couldn't make sense of what had happened to me. Beliefs can hold their integrity through a lot, but chip away and chip away at them, and eventually they start to shiver and dissolve. How much faith we maintain in them becomes dependent only on how tight we hold on. I was white-knuckling by then.

As my body recovered, I dealt with my fear by not thinking about it. I pulled all my notes into bed with me and worked at my thesis with white-hot single-mindedness. When I couldn't read anymore, I lay there with my eyes closed, performing meaningless calculations by importing Mum's lottery numbers into some of my key formulae. By Wednesday, I couldn't bear the thought of another day in bed. So when Gunnar dropped by to tell me that an afternoon tea for Gordon's fiftieth birthday was planned for four o'clock, I insisted that my missing it because of illness would be petty considering the percentage of Gordon's entire life so far which an hour's tea break represented. I got up and dressed.

"Hear that?" Gunnar called to me from the lounge room while I wriggled into my panty hose in my bedroom.

"What?"

"The *Jonsok*. That's the sound of Matthias and Nina leaving."

"So soon?" I called, with a fake tremor of sadness in my voice. I pulled on a turtleneck and a pinafore, carefully tucking the good luck charm out of sight.

"They'll be back, don't worry. They come four times a year."

I was a little shaky on my legs, but I was certain that was attributable to being so long in bed. I joined Gunnar in the lounge room. "Once every thirteen weeks precisely, or at irregular intervals?" I asked.

"Are you sure you're all right?" he said.

"I feel fine."

"You look very pale."

"I'm naturally that way," I said self-consciously. "Do you think Carsten will be cross with me?"

"Attending an afternoon tea isn't particularly taxing," he replied as we closed the cabin door behind us. "I'm sure he'll understand."

Carsten stopped me in the office and insisted on listening to my lungs before letting me go to the rec hall for afternoon tea. By this time, Gunnar had already gone ahead and Magnus accosted me in the galley.

"You're better, then?" he asked gruffly.

It was the first I'd seen him since the accident and I was taken aback by his lack of warmth.

"I'm feeling a lot better, thank you," I said warily.

"Good. I need you back at work on Friday."

"Friday? But you promised five days off."

"You've had four," he said, looking genuinely puzzled.

"Yes, four sick days."

"It's not my fault you were sick on your days off. I'll need you on Friday."

Then he bustled past me and, of course, 1.2 seconds later I thought of the perfect response, which was, "Actually it *is* your fault I was sick on my days off because I had to save your son's life while you were busy shagging the cook." But it was too late, he was in the rec hall and I could hear him laughing and being his usual congenial self with Gordon. I was as baffled by his bluster as I was by Maryanne's pointed frostiness when she offered around the scones with jam and cream.

"Why do you think Magnus and Maryanne are being so cold to me?" I whispered to Gunnar when I could guide him discreetly into a corner of the room.

Gunnar was matter-of-fact. "Frida told me that Maryanne told her that Magnus had confessed to a secret desire for you, and that Maryanne has forbidden him from your company so long as he wants to keep sleeping with her."

It took a moment for all this to sink in. "Gunnar, there's a gossip code of conduct," I said. "If you hear gossip about a friend, you are honor-bound to inform them of it *immediately*."

"I didn't want to worry you. You were sick," he said, and bit off a huge chunk of fruitcake.

"Magnus fancies me," I groaned. "Just what I need."

"Who can blame him?" Gunnar said through a mouthful of cake. A few crumbs sprayed out down the front of his shirt.

"I need a drink of water," I said.

"Get me a champagne, please," he said, picking at the crumbs.

I ventured toward the bar, ably manned by Josef and Alex.

"One champagne, and one glass of your finest desalinated water," I said, resting on the bar.

Carsten leaned over my shoulder. "I wouldn't recommend alcohol just yet, Vicky."

"It's not for me, it's for Don Juan," I said, indicating the corner where Gunnar stood, attempting to cram the rest of the fruitcake into his mouth in one piece.

Carsten moved on. Alex handed me two glasses and leaned close. "Don't eat the soup!" he said, with a dramatic lift of his eyebrows.

"What?"

He flashed his big white teeth and indicated Maryanne. "Whatever food she serves you is bound to be laced with poison."

"Is everybody but me in the loop?"

Josef joined in. "Carsten told me that Magnus told him—"

I held up my hand. "I don't want to know. Thanks for the champagne." Everything I hated about the mating instinct was embodied in Magnus's oiliness, Gunnar's quasi-romantic fumblings, and the eager, knowing gazes of the others, starved for excitement and glutting on speculation about my love life. In those precious quiet moments with Vidar, love had seemed so far removed from such mundanity, it had seemed something divine and eternal and *grand*.

As Gordon's birthday party morphed into Wednesday night drinks and beyond, I remained the only sober soul on a ship of drunken fools, which made for a change if not an interesting one. Josef was scheduled on the night shift, and Alex and Gunnar fetched blankets from the storeroom, proclaiming loudly that they were going to stay up all night in the control room too. Everyone else took this as a cue to go to bed, but I was not ready for my own company yet. I joined them, cautiously sipping a glass of flat, room-temperature champagne while sitting cross-legged on the floor.

Josef switched all the lights out so that the room was only lit by the glow of the computer screens. Gunnar and Alex shared drinking stories until Josef joined us.

"What's the time?" Alex asked, yawning broadly.

Josef checked his watch. "It's after one. You can go to bed, I don't mind being by myself."

"But it's a party," Gunnar said.

"The guest of honor left two hours ago," I noted.

"It's not a party for Gordon," Gunnar explained. "It's a party for you, celebrating the fact that you didn't drown on Saturday."

"I'll drink to that!" Alex said, raising his glass.

Gunnar was too drunk. He was leaning cosily against my shoulder.

"Well, yes, I'm very pleased to be alive," I said, shifting a few inches to discourage him.

"I thought you were going to be victim number three," Josef said.

"Number three?"

"We lost one in the lake in '84, one in the control room in '92."

The numbers poised in my mind's eye, waiting to be

employed in some pointless long division. I drove them out. "I knew about the drowning. But here? In the control room? What happened?"

"None of us were here then, so I don't know," Josef said.

"Wasn't it a heart attack?" Alex offered.

"I doubt it. He was only twenty-five."

"I'm sure I heard it was a heart attack."

"Now how does a twenty-five-year-old man die of a heart attack, Alex?"

They bickered about this for a while, and I tried to hold my uneasiness at bay. I was angry at Gunnar for bringing it up. Denial was my new best friend.

"I bet he was hagged," Alex declared finally, a wild gleam in his eyes.

"Hagged?" Gunnar asked.

"You know. The old bitch that comes in if you dare to fall asleep in here."

Mention of the hag made me feel cold and twitchy. "Yeah, but that's just a sleep disorder," I muttered. "Really common."

"Especially common in here," Alex said, leaning forward. "You're not scared, are you?"

My hand instinctively went to my throat, where the charm rested under my turtleneck. "No. But it's scary when it happens, you'd have to agree."

"I have a confession," Josef said, lying down and resting his head in Alex's lap. "You know the thirty-minute timer?"

We all nodded. He meant the timer that reminded us every half hour to check the wind direction, temperature and barometric pressure. It was the most annoying noise in the control room, intrusive and insistent.

"It has four volume settings. I have it set to the loudest,

just in case I fall asleep in here and she comes. It always wakes me up before she can—"

"Steal your breath," I finished for him.

"Josef, you're so full of superstitions," Alex snorted. "It's just a dream, you know."

"I know," he said.

"The best way to deal with nightmares is to face them head-on," Alex said. "It's unconscious material trying to get your attention. If you ask this hag what she wants, you might get a very insightful answer."

"Listen to us," Gunnar said. "Telling ghost stories in the dark like teenage girls."

"I'm going to bed," I said, standing and hugging my arms around myself.

"I'll walk you back to your cabin," Gunnar said, a hopeful gleam in his eyes.

That gleam disappeared when I left him outside my cabin door without even a kiss on the cheek. I sat on my sofa and peeled off my shoes and panty hose, thinking about what Alex had said. Dreams were unconscious material that needed to be sorted. If I could believe that, then I could believe that Skripi was some kind of metaphor for one of my problems that I wasn't dealing with. Lord knows, there were enough of them. My mother, my love life, my obsessive calculating . . . But could I overcome my natural aversion to all things pop psychology by engaging in some self-directed dream analysis? It sounded like the kind of solution Mum would suggest to a problem. *Ask your higher self, dear.*

What was important here was that I had to do *something*. I couldn't endure another day of math gymnastics. So what if the Queen of the Skeptics intended a little experimental dream therapy? Nobody would have to know except me.

Ignoring my dreams of Skripi was probably making them more insistent. Next time, I would do as Alex suggested, I would face him head-on.

"Take one step toward a mystery, Vicky, and it will take one step toward you." This was my mother's favorite saying to trot out whenever I tried to convince her that supernatural influence was really just coincidence.

"Doesn't it seem odd to you, Mum, that you dreamed your spirit guide was Cleopatra directly after you watched a documentary about Cleopatra?"

"Not at all! Seeing the documentary probably woke my sixth sense. Take one step toward a mystery . . ." And so on.

I vowed I would face Skripi and, shortly after I fell asleep that night, the familiar feeling of blue moonbeams was cool on my face and I wasn't in my bed anymore. I sensed that if I kept my eyes screwed shut and *willed* myself, I could be back there and fast asleep again in seconds. Instead, I gathered my courage in both hands and opened my eyes. I was standing just beside the window of my cabin, on the outside, looking into the forest. Moonlight fluttered above me as clouds swept overhead. I was cold and afraid, but I stood firm.

A rustle in the undergrowth.

"Who's there?" I called, and my voice was a thin, scattered echo in the dark.

"Will you run away this time?" A little voice, childlike and sad.

"Skripi? Is that you?"

He detached himself from the shadow of a crooked tree and tried a tentative smile. "You invited me into your dream."

I studied him closely for the first time. He was the size of a ten-year-old child, but there was something not-quite-human about his face: his irises were oily and black, his teeth were softly pointed, his nose and chin reminded me of a fox, and his hair looked like fine twigs. He wore a ragged brown tunic and pants, and dirty fur boots.

"I suppose I did," I said. I glanced over my shoulder at the window, but the curtains were drawn. Still, I knew that if they were open, I'd be able to see myself, warm and cosy in my bed.

"Why did you want me? Can we be friends?" His eyes lit up eagerly and he took a step toward me, his pointy fingers reaching out.

Instinctively, I flinched backward. "I'm facing my fears," I said. "I'm trying to deal with whatever unconscious material is making you appear." As the words left my mouth I recognized them for the overrationalizing nonsense they were, and I nearly lost my nerve and woke up. "So who are you?" I said softly.

"I'm Skripi. I'm a wood wight. I once lived in Idavíd, a forest in Asgard, but now I live here with my brother and my sister."

"You have a brother and sister here?" I glanced around.

"The draugr and the hag," he confessed, kicking the ground with an embarrassed toe.

"You're related to them?"

"We all come from Idavíd. We'll never get back there."

I thought about asking him if the draugr was the collection of weeds and fingers I had struggled against in the lake. He answered as though I had framed the question aloud.

"Oh, yes, that was the draugr. He would have made you his bride. But Gunnar had *eolh.*" He held his hand up in a stop gesture, and it looked similar to the rune on the stone. "You see, you see? I told you it was important."

"Why are you here on the island?"

"The gods in Asgard put us here, all three. They sent down the hag and the draugr because they were wicked, and I had to go too because I'm related." He shook his head sadly. "We can choose many things, but family are thrust upon us."

"I understand," I said, thinking about my mum. Was this the message my dreaming self was trying to convey to me? "So you're here as some kind of punishment?" I asked.

"Yes, and we're also here to scare the humans away, but they don't scare, they stay. Nobody believes in us anymore." His eyes grew serious. "We are real, and my brother and sister would love to collect your soul."

"What would they do with it?"

He shrugged. "I don't know. Maybe just put it in the lake for always. It's cold down there. And dark." He crossed his hands over his chest and shivered. "You have to listen to me. I'll keep you safe."

I stood there for a few quiet moments, gazing at him, half-formed questions shifting across my mind. I began to feel vague around the edges and realized I might be slipping out of the dream. "Skripi," I said quickly, "is Vidar real?"

With a jolt and a shudder, I felt myself collide with wakefulness. I opened my eyes in my warm bed and took a gulp of air.

Far away, I heard a whisper.

Everything's real.

I flung back the covers, dripping with sweat, and hurried to the window. I pushed the curtain aside and pressed my face against the glass. I could see nothing but moonlight and shadows, and a strange disappointment washed over me.

My breath fogged the glass. "What if none of it's real?" I murmured, and an empty ache for Vidar spread hollow fingers in my chest.

I didn't get back to sleep that night and, at first light, I headed over to the galley to make myself some breakfast. When I slipped through the door, Maryanne was searching for something in the pantry.

"Good morning, Maryanne," I said.

She jumped nearly a foot in the air and shrieked. Then when she saw it was only me, her hand went over her heart. "Oh, you gave me a fright."

"Sorry, I didn't mean to." I noticed that dark circles were smudged under her eyes. "Are you all right?"

A battle between wanting to freeze me out and wanting to confide in me played out on her face. She paused for a long time, blinking rapidly: 1.8 blinks per second.

"Maryanne? Has something happened?"

"I heard the strangest noises last night . . ." she started, in a soft frightened voice.

"Last night?" I remembered Skripi's gleaming black eyes in the dark. "What noises?"

"I'm sleeping in Magnus's cabin at the moment," she said. "It's near the edge of the forest. I heard noises. He didn't wake up. I looked out the window and I saw . . ."

I realized I was holding my breath. "What did you see?"

"I don't know what it was. A twig-man. Then he dived into the bushes and was gone. It was like something out of a nightmare."

An icy shiver tiptoed the length of my spine. "Perhaps it *was* a nightmare."

She shook her head. "There are bad things on this island, Vicky. The forest is haunted."

I couldn't conjure a single logical explanation. Maryanne and I had dreamed the same thing.

"Vicky," she said, her eyes growing troubled, "you didn't see anything, did you? Or hear anything?"

"Me? No," I said too quickly.

She narrowed her eyes. "Because . . . I thought I heard your voice last night, before I saw the twig-man."

"My voice? Don't be silly."

Footsteps and voices in the rec hall alerted us to the approach of others.

She turned away, dismissive. "Forget I spoke."

For an instant I was lost in a frightened stupor. I wondered if I were going insane. I wondered if I'd imagined everything, including Vidar. Somehow my body kept functioning: my heart hadn't stopped, my head hadn't exploded, I was able to put bread in the toaster. Maryanne returned to the pantry and normality seemed to be reinstated for the moment.

"Victoria?"

I turned to see Magnus standing behind me.

"Good morning," I said, attempting to smile.

He didn't respond with one of his own. "Some new transpiration sensors arrived yesterday. I want to install them in the instrument field. It's your area of research, so if you'd like to help . . ."

"I'd love to." Work—that would sort me out. I could add up figures and make observations and draw conclusions and my head could be full of something other than impossible events.

"Vicky should probably have one more day in bed," Carsten said.

"I'm fine, really," I said. "I'm going crazy in my cabin."

"Carsten, give Victoria another physical this morning. Vicky, I'll be heading to the clearing around nine. I'll meet you out there." He strode off, still without smiling at me.

"I'll see you directly after breakfast," Carsten said.

It was only when Carsten and I were safely behind the door of the sick bay, and he was shining that little torch in my eyes again, that I worked up the courage to say, "Carsten, is it possible for somebody to go crazy within a couple of months of arriving on Othinsey?"

He laughed. "It usually happens much quicker than that."

"I'm serious. The isolation. Has it been known to cause psychological problems?"

"What kind?"

"Imagining things? Dreaming strange creatures? A feeling that everything you believed in is made of paper and pipe cleaners?"

Carsten sat back on the edge of his desk. "Are you asking for a medical opinion? Because I'm not a doctor, and I'm certainly not a psychiatrist."

I shook my head. "Just an opinion, then."

"A lot of different people have come to this island over the years. Some of them say it's haunted, some of them don't. Whether or not that's related to the isolation, I can't tell you. But you're certainly not the first person to worry about it." He gave me a reassuring smile. "You've had a shock too. You nearly drowned, you lost consciousness. I can tell Magnus that you need a few more days in bed if you like."

"No, I'd rather be busy." I ran a hand through my hair and sighed. "I'm a bit frightened."

"I'm sure everything will be fine. Perhaps you have been locked away in that cabin for too long." He gave me a fatherly pat on the shoulder. "A walk in the forest might be just what you need."

Just what I need.

I stood at the edge of the forest, knowing I had to go forward, but unable to take a step. I sensed something bad in there, something rotten and cold and primeval that I hadn't sensed before. It was as though last night, calling Skripi, had opened up a gate that had been bolted tight in my mind since I arrived on Othinsey. That forest was haunted. And while this was a notion I would have scoffed at in the past, I knew it to be true with a certainty as deep as the ancient tree roots.

But my boss was waiting, and he was already impatient with me. So I had to go in.

Deep breath.

One foot in front of the other, I counted my way into the trees, estimating distances between trees based on how many footsteps were needed from one to the next, converting the distances to metric, coming up with a mean, dividing it by my age, multiplying it by how many fingers Carsten had . . . And all the while, my breathing shortened, my heart hitched and sped, my shoulders pulled tighter and tighter.

Then Magnus's voice rang out from the clearing. "Victoria? Is that you?"

"Yes," I called, hurrying my footsteps. "I'm coming."

I arrived, flushed and breathlesss, a few moments later. As I crossed into the clearing, my anxiety wound tighter.

Magnus glanced up irritably. "You're late," he said.

"Sorry," I managed, forcing my voice into an even line. My hands felt damp, I wiped them on my jeans. "What can I do to help?"

"I want you to check the temperature and humidity in the moss at ground level," he said, pushing a box of equipment toward me with his toe. "I'm going to take foliage temps in the aspen understory."

All this translated to me crawling around in the dirt while he worked nobly among the trees. Fine. It gave me something to focus on, to drive out the needling anxiety.

I left Magnus sorting out his climbing ropes and harness. A morning breeze moved branches and leaves, the ocean roared in the distance. I breathed deeply, forcing my shoulders to loosen, concentrating on the moss. I moved along the forest floor on hands and knees, taking samples, strip-testing them and writing down the results. A warm sunbeam shot onto my shoulder. Long minutes passed. I looked up and realized that I had arrived at the foot of the anvil-shaped rock.

With sudden brightness, images and sounds and feelings overpowered my brain. For a moment, I wasn't Victoria Scott, I was somebody else. Panic had crushed my lungs, horror and despair squeezed through my veins. I had been running, but now I had fallen. I turned. Silhouetted against the sun was a massive figure, any detail stolen by the bright light behind him, an axe raised above his head. He was huge, male, smelled of sweat and blood and steel. He was bellowing at unbearable volume. In the distance, dogs barked madly.

I screamed, cowering under my arms.

Magnus was looking down at me. "Victoria. What's wrong?"

In an instant, everything returned to normal. There was no mad axe-wielding man, only neat slim Magnus wielding a digital thermometer and wearing a safety helmet.

"I thought I saw . . ." I couldn't finish the sentence. My heart was racing and my throat was dry.

Magnus drew down his eyebrows. "What's all this about, Victoria?" His voice was suspicious.

I could feel my lower lip tremble, but I was damned well not going to cry in front of Magnus again. "I'm sorry, Magnus," I gasped. "I thought . . ."

"Is this some kind of plot? Are you accusing me of something?"

I was genuinely bewildered. "Accusing you?"

"It would be your word against mine and I didn't touch you, and I have a number of people at the station who would attest that *you* have been pursuing *me*."

I sat back on the mossy ground, completely disoriented by the searing moment of terror. "What are you saying?" I spluttered.

"Girls like you don't get far," he said.

"Girls like me? I don't know what you're talking about."

"You think they heard you screaming back at the station? Is that it?"

"No, I screamed because I thought I saw—" A noise in the forest behind me made me whip my head around and shriek. A petrel took to the sky.

"Victoria?" Magnus said, his voice growing concerned. My terrified face finally broke through his self-justifying rhetoric. "Are you sick?" He reached out to touch my shoulder and I flinched away, scrambled back against the rock.

"I have to go back to the station," I gasped, hurrying to my feet. "I can't stay out here."

"Wait, wait," Magnus said, and this time he grabbed my arm firmly and held me still. "Is this the first time you've been out here since you fell in the lake?"

I nodded.

"I think you're having a panic attack, Victoria. I want you to breathe very deeply into your hands. Five times."

"I need to get—"

"Breathe!" he ordered. "Come on . . . one . . . two . . ."

I did as I was told. I focused on Magnus's eyes and breathed into my hands. The dizziness receded. Magnus was right—it was the first time I'd been out here since the incident. I'd been flat on my back in bed for a long time, too. Perhaps it was just a garden-variety panic attack.

"I had a hallucination," I said through my hands. "It terrified me."

"Hallucinations can sometimes happen if you're sleep-deprived. Have you been sleeping properly?"

"No, I haven't," I said.

"I think you'd better have the rest of the weekend off, start work again on Monday." He released me and I dropped my hands. "You shouldn't have come out if you weren't feeling right."

"I was feeling right. Until I came out."

"I want you to tell Carsten what happened, get him to check you over again." Then he added grudgingly, "We can always send you home if you think you need some time off."

That sounded like the best sense I had ever heard. Home. London. Mum. My own bed. No more twig-men and haunted forests.

"I'm sorry if I've upset your plans," I said.

He waved away my apology, and produced no apology of his own for accusing me of a false sexual harassment claim. "I'll walk you to the station. We can finish in here another time."

The thought of returning to the site filled me with horror, but I told myself to be calm and that things might be very different after the weekend.

I was right.

It rained all weekend and I stayed in my cabin. Gunnar brought me food and five-years-out-of-date trashy magazines from the rec hall and offered to keep me company. I told him I needed some time alone to think. I turned Magnus's idea of going home over and over in my mind until I became obsessive about it. This meant I slept incredibly poorly on Sunday night, waking and dozing, never sure where I was or what time it was, plagued by awful dreams about dogs pursuing me, about the forest reaching out to grasp me, about bright-hot blades and big hairy men. When I opened my eyes in the grey dawn, they felt gritty and sore.

I dressed and slipped outside to head to the galley for breakfast. Before I had placed even one foot on the cement slab, I saw it perched on my doorstep.

A wooden carving of a wolf.

And scratched into its jaw was his name. *Vidar.*

Twenty

I was heading for the trees, my dread of the forest suddenly vaporized, when Magnus rounded the corner and saw me.

"Victoria? You're well then?"

"I'm . . ." For a moment I was completely bewildered. I had come to associate Vidar with being alone on the island. Magnus's presence seemed like a mundane aberration; the moment in the cinema when somebody accidentally switches on the houselights. "I'm much better, thanks," I managed.

"Obviously. Off for a walk in the forest?"

"Um. No," I said. Then added, "I thought I saw a cat."

"I'm sure you didn't. There are no cats on Othinsey."

I laughed nervously, wondering how I was going to escape from Magnus to find Vidar. "Trick of the light," I said.

"Just as long as you don't have another hallucination like Thursday's," he said, without a trace of pity. "I'll walk you to the galley. I need to talk to you about today's tasks."

"Today?" I said, following him. How could it be possible that today I had to do anything other than look for Vidar?

"The boreal research unit at Oslo University have asked us for preliminary transpiration and flux figures from our instrument field. I thought you could do the calculations and submit them."

At another time, that task would have been a dream: all day tucked away in a quiet corner with tables and figures and formulae. Today, it seemed like a form of torture.

Magnus walked ahead of me. I lagged back, glanced longingly over my shoulder.

"Are you coming, Victoria?" he called.

"Yes, yes, coming," I said absently. I figured if I could rush through the job, Magnus might let me wander off at lunchtime.

My mind was everywhere but on the task. Magnus explained the process in excruciating detail, then left me alone for a few hours to do the sums and fill out the online forms. By lunchtime I still hadn't finished. Magnus brought a sandwich to my desk, looked over my shoulder at the form I was about to submit and shrieked in horror.

"What's wrong?" I said, nearly knocking the plate off the desk.

"What formula did you use for these?" he asked.

I showed him, he went pale. "Please tell me you haven't sent these."

"I've sent about three-quarters of them," I said.

"Victoria, it's the wrong formula. What were you thinking? That's not even the right table."

I looked at where he was indicating on my calculation sheet, and felt myself grow warm and squirmy with embarrassment. I had been so unfocused, I had made the kind of error a slow-witted undergraduate makes in a first-year exam. "Magnus, I'm so sorry. I mustn't have been concentrating."

"I'll phone them," he said, his voice brusque. "I'll tell them our *trainee* is having a few problems with her math today." He turned to pick up the phone. The conversation that ensued was in Norwegian, but I was in no doubt from the tone of his voice that I was being described in the toadiest of terms to a very eminent climatology professor. I started recalculating, wondering when I was going to be able to get away from all this petty rubbish and out into the forest to find Vidar.

Time crawled. The drizzly afternoon darkened. I fixed the calculations, found myself caught up with Carsten going down the stairs, was dragged to the rec hall by Gunnar for dinner, then finally . . . finally . . .

I got away.

I slipped into my cabin to tidy my hair, grabbed some blankets, then headed off quietly into the forest.

Smells enveloped me: pine needles, damp earth, sea salt, rotting foliage. I can't explain it, but the horror of the forest had dwindled to nothing, as though Vidar's presence neutralized all fear, all danger. I followed the path to his old campsite and was dismayed to find it empty.

I stopped, turned a full circle. Branches dripped, the drizzle intensified, emptiness tapped a finger on my heart.

Then I smelled smoke.

"Vidar?" I called, following the scent. "It's me, Victoria." I hurried through the trees, soon seeing the glow of a fire through shadowy branches.

Vidar was sitting on a log next to the fire, his head bent so that his long hair fell forward to hide his face. Two large animal skins had been strung above him to protect his camp from the rain. He looked up, pushing his hair behind his ear, and gave me a guarded smile. My heart filled with air. *I know him, I know him.* The feeling was so intense that it hurt me.

"Hello, Victoria."

"Hello, Vidar." I moved nearer. He was wearing the strange clothes again. "That's a weird outfit."

"Not where I come from."

I sat next to him, dropping the blankets at our feet. "Where *do* you come from?"

He lifted his eyebrows. "Asking questions already?"

A loud noise from the trees made me jump to my feet, my hand over my heart. "What's that?"

He took my wrist and pulled me gently to my seat. "Don't be afraid. It's only Arvak."

"Arvak?"

"My horse."

"You have a horse in here? How did you . . . ?"

He touched a gentle finger to my lips, then withdrew it reluctantly. "Once more, I can only say that I *will* explain everything to you, but not now."

A horse. Then it was obvious that he had never left, that he must have been on the island all along, living in the forest unnoticed. "When will you explain?" I asked.

He tilted his head as though considering. His black eyes gleamed in the firelight. "That depends on what happens next."

I laughed. "This is crazy. You say crazy things but I keep letting you get away with it. Why do I feel that way? Why do I feel like I know you?"

"You do know me. We met last month."

"No, no. Like I know you from *before*."

"How long before?" he asked, turning to the fire.

"Before . . . I don't know." I watched his profile. "Before everything," I whispered, feeling myself falling out of time again. It didn't matter that the bright lights and humming instruments of Kirkja Station were just twenty minutes away. With Vidar, I felt as though I were somewhere dark and silent and lush; in a place that had long been banished from the busy, chattering world. Anxieties and questions and calculations melted away, became profoundly insignificant.

He didn't answer. Instead, he knelt before the fire and added another log. I could see the muscles in his shoulders through the red-brown cloth of his tunic. Desire caught my breath on a hook, yanked it out of my lungs.

"Did you bring the blankets for me?" he asked, without facing me.

"Yes, I thought you might be cold. Or wet." I looked up at the roof of skins above us. "But I hadn't reckoned with your Boy Scout skills."

He gave me a bemused look. "What's Boy Scout?"

"I'm sorry, you speak such good English that I assume you know everything."

Vidar settled in front of the fire and pulled one of my blankets over his knees. "Will you stay for a while, Victoria?" he asked.

"Oh yes," I replied, and spread out the spare blanket next to him. I lay on my side and gazed at the fire. "But it's going to be a long evening if you don't tell me anything about yourself."

He nodded slowly. "I can tell you some things," he said. "But there are important things that I—"

"Can you tell me about where you live?" I asked. "When you're not here in the forest, that is."

"I live at a place called Gammaldal."

Finally, something to hang on to. Something to know him by. "Go on. What does it look like?"

He closed his eyes to conjure it in his imagination. "It's a tiny farm two miles from a calm bay. A colony of gulls lives amongst the rocky cliffs which lead to the headland. Some mornings it's very misty, as though the clouds have grown weary of staying in the sky and have descended to sleep on the land. My home is behind a deep slope. The grass is lush and green, and in the warmer months wildflowers spring up all over it. On summer days, the sun spends a long time on that slope, and the shadows of clouds race over it, and the birds come from inland, and bees hum and catch the light on their wings. Over the other side is a still fjord. Trees grow all around it, so it's often in shadows. There is a shallow shelf if you enter the water from the east, but it's deceptive. For when you step off the shelf the ground slopes away to a terrifying depth. The water is very dark, still but not serene. I sense there are things moving many fathoms below the surface. It's a mysterious place."

"And what kind of house do you live in?"

"It's just a small house, made of wood. I built it myself."

"You built your own house? Wow. I couldn't even knit myself a pullover."

"I like to be busy. I like to work with my hands and body. Otherwise, I think too much." He sighed. "My mind betrays me."

Moment by moment, he was becoming a person. As he opened up, I felt myself opening up to him. "What do you do all day?"

"There are many tasks to be seen to. Mending the fences, milking cows, sowing in spring and reaping in autumn, fishing and hunting."

"Do you live alone?"

"I have no neighbors for many miles. But I have a . . . friend living with me. Her name is Aud."

I held my breath. He had hesitated over the word "friend." Was she an ex-lover, an ex-wife? "Tell me about her," I said.

"Aud is very beautiful, and very accomplished, but she is very sad. She's a long way from her home and family, and she has come to rely on me very heavily. I think she has feelings for me that I can't return . . ." He leaned forward to poke the fire and I sensed that he was embarrassed. "I can't bear her sadness sometimes, and I try not to see it. Instead I try to be kind to her, but sometimes my kindness hurts her."

"Because she wants more?"

"I think that if she were back home with the people that she loves, she would soon forget about me. She's young."

"So why doesn't she just go home?"

Vidar shook his head and dusted his hands off. "It's too complicated to explain." He nodded toward me. "What about you? Where do you live when you're not on Othinsey?"

I talked a lot. Maybe I talked too much. I told him about the upstairs flat at Mrs. Armitage's, with its peeling floral wallpaper and noisy pipes; I told him about my best friend Samantha and about the mad holiday we'd taken once to Paris; I told him about my years of hard labor toadying to rude tourists at London Bridge Café. I even told him about Patrick and Adam and how I'd agreed to marry each of them simply because everyone around me expected it.

"But you didn't love either of them?" he asked.

We were on dangerous ground, and I chose my answer carefully. "Perhaps I did. But . . . not enough."

"How much is enough?" he asked, his dark eyes holding mine steadily. The rain intensified overhead, dripped mournfully off the sides of the skins.

"I never felt lifted out of my life with either of them," I said. "I never felt as though I were anything more than a collection of flesh and bones named Victoria, wandering about the planet like everyone else. It wasn't enough."

A long silence ensued. Vidar watched the fire, I watched Vidar.

Finally, he said, "Enough love touches your soul." He took a deep breath and his voice sounded sad. "It's older and brighter than the sun, and it's ancient and always new."

"Exactly," I said. Or at least I think I said it. An image laid itself over my vision; another hallucination, but this time it wasn't frightening at all. In it, Vidar and I stood at the edge of a stony beach, the sun setting on us, deep orange and dazzling. My hands were in his and I felt an intense and profound sense of connectedness: to Vidar, to myself, to the sun, to the earth, to time and the tides. Then the vision was gone and I was back in the drizzly forest. I pressed my fingers into my eyes.

"Victoria? Are you unwell?"

"Weird things have been happening to me ever since I arrived here," I said. "It usually frightens me but tonight I'm not frightened."

"Why not?" he asked, though I sensed he already knew what my answer would be.

I met his gaze. "Because you make me feel safe," I said.

His brows drew down and his eyes grew intense. "While

we sit here in the forest together, you are safe," he said. "But, Victoria, I can't protect you from everything."

A cold fear touched me on the toes. "What do you mean?"

There was a sudden thump and rustle which made me gasp and snap my head around. A chestnut stallion emerged from the trees. "Oh, God, he frightened me," I said.

"It's only Arvak," Vidar said, rising to go to the horse.

"I'm afraid of horses," I said.

"Why?" he said, stroking Arvak's nose.

"They're just so big and smelly."

Vidar gave me an amused smile. "Not so loud, Arvak's very sensitive." He beckoned to me with his free hand. "Come here. I'd like you to meet him."

I rose warily and made my way over to the edge of the cover. Arvak was wet and, I swear, giving Vidar a mournful look. I touched his nose tentatively. "He doesn't look happy."

"He's used to a warm, dry stable." Vidar rubbed the horse's ears. "Aren't you, old friend?"

"Have you had him a long time?"

"Since I was a boy."

I didn't know much about horses, but this didn't seem to add up. Arvak was not one of those saggy old horses with grey whiskers. "How old are you?" I asked.

"How old are you?"

"Twenty-seven."

"I'm a little older than that." He smiled, his eyes twinkled.

"You're being all mysterious again," I said. "What's your star sign?"

"I don't know."

"When's your birthday?"

"I don't remember." He patted Arvak on the neck and sent the horse back into the woods.

"What's your mother's name?"

"Her name is Gríd."

"What's your father's name?"

All smiles were withdrawn. "I cannot tell you."

I shrugged. "I can't tell you my father's name either. Mum's determined to keep it a secret, even though I keep trying to frighten her with the possibility of me accidentally marrying a relative one day." I sat back on the blanket. "I'm a Virgo, September 3, by the way. I don't believe for a second you don't remember your birthday."

"Where I come from, only children celebrate birthdays."

"What about Christmas?"

His face darkened. "Nobody celebrates Christmas." He sat on his log again and considered me in the firelight. "Nobody would dare to mention Christ."

The possibilities raced through my head. Religious cult? That would explain the clothes.

Vidar leaned forward and touched my knee lightly. "I can see you guessing, Victoria. And I can tell you for certain that whatever you're guessing is wrong."

I glanced at my watch. "I should go," I said reluctantly. "I'm working tomorrow, and I'm already in trouble with my boss."

"You'll get wet if you leave now," he said, as the rain intensified overhead. "Stay until the rain eases. If you need to sleep, you can curl up there by the fire."

I needed little persuasion. "If you don't mind me staying . . ."

His voice was very soft. "Victoria, I would have you by me all through the night."

A warm flame of longing ignited within me. I was gripped by a desire to go to him, press my mouth against his, slide my fingers under the rough cloth of his shirt to find the hot skin beneath. "I will stay," I said. "Right here. And sleep by the fire."

"Good."

But I didn't sleep, and neither did he. I talked, and he talked too, carefully but warmly. He told me stories from his childhood, stories about his mother, recited me some poetry in his own language, told me how much he despised his brothers, and explained how to build a house. I told him nearly everything that was important about me, and many things that were unimportant. We talked until our voices seemed to detach from our bodies and echo between the trees. We talked until my eyes were gritty and my head ached from tiredness. Strange feelings found paths through my body and mind, and I wondered, cautiously, if I were falling in love.

Pale light streaked the sky and I had to go.

"Tonight," I said. "I'll come back."

"I'll wait for you," he replied.

I reluctantly headed back to the station, hoping to catch a couple of hours' sleep before breakfast.

I slept for four hours; I was late for breakfast. Nobody was in the galley to mind, however, and I still had fifteen minutes before I was due to start my shift. I smeared my toast with marmalade and slurped my hot tea, reliving the night's sweet moments in my imagination.

"Vicky? You're up late."

I turned around to see Gunnar, with four empty coffee cups, making his way to the sink.

"Yeah," I said. "Couldn't sleep last night. I only dropped off around five." I indicated the cups. "Cleaning out your cabin again?"

"Yeah," he said, opening the dishwasher. "You missed all the excitement this morning."

"Excitement?"

"Maryanne's lost her mind," he said, without humor.

I smiled. "What are you talking about?"

"Now she sleeps in Magnus's cabin, she swears she hears noises in the forest all night. She says she's being haunted."

I thought about Vidar and Arvak out there. "Wouldn't it just be the wind making noises? Or animals?"

"I think she's become a little obsessive. She doesn't sleep, she sits up at the window, watching." He sat down at the kitchen table with me. "She told us this morning that she's seen monsters in the forest. She looked insane. Her hair was unbrushed and her eyes were . . ." He did an impersonation of Maryanne, paranoid glance darting all over the room. "She says that she's heading home next time the *Jonsok* comes. Magnus looked positively devastated."

"Do you think he loves her?"

"I think he loves shagging her."

"It's not quite the same thing." I checked my watch. "I have to get to work. I'm in hot water with Magnus." I took my plate and cup to the dishwasher and headed for the door.

"Vicky," he said.

I turned to him. "Yeah?"

"You look nice today."

"Thanks," I mumbled, and left as quickly as I could.

*   *   *

The rain poured down all morning but had lifted by the afternoon. One or two brave stars even managed to peek through after dinner. I made my excuses and went to my cabin, grabbed the extra blankets and sneaked off into the forest.

When I arrived, Vidar was saddling Arvak.

"Are you going somewhere?" I asked, dropping the blankets by the fire.

"We are," he said, adjusting the bridle and patting Arvak's flank. "I've decided to cure you of your fear of horses."

"I can't ride a horse."

"You don't have to ride him. All you have to do is hang on to me."

An ache moved up my ribs. "I can do that," I said.

He turned to me and smiled, put out his hand. "Come on."

The saddle seemed a long way up, but once I had my arms around Vidar's middle and my cheek pressed against his back, I decided the fear was worth it. Vidar pressed his hands against mine on his stomach.

"Hold on very tight," he said. "Don't let me go."

"I won't." *Ever.*

"Are you ready?"

"I am."

His hands withdrew, he picked up the reins and we moved. I held my breath.

"We'll leave the forest slowly," Vidar said. "We can pick up speed when we reach the beach."

Pick up speed? It already felt as though the world were moving past in a blur. I closed my eyes and tightened my hold on Vidar. A few minutes passed like that, then Vidar's hand patted my own again. I opened my eyes. We were emerging from the trees. The ocean was hammering the beach, a pale blue half-moon hung in the sky between silver-rimmed clouds.

Vidar leaned forward and said something to Arvak in his own language, and we took off.

I shrieked, but it was lost behind me. The wind roared in my ears, the tangy air froze on my lips and nose. The ground beneath us seemed to give way, then catch us again. Overwhelmed with sensation, I opened my mouth and laughter poured out of me. Vidar said something to me, but I didn't hear it. The motion and the cold and the sea were exhilarating. We sped through the night like souls escaping the gravity of living.

Finally, reluctantly, we slowed.

"We're about to run out of beach," Vidar said, indicating the rocks a quarter mile ahead of us. "Let's rest and make a fire."

I nodded, heedless of the knowledge that he couldn't see me nod. Arvak stopped and Vidar helped me down. He had brought kindling and firewood, and in a few short minutes had a fire going. Clouds had moved back over the sky and I watched them nervously. Rain would ruin everything.

"You look worried," Vidar said, settling on the sand next to me. Arvak wandered back toward the trees.

"It might rain," I said.

"It might not." He smiled at me, and I sensed that he was growing much more relaxed in my company. He stretched his arms above his head and heaved a sigh. "I love to ride. It fills me with wild feelings."

"Wild?"

"Wild and melancholy. Like happiness."

"You think happiness is wild and melancholy?" I asked.

"Don't you?"

I considered for a few moments. Then said, "I don't know. I'm not sure if I've ever been happy. I mean, it's more than just the absence of sadness, right?"

Vidar took my hand in his and turned it over, palm up. "Of course it is. It's wild. And it's melancholy." He traced a tiny circle on the inside of my wrist. "Your skin is so soft."

"Thank you," I said, but my voice seemed to come from a long way away. I wondered if he would kiss me. I was convinced that if he did, I would probably die.

He didn't kiss me. He dropped my hand gently and wrapped his arms around his knees, almost as though he regretted touching me in the first place.

"Why melancholy, though?" I asked.

"Because anything that causes deep joy casts the shadow of its possible loss." His gaze was far away to sea. I knew for certain one of those shadows preoccupied him at that moment.

I watched his face for a long time: his straight nose, his broad forehead, his serious eyebrows, and his soft dark eyes smudged with some weary anxiety he wouldn't disclose. I felt wild feelings, and melancholy ones too.

He turned, saw me watching him, and an expression crossed his face: intense, desperate, lonely. I was certain he was about to say something to me—something profound and familiar that might reveal a hidden truth about the universe—but he said nothing.

Instead, he said, "Tell me why you're so fascinated with the weather."

I found myself talking again, trying to cajole more details out of him with limited success. The rain set in around midnight, so we went back to his campsite and curled up among the blankets. We talked and we shared long silences, and he didn't touch me again, nor mention happiness. I spent the entire night in a state of heightened physical awareness, as though my body were preparing for any possibility: to run away, to make love, to die. Dawn threatened a grey glimmer through the drizzle and it was time for me to leave again.

Vidar stood when I did, and hovered uncertainly while I packed up the blankets.

"I'll be back again tonight," I said.

"Victoria, how do you feel about me?"

At first I thought I hadn't heard the question right.

I paused, a few silent moments. His face was soft in the firelight, shadows gathered around him.

"I shouldn't have asked," he said quickly.

"No, no," I said. "I'm glad you asked."

He took a step forward and picked up my left hand. He pressed it against his chest, his heart beat beneath my fingers. "Victoria," he said again. "How do you feel about me?"

I was overcome by conflicting thoughts and couldn't make a coherent answer. Part of me, the part that had two broken engagements behind her, warned me to be wary. "I don't know, Vidar. This whole thing is mad. I feel like I've known you forever and yet I know so little about you."

"I've told you many stories now," he protested, dropping my hand.

"But you've kept so much a secret," I said, feeling that this exchange was going very badly, that I'd ruined something beautiful and perfect.

He shrugged. "I understand. I will see you again this evening."

"Good night," I said softly.

"Good morning," he said, smiling ruefully.

I turned, I walked away, I took a deep breath. I felt wild and I felt melancholy.

It wasn't happiness; it was love.

I stopped, glanced over my shoulder. Vidar was tightening the knots on the animal-skin tarpaulin above him.

I wavered a moment.

Then walked back to him.

"Vidar?"

He saw me and dropped his arms. "Victoria?"

It seemed that even the dark forest held its breath.

"Vidar," I said, reaching for his fingers and for my courage. "Vidar, I love you."

With a sharp breath, almost as though I had wounded him, he seized me violently in his arms. I could hear his pulse thundering through his veins as he pressed me against his chest. Then he tipped my face upward and placed one hot, gentle kiss on my chin. I tried to return his kiss, but he pulled away sharply and touched a finger to my lips.

"No," he said, "not yet."

"Not yet?"

"Tonight," he said, his dark eyes glinting in the firelight. "Tonight I'll tell you everything."

Twenty-One

I walked, dazed, back to Kirkja, going over the possibilities in my mind. He was royalty, he was a fugitive from the law, he was escaping from a cult, he was a figment of my imagination. I wondered if my feelings for him would change once he had revealed his great secret. The old me, the love-shy London girl who had arrived at Othinsey a few short months ago, would have a cynical quip waiting on her lips for fools like me. *You don't even know him. He could be a murderer. You're thinking with the brain between your legs.*

She would be profoundly wrong. The love I felt was deeper than the Atlantic, and more powerful than its fiercest currents. The sight of the station up ahead between the trees confounded me for a moment. My mind had to force the connection between my night in the forest with Vidar and the daytime mundanity of my work. I shook my head to clear it, felt in my pocket for my key.

Just as I broke from the trees, Magnus stepped out of his cabin and spotted me.

"Victoria?"

"Good morning, Magnus," I said, and I know that I looked guilty. I know that my eyes didn't meet his, that I kept my head too low, that my voice gave away my desire to pass unnoticed. None of these things were lost on him.

"What are you doing in the forest this early?" he asked.

"I've been out for a walk."

"It's barely dawn."

"You're up," I said, as though that explained everything. If he was out of his cabin, then why shouldn't I be?

"I'm getting tea for Maryanne. She's had another terrible night." He nodded slowly. "And I'm starting to think I know what caused it."

If I'd slept at all, I might have retained enough wits to grasp what he was implying and neutralize his impression immediately, but I shook my head, and in a too-innocent tone said, "What do you mean?"

His eyes flared with suspicion. "In my office. Thirty minutes," he said, pointing an accusing finger at me.

"What?"

"You heard." He was stalking away from me in the grey half-light.

I watched him go, realized that he meant he had identified me as the nighttime menace about whom Maryanne had been complaining, and called out, "No, Magnus, it's not me." He didn't hear me. "Shit," I said, unlocking my cabin. I had really been hoping for a nap before work. I was absolutely knackered. I gazed at my bed longingly with my gritty eyes, as I changed and tried to tidy my hair. Sleep, sleep, I needed sleep. I needed Vidar. I needed to curl up in his arms in front of the warm fire. The last thing I wanted was a confrontation with Magnus.

I hurried over to the station. Magnus sat in his office chair, fingers steepled together like he was some international criminal mastermind in a James Bond movie. I don't know whether the pose was genuine or an affectation. I sat down, tense and cautious.

"I know it's early, but I thought I'd save you the embarrassment of seven other people witnessing this. And besides, you were already up."

"I was hoping to get some sleep before work," I said.

"So you were up all night?"

"You know that I sleep poorly. I went for a walk early. Magnus, I hope you're not implying that I'm deliberately trying to upset Maryanne because—"

"I'm not implying anything. I *know* what's going on. It's quite clear. You're trying to scare her with strange noises in the night. You know she's gullible."

I shook my head vigorously through this whole tirade. "No, no! Magnus, I swear to you, I've not done anything to Maryanne. I've not been making strange noises near your cabin, I've no reason to do anything like that."

"No? Not jealousy?"

I was stricken into complete silence for four heartbeats. "Jealousy?" I gasped at last. "Magnus, you're nearly twice my age."

This was entirely the wrong thing to say. His face flushed deep red.

"Victoria, the facts before me are these." He struck them off violently on his fingers. "Maryanne moved into my cabin; she started to hear frightening noises in the forest directly afterward; she mentioned having heard your voice once; I caught you this morning in the forest near my cabin before dawn. I may be an *old man*, but I am not a stupid one."

I was too tired to gather energy for a fight, even in the face of his infuriating allegations. I shook my head again. "No. Not me. I sometimes hear noises in the forest too. You're neither an old man nor a stupid one, Magnus. I don't mistake you for either. I'm tired. I just want to go to bed."

His lips twitched into a cruel smirk. "It's nearly time to start work."

"I've got four hours—"

"I'd like you at work at seven. I have a lot for you to do today. It's nearly six, so you'd better have some breakfast." He shot out of his chair. "I'll speak with Maryanne. I expect you to be here waiting on my return."

So he was going to make me do penance. I returned to my cabin for a quick shower and a cup of coffee to wake me up.

A helpful Gunnar brought me breakfast in the office before leaving me alone with snake-eyed Magnus. He was smart enough not to give me any tasks that involved complicated thought processes. Instead, I spent the day rewriting file labels in the storeroom, yawning until I longed for bed. The hours crawled, time lost its shape, and my head throbbed. By afternoon tea, I could see the prize: quitting time, bed for a few hours, then back to see Vidar.

But Magnus still had another surprise up his sleeve.

"Victoria," he called archly, as I was heading to the rec hall for more coffee.

"Magnus?" I replied, turning and forcing a civil expression.

"Gordon is ill," he said. "He was scheduled on the night shift."

My mind tried to grasp the personal ramifications. "And . . . ?"

"I'd like you to do it instead."

"But I've just worked all day."

"Go to your cabin now, have a few hours of sleep," he said. "I just want to make sure that you're not free to go wandering in the forest tonight."

"I keep telling you, Magnus—"

"If you're so adamant it's not you making the noises, then you should be happy for a chance to clear your name."

I fought to comprehend. No sleep. Work all day. And now the night shift? What about Vidar? What about his secret? What about the hot kisses he promised me?

"Victoria?"

"I simply can't, I—"

"Refusing isn't an option," he said, leaning close and dropping his voice to a harsh whisper.

"But Carsten always schedules at least—"

"Carsten is not the station commander. You are not the station commander. I am."

I held up my hands and took a step back. "Fine. Send Gunnar over to wake me at seven."

A combination of caffeine and frustration made sleeping difficult, and I only managed half an hour before my wake-up call.

This meant that as I sat down at the desk in the control room and logged on for my evening shift, I had slept only five hours in the last forty-eight.

I heard footsteps on the stairs and braced myself for another appearance by Magnus. It was Gunnar.

"I brought you some dinner," he said.

"Is it dinnertime? I've lost track."

He put a bowl of undercooked ravioli in front of me. "This is illegal, you know. He can't make you work this many hours in a row."

I waved his comment away. "It's probably a good thing. At least he'll know that it's not me frightening Maryanne."

"He's an idiot," Gunnar said, settling on the couch. "Maryanne's obsessed with a stick-man she says she's seen. That's obviously not you." His eyes twinkled. "Or is it? Should I be checking your cabin for a costume?"

"I've dreamed about the stick-man too," I said. "Remember?"

"Have you told Maryanne that? You're both from England, so maybe it was something you saw on TV as kids."

"I can't talk to Maryanne," I replied. "This ravioli tastes like cardboard."

"Mmm, cardboard," he said, rubbing his stomach.

"I hadn't thought of that, by the way. That it was something we both saw as kids. Though Maryanne's older than I." A flutter of relief, a flutter of disappointment; too tired to process it.

He shrugged. "Reruns. Can't escape them."

"So, why are you here?"·

"To bring you your dinner. And I thought I'd stay a while. Keep you company."

"That's very sweet," I said. But he wasn't Vidar, and I glanced out the big glass windows at the forest below. Was he waiting for me? Did he think I'd changed my mind?

Gunnar chatted to me while I worked, made me coffee, entered some data for me. I was finding it increasingly hard to concentrate so, around 1:00 A.M., I sent him off to bed. He left, I sensed, reluctantly. I dimmed the lights and stepped outside onto the observation deck. Visibility good, light drizzle, wind from the northwest, heart sick with longing. It was cold, like summer had changed its mind about coming. I shivered and backed into the heated control room, sliding the door shut. I had half an hour before my next entry was due, and Magnus had left more files and blank labels for me. I turned up the lights and sat on the sofa to start work.

My head was heavy. I rested it just for a moment on the back of the sofa.

Sleep rushed upon me, and I startled back toward wakefulness.

But I couldn't wake up and I couldn't move. My body was unconscious around my panicked brain. I tried to sit up, but my limbs were encased in concrete.

Not this again. I remembered taking the ward off that morning to shower, but being so tired I forgot to put it back on. I forced my eyes, but the lids wouldn't budge. And yet, with a peculiar tickling sensation on my forehead, I could perceive the control room, albeit in nightmarish colors and shadows: blues and purples and greys. And a strange emptiness lay over it all, as though nobody had set foot there for centuries. It was at once familiar and unfamiliar, and it unsettled me. I wanted to shake off this sleep paralysis and see everything as it really was: bright lights and coffee cup rings and other mundane things. I wondered whether every ordinary setting had an empty, surreal form within it, ready to reveal itself in nightmares.

I struggled against the inertia to no avail. My best hope was that the thirty-minute timer would go off before the hag came.

Then I heard the door slide open.

"Wake up, wake up, wake up!" I shouted in my head. My

new sight ranged out and found her, sidling toward me, her hands folded behind her back like a schoolgirl hiding something. "Wake up, wake up."

"You must stay away from him!" she hissed, dropping to all fours and crawling the remaining distance to the sofa. Her lips didn't move when she spoke, the words appeared in my head like dull echoes.

In my mind's eye I could see the ward on the bathroom sink. I longed for it. "I don't know what you mean."

She pulled herself up, using my knees, and leaned forward. Her breath was rancid, her eyes were black and her fingers dug into my flesh. "He is the son of a mighty man. A wise man." She averted her eyes, and her face took on a sad expression. "A man surely wise enough to call me home one day."

"Get off me! Wake up, Vicky, for God's sake, wake up!"

The hag's face swooped up to mine, all bruised colors and purple shadows. "Stay away from him," she repeated. Then her crooked hands grabbed my hair and yanked my head forward so that my mouth was pressed against hers. I tried to breathe, but she was sucking the air out of my lungs. My chest ached, and I was momentarily convinced that this was real, that my poor limp body would be found here in the control room in the morning and nobody would know what had happened.

Beep, beep, beep, beep.

I sat up and gasped. The control room, the bright messy version, was back. I could move and nobody was there but me.

"Thank you, Josef," I said, head in hands, leaning on my knees. It took me a full minute before I realized my skin hurt where the hag had clawed me. I stared down at my jeans, wondering if I'd find two bruises beneath the denim. I decided not to look. Until Vidar had spoken, everything was on hold.

I guess I already knew the mysteries would all link together, somehow.

I managed to stay awake until four. I changed shift with Alex and headed outside. It was raining, I had my head down, and ran straight into Gunnar.

"You're up early," I said.

"I came to find you. I need to talk to you about something."

I glanced over my shoulder at the growing light in the east. Was Vidar waiting for me? Perhaps, if I wandered into the forest, I would find him, curled up asleep under the animal-skin tent. Perhaps I could curl up next to him, feel his warm, strong arms around me . . .

"Vicky?"

"Can it wait, Gunnar?" I asked, trying to sound patient and warm. And failing.

"I know you're tired," he said, "but I only need five minutes."

I simply couldn't respond. So many things were prioritized above Gunnar—Vidar, food, sleep—but he was always so good with me, so kind and thoughtful.

"Vicky? We're getting wet."

"Of course," I said.

"Come back to my cabin," he said, smiling his relief.

We hurried inside. Gunnar indicated I should sit on the sofa while he made me a hot cup of tea.

"Magnus shouldn't be allowed to get away with scheduling you day–night," he called from the kitchen.

"I'll get over it."

"Will you? He's got you scheduled on again tonight."

"Again?" I nearly jumped out of the sofa. If I was supposed to be working again tonight, then I had to see Vidar immediately. I told myself to sit still and be patient with Gunnar. Vidar would still be there in an hour. There was no rule about me only meeting him in the dark.

"I think so. You'd better check." He put a steaming mug in front of me and sat opposite.

"So what do you need to talk to me about?"

"I got an e-mail this morning from the New Zealand Meteorological Service."

"New Zealand?"

"I applied for a job there. Vicky, I've only got a month left on Kirkja."

I was bewildered. Gunnar was leaving? "Have you? Why didn't you tell me before now?"

He shrugged. "It seemed a long time off when you first arrived, and since we've become closer I didn't want to mention it in case you thought . . ." He trailed off, but I filled in the blanks. Gunnar didn't want me to think he was using his imminent departure as a way of pressuring me into romance. "You know I like you, Vicky. We make jokes about it, but you're more than just my mate."

"I'm sorry, Gunnar." Gunnar was one of the nicest people I'd ever met: genuine and smart and funny and warm.

"I know you said when you first arrived that you were still hurting from the others. It's been a few months now . . . that hasn't changed?"

"Gunnar, it's not even that. It's just . . . I don't feel that way about you. I don't know why." I thought about Vidar, and felt the pull of the moon on the tide. I had never experienced attraction like that before, and certainly not with Gunnar.

He smiled and propped his feet on the coffee table. "So I may as well head off to New Zealand?"

"I'll miss you. Really, I will."

"You can come and visit. It's very pretty." He shot out of his chair. "Do you want to see some pictures?"

"Um . . . sure."

He paused. "Look at you. You're so tired and here I am being an idiot."

"You're not being an idiot. I'd love to see pictures of New Zealand."

"Lie down. I printed them off the Internet and they're under a pile of work orders. Take me just a moment to find them."

I lay down and pulled a cushion under my head. "Take your time. I've got all day."

That was the last thing I remembered until I woke up nine hours later.

Gunnar had left me a note, telling me how peaceful I'd looked and he hadn't wanted to wake me. I screwed it up with one hand and lobbed it across the room. Damn it! I had woken in time for the staff meeting, then, if Gunnar was right, my night shift. And I still hadn't seen Vidar.

I raced over to the station to check the schedule, praying, crossing every finger, saying *please, please, please* in my head that Gunnar was wrong. But he was right. Magnus had crossed out Gordon's name and put mine in. It was all too much for me to bear. I burst into tears.

"Victoria?"

I spun round, sniffing back my tears and forcing a smile at Carsten. "Hello."

"What's wrong?"

"Nothing, nothing."

He peered over my shoulder at the roster. "Is that right? Did Magnus make you work day–night yesterday?"

"We had a disagreement," I said, hearing my voice tremble. "He wants me on night shifts for a while."

He shook his head. "No, no, that's not right," Carsten said. "I won't allow it."

"He's the station commander."

"I'm the medical officer. It's an occupational safety risk. You go back to your own cabin. Go to bed and have a long rest. Let me take care of Magnus."

I could have kissed him. "Really?"

"Really. Go on."

"But the staff meeting?"

"Forget the staff meeting. You need to rest."

I raced off to change and moved into the woods.

"Victoria. I thought I'd scared you away."

"I had problems with my boss," I said, standing uncertainly before him.

Afternoon sun revealed to me a warmth in the color of his eyes and tawny highlights in his dark hair I hadn't seen before. I realized that the sunlight might be less kind to me with my pale coloring. My hands went self-consciously to my hair, pulling it over my cheeks.

"You are beautiful," he said, as though reading my thoughts. He pushed my hands away and swept back my hair. "I could look at you forever."

I fell into his arms and it felt like the safest haven I would ever know. Silence settled on us. I wished I would never have to speak or think again. This moment in his arms, just breathing, was too precious to ruin with anything so coarse as language and logic. He started pulling away and a sense of dread descended, as though I knew that what he said next would change everything.

"We cannot proceed another step until I've told you my tale," he said, touching his lips to my hair.

My heart rose in my chest. It was ridicuous; why was I frightened? "Go on, then."

"Let us sit down. Victoria, I will tell you things that might seem impossible at first, but if you listen and don't push my story away, eventually you'll start to believe."

I lowered myself to the fur he had spread next to the fire. I felt like a small child, afraid of stories and words. "What do you mean?"

"Some of these memories are yours, but some belong only to me," he said. "You need to hear them all."

"Memories?" The familiarity of the forest deepened to such an intensity that my senses flared into hyperdrive. Everything grew brighter and louder.

"What's happening to me?" I asked, and my own voice frightened me.

"Memories of us," he said, grasping my fingers. "You know, don't you?"

I tried to take comfort in his warm, firm hands. I wasn't sure what he meant. "I don't know anything."

"Then listen," he said. "Don't say a word, just listen. And remember."

Twenty-Two

[1004 Anno Domini]

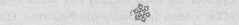

I have done many things of which I am ashamed. I have waded deep in cruelty and pain, without an eye blink of thought for consequences. I have tasted much blood and breathed much battle dust. I don't tell you this to frighten you, or to make you feel awe. I tell you this because it is true and I want to tell you only the truth.

My family are the Aesir. You may not have heard much of them in this life, but you knew them once. My father, Odin, believes himself a god. My brothers, uncles, sisters and aunts believe it too. I once believed it of myself, for we age slowly and only die if careless, but I no longer believe we're gods. I know now that we are just a race of people; petty, brutal, stupid people. Centuries ago my family had many men to worship us. They built temples in our name, sacrificed their livestock, fought wars and had children for our honor. Every man in this part of Midgard had a story on his lips of us. Then, spreading from the warm parts of the world and moving up slowly through the rain and snow, came word of the man we called Hvítakristr: the White Christ. It wàs a tide that we couldn't hold back.

Odin hated this new way of thinking. A god who rewarded meekness, gentleness, turning away from confrontation! He watched events on Midgard with horror. The king of Norway, Olaf Tryggvason, declared his kingdom part of the Christian kingdom, but many ordinary folk kept up the old faith. With Olaf's death the country slid backward. The missionaries redoubled their efforts, taking the Christian faith to the new settlements. One of these missionaries was named Isleif Grímsson. I see a flicker around your eyebrows, Victoria, you recognize this name. This was your mother's brother, and it was with him that you first came to Odin's Island.

This island does not belong to Midgard, nor does it belong to Asgard. It lies between the two worlds, much as a stepping-stone lies between two banks of a stream. Odin had long used it as a place to exile the smaller creatures of Asgard who angered him, like your friend Skripi. By leaving them here, he hoped also to discourage settlements of mortals, and that has mostly worked for the last two thousand years.

Isleif Grímsson was young, energetic and extremely charming. He had brought Christ to many settlements in Iceland and the Faroe Islands, but he was very ill. A cancer grew inside him and he knew that it would kill him within a few short years. The turn away from Christ in Norway dismayed him and he wanted to finish his days in a Christian place, surrounded by Christian people. Odin's Island already had a reputation among the folk of Norway as a place where any new settlers would be punished severely if they dared to make it a home. Isleif, I presume, did not believe in these

folktales. He brought seventeen members of his family here,
he built a church and he renamed the island Church Island.

Odin was at first unconcerned. He had creatures on the island to frighten the new mortals, he had a groundswell of renewed love for him in Norway. He thought the Christians
would leave. Even after the church was built, and the three
little wooden houses sprouted by the side of the fjord, he
thought they would leave. The months went by and they did
not leave. The wood wights frightened them, certainly, but
rather than run away, the Christians began to ring their bells,
morning and night, in the forest, over the water, so loudly
and vigorously that we could sometimes hear it in Asgard,
echoing over Bifrost on random updrafts.

At the time I lived in my father's home at Valaskjálf. I
had just returned from a battle on the borders of Vanaheim
and barely had time to wash the blood from my hair before
I received my orders from Odin.

Go to Odin's Island, and put all mortals there to the
sword.

I was once my father's favorite son. I know this because he
told me and everybody else, including his other sons. But
don't imagine some fond scene where he dandled me upon
his knee and sang me nursery rhymes because of a special
connection he felt with me. No, I was his favorite because I
was marked out by fate. My destiny is one day to save his
life at Ragnarok, the prophesied end of our world. So he
took particular care in my education, taught me swordsmanship himself, kept me close by him. As I grew into a man, I
could see how my brothers despised me for this, but Odin
would not let them lay a hand upon me. I was too important.

For a long time, I was completely unaware that his affection

relied on necessity. I gloried in his favoritism, I rose to his
faith in me time after time. I killed for him, over and over.
And this went on for many years and I never questioned it,
just as I never questioned breathing.

At around the time when Christ's name was first mentioned in our home, the questions began to bother me. If
Odin was all-powerful, why was he so anxious? Some nights
he would worry until he had to bend his head to the fire and
vomit. If Odin was all-wise, why couldn't he explain what
would happen to us if Christ's word did take hold in the
northern lands? Instead, he would grind his teeth at the question and promise to hack the head off the next person who
asked it. And if Odin was all-knowing, why didn't he know
that I had begun to doubt him and the life he had laid out for
me? In my desire to please my father, I had turned my heart
into a stone. And yet, somehow, it had begun to beat. In my
last campaign, I had offered mercy to some of my enemies
if they were old or frail. I had started to think about my
mother and wondered about her life in exile. I was waking
out of a long, dark dream.

Still, the idea of butchering mortals caused me only the
faintest disquiet. It would be unpleasant, but I would do it
quickly and keep the peace at Valaskjálf. When I arrived on
Odin's Island I was not the man I should have been; my resolve was vulnerable, and I had not reckoned with meeting
you.

These are your memories too, Victoria. I've held them for a
thousand years. As they unfold back to you, you may feel
strange or even frightened. It is all past, now. The threads
have been unraveled and cast back into the dark. There will
be time for fear, but later. Not now, not here with me. Close

your eyes if you wish and see yourself as I saw you that first morning in autumn.

I had arrived the previous night and camped. When morning came I set out toward the settlement with my sword in my hand. You must imagine it, a gleaming immortal sword with a broad flat blade, perilously sharp and battle-hardened, forged by fire giants and called Hjarta-bítr, the heart-biter. Mortal flesh would be butter beneath it.

As I approached the lake, a flash of dazzling white caught my eye and I paused among the trees. The dappled light illuminated you there, kneeling by the lake. You had been drawing water, but had stopped to watch your own reflection. At first, it was only curiosity that made me wait and gaze at you. Your hair and skin were so fair and the effect of the sunlight on you was to make you look like a carving. You wore a dress the color of the leaves fallen around you. You were stiller than the surface of the water, but then a breeze picked up your hair, trailing a strand across your face, and you brushed it away with your fingers and sat back, looking up toward the branches moving above you.

I could see your pulse beating in your throat and the faint blue lines of your veins. And a sudden understanding was upon me. *Mortal.* You were so vulnerable, only a soft blink away from death at any time. All I had to do was spill the blood in those veins, still the pulse in that throat, and your light would be extinguished. An unfamiliar ache swelled inside my chest and I dropped my sword.

"Is someone there?" you called as the weapon landed in the undergrowth.

I stepped out from my cover. A sunbeam flared in my eyes and you were swallowed by light. I shielded my vision with my left hand and saw that you were smiling at me.

"Who are you?" you asked. "Have you just arrived on the island?"

"Yes," I said. "My name is Vidar."

You rose and brushed a fallen leaf from your skirt. "I'm Halldisa Ketil's-daughter. Everyone calls me Halla."

I see the twitch of recognition on your brow again, Victoria. You recognize the name by which you were once known. By now, I hope, this story has begun to seem real to you and not the mad ramblings of a desperate man. Though I am desperate, make no mistake.

Still, you were smiling at me, and I wondered at how trusting you were.

"What are you doing here on Church Island, Vidar?" you asked. "Have you come to join my uncle's mission?"

I recoiled involuntarily and you laughed, freely and beautifully, as though we had known each other for years. "So, Vidar," you said, "you must learn to hide your reluctance to be part of Isleif's good Christian kingdom. All my brothers and I have. You must simply make a very somber face and talk endlessly about damnation. That keeps him quiet."

"I do not know Isleif," I said. "I am a stranger here."

You tilted your head. "We are all strangers here, Vidar." You sighed. "I yearn every day for my home and my friends, but that life exists many miles over the sea. It goes on without me."

I was fascinated by you. I had never talked to a mortal before and the idea that you yearned for something touched me unexpectedly. "What does it feel like when you yearn?" I asked, moving closer and putting the sun at my back.

"That's an odd question," you said.

"Can you answer it?"

You closed your eyes and drew down your brows. "It

feels like my heart is being pulled from somewhere far away." Then you opened your eyes and laughed again. "That sounds like nonsense."

"No, not at all," I said. "That's how I feel when I yearn."

You sat on the ground among the fallen leaves. "What do you yearn for, Vidar? Sit down and tell me."

I shook myself. A few minutes ago I had been prepared to murder you, but now I was being invited to sit by you and tell you what I yearned for. Confusion held my tongue.

You scooped up a handful of leaves and threw them at me. "Come on, we'll be here until Michaelmas."

"My family doesn't celebrate Michaelmas," I said.

You shrugged. "I don't care what your family does. I asked you a question."

I was overwhelmed with strange feelings. All I knew to do in such a situation was kill something or retreat. I turned and, without a backward glance, walked away.

"Vidar, where are you going?" you called.

I scooped up my sword and disappeared into the forest. You didn't follow, and for that I was glad.

I spent the day pacing the beach, trailing my sword in the wet sand. I felt the keen discomfort that only a man who brings shame upon his family can know. My brothers would laugh at me, my father would bellow until the hall shook. I could not kill you. I recalled the light in your eyes when you laughed, and knew it was too precious a thing to extinguish. Confusion drove me up and down the water's edge. My father's hall and all the brutal laws that filled it had seemed as fixed as ancient stone, and yet the sand was moving underneath them, just as it slid and skidded under my feet. Why kill the mortals? Why spend my days winning battle glory against the Vanir? Why snarl and set my eye only on the honor of my family, when my family had so little to honor—their petty quarrels, their trivial desires, their cruel humor?

I began to shed my family that day, adding up their wrongs, finding the sum too great to measure. The tide crept in. I thrust my sword up to its hilt in the sand and sat back on the beach to watch as the sea swallowed it. The afternoon grew pink and mauve, the wind was cold, the sun disappeared.

Odin would know, of course, that I had not killed you or your family. I believed I would have to convince Isleif to leave the island and take his followers with him. The next morning, I dressed for battle and rode Arvak down the edge of the fjord toward the church. Three little girls played in the grass, an elderly woman hung wet blankets over a tree's branches, and Isleif Grímsson stood at the entrance to his home—one of three unfinished ash cabins—at the side of the water.

"Ho, stranger," he called. "Have you come to find God?"

I did not reply. I rode up to him, and I could see unusual strength in his face. He must have been frightened of me: I was a stranger, I wore a bloodstained coat of mail and a scarred iron helm. Isleif betrayed no fear. Rather, he emanated an odd serenity, a bemused acceptance of whatever it was that I was bringing to his family.

"You must leave this island," I said as I drew even with him.

The elderly woman had paused to watch from a distance. One of the little girls ran toward us and the woman tried to stop her.

"All is well, Gudrid," Isleif said to her. "Let the child come. This man means no harm."

The little girl snuggled under Isleif's elbow. "Who are you?" she said to me.

"My name is Vidar," I said, without dropping Isleif's gaze. "I bring you a grim warning. You must leave this island. This island belongs to Odin."

"Odin isn't real," the little girl said confidently.

"I assure you he is," I said.

Isleif patted the child's head. "Odin only exists because God permits it," he said. "I am not afraid of him or of his family."

"You must be," I said, "for you have angered us greatly by building your church here. You and your settlers are all in danger." I looked around, and noticed that one of the cabin doors had opened and two young men peered out. You were with them and you were still smiling.

"God will see to it that no harm comes to us," Isleif said. "Would you like to give yourself to God, Vidar?"

Anger tightened my guts. I spat on the ground. "No, I would not," I said, "for among my family, God's name is abhorred."

"If you change your mind, I'll still be here," Isleif said, and turned his back on me, still with the little girl under his wing. I had never seen anyone turn his back on me before, leaving himself so vulnerable to the point of a sword. I had little time to wonder if Isleif were brave or foolish, because the two other little girls had run toward me and were asking me if I'd let them ride my horse. Arvak whickered anxiously— he was used to armed warriors, but little girls' probing fingers were new to him—so I turned him sharply and rode out of the mission, into the trees.

I paused when I was out of sight and rested my face on Arvak's mane. What had just happened? I had ridden in like

Death himself and none of them had flinched. How was I to convince these people that they must leave?

I heard a voice then, from the edge of the forest.

"Vidar?" It was you, following me into the trees.

I dismounted and pulled off my helm, waiting for you among the shadows. "What do you want?" I asked as you drew closer.

"I'm not afraid of you," you said.

"You should be."

"I believe in the old gods," you said. "I believe in them more than I believe in Isleif's God, because he's mysterious and nobody has ever seen him, but my brother, Hakon, once saw Thor on the battlefield at Gokstad."

"Then why aren't you afraid?"

"I said I'm not afraid of *you*," you said. "There are many things I'm afraid of, but as for Odin or Thor or God"—you lifted your shoulders—"who knows what they want from us?"

I took a step forward. I wanted to seize your shoulder, but I was afraid to touch you, to feel the warmth radiating from your skin. "I know that Odin wants you to leave. You must convince Isleif."

You smiled mischievously. "You seem very sure, Vidar."

"This is not a joke," I said.

"I'll tell him," you said. "Will I see you again?"

"You must leave," I said. "You must never see this place or me ever again." As I said it, an unexpected melancholy descended and I had to turn my back on you. "Go, Halla. Tell Isleif to leave this very night or tomorrow. I can't guarantee your safety any longer than that."

"Vidar, don't go," you said.

But I jumped on Arvak's back and urged him away at speed.

My plan had been to wait until nightfall to return to Asgard. Now a seed of some new dissatisfaction had been sown within me and I found it impossible to imagine myself leaving just yet. I felt impatient, and vulnerable, alternately filled with energy or gripped by torpor. I wanted to range the forest all night, then I wanted to lie down on a bed of skins and think about the soft curve of your throat. Sleep was unthinkable. Returning to the mission was out of the question. I settled for a compromise. When evening descended, I sat at the outer edge of the fjord and watched the church and the three little houses, knowing that you were inside one. Perhaps you sat by the fire spinning, or perhaps you were eating, or sleeping. I sat for many hours in the cold and the dark, while the black water rippled silent and deep at my feet. A snatch of an old tune stuck in my head, a love song that one of my father's servants always sang. The night soaked me up, its gloom suffused me. I pulled my cloak tight around myself and wondered what was happening to me.

Then I saw a figure approaching. Your fair hair caught the starlight and at first you didn't see me, and then I must have moved just enough to draw your eye. You revealed no surprise, but you were more cautious than you had been in the daylight.

"I thought about you and you appeared," you said.

"Good night, Halldisa Ketil's-daughter."

You approached and sat next to me. "Good night, Vidar Odin's-son. For I know for certain that is who you are."

"It's true. There's no point in denying it. I was sent from Asgard to persuade your family to leave."

"What does it feel like to be a god?" you asked.

"I don't know if I am a god. I know what it feels like to be Aesir. It feels like shame."

"You feel shame that you come from a great and powerful family?"

I turned to you, impatient. "What are you doing here?"

"I have thought about you all day."

"Because I am Aesir?"

"Because you are Vidar. Because you have hard hands and soft eyes. I could fall in love with a man with such hard hands and such soft eyes," you said. Then you burst into laughter and I found myself laughing too.

"You speak very plainly," I said.

"I see no use in doing otherwise. Tell me, if Odin has only one eye, is he always bumping into things?"

I laughed so hard I couldn't answer.

"And Thor? He must smell like a goat."

"He does. And has the manners of one." Nobody had ever made jokes about my family before.

"Heimdall's beard, from the stories, must be long enough to trip over."

"Not yet," I said, "but it prevents any of the ladies of Valaskjálf from finding his face beautiful, and so he is forced to observe them from afar."

"Your smile suggests the ladies do not know he watches them." You leaned down and picked up a stone, which you skimmed across the water.

"He keeps his hands occupied," I said, and felt a wave of fear and guilt. I banished it. Nobody in Asgard could hear me now.

You laughed and pushed your hair off your face. "It sounds just as petty and boring as families in Midgard."

"I would rather hear of your family," I said. The chill air and the distant stars were already weaving magic between us. "I grow tired of thinking of my own."

"Mine are worse," you said. "Isleif dragged us all here to be good Christians, but half of us still worship the old gods or nobody at all. He'd be appalled at some of the things I've done." You raised your eyebrows knowingly. "Would you like to hear?"

"Of course."

You reached inside your dress and pulled out a moonstone set in silver on a fine chain. "Thou shalt not steal," you said. "I stole this back in Egersund, before we came on this hellish trip. It's to remind me of everything I had to leave behind."

"Stealing is forbidden by your God?" I asked.

"He's not *my* God," you replied. "He's Isleif's." You held up a pale finger. "Thou shalt honor thy mother and father. I call my mother a fool and a coward, and if she had any mettle we'd be back home with all my friends, but Isleif is her brother and she quakes when he speaks. As for my father, well, he's been dead six years, but he was a liar anyway."

I smiled at you. Your irreverence was gentle, not savage. Your voice was infused with warmth, even as you told your tales of mischief. "Any more?" I asked.

You lowered your voice, pretended to look around for listeners. "Well . . . I don't know if I should tell you . . ."

"Go on."

"Thou shalt not commit adultery," you said, "but I once lay with my cousin Asbjorn, on my sixteenth birthday."

New desire stirred within me. "You did?"

"Just to see what it was like," you replied lightly. "Asbjorn has since taken a wife. The three little girls you saw today are his. But he hasn't forgotten." You bit your lip to still a laugh. "I'm too wicked, aren't I?"

"You are far from wicked," I said, thinking about my sins and what they amounted to.

"Asbjorn is one of the most pious of Isleif's followers," you said. "No doubt his feelings about me are what leads him to press so hard that I marry Ulf."

"Who is Ulf?" I said, ready to tear out his heart.

"One of the others. He's too old and too pious for my liking, and Isleif would never force me." You grew serious. "What of you, Vidar? Does your family try to marry you off?"

"I have lived the life of a warrior," I said carefully. "Marriage and children have not been spoken of."

"Though you must have loved?"

I thought of all the women I had desired, how easily those desires had been satisfied, and how quickly the women were discarded. "No," I said, almost surprised to hear myself say it. "I have never loved."

"Nor have I," you said softly, "though I can imagine it well enough." You leaned toward me and turned up your face. "If you kissed me . . ."

I placed a hand on your hair, trailed the silky strands through my fingers. "You are so mortal, Halla," I said. "I don't understand you."

You smiled. "I didn't ask you to understand me. I asked you to kiss me."

Savage desire gripped me and I kissed you. You wound your arms around my neck and I pressed your body to mine, and it felt as vulnerable as a bird's with its speeding heart and its fine bones. I was intoxicated and I felt myself letting go of my family, my past, my blood. I was free, after a life-time trapped by the Aesir name.

You pulled back and murmured against my cheek, "I think I am in love with you, though I only met you yesterday."

I thought about our first meeting, with Hjarta-bítr in my fist and Odin's orders in my heart, and fear chilled me. "Halla, you must convince Isleif to go. I cannot safeguard you from my father, and he wants you all gone."

"I'll see what I can do," you said.

"And I'll see what deal I can make with Odin," I said. "Will you meet me again, here, tomorrow?"

"I would meet you whenever and wherever you asked, Vidar." You kissed me again, then climbed to your feet and, with a wave over your shoulder, headed home.

I returned to Valaskjálf, but my father was too drunk to speak to me. I left word with one of his servants that most of the settlers were his worshippers, so I had not wanted to kill them and had chosen to warn them instead.

"They will be gone before winter," I called over my shoulder, eager to be back in Midgard with you. "Tell him he can trust me, tell him it's all at an end."

But it was actually only the beginning.

Twenty-Three

I felt hope and I felt at liberty as I returned to Midgard the next evening. You had until winter to convince Isleif and his followers to go. And then? When you went with them? These feelings were still too new to me to understand, so I ignored the questions they provoked. Winter was many weeks away, the answer would come. I had time to spend with you, to test if my wild emotions would lose their brightness.

I waited for you that night by the fjord, but you didn't arrive. My disappointment overwhelmed me. I was angry and confused. The long night grew cold and still you didn't come. When the first glimmer of dawn touched the sky, I cursed you as a harlot and pulled myself to my feet. Only moments remained for me to cross Bifrost, and I was heading into the trees, whistling for Arvak, when you came running up the bank of the fjord.

"Vidar, wait!" you called. Your cheeks were flushed and your eyes watered from the cold morning air.

"I won't wait any longer, Halldisa Ketil's-daughter," I said, "for I have waited all night."

"You waited all night?" you said. "Really?"

"And you did not come, so now I will return to Asgard while some dark still stains the sky."

"No, don't go." You caught your breath. "I'm sorry. I couldn't get away. I share a cabin with my mother and three of my idiot cousins. I intended to leave as soon as they were all asleep, but Olrunn has been vomiting all night and whining and moaning and wouldn't let me go." You nodded, that mischievous smile finding its way back to your face. "I believe she is with child to my brother Hakon, although they are not husband and wife. Perhaps when Isleif realizes how much adultery is being committed on his island, he might throw his hands in the air and leave without my persuasion."

I was still angry, but not sure how to express it.

"Come. Vidar, don't be so cross." You took my hand. "I wanted to come. I thought about you all night, and all day yesterday too. You look so grim. Perhaps you are too used to getting your own way?"

I found your irreverence beguiling. You charmed me, you fascinated and intoxicated me. "Halla, before I came to Midgard, I can't remember the last time I laughed."

"I'm glad you find me amusing," you said. "Would you allow me to amuse you this morning?"

"Certainly."

"Come. Let's walk in the woods. You can tell me stories about your brothers." You held out your hand and I closed it in my own.

"First, tell me that you warned Isleif to leave the island," I said.

We moved into the trees, leaving the mission and the cold water behind. "I mentioned it. He wouldn't listen."

"You must keep trying."

"You have not reckoned with Isleif Grímsson," you said. "He is determined to live out his days here, and he is determined that we all die of boredom along with him."

"But you must—"

"I will keep trying, Vidar."

"You only have until the winter. Odin expects you to go or he'll . . ."

You let the silence stretch out a few moments, then you stopped and turned to me. "What *will* he do, Vidar?"

"He will have you all killed."

Your eyes held mine and I saw realization dim them. "Oh. He sent you to kill us, didn't he?"

"Yes, he did."

"But you didn't kill us."

"No. I couldn't."

"Now I'm frightened of you, Vidar Odin's-son."

Your words cut me deeply. "I would never hurt you, Halla."

"But that first time we met?"

"I was armed. I intended to fulfill my duties. When I saw you, things changed." I squeezed your fingers gently. "Everything changed."

We watched each other in the dark wood for a few moments, while the sky brightened behind me. Your eyes were intense, your brows drawn down, I could almost see your mind working. "I have been a fool," you said softly.

"I promise you, you can trust me."

"I believe that, Vidar, but what of the rest of your family? I have been a fool to take your kisses so lightly. You are something so different from me. You bring danger to us, un-willingly, but certainly. And I have behaved like a silly girl."

"I have enjoyed your laughter."

"Vidar, I will get Isleif to go. If I have to set fire to the church and all the cabins myself, I will get us off the island. Give me a few weeks to work on him." You shook your head sadly. "I think that we should not speak again, you and I."

The first sunbeam broke through the canopy and speared the ground beside you. Your hair was lifted by a morning breeze, which sent leaves spinning in its wake. The thought of never seeing you again hurt me, as though one of my brothers had punched me between the ribs. I gasped. "Halla, I would see you every day of my life."

You couldn't help yourself, you smiled, tried to bite your lip to keep it in check. "You flatter me."

"I love you."

"Can you be certain?" You pulled your hand out of mine. "Is it worth the trouble?"

"Halla, I—"

"You're not used to talking of your feelings. Let's not mention it again. Let's spend the day together as though the whole world is on our side, then when night falls we can think about this some more. About what is the sensible thing to do. I'm a sensible girl, Vidar. You should remember that." You touched my cheek lightly. "You are not to say you love me again until you are very, very certain. And nor shall I."

That day was bliss. We walked in the woods, we rode Arvak, we built sand houses on the beach, and you made me laugh over and over again. I tried to match your humor with my own with very little success, until you cried laughing every time one of my jokes failed. I had never seen anyone cry laughing before. Your face flushed pink and hot tears rolled down your cheeks and settled in the upturned corners of your mouth, waiting for me to kiss them away.

Your soft skin seemed to beg for my lips to press it; your body sizzled with an irresistible sensual energy, so that my hands were useless for any other task but smoothing its contours. You forbade me, however, from knowing it the way your cousin had known it. Once again, you cited your sensible nature. "You may be gone at the end of the day, Vidar. Or at the end of the week. Next time I lie with someone, it will be every night, forever."

Every night, forever.

I had never been so enchanted with an idea. To have you by me, enclosed in my arms, as I fell asleep each night, your warm, scented hair and soft cheek on my pillow in the morning was the only bliss I could imagine. My life before you seemed bled of all its color. Empty, violent, brainless. I knew then, with great certainty, that I did love you, and I knew this meant I would have to reason with Odin. Then I would bring you back to Asgard with me, make you my princess, build a little house on the shores of the bay, far from my family.

So as the sun dipped once again into the sea, I held you and I swore to you that I loved you, for certain, forever.

"Is that wise, Vidar?" you asked me. Your eyes were hopeful, trusting.

"I don't care if it's unwise," I said. "I have done everything my father has ever asked of me until now, and that must count for something. His quarrel is with Isleif, with Isleif's God, not with you."

"Let's not proceed in haste," you said. "We have time. We have weeks and weeks until winter is here. If we spend every hour of every day together, perhaps we will get sick of each other and there it will all end." You were laughing as you said this, and your laughter lightened the dark wood and the foreboding ocean and filled me with hope.

I often wondered if Isleif and the others suspected what you were doing in the weeks that followed, for you were hardly ever at home. You met me in the morning and you sometimes didn't return home until sunset. When I asked, you waved the question away and said that Isleif didn't care what you did as long as you prayed every morning. The season grew cold and damp, and so I built a tiny cabin in the woods for us, and a shelter for Arvak. I had little inclination to return to Asgard, and the longer I was away, the weaker grew my ties to the Aesir. I confessed all their sins to you, and some of mine too. I was ashamed of my past, and felt certain that you would reject me or, worse, fear me once you'd heard of it.

"You were a warrior, Vidar," you said, smoothing my hair from my brow as we lay beside the fire in the dark little cabin, "and now you are a lover. What you have been matters far less than what you're becoming."

Your words awoke something within me. You were right: I could *become* something different. I wasn't constrained by my blood. I had a free will. If Odin wouldn't let me bring you back to Asgard, then I would simply stay in Midgard with you. The solution was so blindingly clear that it took my breath away.

And still you said, "Wait, Vidar. Let's enjoy these last weeks and not talk about the future. Be here with me now."

This made me suspicious. "Don't you see a future for us, Halla?" I asked. "Is your love for me only *now*?"

You touched my face with your soft fingers and an expression of deep sadness filled your eyes. "Oh, no, my love," you said, "this love is past, present and future. This love is eternal and mighty, but I dare not long to be so happy beyond a few short weeks. You are different from me, and I fear that difference will drive us apart."

Whatever struggle I felt between familial duty and the call of my heart, I didn't realize for a long time that you were struggling too. You rarely mentioned your family, and when you did you were dismissive. Every afternoon, you dutifully returned home to them, though I sensed your reluctance growing greater and greater as the weeks passed.

One afternoon, three short weeks before winter's date, you were in a somber mood without explanation. I allowed you to be silent, and I was silent too. Shared silence with you was sweet and warm.

"We should watch the sunset," you said. "This might be the last clear day for many months."

So we walked out through the golden haze that misted between the trees, until we found the beach. You turned to me, nestled into my body with your ear against my heart.

"What troubles you today, Halla?" I asked over the roar of the sea.

You didn't answer for a very long time. I held you and the sun fell into the water, fracturing into golden shards. As the last of them dissolved into the ocean and night spread from the east, you looked up, and you said, "I want to be with you always."

"And I want to be with you always."

You stepped back and took my hands. "To be apart from you is to fall all to pieces. There would be no center left inside me. You are my heart, Vidar." Your eyes went to the sea. "You are my heart," you murmured.

I couldn't think of words enough to answer, so I stayed silent.

"Tonight, I will not return to my mother. Tonight, I will spend next to you, and give my body to you as I have already given my soul."

Your words warmed my blood to fever and I found myself laughing.

"Are you mocking me?"

"No, my love. I wonder at how you have managed to make an Aesir warrior feel like a blushing virgin."

You laughed then, and fell into my arms. I squeezed you hard.

"Tomorrow, when I wake in your arms, we'll make plans," you said, your voice muffled against my chest. "Plans for the rest of time."

"Sensible plans?" I said.

"Yes," you said, "in spite of our stupid families."

I took you back to my cabin in the woods, and as night fell and a chill deepened among the trees outside, you laughed and said you were "wicked" for missing the evening meal at home, and I couldn't keep my lips or my hands away from your warm body. And when the time approached, you knelt before me and you unfastened the clasps on your clothes and slid out of them as easily as a petrel takes to the sky from the treetops.

"I love you, Vidar," you said, sinking into my arms.

"I love you, Halla," I replied, losing myself in your warm skin.

The wind moaned outside and the fire cracked and popped beside us. It was the last moment of true happiness that I knew. Before we could proceed another moment, I was alerted by thumping footfalls in the woods.

Your eyes went to the door. "Who is that?"

"Halla, you must get dressed. Someone's coming," I said.

You sat up and felt around for your clothes while I went to the door. A man, fair and broad with a bushy beard, stood in the trees about twenty feet away.

"Who are you? Where is my cousin Halldisa?" he said.

"Halldisa is safe," I answered. "She is here with me."

You appeared at the door then, flustered and disheveled. "Asbjorn!" you exclaimed. "What are you doing here?"

"Looking for you, harlot. How dare you bring such shame on your family with a heathen man?"

You looked at me with raised eyebrows, barely taking him seriously.

"Well, Asbjorn," you said to him, "it would hardly be the first time, as you know."

He advanced and I saw that he had pulled out a sword. I grabbed you to push you back inside, but you fought me off.

"Asbjorn, put down the weapon, you fool," you said. "Vidar, ignore him. I'll go home with him, and I'll explain that I intend to take you for a husband, and they'll all just have to accept it. Don't worry. I'll be back tomorrow."

Asbjorn looked glum, his sword pointing impotently at the ground. "You bring great dishonor to Church Island, Halla," he said.

"Yes, yes. Come on, let's not waste any more time. It's cold." You took his arm and turned him around, smiled at me over your shoulder, and mouthed the words, "I love you."

The struggle with my impulses, which dictated I should seize Asbjorn and hack off his limbs, kept me silent. I said nothing as you left. Nothing. That nothing has plagued me for a thousand years. I wished every day that I had said, "I love you, Halldisa. I will be yours forever. No matter what happens I will make certain that we are together. Do not be afraid, not of death, nor of silence, nor of my father. I will find you, I will bring you back to me, this I promise you with all my heart."

But I said nothing.

You didn't return the next day, but I allowed that you needed time to explain your intentions to your family. I passed the long lonely hours in carving, keeping my hands busy so that my heart and mind couldn't plot against me. When you didn't arrive again the following day, I quietly dressed and, with axe and spear, strode off to find you.

When I walked into Isleif's camp, two of the little girls were playing in a tree house, Isleif was talking to a woman who I guessed was your mother, and Asbjorn was fixing the beam over the door to the church. One of the girls saw me first and came running over, shouting, "Where is your horse today?"

I put my hand out to stop her coming near me, and I must have looked serious and frightening enough because she pulled up and glanced uncertainly from Asbjorn to me.

"Come here," Asbjorn said, and the little girl went to him. By this time, Isleif and your mother were watching me. Isleif said something inaudible, and your mother seized the little girl's hand and took her inside. Asbjorn stayed on my right, trying to look threatening.

"You visit us again, Vidar," Isleif said, smiling. This time, though, I could see something beneath the smile. Fear, yes, but also self-righteous piety.

"I want Halla," I said.

"You can't have her," Asbjorn said. "She belongs to our family. Go back to whatever heathen place you came from and leave us be."

I ignored Asbjorn; he was not the person who held the

power in this community. "Isleif, Halla and I are in love and intend to be husband and wife," I said. "Hand her over to me. You hold her against her will."

"Her will has been infected by you," Isleif said. "Halldisa is a Christian woman, and as soon as her right mind is returned to her, she intends to take my dear friend Ulf as husband. You must leave the island so that Halla can recover her senses."

Anger burned brightly inside me and a flash glimmered behind my eyes. I knew that feeling too well, the rush of blood to my brain before battle, where images and sounds became sharp and hot. "Halla is mine," I said. "As I am hers. Bring her out here to explain."

"No, she is with her family. She will not see you again. Return to . . . your home. Work no more of your devil's magic here on Church Island."

"It is Odin's Island," I bellowed, and Isleif took a step back. My hands tightened on the haft of my axe. I knew precisely how it would feel to lift it and split Isleif's head open with the blade. I knew the exact weight of the swing, the sound it would make, the shudder of resistance vibrating up to my shoulders . . . Then I thought about you, somewhere inside, held against your will and commanded to keep very still and quiet. You would not want me to kill Isleif. You would want me to be sensible and try to solve this problem with my brain.

I took a deep breath and forced my arms to relax. I could see Isleif relax too.

"I will return," I said, "and I will make Halla mine. But I won't spill your blood, Isleif. Tell Halla that she need not fear me."

"Give yourself to Christ, Vidar," Isleif said. "It's the only way."

I bit my tongue and walked away. Shame tickled my face and neck. If my brothers could see me, backing down from a fight, letting a Christian bully me into meekness! Then I realized what my brothers thought of me was no longer my concern, and I felt liberated. Under the most pressing of circumstances, I had kept my wits and I had controlled my urge to kill. This meant for certain that I was shedding the curse of my blood. This meant for certain that I was worthy of your love and trust, that I was *becoming*.

I had never turned from a battle before, nor had I ever tried to reason with my father. The first experiment had been successful, and that success heartened me for the second.

Wisdom is not a lover's strength.

As soon as the sun sank I returned to Asgard. The long hall at Valaskjálf was alive with fires and music and chatter. From one end to another, members of my family, their friends and servants, warriors visiting from Valhalla, captives, concubines and Vanir slaves talked, laughed, sang, cooked, scowled, kissed, fought, ate and drank. These were our golden days, when my father's hall was bursting with warmth and company, not the unhappy place it is now. Smoke from the fires collected in the cavernous ceiling, escaping slowly through small holes in the silverwork. I stepped inside and looked around for Odin. He was nowhere in view and I grew irritated. I wanted to speak with him while my nerve still held, while the carefully rehearsed address was clear in my mind.

My eyes found my brother Vali across the hall. I weaved

through the tables and the people and laid my hand on his shoulder.

"Brother!" he exclaimed, grabbing my hand and squeezing it firmly. His tongue slurred on the ale he was drinking. "You are returned. It has been too long since we have seen you. Come, sit, drink."

"Vali, I need to speak with Odin."

He fixed me with an amused gaze. "Really now? It sounds very serious."

"It is serious. Where is he?"

"Indisposed."

"Drunk?"

"We're all drunk." He gestured around the room. "Perhaps you wouldn't feel so serious if you were too?"

He was gazing at me unevenly, a smile on his lips. I returned the smile. "It's serious enough to wait until he's sober. I'll speak to him in the morning," I said.

Vali pulled me down next to him. Two Midgard warriors were demonstrating a combat routine to a small group. I watched them battle, their spears and axes glinting in the firelight. One ran the other through and a great cheer went up as the victim fell to the floor with a crash and a groan. The victor reached for a mug of ale while his companion was dragged out in a smear of blood.

The entertainment over, Vali turned to me. "So, brother, what is this serious business? Something to do with the Christians on Odin's Island?"

"Yes, and no. They are bothersome, but not all Christians. There is one woman in particular . . ." I had no idea how to articulate to my brother what I felt. I knew that every attempt would sound to him like I was speaking a foreign tongue.

Vali grinned suggestively. "Pretty, is she?"

"I should like to take her as wife."

"A Midgard woman?"

"I'm in love with her." I couldn't meet his eyes, braced myself for the barrage of mockery.

"He won't let you," Vali said dismissively, draining his mug.

"He has to let me," I said.

"Why can't you find somebody here?" Vali said, indicating those around him. He singled out a dark-haired woman near the roasting spit. "How about her?"

"She is nobody. She is anybody. Halla is irreplaceable; she is always and forever all I will ever love."

"Good luck," Vali said coldly, with a derisive snort.

"If he won't let me bring her here, then I'll go there and stay," I declared, pounding a clenched fist on the table. "I'm not a prisoner."

"Of course you're not," Vali said, meeting my gaze unevenly.

I pulled myself to my feet. "Brother, I will save the rest for Odin. I have no heart for celebrating, so I'll go to my bed now."

Vali nodded, already turning away. Another fight was about to commence. "Sleep with your problem, Vidar, and perhaps by morning it will be solved."

My room was in an outbuilding at the western end of Valaskjálf and north a hundred paces. I lit the fire and lay down next to it, watching the flames for many long hours while I turned my problem over and over in my mind. I missed you wildly. I hadn't known that somebody's absence could create such an ache in my bones. I had to be with you, and in order to be with you, I had to gain my father's permission to bring you back to Asgard. Isleif could not attempt to control you here in my father's hall, nor could your actions bring dishonor to your family. I closed my eyes and imagined you next to me. Despite the echoes of revelry that occasionally drifted to my ears on a gust of sea air, I fell asleep.

When I woke, it was with disquiet in my belly. A sound had disturbed me. What was it? It was still dark, but birdsong told me day was bare moments away. Then the sound again.

Dogs.

Wild dogs, released from the pit. Odin's dogs, his war companions; four feet at the shoulder and ravenous for warm flesh, and only Odin could control them. Their savage loyalty meant that anyone else who approached would lose at least a limb. If the dogs were loose, their master was not far behind.

I started upright, leaped to my feet. Odin's horn sounded. The dogs barked in frenzy. I ran to my door, but found my way barred by some unseen object. I turned to the shutter and lifted it, eyes straining to focus in the mist.

A blur of animal bodies streamed past. Then Odin, on top of Sleipnir, twice as fast as any other horse known to the Aesir. His torch glimmered off his helmet, his hunching shoulders were clothed in fur, his axe gleamed. Vali, my traitorous brother, rode in his wake.

"Odin!" I cried, hoping vainly that he wasn't taking the dogs to Bifrost. To Midgard and Halla. The last shred of night was unraveling, Bifrost would be closed at any moment, and the door defied every attempt I made to open it.

"There is no love, Vidar," Odin called, and his voice whipped behind him on the wind. "There is only fate."

* * *

How can I describe to you the agony of anxiety that day brought me? By the time I had hammered my way out of the room—an oak table with a boulder upon it had blocked the door—it was daylight. Bifrost was closed.

I saddled Arvak and waited all day by the gleaming stone towers for the first shadow of night to come. Thoughts burned in my brain amid confusion and terror. Somewhere, under layers of hope and denial, I knew you were already dead, but still I constructed detailed fantasies, where Odin killed every member of your family but spared you. The sun sank behind me. Heimdall arrived, grinning at me knowingly. My panic was too focused to allow another thought in. The bridge opened, I plunged down its colored contours toward Midgard.

The world was all torn to pieces.

I could smell smoke and blood. Ice hung from the trees. A wind howled down the ragged corridors between their trunks. My heart weighed in my chest like a stone, sick and frozen.

"Odin?" I called. "Vali?" I tentatively moved Arvak out of the wood, toward the camp. There was a horse's screech behind me, the whimper and thump of brainless dogs. Somebody laughed, then the laughter faded. My family, disappearing to Bifrost and home.

The panic was hot and heavy in my mind. Arvak broke the cover of the trees and the camp was laid out before me.

There was hardly a thing left of it. The three cabins were razed and smoldering. The church burned slowly. I dismounted and moved closer to inspect it. My father or my brother had soaked the wood on the west wall so that the flames were low and green. Hanging from the wood, pinned up with spears, was Isleif's corpse. I kicked open the door and peered inside, then turned instantly and tried to forget what I had seen. The women and children, hanged and burned, like ghastly dolls. Among them, no flash of white hair. You weren't there. I felt my lungs expand. Perhaps you had escaped.

I moved through the choking ruins toward the fjord and down into the trees again. I found the remains of the men near the water. Had they tried to fight, or had they stood like hapless deer while Odin's dogs ripped them to pieces? A groan nearby made me catch my breath and spin around. Asbjorn, pinned to a tree. The dogs had started on him but not finished. I approached. His pale eyes met mine, but there was no recognition in them. He was not dead in body, but I suspected Asbjorn had long since ceased to be in mind. I carefully placed the tip of my spear over his heart and ended his suffering. He shrieked and twitched, the last mortal instinct, then fell slack against his bonds.

Still, I had not found you.

I took a deep breath. "Halla?" I called. "Halla?"

Maybe you were with my father and brother, a captive in Asgard. Even though I knew how captives were treated at Valaskjálf, the thought gave me joy. Alive, I could help you, I could speak to you and hold you. Dead, you were separated from me forever.

I gathered my courage and moved into the woods, scanning every inch around me for a glimpse of you. Until the very last moment I thought it might be possible you had survived; convinced myself of it so deeply that the sight of your hair, catching the moonlight at the foot of a rock in the clearing, almost failed to register.

But it was you. I ran to you and skidded to my knees.

Odin had done this, I knew his work. You had run from him, he had chased you here out of the cover of the trees, and he had killed you with an axe blow to the back. Blood stained your hair, but the dogs hadn't found you.

I removed the axe and turned you over, pressed myself against you and sobbed like a child. As the night deepened and the ice melted from the trees, I held you. You were cold and your head flopped about and your skin was blue instead of cream. I was covered in soil and moss and blood, my clothes were damp and I shivered with the cold and the shock. Every possibility of comfort had evaporated eternally. I laid your body down and sat back to stare around me like a simpleton.

A gleam of steel caught my eye. I rose and moved toward it.

Hjarta-bítr, rescued from the sea, thrust into the ground a bare five yards from where you had died. My hand closed over the crosspiece and I pulled it from the ground and felt its familiar weight in my hand. In an instant, I had thought of the one thing that might bring a glimmer of satisfaction.

To take this blade and plunge it into my father's heart.

I released Arvak near the stables of Valaskjálf. The salty wind leaped down my throat and dried the last of the tears on my cheeks. As I strode up toward the hall, my heart pounded in my ears. Dark clouds gathered out at sea and crowded in on me, blocking out the stars. I trudged up the hill and saw the outline of the hall, and it seemed as though the walls themselves were quaking. My intention, to kill my father, was poison and ruin to our world. Lightning flashed, illuminating figures running from the hall. Odin knew I was coming, he was clearing out the usual crowd of revelers. By the time I flung the door open, the sky had fallen all around me. Hail began to beat off the roof, thunder split the heavens.

Fires still burned, mugs of mead littered tables, half-eaten meals cooled, but the hall was as silent as death.

Outside my father's door, twenty of his servants formed a barrier.

"Stand aside!" I shouted, drawing my sword and noticing a smear of your blood on my wrist.

They all gazed at me mutely.

"Stand aside at once or I will remove your heads from your bodies."

A man, grey and stooped, stepped forward. "You will not enter your father's chamber," he said.

"Stand aside, old man."

He shook his head, planted his feet. I felt the hurricane of pain and anger and injustice tighten within me, lashed out and felled him. When I kicked the body aside, another took his place.

"You will not enter your father's chamber."

One after the other they stepped forward, and I mowed them down without thought, tasting the satisfaction like a drowning man tastes air, until there were only five left. Then Odin's door quietly opened. My heart jumped, but my father did not appear. Instead, another ten servants filed out.

It finally occurred to me what was happening.

My sword, waiting for me in the clearing.

These willing victims, falling at my feet in a pool of blood and sad resignation.

Odin *wanted* me to kill them. He wanted me to be a killer again, to be the son he had nearly lost to love. I gazed around me with a sick heart. Blood zinged on my tongue, my hands were smeared, my shoes were soaked in it.

I had tried to become something different, and with the tiniest effort my father had drawn me back to him.

My breath stopped in my lungs. I surveyed the sullen faces of the servants in front of me.

I quietly turned and strode from my father's hall.

Twenty-Four

Victoria, that is where your memories cease. You had been plunged into that dark world that allows neither thought nor remembrance, neither pain nor love. Like all those left behind on the living side of the veil, I had to continue breathing. I trust you will allow me to finish this tale.

Outside Valaskjálf, rain still thundered down. I left Arvak in the warmth of the stable and made toward the drenched woods. You must understand that I was not in any rational state of mind. Only the rhythm of my footsteps held my thoughts together; without them, I would have descended into the madness of formless grief. Instinctively, I headed west, to the place where fate is made, to the World Tree. As the night deepened, the rain eased and the clouds opened on cold stars. My breath came in short gasps, my whole body ached. Miles from home, the ugly arms of the tree beckoned. The valley opened and I descended, one foot after another, until I stood at the base of the tree. I leaned for a moment, my hands pressed against its rough, lichen-dotted bark. The lack of motion irritated me; I began to circle the tree, climbing over roots and hacking at drooping branches.

My thoughts circled too. I thought about all the widows I had made over the years, and how their wailing had not touched me. I considered the way I had let my weapons think and speak for me. I resolved that I would become the man you had seen in me. A lover. I vowed I would never wield Hjarta-bítr again.

Around and around I went, hours and hours, until the sky spun and my mind began to trip over itself. Knots in the bark became grotesque faces that seemed to laugh at me. The wind in the branches seemed to be whispering mockery.

"What did you say?" I shouted at the branches above.

The whisper came again, clearer. *You are the plaything of fate.*

I stopped. "Is that so? Then I disavow my fate and my blood. I go unarmed now into the future." I drew my sword and held it two-handed above my head, then thrust it with the full weight of my body into the roots of the tree. The tree shuddered once, but it was as a pin to a bear, soon forgotten. The World Tree and the fate-spinners in it cared nothing for my resolution.

One way or another, our paths always lead us back to our fate.

Now I had stopped moving I could feel the weariness in my bones and gristle. I cast a long gaze out over the cold bay to Jotunheim, the shadowed wilderness on the other side. Somewhere beyond those landmarks lived my mother, the other half of my blood. I knew little of her. She was exiled while I was still a child, and I was raised at Valaskjálf. My early years with her were lost to my memory. I sought some connection, some comfort; I sought escape from the pain of your loss. I had not realized such a blow could be struck to me outside the defendable limits of my body. And I sought to move again. I was afraid that if I stood still, I would die from the pain, so I kept traveling—across land and water, forest and field—into the night.

Finally, daylight bled into the sky behind a veil of drizzling clouds. Beyond the woods were the last of a field of drooping flowers, petals in incoherent patterns on the cold grass. I had heard that Gríd grew flowers and followed the field around its edge, down into a hollow where I saw her house, warm and safe like a plump nest. Tightly woven twigs and mud kept out the rain, and a slender curl of smoke emerged from the roof. I was tired, I stumbled and slid, then lay on the ground a few moments, grateful for the enforced end to my traveling. My heart thudded in my ears.

"You must keep going," I said, my mouth full of dewy grass.

I climbed to my feet, aching all over, and went to her door.

She glanced up as the daylight fell onto her hearth, her eyebrows twitched in surprise. "Come in, child," she said. "Be warm and dry."

I hurried inside. She helped me to peel off my wet clothes and gave me a blanket and a cup of warm soup. When I had settled next to the fire, she said, "You're my son, Vidar, aren't you?"

"I am, though I'm surprised you recognize me."

"A mother always knows her children," she said. "I am thrilled that you've come, but I'm wise enough to know that you are here for a reason. You want something from me?"

"I want . . ." My tongue froze. Language collapsed under the weight of grief.

She knelt next to me and her warm hand closed around my arm. "Vidar? You look like a man full of sorrow."

"I am," I said. Her warm touch and her soft concerned voice undid me. I bent my head and tried to swallow a sob.

She closed me in her arms. "Ah, hush, my boy," she said, smoothing my hair.

But I could not hush. My body felt as though it would shudder to pieces, and only Gríd's warm embrace held it together. She let me cry, then, when I had vented some of my sorrow, she made me sit back and tell her the whole tale. She condemned my father, stroked my hair, and said, "Poor boy," and I knew that I had found in my mother a strong new ally.

After three days, the storm of sorrow and shock passed and the dark rain clouds, which I anticipated would surround me the rest of my days, set in. In the evening, as I sat by the fire eating my mother's lamb stew, I said to her, "Perhaps I was foolish to fall in love with a mortal."

Gríd sat beside me and held my gaze in hers. "Vidar," she said, "you didn't lose her to her mortality. You lost her to Odin. We are all mortal. Certainly, Midgard mortals are more vulnerable, but how many Vanir folk have you killed? And what of your brother Baldr, killed with a dart of mistletoe? And what will befall us if Ragnarok should come? We can all die, Vidar. We probably *will* all die. Don't allow your father's blindness to become yours. You are not invincible."

Her words sank in, and rather than being frightened I felt relieved. Eternity is too slow, too empty to contemplate. "What do you think of Ragnarok, Gríd? Do you think it will really happen?"

"I think our time will end, as all times do," she said, "but I think it will happen slowly and feebly. As men on Midgard stop telling our tales, we will fade to sad shadows and dissolve."

I stared into the fire, turning over what she had told me. "Is there something beyond this life, Gríd?"

"I don't know. Nobody comes back to say."

"For mortals? I mean, Midgard mortals? Where is Halla now?"

"She is deaf and blind to any world, in a long and profound sleep, a shade in the keeping of the mistress of the underrealms." She patted my knee. "She doesn't suffer, Vidar."

Gríd stood and moved away, making herself busy collecting plates and cups. Her words vibrated in my mind, sharp and urgent. *A shade in the keeping of the mistress of the underrealms.*

"Vidar?" Gríd said. "You've gone very pale. I didn't mean to frighten you."

I shook my head. "I'm not frightened, Gríd. I'm excited."

"Why so?"

"In a day or two I will leave you for Niflheim. I'm going to ask Hel if she'll give Halla back."

Gríd did not behave as some mothers might, wringing her hands and wailing and discouraging me. Instead, she asked me if I was very sure, and then set about offering practical help. She sewed me a woollen cloak with an oilskin overlay; she packed me a bagful of salted meat and dense black bread; she made me a fur hat and resoled my shoes. As she bustled about, she told me of Niflheim, of the obstacles along the way.

"You'll have to walk for many weeks across the barren plains," she said. "So ration your food carefully, and drink wherever you see clear water, because the hot springs closer to Hel's cave are poisonous." "Try to keep warm, though there is very little shelter." "The journey down, I've heard, is very taxing and you might feel as though you're wandering forever." "Don't miss the entrance to the cave; it's tiny. Many have gone before you, looking for a mighty and grand gate, and have wandered farther and farther down the path past the entrance and died from hunger weeks later." "Watch for Garmr, the ferocious dog who guards the cave." "Don't try to swim the river Slíd. It's full of dead men who have tried before you. Use the bridge, but beware. Those in the river will be jealous of your beating heart." "I have heard that Hel lives behind a gated wall, but then who knows which of these stories are true?" And interspersed with all this advice were her constant self-reassurances. "You are brave and strong, Vidar. I know you'll come back to me."

She knew, as I did, that the journey was dangerous, that many had attempted it and lost their lives. I accepted that I might die, but the symmetry appealed to me, Victoria: at the end of this venture, we would either both be dead or both be alive. There was no pleasure in having one of us on either side of that divide. Wherever you were, was precisely where I wanted to be.

On the morning of my departure, I noticed Gríd pulling on her own cloak and thick shoes.

"Where are you going?" I asked.

"I'm accompanying you down to the water," she said.

"You don't need to."

"Yes, I do. You need me to help you across to Niflheim."

"I will swim across to Niflheim."

She shook her head. "Vidar, a freezing sea lies in your way. Not the mild little bay between Asgard and Jotunheim."

"Then I will stay a while longer and make a rowing boat."

"The waves would crush it. You need a longship."

"I can't row a longship by myself."

"I know. That's why you need me." She smiled. "Trust me, my son. Now, are you ready? Do you have all your things? Where is your sword?"

"I left it behind in Asgard," I said. My stomach turned over as I remembered the last time I had used it.

"Then do you have a spear? Or a knife?"

"I have no weapons, Gríd. I go to Niflheim unarmed."

An expression of fear and sadness crossed her face, then was banished. "If you are very certain—"

"I am."

"Then let's be on our way."

The edge of the water was a six-hour trek from Gríd's house, and as we made our way we talked lightly and lovingly. All our exchanges so far had been full of sorrow, of longing and loss. Now we took the time to know each other better, to fill in the details of a lost history. I would often catch Gríd looking at me, as though she were trying to memorize my face and voice. I knew she thought I would not be returning, and perhaps I thought that too.

The sun was low in the sky when I heard the first strains of the ocean's roar.

"I need to explain something to you, Vidar," Gríd said, "for we are fast approaching the shores of the sea. Some years past, when your father had taken a lover but I had not yet been exiled to Jotunheim, I was very angry with him. I went to Midgard, intending to raise an army against him. The first willing warriors I found, about two dozen, I swore into my service. Then, as my temper cooled, I thought better of the idea and forgot about those warriors, until the first of them appeared at my door here in Jotunheim. He had been killed in battle, and turned away from Valhalla because he had sworn himself Odin's enemy. He was mine. Then another appeared, and another. I sent them to wander in the woods, but they kept reappearing, asking me for orders. When all had come to me, some killed in battle, some dead from age and disease, I sent them down here to build a long-ship."

We crested the rise and the landscape before me was layered thickly in mist. The water scraped and frothed on the pebbled shore and the long grass stood sentinel in the still air. Gríd raised her fingers to her lips and whistled once, loudly. I tried to focus through the mist, out to sea. A horn blew in response.

"They wander the sea, to and fro, with empty eyes and souls, which cannot rest until Ragnarok. This is my fault, my carelessness. I am responsible for them until that day, though they require nothing from me but orders."

The slender prow of a warship cut through the fog, a painted dragon's head with its tongue lolling forward. Round wooden shields lined the sides and dark shadows of men pulled the oars.

"They will take you to Niflheim and wait, either for your return or . . ."

I turned to her. Her skin was washed in pale amber colors by the setting sun. I took her hand. "Allow until the first shoots of green appear on the elms near your house, Gríd. If I haven't returned by then, you may call them back and mourn me."

She squeezed my fingers. Her black hair whipped behind her in a sudden gust of wind. "I will, Vidar."

The ship grated to a halt on the pebbles and Gríd led me down to the water.

Each pallid face was turned toward me, with hollow eyes and motionless blue lips. Some were young men, scarred and maimed by battle. Some were old and crooked, with palsied hands that shook on the oars. The stout, bearded steersman had a horn hung around his neck and sat in the stern of the ship. Gríd waded out to speak with him while I waited on the shore, trying to avoid the warriors' empty stares. Then she turned to me and indicated that I should climb inside the ship.

Gríd came to the side as I settled on one of the boards between two oarsmen. "They will take you to Niflheim. It is seven days' journey if the weather is in your favor. Don't bother trying to speak with them, they won't answer you. Don't give them any further instructions, I have told the steersman all he needs to know." She kissed her palm and held it up to me. "Good-bye, my child, and take my blessing with you."

"Good-bye, Gríd," I said, reaching out to touch her fingers with my own. My arm brushed against the arm of the man next to me and he was as cold as a stone. "I hope I will see you again."

The ship moved off, the water caught its weight and the oars began to draw.

"I hope so too."

I watched her standing on the shore until the mist swallowed her.

All around me, dead men rowed in silence as if of one mind, with no need for orders or discussions. The wind picked up and we sailed out of the fog. Far from the cover of the coastal waters the sea rolled and tumbled beneath us. The sun sank and dark clouds moved in. The only light was the pale splash of the water against the prow, fainter than starlight. I huddled into my cloak and tried to stay warm, but it seemed that the cold flesh surrounding me leached my own body of its heat. The sea roared, the wind moaned, the smell of salt was thick on the air. Beneath the boat, I felt the occasional bump and slither of a lost thing, and sometimes thought I heard the splash of a creature's tail or limb just off to starboard. None of the crew spoke or looked around, nor did they move from their seats or drop their oars. I might as well have been utterly alone. Land receded completely, and mine seemed the only beating heart in the universe.

The sun rose weakly and set dimly day after day on this ship of ghosts. The rhythmic movement of the water and the unbroken silence of the crew worked on my mind, lulling me into a semidaze, where I cannot remember sleeping or waking. But I do remember the nightmares: the moment of finding your body over and over; or sometimes seeing your pale hair floating in the water beside the ship; or hearing your voice on the wind and turning around, expecting you to be there, and finding only the grim, blank gaze of an oarsman. I am certain that by the seventh day my gaze was equally grim, but the seventh day was also the day I saw land again and my thoughts began to wake within me. A journey awaited me, and at the end of it I hoped to see you and hold you again, or I hoped I would die. Either way, I believed my suffering was drawing to a close.

All morning the land drew closer and closer and I itched with excitement. The clouds hung low and the air was cool. The wind dropped and the oars were picked up again and the twenty-four dead men rowed me to shore.

The ship skidded up onto grey sand and stopped. I glanced around me. Every man still faced directly ahead of

him. Not even the steersman turned my way. I climbed out
of the vessel and landed on the sand.

"You will wait here for me?" I said, even though Gríd had
said there was no need for further orders.

The steersman didn't answer. A breeze picked up and
flapped the corner of the sail. I turned to survey the area
around me. Black rocks waited ahead, a steep climb. Rain
fell. My nerve fluttered but didn't fail. I took a deep breath
and a first step, unarmed and alone on the shores of
Niflheim.

Niflheim is the northernmost of the lands that surround Asgard. Beyond it, there is **a** freezing void that spews mist and
ice back toward the south, so Niflheim is very cold. The land
appears flat and treeless, apart from a few brave pines here
and there, but the land isn't flat, it slopes downward, imperceptibly at first, then opening into ravines and gorges where
icy water moves and freezes. The path to Hel is not marked,
but if you follow the source of the icy wind which buffets the
beach, with not a degree of movement west or east, you will
eventually happen on the narrow black road that winds down
into the realms of the dead.

Of course, the easiest way to get there is to die, as you
had. You wouldn't remember the journey, Victoria. Souls
need not concern themselves with distances and directions;
every place is one place, and Niflheim is just a point of
access.

I left the beach, climbed the black rocks and set myself
on a northern path. My feet crunched on the black gravel,
the rain was gentle and I felt strong and hopeful. I had been
a warrior and I was accustomed to hardship, to traveling
great distances on foot and rationing my food. As the rain set

in over the coming days, I pulled my oilskin close and endured. Sometimes the mist was so thick that I couldn't see the path in front of me. Yet, with one foot in front of the other, I continued to make my way forward. I thought back on battles I had fought and the discomforts I had suffered, and I made light of the cold and the damp and the mist. I ate frugally and kept hunger at bay, and there was enough fresh water to satisfy my thirst. Those first few weeks were easy on the warrior in me for all that I no longer carried a weapon.

The journey continued, the harsh conditions intensified, and I had to remind myself I was a lover and there was nothing more precious than the reward I would claim if I could just push myself forward. As the rocky plains fissured and cracked around me, I began to despair of ever being dry again. The oilskin could not protect me from those drips that trickled down my neck, or the damp which seeped into my boots, or the way the rain sometimes caught on a swirling wind and found its way under my protective clothing, then clung obstinately in the wool. My fingers were puckered and my ears ached. The ground had started its downward slope, and sometimes the gravel on a steep downpath was loose and treacherous.

By the end of each day my feet were aching from trying to cling to the path. Each morning when I rose from my cold, damp bed I found it almost impossible to stand: my feet felt bruised and shredded. The sulfurous air nauseated me and clogged my lungs. Sometimes, when the mist cleared and I saw the path snaking away from me toward the endlessly receding horizon, my heart grew as heavy as lead. I rationed more carefully, fearful that my journey would take much longer than I had anticipated. Hunger ate me more often than I ate my bread, and before two weeks had passed my clothes were hanging off me like they might hang off my hunting bow. But I was a lover, and a great love was worth any suffering.

Then the snow came.

And I was an animal—a skinny, wet, filthy animal—all of its energy concentrated on simply trying to survive. My knees burned, my back ached, I couldn't feel my feet: I might as well have been walking on my bare anklebones. The path deepened, winding passes cut narrowly along the edges of black cliffs, which dropped vertically into a dark, mist below. Only an animal could survive the blizzard I survived on the side of that dizzying ravine, an animal clinging tooth and claw to life with no man's intellect to surrender to despair.

Finally, after the snow, as all the black twists in the road became one, as the emptiness of Niflheim permeated my skin and possessed me, I became nothing. What did it matter that all my food dropped in a dark lake while I was bent there drinking? Nothing needs no food. What did it matter that the gusting winds out of the deep gorge tore my fur hat from my head and carried it miles away? Nothing suffers no discomfort. I could not remember entering life, so perhaps I never had. I could not see an end to the path in front of me, so perhaps I never would. If my body moved, I don't remember it. If I had a thought or spoke a word, I didn't hear it. Nothing roams empty in the wilderness, and the wilderness and the emptiness neither sees it nor cares.

Only in this state of mind, stripped of my pretensions to be a warrior, or a lover, or even an animal, did I finally make my peace with the mystery of my existence. I was born, and I live, and someday I may die, and this is utterly baffling, but

I accept it. I have loved, Victoria, and love infuses everything else, infuses the confusion and the blankness and the fear of emptiness, and brings to it a glimmer of meaning. Enough meaning to move forward, to keep moving, until I found that tiny cave hollowed into the cliff, small enough almost to escape my notice.

I had arrived.

A flurry of snow whirled around me and cleared, and I found myself staring at the entrance to the realms of the dead.

Twenty-Five

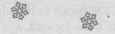

I hurried down the slope and climbed into the mouth of the cave. Strewn on the dusty ground were dozens of bones and three cracked skulls. I paused to listen, but heard nothing except the *drip drip* of melting snow outside. The cave narrowed into the dark, but I had traveled months in the rain and cold and had only one priority: to become warm and dry. There was no wood for a fire, so I stripped off my clothes and hung them on the rocks around me. Near one of the skulls I found the moldering scraps of an old tunic, and I put it on and curled up on the floor in the soft dirt, and slept.

I don't know how much later I woke, but it was with a start. My mental senses, long confused by a veil of physical suffering, sprang sharply to life. I sat up and strained to hear. There was a scuffling and scratching, seemingly just past the bounds of my seeing, in the dark end of the cave. I looked at the bones around me with fresh eyes. Men had died here, trying to get past Garmr, Hel's hound who guarded this entrance. I was unarmed, weak and hungry. What chance did I stand?

Still, I imbued my voice with courage. "Who is there?" I called.

A deep growl thundered around the cave. I climbed to my feet, horribly aware of my vulnerability; the threadbare tunic was all that stood between my flesh and the teeth of this animal. I considered reaching for my other clothes, afraid to turn my back on the dark tunnel for even a moment. The scuffling approached. A huge figure loomed in the dark, its eyes glowing dimly, and I braced myself for the arrival of Garmr.

The hound emerged. Glittering eyes, ferocious teeth, a snarling maw, powerful shoulders; but he met my gaze, then sagged forward. In an instant, he was not a vicious beast at all. He was an old, old dog, with rheumy eyes and a grizzled nose. I took a step back as he approached, wondering if this were a trick to unsettle me. The enormous creature lay down, head on his paws, and looked up at me sadly.

"Garmr?" I said.

His tail thumped in the dirt. I sat and touched his ears, then gave his head a rub. He closed his eyes happily.

"You aren't a ferocious beast," I said.

He growled, low in his throat, and I pulled my fingers away sharply, but still he didn't rise, nor make any movement to stop me.

"Can I go to see Hel?" I asked. "Will you let me through?"

The tail thumped again. I scratched behind his ears and he sniffed near my pockets.

"Sorry, old boy, I haven't any food for you. Are you hungry? Do you get much to eat here?"

He lifted his head and nosed at the corner of my tunic, where a bloody rip had pulled the corner away. So Garmr had eaten the previous owner of these clothes; why was he not eating me?

"I don't understand," I said, "but I have to keep moving."

He rolled over with his legs in the air and closed his eyes. I rose and changed into my own clothes—still damp and cold, but not wringing wet—and Garmr went to sleep. He was whimpering in a dream as I filled my water bottle from the melted snow outside, then headed back toward the tunnel.

I walked for half a mile and the light faded behind me until I was walking entirely in the dark. For the first time in many months I thanked my Aesir blood, for we can see, if dimly, even in the darkest place. The tunnel narrowed. I had to bow my head to keep moving, then I had to bend my back, then I had to crawl on my hands and knees, and then I had to slither on my stomach. The rocky walls scraped my shoulders and back, and in some places I had to turn my head to the side and squeeze my body through narrower and narrower openings. Four hours later I had wriggled through the worst of the tunnel and could hear the nearby rushing of a river. The Slíd. A breeze coiled down the tunnel and lifted my hair. I was not far from open space.

I moved forward, the tunnel widened, and I was on my feet when I came to the opening. The ground dropped out in front of me. I cautiously peered out and down.

And down and down.

A giant cavern spread out before me, hundreds of feet below. Through it ran a roaring river at least half a mile wide, the water glowing faintly green, lending an eerie light to the cavern. The river snaked off into misty distance in both directions, but to the east I could see the outline of a bridge. A narrow ledge, not more than six inches across, jutted out below me. It sloped steeply toward the floor of the cavern. I made my way down.

The banks below plunged into the furious icy water, which was pale green and choked with clattering objects. Bones, spears, helmets, skulls, pots and silver jewelry. I watched for a few moments and thought I saw the flash of a limb, then streaming hair. With a splash, the water broke and a man launched himself out of the river and toward the bank. I scrambled backward, and he was pulled under and carried away, but not before I had seen his bloated face and purple lips. He had drowned in this river and, like all drowning victims, remained in the water hoping to lure another victim to his death.

Keeping a safe distance from the bank, I headed toward the bridge. From time to time a howling wind would surge down the river and I threw myself on the ground until it had passed. On two occasions, a grasping hand reached out of the water as though it wished to seize me and pull me nearer. I kept moving, determined, knowing that my goal was just across the raging waters.

Yet it was three hours beyond the river, through a high tunnel, that I finally knew I was approaching Hel's abode. Burning torches hung on brackets and the cold lost its bite. The tunnel inflected sharply to the east, and I rounded the corner and was confronted by a gate. It was some hundred feet high, built from bones and skulls that had yellowed with age. A moldering plaque set into the bones read NÁGRIND: corpse-gate. This was the end of the tunnel; there were no other passages or crooked paths to explore. I approached and tried the gate. It wouldn't move. I pounded it and cried out. Nobody came. For more than an hour I tried to open it. I had arrived, but it seemed my arrival meant nothing, would avail nothing. The discomfort in my body grew less and less bearable as the realization sank in: perhaps this journey was meaningless. Perhaps I would have no satisfaction for my suffering.

I huddled in a ball on the ground in front of the corpsegate and clutched my stomach and let the sobs tear at my throat. How careless I was to lose you. How empty eternity seemed. I would have been luckier if the drowned soul had pulled me under the water, or if Garmr had eaten me, or if the blizzard outside had claimed me. Exhaustion overwhelmed me and I lapsed into a deep sleep.

A touch on my cheek woke me. I opened my eyes and tried to focus, reminding myself where I was. I saw a woman, ageing and plump, smiling down on me.

"Come in, Vidar," she said.

I sat up and looked around. The gates were open, the woman was holding out a warm blanket.

"My name is Hel," she said. "Come in, your journey is at an end."

On the other side of the gates lay the fields of the dead, a nighttime pastoral scene lit by bonfires. Meadows and wheatfields stretched out under the livid light. I saw sheep and cows wandering in and out of the dark. She led me to her hall, little more than a cabin on a rise of rock.

My relief at being found was immeasurable, even more so because of Hel's warm greeting. She allowed me to sit silently as she stoked her fire and ordered her maid to make me a meal. Hel herself fetched me warm skins to rest on, and blankets to heap on my cold, aching body. She clucked the whole time about how brave I was, what a handsome fellow I was, and on one occasion even bent to press me against her enormous bosom and reassure me that I was safe and warm and needn't worry about a thing.

When the maid had brought me a trencher filled with hot rabbit stew, Hel sat cross-legged beside me. As she did, her skirt flipped up far enough for me to see her ankles and they were mottled and moldering. I remembered the stories that said she was half-alive and half-dead and shuddered.

"Still cold, Vidar?" she asked. "Shall I get Ganglöt to fetch you another blanket?"

"No, I'm fine now," I said, falling on the food. "I can't find the words to thank you for taking me in. You are not what I expected."

"Oh, those stories! That I'm a fearsome scowling goddess who tears men to pieces!"

I tried a laugh. This doughy, gentle woman was far removed from that description. "Yes, those stories."

"I'll show you something, Vidar," Hel said. She took a breath, and as the air filled her body a horrible transformation crept over her. Livid shadows deepened around her eyes, her lips pulled back in an animal-like grimace and her hair began to writhe like serpents. Even her body drew up taller and I realized she was easily powerful enough to crush a man. I flinched away from her, but then she released the breath and the frightening countenance melted away.

"You see?" she said. "I am that fearsome monster, but not to everybody."

"Like Garmr."

"Precisely like Garmr. I'll explain. Don't stop eating, poor boy, you must be starving." She patted my knee. "Garmr is me, or at least a part of me. He's my eyes and ears out there. There's nothing either of us likes better than ripping a man to pieces and eating his liver." She laughed. "So many come, more every year. Armed like warriors to force me to do their bidding. I relish seeing them die. But you, you came unarmed, poor boy. Such a famous warrior, you sent me many new souls to keep, but you came to me unarmed. You won't stand there and command me on the point of a blade, will you?"

I shook my head, devastated to have finished the stew. Ganglöt stepped in and ladled some more onto the plate. "I'm not a warrior anymore," I said. "Those days are behind me."

"What does your father think of this?"

"I am not the keeper of my father's opinion."

Hel smiled. Her teeth were small and grey, but slightly pointed. "Tell me why you're here, Vidar. I will listen."

Every time I had to tell what was in my heart, I had to suffer the pain all over. It took me a moment to steel myself to the task.

"I loved," I said to Hel. "I loved a Midgard woman so dearly that my heart transformed from stone to flesh. I loved her so dearly that I was prepared to give up everything to be with her. I loved her so dearly that my hands shook while I waited for her to arrive, afraid she would not come at all. I loved her . . ." My words wavered, bent too hard over my sorrow, and I checked myself. When my voice was even again, I continued. "Odin discovered this love and slew her."

"Oh!" said Hel, her eyebrows quivering. The fire popped and shadows fluttered on the walls.

"My existence is meaningless without her. I can't go back to being what I was, I despise it now. I want her back, Hel. I've traveled for months and endured many hardships. I am starved and frozen and battered and heartsick. All because I cannot endure a life without her in it."

Hel gazed at me, her eyes filled with tears. "You came all this way for her?"

"Yes, I did."

She shot to her feet and walked away a few paces. I could see her fists ball up and felt a flutter of wariness.

"Hel?" I ventured. "Have I offended you?"

Hel spun round and her face was the monster's expression I had seen earlier. "Why *her*?" she screamed. "What's so special about *her*?" Then her features relaxed and became gentle once more, and she sagged into her chest. "Oh, oh. It's not your fault."

I wasn't sure what to do, so I remained silent.

Hel raised her head and met my eyes sadly. "I loved once," she said, "and what is left of the lover in me wants to grant your wish. My beloved promised to come for me, here to Niflheim, after my exile." Her eyes dropped, and she whispered, "He never did."

I waited.

"The woman in me who was betrayed wishes you to be as unhappy as I am."

This last declaration galvanized my tongue. "Please, Hel. I am sorry that you were let down—"

"Why her, Vidar? Why is she so special, and why was I so . . . disposable?" Her eyes began to glitter and I feared she would transform again.

"You are not, Hel," I said quickly. "He was simply not capable of estimating your worth."

"Rubbish. You don't believe that. I'm a fat old cow with the legs of a corpse."

"No, no, you—"

"Enough!" she shouted, flinging out her right hand. "Don't insult me with your false flattery. What was your woman's name?"

"Halldisa," I said, my breath caught in my throat. "Halldisa Ketil's-daughter."

Hel paced the room three times in the firelight, her shadow growing and shrinking on the walls.

"Vidar, I want to reward you for your own true heart, but I must punish you for *his* false heart. I know this isn't fair, but I feel too. I hurt too." She paused and sucked her lips together, holding back tears. "Halldisa will come back," she continued, "but not now. She will enter Midgard sometime in the far future. I'd like to see if you will remain faithful to her memory once time wears you down."

"I will remain true forever," I said, my heart heavy. "Please, let me have her now. Let me take her back with me."

Hel shook her head. "No. I will let you have warm clothes, new shoes and food for your journey, but you won't have your beloved, not yet."

"How will I know when she is reborn?"

"If your love was true, then your souls have touched and saved the imprint of one another. They will always be drawn to each other—across miles, across centuries. When it's time, you'll know." She held up a warning finger. "She won't remember you. You have to woo her all over again before you remind her. That will also test *her* love. If she doesn't respond to you, then perhaps you overestimated the depth of her feeling."

."I can't bear the years without her!" I cried, despair flooding into my throat. "Please, Hel."

"Be glad for what I've granted you. It's much more than

most people take from this place," she said. Her voice grew gentle and kind once more. "Rest here a night or two, regain your strength, set your mind. She will come again; your heart must ache until then."

This is nearly all I have to tell you, Victoria. I returned from Niflheim and took my mother's advice to exile myself from my family, and I have been true to you for a thousand years. Our story, my story, ends here. You've asked me for it many times: what will you do with it, Victoria? What will you do with me now you know the truth? Everything depends on your answer.

Twenty-Six

[Midgard]

The silence that followed Vidar's voice rushed upon my ears and grew heavy between us. I opened my eyes. The forest had grown dark and gloomy shadows had gathered. Vidar waited. He had waited a thousand years.

It seemed I had lost the ability to speak. Formless thoughts clustered and shifted in my mind. Logic had completely disintegrated. During Vidar's rehearsal of his tale, I'd recognized every word as a faithful account of my own memories—but memories that weren't my own. Looking at him, his sad eyes black in the firelight, I knew that he was a supernatural creature utterly alien to me, but I had never felt closer to anyone in my life. My body had responded to his story with rush after rush of adrenaline, like riding on a fairground ride for so long that standing on solid ground seems all wrong and flat. Here I was, Queen of the Skeptics, dethroned by my own history. Irony or destiny?

Vidar still waited.

I sat up and he moved to sit beside me, our arms touching. "I don't know who I am," I said. "Or, at least, I don't know whom you love."

"I love you."

"Halla? Or Victoria?"

"You're the same person."

"I'm not. I'm Victoria." As I said this, the echo of my previous existence resonated on top of me and I had to catch my breath.

"It's only a name. It's your soul, your spirit—"

"I don't even believe in souls. Or at least, I didn't."

"You believe in me, don't you?"

"With all my heart."

"I need to speak to you seriously," he said, his eyebrows drawing down. An image of him overlaid it and I knew it was one of Halla's memories: he had spoken seriously to me long ago. "If my father finds out, he will kill you. You have to leave the island, go as far away as you can, far enough that he will not bother to follow you."

"And you'll come with me?"

He shook his head. "I cannot."

The earth seemed to shudder. "What do you mean?"

"Because he would bother to follow me. To the very edges of civilization. Victoria, I have come here to save you, not to be with you. We can't be together."

"No," I said, as my already overtired brain tried to process this new flood of feeling. "We're meant to be together. We've waited forever." I could feel the years that had passed, century on top of century like layers of thick cold soil, heavy on my chest. I forced a breath.

"My father—"

"Save it, Vidar," I said, resting my finger on his lips. "Tell me tomorrow. Be with me tonight."

His eyelids fluttered closed and I could feel the shuddering breath he drew.

"Vidar?"

Vidar opened his eyes and held my gaze and my body swirled with warm shivers. He turned and pulled me close against him, and I could hear his heart pounding and feel the heat of desire rising from his skin. He drew me into his lap and pushed my hair off my face and we froze there a moment, watching each other, and it seemed that the sun rose and set for an age; each cloud and shower of rain, each glimmer and beam of the daylight, counting all the days between us, between this love and the last. I felt something eternal and something sacred, and I recognized everything I had felt before as a mere shadow of real love. The ocean I had plunged into with Vidar was deep and thrilling, and the bottom was so far beneath me that I was terrified. To lose him again? To go back to my ordinary, flat world of shallow concerns? I would sooner die.

I touched his face. He made a rumbling sound deep in his throat: half a growl, half a groan. His hands still in my hair, he pulled me forward and kissed me violently. His beard was rough, his lips were hot and laden with frantic passion. He pressed my body against his as though he wanted to crush me to pieces, dissolve into me. When I drew a sharp breath of pain, he released me and proceeded more gently. Tiny kisses on my chin and ears, down my neck. I was unfastening our clothes as quickly as I could, shedding mine awkwardly, having no idea how to get him out of his. He helped me and we ended up on the forest floor among the animal skins he slept on. Warm blood, hard kisses, and smooth hot flesh over his ribs under my fingers. He covered my body with his and slowed: his breathing, his heart, his mouth. I looked up at the dark branches above us, the scudding clouds. Vidar warmed my skin with his touch and trembles started deep inside me.

"Remember to breathe," he said.

Centuries of desire weighed down his fingertips, the yearning of ages about to be dispersed. His body moved into my body. Intense feelings threatened to break each of us out of our skins, to achieve the impossible and melt us together.

One of us cried out. The dark forest did not respond. Far away the clouds parted on distant stars and Vidar's hot skin soaked up the light and transferred it to me. It seemed to last forever and yet be captured in a moment. I sobbed and clung to him and he held me and drew up a blanket to cover us. I came all the way back to my own body and Vidar was kissing my shoulder tenderly.

"I love you," I said, but it seemed impossibly inadequate to say, *I love you.* Drunkards and novelists had been using those words for too long. What I felt was so much more than that random collection of blank syllables. The meaning spilled over the edges and disappeared, unvoiced, into the forest.

"And I love you," Vidar said. "Forever."

"Stay with me."

"I can't."

"I'm not afraid to die," I said, and in that instant it was true, though it would not always be so.

"I'm afraid of you dying."

"More afraid of that than of us being apart?"

He bent his head and pressed his lips into the hollow of my throat. "It's impossible." He sighed, his breath warm on my skin. "It's all impossible, Victoria." He raised his head.

"If I must lose you, then I would rather you were alive, here, with some hope of happiness for—"

"There's no hope of happiness without you," I said, sitting up and turning on him. "Now I know, I can't go back to what I used to be." I realized that I had shouted, that my voice had sounded shrill and desperate. I shook my head and laughed. "Look what you've done to me. You've turned me into a crazy person."

"Victoria—"

"No, no," I said. "Not now. I can't bear to hear it. Stay just until tomorrow night. Just one day, Vidar. Please." I secretly hoped that if I could make him stay until then, we could conjure a way to be together. I had transformed from the girl who believed in nothing to the girl who believed in miracles.

Vidar had his lips pressed together in consideration. His eyes undid me, so deep and sad and full of passion.

"Vidar, please?" I whispered. "Just one day."

"Victoria, it cannot be," he said quickly, as though he wanted to have it out before he changed his mind. "I must go tonight, and you must leave tomorrow."

The real world swerved in on me. My job, my future. "I can't leave until Wednesday when the boat comes," I said.

"And what day is it now?"

"Thursday . . . nearly Friday."

He sat up next to me and looked bewildered, afraid. "Then I will stay with you until Wednesday, and keep you safe from him."

"But you don't know for sure that he'll come?"

Vidar shook his head. "No. I hope he will never find out. However, now we have been together, he could sense you, and he has scrying water he could use to find you . . ."

The first cold tendril of fear touched my heart then, mortal fear. I remembered the dreams I'd had of the dogs chasing me, the man-monster with the cruel axe. Now those fragmented dreams had a deeper texture, fleshed out by Halla's memories.

"I will keep you safe until then," he said firmly. His right fist was clenched.

"I trust you," I said, touching his hand.

He looked at me, slowly releasing his fingers. "I won't let it happen again," he said.

I folded him into my arms and pulled him down so we lay among the furs and blankets. "Vidar, imagine if we could stay together."

"I dare not."

"Please, just for tonight. Let's imagine what it would be like. Perhaps we'll discover we're completely incompatible, then you'll be happy to go home without me."

"Don't joke about it, Victoria."

"Lighten up," I said, snuggling against his chest. "Go on. If you could, what would you do with me?"

His skin was very warm and his voice vibrated in his chest. "I'd build you a little house here in the forest." His tone was so sad that I regretted asking him. "I'd gaze at you every moment and cover you in kisses, and every night we would sit by the fire and tell stories, and every day we'd walk along the beach or in the forests and nobody would ever disturb us."

"It sounds wonderful. But couldn't we leave the island? I'd miss my mum. Imagine, we could get a little flat together. You could bring me a cup of tea in bed every morning. We could have a little family."

His body tensed. "No, Victoria, your blood and mine can't mix. There could be no children from our union."

I was surprised by how sad that made me. "Oh well . . . Dogs, then. Spoiled yappy ones."

"We would have so much love, the two of us," he said, stroking my hair. "Enough to make the universe spin and all the stars glow until Ragnarok . . . but it's dangerous to say such things."

"They're only words," I muttered, as sleep slipped over me. But they were more than words. They were compelling fantasies, persuasive enough to lead lovers into foolish decisions.

Dawn crept under my eyelids a few hours later and I woke with a horrid churning in my guts. Lack of sleep, lack of food, the shock, who knows? I sat up, felt my whole stomach start to rise, and dashed into the woods with a blanket around me to hurl it all out.

Vidar was behind me a second later. "Victoria? You're unwell?"

"I'll be all right," I said, waving him away. "I've got a weak stomach."

"A weak . . . ?"

"I get sick easily. I'll be all right. I just need to eat something, probably. Please, let me upchuck in peace. It's not how I want you to remember me."

He quietly took himself back to the campsite and I threw up a few more times, nothing but bile, and felt a little better and joined him. He offered me some water, which I gulped down, and a piece of hard dark bread. I chewed on it dutifully, but was longing for a hot cup of tea and some toast with marmalade. I lay down and groaned, my hands over my aching stomach.

"I don't understand, Victoria. Hunger makes you ill?"

"It's probably a combination of things," I said. "I'm tired and maybe a bit shaken up still. Shock can do strange things to your body." I smiled. "Well, my body at least. I'm sure yours is built to withstand more than mine. Look what you did to me last night." I slid the blanket off my shoulder to reveal a purplish bruise.

"I did this to you?" he said, his eyes round with bewilderment.

"Don't feel bad," I said quickly. "If I'd wanted you to stop, I would have said."

He frowned. "I forget how mortal you are," he said. "Your spirit is so strong, but your body . . ."

"I'm all right, really," I said, patting his hand. "Thanks for being concerned." I closed my eyes, and when I opened them again a few minutes later he was still looking at me, worried.

"Vidar?" I said, sitting up.

"You're so vulnerable," he whispered. "I should never have come near you. I should have let you live your life in peace."

"I would have lived my life in sadness had you not come," I said, putting my arms around him. "Peace is well and good, but I'd give it away to be with you." I sat back. "Now, we have to make plans. I'm expected at work today, but I won't go. I'll say I'm sick. You can come back to my cabin. I'll get us some food and see if I can steal some of Gunnar's clothes from the laundry."

"You are still a sensible girl, I see," he said. "Making plans."

"I just want to be with you," I said, my lips finding the tender skin at his earlobes. "If fate has decided that we only have until Wednesday, that means we have to fit two lifetimes of love in."

"That's a lot to ask."

"It's all I'll ever ask for." I paused, an idea glimmering in a far corner of my brain. "Vidar, is it possible for you to change your fate? Then your father would have nothing to hold you by."

Vidar looked perplexed. "One can bargain with the Norns," he said, "but I don't know where they live."

He paused and I opened my mouth to say something, when he continued: "At present," he said. "I don't know at present where they live."

"But you could find them? Hypothetically speaking?"

"Many men have wandered for years and grown old in the roots of the World Tree, looking for the spinners of destiny," he said. "I fear we don't have that much time on our side."

I stood gingerly and stretched my legs. My stomach was beginning to settle again, but I wanted to be inside. The forest had its charm; the cabin had central heating and a shower.

"Come with me," I said. "Be careful. Don't speak and if you hear somebody approaching, you have to be really quiet."

"Wasn't it me who taught you to be quiet?" he said, laughing. "Let's see who makes the least noise on our way."

"It's a bet."

He won, of course, because I broke a twig within forty seconds of leaving the campsite behind. As we walked beside each other in the forest, with the warm sunbeams bouncing between the new leaves and my hand enclosed in his, I felt a shudder of such exquisite happiness that I wanted to sob. At last, life made sense. At last, there was a meaning, a shape to my existence. Although I accepted that I might lose him, that I could die if I wasn't prepared to let him go, the fear seemed distant in the morning sunshine, a cold thing to be considered only at night.

I could almost feel the cogs and gears of my brain whirling over, processing the problem. There must be a way around it, there must be a way we could be together. Vidar was a supernatural being, there must be supernatural logic somewhere in there, and why couldn't it work in our favor instead of just against it?

We drew near the hem of the forest and, remembering Magnus spying me there, I slowed.

"We have to be careful now," I said.

"I'll follow you."

I took his hand and we crept to the edge of the slab. I peered left and right. Nobody in sight. Squeezing his hand, I led him quickly to the back door of my cabin, fumbled the key, pushed the door open, then slammed out the outside world.

"Home safe," I said.

He hesitated in the hallway. "Make yourself comfortable," I said. "I'm going to sort out a few things."

"Don't be long," he said, reluctantly letting my fingers go. "Every moment is precious."

I hurried over to the admin building, first stop the laundry. Gunnar always left his clothes in the dryer for days after he'd washed them. I found a shirt and a pair of checked pajama pants which I thought might fit Vidar, and stuffed them into a laundry bag. With that under my arm, I went to the galley. Empty, but not for long. I could hear Frida and Carsten talking in the rec hall. I threw open the doors to the pantry and grabbed four cans of soup and a leftover half loaf of bread, a bag of chocolate cookies and a packet of Weet-abix. I was in the cold room stashing a carton of milk in the laundry bag when I heard someone in the kitchen.

"Hi," I said, peeking out. It was Gordon.

"Morning, Vicky," he said cheerfully. "How are you?"

I closed the cold room door behind me. "Terrible. Really, really sick. That bug that you had—"

"You must have caught it. So sorry. Vomiting?"

I nodded, trying to look pale and trembly.

"Diarrhea?"

I nodded again, hoping he wouldn't probe much further. I didn't want to talk bodily functions with Gordon.

"You'll be better in a day or two. I feel fine now."

"Thanks. I came over to get some breakfast but I'm not feeling up to work. Could you let Magnus know?"

"That you're sick? Of course." He gave me a theatrical wink. "Let's hope we spread it around. No point in keeping it to yourself, eh?"

"That's right," I said, not a hundred percent sure what he meant because half my mind and all of my heart was back at the cabin. "I might go back to bed." With that, I was out the door, my booty under my arm and my heart thudding with excitement.

I found Vidar in the kitchen, freshly showered with a towel around his waist and his hair trailing damp on his warm shoulders.

I caught my breath. He turned around.

"I got milk," I said, offering the carton as proof.

He took my wrist, cast the carton of milk aside and

dragged me to the sofa. I was utterly helpless in his hands, partly owing to his irresistible, hot skin, and partly the unyielding power of his body. Only his fingertips knew how to be gentle and my flesh responded to the combination of relentless and tender with greedy longing.

Then, dressed in Gunnar's long-sleeved T-shirt and the checked pajamas, Vidar was treated to his first-ever breakfast of Weetabix, which he liked well enough. I showered, we tumbled into my bed and idled the hours away in conversation, kisses and long dozes.

I woke in the late afternoon. The last beam of sunlight diffused through the curtain. Vidar was still asleep. I had dreamed of my old life, the one where nothing supernatural had ever been admitted. It had been a simple dream, not a sad one. As I watched Vidar's face, made soft and boyish by slumber, desire glowed in my heart, but the first thought to chase it was fear. Oh, I had got myself into a big, *big* mess. We had spent enough time in the lull of each other's company. I had to start working on a solution.

A knock at the cabin door broke into my thoughts. Vidar's eyes flew open. I was out of the bed and pulling on my dressing gown. I held my finger to my lips for him, then rushed to the door.

"Gunnar, hi," I said, blocking the doorway with my body.

"Hi, Vicky. I brought you some dinner." He held out a plate with aluminum foil over the top.

"You didn't have to," I said, taking the plate.

"Can I come in?"

"You'd better not. Wouldn't want you to catch this bug."

"You look fine. It's probably not contagious."

I held up my hand to stop him advancing. "Really, Gunnar. I'd rather be alone in my misery."

"Sorry," he said.

I felt a pang of guilt. "We'll catch up in a couple of days," I said, "when I'm feeling better."

"Okay." He raised his hand once, then dropped it, backing away. "Sleep well."

I closed the door and returned to the bedroom. Vidar waited, an expression of curiosity on his face.

"Who was it?"

"Gunnar. My friend." I laid the plate on the bedspread. "He'd like to be more than my friend."

Vidar's eyebrows drew down. "What would he like?"

I whipped the aluminum foil off: fish and chips, with Maryanne's special seafood sauce. "He's a nice guy, don't worry," I said. "You're wearing his clothes."

He reached for a chip and tried it. "I like Midgard cooking," he said.

"This is Maryanne's cooking. I promise you mine isn't as good." I sat cross-legged on the bed while we shared the meal. "Now, we need to work out what we're going to do."

He shook his head sadly. "It's too late. I have marked you, now he can find you."

"You need to lay it all out for me, Vidar. The logic of it. You waited for me for a thousand years. What did you think would happen? Didn't you have a grand solution?"

"I had a simple solution. I thought that I would find you, keep you secret from my father, be with you."

"That's it? Just keep me secret?"

Vidar averted his eyes and his voice became soft. "It isn't the kind of secret I could keep for eternity, but we don't have eternity."

It took a moment for this to sink in. Of course. He would live long after I had grown old and died. "You mean—?"

"Only the length of a single human life span. Last time, it all went wrong when I told Vali. This time, I intended to tell no one. The years would pass unnoticed by my family. But I said a rash thing last time; that I would run away to Midgard forever. That is what my father fears so much . . ."

I paused for a few seconds, the knowledge of my inevitable death blistering hot in my brain. A rough wind shook the windowpane, a flurry of raindrops. It seemed I had little time left. Fifty or sixty years perhaps? Half of that as an old lady, full of aches and pains, wrinkled and saggy. Measured against his life span, it was infinitesimal.

"Vidar, you waited a thousand years to be with me for just a handful?"

"Love is eternal," he said, and his words hung in the air for long moments afterward. Gradually I became aware that I had not finished asking him all the questions I had thought of.

"Did you think we'd be together here or in Asgard?" I continued.

"Here. My father would find you in Asgard. He rarely turns his attention here anymore."

"Then what's your specific concern?"

"I've been with you. We've created a spark that he may sense. If he suspects, he'll go to the seeing-water and know everything."

"You didn't think of the spark before?" I said gently.

"I didn't know it. The first time I came, I remembered how vulnerable you were and became frightened. I went to my mother for advice and she told me to beware."

I processed all this as I wiped my greasy fingers on a napkin. "So, how did you know I was here on Othinsey?"

"I sensed you. One morning."

"You *sensed* me. What does that mean? Specifically."

"It's like a prickle of awareness. As though someone is in the room with you that you can't see."

"And you're afraid that Odin will feel this prickle?"

"Yes."

"How long had you known I was back here on Midgard?"

"Since that morning."

"When was it?"

"A few weeks before I came for you."

A light glimmered on in my mind. "Not before?"

"No."

"Not at all?"

He looked puzzled. "No."

I nodded slowly. "So tell me about this seeing-water. Odin can use it to see what's happening here on Midgard?"

"Yes. We all can. I have used it many times to look for you. Then to see you, when you returned to Midgard."

"When I returned to Othinsey," I corrected him. The thrill of possibility bubbled inside me. "Do you not see the difference?"

"The difference?"

I leaned forward and met his gaze. "Vidar, I'm twenty-seven years old. I've been back here on Midgard for nearly three decades. You only sensed me, you could only see me, when I came to Othinsey. Your sixth sense and your seeing-water . . . they don't work outside this island. It's a stepping-stone, like you said, and your father's magic doesn't work beyond it. If you and I got off Othinsey, I bet he couldn't find us."

I could see this sinking in.

"There are six billion people in Midgard, Vidar. There are

vast places you haven't even dreamed about. We could disappear."

"What if you're wrong?" he said. "I share his blood. Perhaps the connection is strong enough to work throughout Midgard."

"But he can only find you in the seeing-water, right? If he doesn't have that—"

"He'd have to come here. He'd have to get off this island, travel in a world where he no longer belongs, find his way through all the continents and all the people . . ." Vidar's eyes were alight. "I could poison Sjáfjord. The water would take centuries to clear. Enough time for us—"

"The boat goes on Wednesday."

"I'll return to Asgard tonight."

The rain set in shortly after nightfall, cold and insistent as we hurried into the forest away from the eyes at Kirkja. I waited under an umbrella while Vidar packed up his camp and saddled Arvak. All the while my chest ached with fear and yearning. The possibility of our being together was too precious; there was so much at stake.

"Please, please be careful," I said as he tightened Arvak's saddle.

"I will. You too."

I nodded. "I'm afraid of letting you out of my sight."

"I welcome the separation if it means we'll be together a lifetime."

I frowned. "Vidar, will you still love me when I'm not young anymore? When I'm a wrinkly old woman?"

He touched my face with the back of his hand. "Victoria, I would love you under any circumstances."

"But you'll stay young and strong."

Vidar seemed bewildered. "All the better for taking care of you when you are old and frail."

"There's a romance in growing old together, Vidar," I said, trying to laugh it off but finding a lump in my throat.

He leaned under the umbrella and kissed me, then said, "Let each season come when it comes, Victoria. Do not fret about winter while spring blooms around you."

I smiled. "I'll arrange everything. Be back by Tuesday night. I'll work out a way of getting you on the boat, even if I have to pack you in a crate myself."

He pulled me into an embrace and I dropped the umbrella in the mud. "Victoria," he said, his breath hot in my ear, "if I haven't returned, you must go without me."

"I know," I said reluctantly.

"If I'm not here, it means things have gone wrong, that you're no longer safe."

"I know," I repeated, more firmly. "I know." I stood back and gazed at him. Raindrops clung to his hair and eyebrows. "But you'll be back."

"I love you," he said.

The ground shifted underneath me as a sick fear of loss swirled in my stomach. "And I love you. Go on. Leave fast, return faster."

He held my gaze a few moments longer, then turned and climbed onto Arvak's back. "Come on, Arvak. Quickly now."

Arvak snorted and sped forward. I saw them plowing between the trees, I saw a shiver of amber and violet light, then they disappeared and I was all alone in the rain with a muddy umbrella and a vague presentiment of ill fate ahead of us.

Twenty-Seven

I returned to my cabin and changed into dry clothes, mulling over possible escape routes in my head. Assuming I could smuggle Vidar onto the boat without anyone knowing, what then? When we arrived in Norway, where neither of us spoke the language, how would I get him to England without a passport? I supposed I could learn Norwegian and try to get by in a strange land, but it would limit my ability to earn us a living. Could Vidar work? Without references, a history, a birth certificate? It looked impossible, but I refused to accept that it was. I did know that I couldn't plan this escape alone, and I paced up and down my hallway seventy-four times before I decided that I would have to ask Gunnar for help. He knew Norway, the language, the systems. He knew about getting cargo on and off the *Jonsok*. He knew about computers and networks and information. And, I was almost certain, I could rely on him not to ask too many questions.

"I thought you were sick," he said, leaning on the open door.

"Maryanne's cooking made me feel better." I smiled. "It's raining out here."

"Come in," he said. "I've got the heater on. It's cold tonight."

"It's always cold. We're in the middle of the bloody Norwegian Sea," I said, hanging my raincoat on the back of a kitchen chair. "Could we have a cup of tea?"

"Certainly, my lady. Make yourself comfortable."

I sat on the sofa, warmed my toes in front of the bar heater. On the scarred coffee table he had a stack of books and drawings. I picked one up to examine it. A Viking warrior. "How come this chap doesn't have horns on his helmet?" I called.

"Vikings didn't have horns on their helmets. It's a common misconception." Cups and spoons clinked. "You can move those papers if they're in your way. Put them on my desk."

I picked up the books and carried them to the bookshelf, then gathered the papers and found I held in my hand the photocopy Gunnar had read to me once, about the day Odin had come to the island. I scanned it, but it was in Norwegian.

Gunnar put a cup of tea in front of me. "Find something interesting?" he said.

"Please read this to me again," I said, thrusting the photocopy into his hand.

"Why?"

"Just interested." I sat on the sofa and cradled my cup of tea. Now that I had access to some of Halldisa's memories, I wondered if Isleif's writings would stir something in me. "That bit about the last day . . . the weather."

Gunnar sat opposite me and, as he read, fragments of memory fluttered light and dark in my mind's eye.

"The late morning grows hot. The children paddle naked

in the water. I have never experienced such a heat, even in the middle of summer. The fires of hell itself could not be warmer."

The little girls calling to each other, playing a game. Me, trapped inside, wondering when Asbjorn would grow tired of this game and let me free to find Vidar. Frustration upon frustration. Sticky heat clinging to me, poaching my eyes.

"At dusk, the heat drained suddenly and sharply, and across the whole island stole a great frost. The trees are white, the lake has frozen over and the ground is covered in crystals."

The creak of heat transforming to ice. My skin cold, my innards yet to catch up. Superstitious murmurings from my mother. I venture a glance outside. Ice everywhere. The first glimmer of fear. Asbjorn slams the door on my fingers. "Stay inside, whore." A distant howl, the wind spinning off the sea.

"It is now dark and there are fearsome sounds in the forest. A cruel wind gathers force and we all huddle inside by the fire in fear of what may happen next."

In the church, Isleif is pale with fear. Hakon screams about letting the blood of one of the cows to appease Odin. Asbjorn clutches his three little daughters to him and prays until his eyes are glassy. Something bangs on the door. Dogs howl, the wind shudders over the roof. "Send the whore outside, that's what they want!" Asbjorn shrieks. Isleif wrenches my arm, throws me out into the storm. At once, the wind drops to an eerie, expectant stillness. I draw a breath. A dark, hulking figure moves in the distance. I see the glint of steel . . .

"Vicky? What's wrong?"

Gunnar was leaning across the coffee table, trying to get my attention.

"Nothing's wrong," I managed.

"You zoned out."

"It's very evocative, isn't it," I said, feigning a casualness I didn't feel. "The description."

Gunnar settled back in his armchair and slurped his tea. "You didn't think so last time I read it to you."

"I've changed my mind." It was suddenly achingly clear that everyone else here at the station was in danger. Vidar and I had to get off the island before Odin sensed us. "Gunnar, I need your help."

He looked at me over the top of his cup and his eyebrows twitched. "You sound really serious."

"I am. I have to leave the island."

"Ah." An expression of sadness lit his eyes and then passed. "Too much of Magnus?"

"Yes, I suppose. And other things. Too complicated to explain."

"Not me, though? I haven't scared you off by asking you to run away with me to New Zealand?"

I smiled and shook my head. "Not you. You're a good reason to stay."

"Have you told Magnus yet?"

"Not yet. If I wanted to get something large off the island—secretly—how could I do it?"

"Smuggling, Vicky? Do I get a cut of your profits for helping? Is it drugs or diamonds?"

I shrugged. "I can't tell you any more than I already have. Sorry."

He sipped his tea and cast his eyes toward the ceiling. "Let me think . . . how large?"

"About as large as a man."

"And how heavy?"

"About as heavy as a man."

Gunnar met my gaze. "I see."

"Please don't ask any questions."

"We have six-foot crates in the storage shed. They came with the struts for the satellite dish. If you were leaving, you could say you needed one to pack all your belongings. You'd put your diamonds in the crate, and you and I would carry it on to the *Jonsok* claiming it's fragile and you don't trust the deckhands."

Six feet. Might be a bit cramped, but I was sure he could endure it for ten hours.

Gunnar continued: "I'll pack up all your things after you're gone and send them to you by mail over the following weeks, so as not to attract suspicion. Tell me, do we need breathing holes for these diamonds?"

"We might," I said guardedly.

"Then we'll have to drill those in before we pack them."

"Can we do it this weekend?" I said. "I want to be out of here on Wednesday."

Gunnar shook his head. "Sorry, Vicky, no matter how well prepared you are, you're not going anywhere on Wednesday."

"What do you mean?"

"Magnus is scared that Maryanne will leave because of the haunted forest. He's canceled the *Jonsok* for this week."

An electric shock to my heart. "He's *what*?"

"He has canceled our supply boat so he can be certain of Maryanne's continued sexual favors. That's just one of the good reasons you can give for your resignation."

"How are we supposed to eat?"

"He's crafty. He ordered a double supply as soon as Maryanne started getting ghost-shy. Blamed it on an administrative error and canceled the next delivery to re-balance the budget."

I let all this sink in, trying to calm myself. Just because the *Jonsok* wasn't coming didn't mean that Odin was neces-sarily going to discover Vidar and me. We'd probably be perfectly safe for another week.

But if Odin did sense us, if he felt that prickle that Vidar had spoken of . . .

Then we were trapped there, miles from anywhere. At his mercy on an island in a freezing sea.

At the fund-raising table tennis match on the weekend, I sat in a corner of the rec hall nursing a plastic cup of rum, glow-ering at Magnus. He glanced once or twice out of the corner of his eye, but continued chatting with Frida and Carsten, his arm around Maryanne's waist. He was pretending he couldn't see me. That idiot was going to ruin everything, thinking with the tiny brain in his tiny penis.

I had been knocked out of the match in round one, trounced by a frighteningly overcompetitive Frida, who had been trounced in turn by a frighteningly overcompetitive Josef. Now it was just Josef and Alex left, lovers in life, bit-ter rivals on the table-tennis court. Since my disqualifica-tion, I had been drinking steadily. The rain hammered on the tin roof of the rec hall, drowning out Gunnar's U2 album. The more I drank, the more anxious and irritated I grew.

"Match point!" called Gordon, who was umpiring. "Come on, Alex, you can beat him."

"I need another drink," I said to nobody, and tottered to the galley, where Carsten had hidden the alcohol in a vain at-tempt to slow me down. I was sloshing some rum into my plastic cup when I heard somebody enter the room behind me.

"Victoria," Magnus said.

I turned and felt my hands automatically ball up. "What?" I asked.

"You've been glaring at me all afternoon. You insist you aren't jealous of my relationship with Maryanne and yet—"

"I'm not jealous," I shouted, and felt the world shift a little to the left. I steadied myself on the bench and advised myself not to act like a drunken fool.

"Then what's all this about?"

"I'm angry at you for being a small-minded control freak."

Magnus blinked at me in shock. Though why he should be shocked was beyond me. Surely I couldn't be the first person to point out this indisputable fact.

"I will let that pass, Victoria, as I can see you've drunk too much—"

"Why did you cancel the *Jonsok*?"

"An administrative error occurred which extended our budget. I merely addressed that error. I'm the station commander, the buck stops with me."

"Are you really thinking about bucks, Magnus? Or fucks?"

"I'm warning you—"

"Warning me? You think I'm afraid of *you*? I've got plenty of other things to be afraid of."

"This is your final warning. I can dismiss you for insubordination."

"Go ahead and dismiss me, then."

A silence ensued while Magnus fought with the redness

in his face and I wondered why I hadn't heeded my own advice about being a drunken fool.

"Victoria, we'll discuss this on Monday morning, both sober, in a work setting." He turned to go. I felt like I would burst.

"Please, Magnus," I said. "Make the *Jonsok* come on Wednesday. I have to get off this island."

He stopped, turned to face me. "Victoria? You're not succumbing to the same superstitions as Maryanne, are you?"

"I want to go home," I said, and my voice shook.

"You're drunk," he said impatiently. "We'll talk on Monday."

"Please, Magnus."

Magnus left without another word and I sagged against the bench with my rum, light-headed and dissociated, wondering what Vidar was doing now. A loud cry of triumph from the rec hall alerted me to the fact that the table-tennis champion had been crowned. Gunnar poked his head into the galley.

"Are you all right?" he said.

"I fought with Magnus," I said miserably.

He approached and put an arm around my shoulders. "You stink of rum."

"I spilled some on my top."

"Vicky Scott, no matter how posh you sound, no matter how many degrees you accumulate, you will always be a scrubber from South London."

"Don't say that."

"Don't worry. Nobody knows it except me," he said, stroking my hair.

I leaned into him, woozy with alcohol and irrationally teary as only drunks can be. "It's true," I said, "there's nothing special about me." Then why did Vidar love me? Why had he waited a thousand years to spend a bare half century with me?

"You don't even know, do you, Vicky?"

"I don't know anything."

"You are so beautiful," he said. "You're funny and complicated and warm and beautiful."

I pulled away. "Don't, Gunnar. You make me feel so sad."

Josef and Alex came in. I sat on the kitchen floor and slurped my rum. Voices whirled around me. I was starting to feel like I could lie down on the cold tiles and lapse into sweet unconsciousness for a few hours.

Josef crouched in front of me. "Vicky? Are you all right?"

"She's just drunk," Gunnar said from far away.

"I'm sad," I said.

"I've got to tell you something. It's going to sound crazy." Josef's smooth white skin and rosy cheeks made him look like a painting to my drunken eyes.

"Go on."

"I dreamed of the hag on last night's shift."

I felt an itch of unease. "And?"

"And before I woke up, she said something to me . . ." He trailed off, as though embarrassed.

I leaned forward, my skin hot with fear. "Go on," I said.

"She said to tell you something . . . She said, 'Tell Victoria that I'm going to tell his father.'"

My heart picked up its pace. I tried to stand but couldn't make my feet work.

"I know it's just a dream," Josef was saying, "but I had such an important sense that I should tell you." He shrugged. "Alex would think it was nonsense."

"I'm glad you told me," I managed, pulling myself up on the bench. "I have to go."

"Vicky, you should lie down." This was Gunnar. The room was full of people, pink faces leaning toward me.

"I'm fine," I said, brushing off their concerned hands and hurrying away. "I'm going for a walk to clear my head."

I burst from the galley into the rainy afternoon, stopped and let the cold water drench me. "Oh, Vidar," I whispered. "Please hurry, please hurry."

The possibility of my ever sleeping again was so remote that I didn't even try. I may have dozed a little in the early hours of Sunday morning, then again for a few hours late on Sunday night. My body was tense the whole time. Was the continuing rain the start of something more sinister? Were the sounds I heard forest animals? Or Vidar returning? Or something far worse, something brutal and hulking and hypermasculine with a gleaming axe and an empty eye socket?

At three o'clock on Monday morning, my light doze lifted and I found myself once again staring at the perfectly regular ceiling of my bedroom. I sighed and threw back the covers, went to the window and gazed out into the forest. The rain had cleared and I could see stars above the trees. It was very still outside, as though poised and waiting for something. Deep shadows sat motionless in the grey gloom. The eerie outline of a bony twig jolted my brain and a very obvious solution occurred to me. Skripi. The hag was his sister. I pulled on my anorak and boots and headed outside.

The ground was sodden, the branches damp and the leaves dripped on me, but I made my way into the forest until I was certain I was out of earshot of Magnus's cabin with nervous Maryanne inside.

"Skripi?" I called, and my voice echoed lonely in the stillness.

Nothing happened for long seconds. I called again. I heard a rustling in the distance and became terrified. "Skripi, is that you?" I said, every muscle in my body poised to flee.

"It is me," he said, ambling out of the shadows to stand ten feet away. "Hello, Victoria."

"I need your help," I said.

His face broke into a smile, his shiny black eyes crinkled and his sharp little teeth were exposed. "I'd love to help you," he said.

I shuddered. It wasn't that he was hideously ugly; it was simply that he was so impossible, a bizarre puppet brought to life. Such things shouldn't be real, and yet they were.

"It's about your sister. The hag."

The smile was withdrawn. "Why do you make me sad by mentioning her?"

"She told one of the others that she's going to report back to Odin about Vidar being here. Odin can't find out. He'd come here and kill me. Maybe kill everybody."

"No, no!" Skripi said, clasping his hands together.

"Can she do that? Can she tell Odin? I thought you were all in exile?"

"She'll use it to get his favor. She'll call up to him."

"What does that mean?" I asked, exasperated by all this supernatural logic, which was not logical at all. "How can she call up to him?"

"We're all his children. He can—"

"Sense you . . . yes, I see. Like a prickle."

"If she concentrates hard enough, she can get his attention."

"She could have done this already?"

"She hasn't. I would sense it too."

"Then how do I stop her from doing it?"

Skripi looked at me, silently, for nearly a full minute. His eyes were round and his brows turned up.

"Skripi?"

He sat down and crossed his legs. "I'm thinking."

I let him think. A breeze licked through the trees and I wished I was inside where it was warm. I sat down with him, immediately regretting it as the damp seeped into my pajamas. I shrugged out of my anorak and tucked it underneath me.

"You see," said Skripi, "I know the answer, but I don't want to say it."

"Why don't you want to say it?"

"It will frighten you."

"I'm used to being frightened."

He nodded. "Then I'll say that the only way to stop the hag is to kill her."

I felt a wave of profound tiredness shudder over me. "I have to kill the hag?"

"It's the only way. She can't be reasoned with."

I wrapped my arms around my knees and leaned my head on them. "How do I kill her?"

"The same way she tries to kill you. Steal her breath."

I glanced up over my folded arms. "You'll have to explain."

"When she puts her lips over yours, inhale very slowly."

"If it's that simple—"

"Nobody ever thinks of it," he said. "They panic and hold their breath, making it a parcel for her to yank out easily."

I sighed and leaned my head down again. I heard a rustle, then felt his cool hand on my hair. I flinched.

"Do not be afraid, Victoria."

"I just want Vidar to come back," I said. "We have to get away from here."

He sat in the mud next to me, and said mournfully, "Oh, yes. How I would love to get away from here too, but I can't leave until Odin says so. Or until my siblings are dead, because it is only their guilt that keeps me in exile."

I felt a pang of sympathy for him. I made room on my anorak for him and he moved onto it gratefully. I inspected him closely, pity displacing my fear. Perhaps he wasn't so bizarre after all. Just because I hadn't known such things existed, it didn't mean that they couldn't.

"How come you can speak my language?" I said.

"I had a friend here. Many years past. He was a scientist like you, and he taught me his tongue. Your tongue. I tried to warn him about the hag, I tried to find him a ward—"

"He was the man that died?" I shivered.

"Since then that room is her hunting ground. If you are afraid, it will be so much harder." He stood and offered me his hand.

I let him help me up and shook out my anorak. "I am afraid," I said. "I can't help it."

"The hag is not as frightening as Odin," he said, his face serious. "Remind yourself of that, and breathe slowly. You have *eolh*. *Eolh* will help to keep you safe."

I nodded. "Yes," I said, "I'll breathe slowly."

But first I had to deal with Magnus.

I dressed soberly and tried to look contrite when I appeared at his office door at 8:00 A.M. Somehow, I had to take the night shift that night, and getting myself fired would be counterproductive. Magnus glanced up from his desk, asked

Carsten if we could have some privacy, and closed the office door.

"I'm sorry, Magnus," I said immediately. "I regret very much what I said and—"

"Then why did you say it?" he asked coldly, standing directly in front of me, glaring down.

"Because I was drunk," I said.

"That's not an excuse. Alcohol loosens people's tongues, but it can't make them say something they don't believe."

I looked up at him and said the only thing I could think of. "Magnus, you were right. I am jealous of Maryanne."

Underneath the frown there was now the hint of a smile. "I see."

"Try to understand. It's not easy seeing you two together. Then when I found out that you canceled the boat to keep her here . . ." I dropped my gaze. "I'm not proud of myself." My face was flushed with humiliation and anger, but I hoped he would interpret that as girly shyness.

His voice was soft in response. "Victoria, didn't you know I'd understand if you just told me the truth?"

"But I'd turned you down before."

"The heart is fickle. Who knows how much longer Maryanne and I will last? And then, perhaps, there will be a time for you and me."

I suppressed a full-body shudder. "Can I go now?" I said.

"I'm glad we sorted this out, Victoria," he said, returning to his desk and making a pretence of businesslike behavior. "Don't let it happen again."

"I won't. Oh, Magnus. Is it all right with you if Josef and I swap a shift?"

"Which one?"

"Tonight's night shift."

"If Josef agrees."

"He has. Thanks."

I closed the door behind me and hurried up the stairs to the control room. Gunnar was upstairs with Josef.

"Is Magnus still mad?" Gunnar asked.

"No. It's sorted," I said.

Josef spun his chair around. "I'm glad you told him off," he said. "He had it coming."

"Josef, can I do your night shift tonight?" I said. "I'm having better luck sleeping during the day at the moment."

"Which shift am I swapping into?" he said.

"Swing," I replied.

"I don't know—"

"Please," I said. "It's important."

Josef met my eyes and I think he knew I was concerned about the message from the hag. He shrugged. "If you like." He turned back to the radar display. "She's mysterious, isn't she, Gunnar?"

"I'm still trying to figure her out," Gunnar replied.

"Thank you. I'm going to bed," I said.

Of course I didn't go to bed. Far from it. I did everything within my power to make myself sleepy but not actually go to sleep. I had to be able to sleep in the control room that night to make the hag come. Luckily for me I could have written a book about insomnia cures. I drank herbal tea; I went for a long walk along the beach; I turned off every thought that came screaming into my head; I breathed slowly all day. When it came time to start work, I made myself hot milk with honey and set about turning off every instrument in the control room that could possibly make a sound that would wake me.

It was eerily silent and dark as I lay on the sofa and closed my eyes.

I couldn't sleep. I had the equivalent of a loaded gun pointed at my head. The hag or Odin. Which one would get me first?

But I had to do it, so I lay very still and counted backward from ten thousand.

Ten thousand, nine thousand nine hundred and ninety-nine, nine thousand nine hundred and ninety-eight, nine thousand nine hundred and ninety-seven . . .

What was Vidar doing? Was he saddling up Arvak, ready to come back for me? I thought about his serious face, felt a flutter of longing. How gently he spoke, how violently he loved me.

. . . nine thousand nine hundred and sixty-four, nine thousand nine hundred and sixty-three . . .

How had my life taken such a sudden curve? How was it that I was preparing to do psychic battle with a nightmare hag, on the advice of a wood wight, to keep secret my reincarnated love for a Scandinavian deity? Under other circumstances I could have laughed. Perhaps one day I would laugh, but now it was almost too overwhelming to bear. I cleared my head and thought about Vidar again. Reliving that last day together, wrapped around each other, warm skin and soft voices.

. . . eight thousand five hundred and twelve, eight thousand five hundred and eleven . . .

I had always known that love was meant to feel that way. Sunshine seemed to drift into my mind's eye, numbers stopped making sense, a warm shiver of memory from the forest, mine or Halla's, I didn't know. The image dissolved, a cool darkness waited beneath it.

A sigh.

I was asleep.

Breathe slowly, breathe slowly.

My body was encased in rock, I couldn't move, I couldn't wake. I heard the door to the observation deck slide open. I forced my breath to be regular, I willed myself to be brave.

"You?" she said, slithering across the floor in the livid night world of the control room. Although my eyes weren't open, I could see her, a cruel sneer curled on her lips. "I thought I told you to leave Vidar alone. Too late now. Odin will be pleased when I tell him I got you."

She climbed onto my chest, her white hair trailing onto my face. My nerves were all singing with fear. This time I knew it was real, this time I knew she could kill me.

Breathe slowly.

Her face descended, her lips peeled back and I could see into her mouth and down her throat as though it were a tunnel into the grave. Her mouth pressed mine, her jaws forcing my jaws open, and she started to suck. I let her have two seconds of my breath, then I slowly inhaled.

We were locked together at the lips; she grunted, I held firm. My breath came back, then hers grafted onto it. She shrieked in the back of her throat as I inhaled slowly and gently. Her breath tasted foul, like old mud and rotting leaves, but I drew it in, gasp by gasp, until my lungs shook. She struggled, she clawed at my face. I pinned her to me, my fingers digging into the rough, damp clothes she wore. Her grasp grew weaker, her breath thinner, her cries softer.

Abruptly, her struggling stopped. Her eyes rolled back and she fell off me and hit the floor with a thud.

I gasped and sat up, fully awake, coughing and choking. The ordinary control room was restored. My eyes were watering and my lungs felt like rock. I glanced down to look for the hag, but saw nothing.

No. I saw a little pile of dust and rags.

I slid to the floor and poked at the pile. It smelled the same as her breath: mud and leaves. I gazed at it, astonished, for a few moments while I regained control of my lungs.

"Oh, my God, I think I killed her," I whispered in the dark.

I brushed the dust and rags into my hands and went to the door, sliding it open with my foot. I released the bundle off the edge of the observation deck and watched the wind carry it away to the north, then sagged against the railing. I realized I was sweating. The fear? Or something else? I checked the digital thermometer on the glass. Twenty-nine degrees.

"What?" I gasped, tapping the thermometer. A misreading, surely.

I dashed inside and switched all the instruments and computers back on. Barometric pressure falling rapidly. Thermometers going out of control. The wind direction reading blinked and wouldn't settle. I stepped out on the deck again and dropped a piece of paper. It blew to the south, in a different direction to the dust I had let loose just two minutes before.

Then, a sound to send electricity to my heart. Thunder, far away. The thermometer now read thirty-two degrees. That afternoon, it had been twenty degrees cooler. I glanced all around me. Lightning shivered under the clouds. The wind picked up in the treetops, tearing them one way, then the next.

The weather had gone mad.

III

No one should speak with certainty of
what is possible for people in love.

—Oddrúnargrátr

III

Twenty-Eight

[Asgard]

On the fifth morning of her stay at Loki's house, Aud woke cold.

She had not returned to Gammaldal to spend her time alone. She feared that the emptiness created by Vidar's love for another would slither inside her and break her heart. Instead, she had found an uncertain solace in Loki's cool arms. He still treated her like a servant; but he was affectionate and sympathetic and teased her only gently, instead of savagely. Aud had been content as far as contentment was an absence of suffering, then the fifth morning had come.

It was not a coldness of the skin and bones, because she was buried deep under blankets next to her sleeping lover and it was midmorning outside. It was a coldness of the heart, as though a cup of icy water had been trickled into her veins. Dread, dark and chill as the grave, descended and she said his name aloud in a gasp.

"Helgi."

Loki stirred next to her. Aud rose and dressed, shivering with fear. Something was wrong with her son; she sensed it in her heart the way that a wolf senses a thorn in her paw. Although forbidden from practicing her Vanir magic, the sensitivity of spirit she possessed was still keen. Helgi was certainly in danger and she could not be still until she knew what that danger was.

"Aud? You haven't stoked the fire."

"I must go."

"Go where?"

"Home. To Gammaldal," she lied, hoping her hair falling forward as she pulled on her shoes would hide her flushed face.

"I thought you liked it here."

"I've been here long enough. I must prepare for Vidar's return."

"I see. And will I get a good-bye kiss?"

Aud had no time to banter with him. "I have to go," she said, and stepped out into the cold morning. Mist lay in the valley and the trees were dim, bent shapes that seemed to mirror her own dread. One foot in front of the other, she started her long journey to the World Tree. Past deep cliff faces that still ran with the previous night's rain, past a thousand mossy trees and rocks, and all the whispering shadows between them. As the mist lifted and the weak sunshine glanced off her cheeks and dazzled the corners of her eyes, she drew closer and closer to the edge of Asgard. The panic twisted up inside her, pushing her forward, forcing out a periodic helpless sob. *Helgi, my Helgi.* If she were with him, as a mother should be with her child, she could protect him from any danger.

That wasn't right, though, because she was the one who had led him into danger in the first place. She was the one who had placed him on Steypr's back, had not managed to hold the reins. Accidents are forgivable in others, but there are no accidents for mothers; only heinous carelessness.

Aud paused at the crest of the rise, gazing far out over the waving grass plains of Vanaheim. If she just kept walking, another half a day's journey, she could see him in the flesh, rather than the pale, teasing pictures in the enchanted crystal. But the consequences were too great. So she descended the stairs and crossed the valley, wound into the intestines of the World Tree and eventually came to the Norns' abode.

"Aud? We were not expecting you," Verda said, glancing up from her loom.

"Helgi," she said, falling to her knees in front of Verda. "I must see him. I have an awful foreboding."

Skuld tut-tutted as she spun, but did not forbid it. Verda fetched the brooch and passed it to Aud, who huddled over it with her heart in her throat. The mist swirled, then the image formed, and Aud cried out.

Helgi, lying on blankets near a fire, eyes closed, skin pale and sweating. Thuridh knelt next to him, weeping. His skinny chest rose and fell, but he was insensible to the world. Mímir was a shadow in the doorway, hovering, uncertain as all men are at births or deaths.

"He is ill!" Aud cried. "No, no. He is ill and he is dying!"

"He is not dying," Skuld said.

"He is! He is near to death and here am I so far from him." She collapsed forward and sobbed. A cool hand touched her neck.

"Aud," Skuld said, "look up. Listen to me."

Aud sat up, gazing at Skuld while sobbing breaths shuddered in and out of her lungs. Skuld rarely left the distaff.

"He is not dying," Skuld said.

"Skuld!" Urd called. "Don't you tell her anything."

"She's not allowed to know," Verda echoed.

Skuld crouched in front of Aud and touched her hair lightly. Her pale eyes were serious. "He is not dying, and he will be well in three days." She held up three narrow fingers. "He will be well and Thuridh will laugh about how she wailed at his bedside. He will wake from this fever and ask for honeycakes. Your son will not die this day, or the next. Your son will be well."

Urd and Verda made irritated noises.

Relief spread through Aud's body. "In truth?"

"I can speak nothing but truly," Skuld said, rising and returning to her distaff.

"Why don't you just tell her everything?" Urd said sarcastically.

"Yes, why stop now?" Verda said.

"Hush, you two. You know I hardly ever open my mouth. Trust me to be wise with my tongue."

Aud palmed tears off her face and bowed her head. "Thank you, Skuld. Thank you."

"Thank me for this advice, Aud. That little boy is lost to you. You ensured that on the day you came to us and made your bargain. Helgi is not your child to mind, to fret over, to keep well and happy. Accept this and you will find some peace." She shook her head as she returned to her work. "I've a good mind to break that brooch."

"No!" Aud cried, clutching the brooch against her chest.

"I won't let her," Verda said. "The brooch is mine because you made the bargain with me."

"Can you not see it makes matters worse for her?"

"At least she only sees the present in it," Urd said, "rather than laying out the future as you just did."

They quarreled for a minute and Aud gazed again at her pale, sick son and reassured herself that he would be well.

"Aud, I hope you understand what I have told you today," Skuld said.

"I have," Aud said, nodding, "but I don't know if I can accept my lot so easily."

Verda held out her hand and snapped her fingers. "The brooch, please. We are busy. Come again in a few weeks. Bring us flowers and something that smells like sunshine."

Aud reluctantly handed Verda the brooch and stood up. Skuld gave her a stern glance but Aud couldn't help smiling in return. "I am sorry to have disturbed you," she said.

"On your way now," Urd muttered.

Aud weaved back through the maze, mulling over what Skuld had said. *That little boy is lost to you.* How could he be when his blood still sang to her blood? How could she ignore a presentiment like the one she had felt this morning?

A sound up ahead made her stop and catch her breath. Normally the passages were silent. It had sounded like a small rock, dislodged by a careless step. She held very still and listened, heard a scuff. Somebody was in the passage.

"Is there somebody there?" she called into the dark.

"Only me," came a mock-frightened voice in return.

"Loki?" Her skin prickled. Had he followed her?

Aud heard the sound of running footsteps and hysterical laughter disappearing ahead of her, and realized that she had accidentally revealed to Loki the home of the Norns.

Loki was two hundred feet ahead of Aud all the way back. If she ran to catch up, he would run too, calling insults and laughing wildly. Finally, she lost sight of him in the forest north of Gammaldal. She slowed her pace and sat for a moment in the grass, gazing above her. The dying embers of the day glowed around her and birds soared overhead on the way to their warm nests. She had a sense that everything important had been stolen from her control, that she had no choice but to surrender to whatever dread thing would happen next. She sighed and leaned her head against a tree trunk, and let a few tears fall for everything she had lost.

Loki detached himself from a shadow and stood in front of her. "Have you given up?"

"Given up what?"

"Our game."

"I don't know of which game you speak. Perhaps it was not a game to me."

"Why did you lie to me?" he asked, and he seemed genuinely puzzled.

"You lie to everyone. Why do you deserve honesty?"

"You are a bad girl, Aud. You are full of secrets, and I didn't know. I thought you were just full of Vanir ill manners." He crouched next to her and dipped his head to look into her eyes. "What did they hold over you that you kept it secret from me?"

"I need no reason to keep a secret from you."

"But they do hold something over you?"

Aud dropped her gaze. "Yes. An image of my son."

"Only an image? That's all they give you, with the power that they possess?"

"That's all."

"So it puzzles me that you hid them all this time. They are nasty old hags and they owe me."

"Loki, if you go to them, they will take away my last link to Helgi."

He shrugged. "I heard Skuld's lecture and your pitiful weeping. Perhaps it wouldn't be such a bad thing."

"It means something to me!" Aud shouted, flinging out her arms. "Do you care nothing for how I feel?"

Loki sat back on his haunches. "There's a temper."

"Don't mock me," she said, rising and heading toward home.

Loki scrambled to his feet and came after her. "Am I not your friend?"

"I don't know. I don't know if you're my friend, or my lover, or my master, or my torturer."

"You trust me so little?"

Aud paused to look at him. "Are you making a joke? What reason have you given me to trust you?"

"I love you, Aud," he said.

"No, you don't," she scoffed, taking to the path again. "What rubbish."

"Yes, yes, it's rubbish," he admitted. "I don't love you. But I do like you. At this moment I like you more than anyone else in Asgard, and that's something."

"If you like me, you'll stay away from the Norns." They were emerging from the trees, and the deep slope near Vidar's house fell away before them. Night had closed in and the first light of the stars glimmered. The carved crossbeams above the gable were silhouetted against the deep sky.

"Now, how can I promise that? I have been hunting for them for so many long years. The hags *owe* me, Aud. Why shouldn't I have what I'm due?" He glanced at Vidar's house. "Come home with me, Aud. We'll talk about it some more."

Aud wavered. Perhaps she could convince Loki not to

collect his debt. Perhaps it was possible that he liked her enough to be considerate.

He leaned close to her ear and licked her face. "Come home with me, Aud," he repeated.

A sound from the east attracted her attention. They both snapped their heads around as Arvak galloped toward the house, Vidar on his back.

"Vidar," she whispered.

"Oh, dear. Not him again." Loki seized her wrist and pulled her close. "You won't revert to pining away for him, will you? Not now you've been with me?"

"He's my master," Aud said, attempting to wrench herself away. "I haven't even prepared the house for his return." The last few days now seemed like a very bad idea.

Loki released her and pushed her forward. "Go on, then. I see it in your face. You're a bitch in heat when he's around."

"I'll come again soon," she said, mindful of the power that Loki held over her.

"I'll make sure of it. It's time I negotiated with Vidar for your company." He urged her forward. "Let us greet him together."

They met Vidar returning from the stables. Aud's breath wedged in her throat to look at him again, dark and serious, his eyes wild. Something troubled him.

"Vidar? I'm pleased that you've returned," she said.

Vidar looked at Loki without greeting her. "What are you doing here, cousin?"

"Aud and I were out for an evening walk together. We weren't expecting you."

Vidar gave Aud a wary look.

"I have been at Loki's the last week," she said. "I haven't prepared for your return."

"I need you to be here tonight," Vidar said. "I have something important I need you to do."

"I want her to come home with me," Loki said, drawing himself up to his full height. "You cannot make unpredictable demands on her."

"And you cannot tell me what I can and cannot do. Aud is my bondmaid." Vidar touched Aud's shoulder gently. "Go inside, Aud. I'll join you shortly."

"You took her from Valaskjálf because they were treating her poorly. Well, now I want to take her from you for the same reason," Loki said. "I'm Aesir too. I've just as much right to command her."

"Aud stays here with me."

"She owes me for the breakage—"

"Forget the breakage. She stays here with me. She won't be returning to you again until I say so. You should leave us now."

Loki's nostrils flared and his pupils contracted to pinpoints in his pale eyes. "Vidar, you anger me."

Aud felt a shudder of unease. Loki had too much power over them both. He had to be kept happy. "I'll go with him, Vidar. I don't mind," she said.

Vidar shook his head. "I need you here for now. Whatever attachment the two of you have formed will have to wait." He spoke as a father might speak to two children, and Aud felt ashamed and annoyed all at once.

Loki relaxed into a smile. "Have it your way, cousin. I shall go." He turned his attention to Aud. "Aud, I've enjoyed our time together, but it seems that Vidar has declared our love forbidden and one shouldn't quibble with authority on these things." He turned and trudged away up the slope, disappearing between the shadowy trees.

Aud watched him go.

"I'm sorry, Aud," Vidar said. "You can go to him soon, but I need your help with something very important, and I need it quickly."

"Of course," she said, forcing a smile. "What would you have me do?"

"Let's go inside," he said, his arm around her shoulders. "I need a meal and a moment to catch my breath by the fire."

Aud cooked potato soup while Vidar unpacked and changed into fresh clothes. She watched him from the corner of her eye, and knew that matters had become desperate for him. When they sat down to eat, he met her gaze and confessed everything.

"Aud, I'm going away soon and I'm not returning for a long time."

"You are going to be with her then?"

He couldn't control a smile, almost boyish in the firelight. "She loves me, Aud, and I love her."

Aud tried to keep disappointment from appearing on her face. "Is it safe to love each other?" she whispered.

"I have returned to make it safe, and I need your help. I can trust you, Aud. You've proven that to me."

Aud thought about Loki but said nothing. "You can trust me," she said, then, before good sense stopped her, "but it pains me that you love another."

Vidar put aside his bowl and crouched in front of her. "Aud, Aud, you are a dear friend, you are a beautiful and accomplished woman . . ."

Tears brimmed. "Don't, Vidar, I can't bear your tenderness."

"I'll see that you'll be safe. You can stay here at Gammal-dal, or you can go to Loki, or I can arrange for you to stay with my mother."

"I have to stay in service to the Aesir."

"I have cousins in the north who would treat you decently."

"Don't worry about me. I will be fine," she said, brushing him off and moving away. "I must pay the price for the deal I made with fate. I have been lucky so far and perhaps I will be lucky again. You said you need my help." She pulled out some mending and settled in a far corner of the room so she wouldn't have to meet his eye.

He paced the floor. "Your family are different from mine, Aud. We have always concerned ourselves with battle, your family knows magic, secrets, mysteries. I need to poison Sjáfjord so that Odin cannot find me on Midgard, but I have no idea where to start."

Aud considered for a few moments. To make magic again would be wonderful, but did she still possess the skills? "It has been a long time since I made any kind of magic," she said softly.

"Could you do it?"

"I'm forbidden from using magic against the Aesir but the seeing-water has been blessed by the giants. It would have little defense against a very simple curse poison."

"And you could make that?"

"I could. It would take several days."

His eyebrows shot up. "Several days? Why?"

"I need to steep the wolfsbane for three nights; otherwise, it won't have the power to infuse the whole fjord. It's very deep."

He tapped his fingers against a carved pillar. "Three days."

"If I go to collect the wolfsbane tonight."

"Would you? I'll come to help."

"I can do it alone."

"Good, good, because I have other things to prepare." He paced again, and she stole a longing glance at his powerful back and shoulders. Had he had the Midgard woman then? Had his long vow of celibacy come to an end? She felt something move inside her and didn't know if it were desire or anger. Still, she was bound to help him now; Loki was an unreliable repository for any secret.

"Three days, then. It still gives me time. Three days isn't so long to wait."

"And then you'll be gone for good?"

"For a long time." He glanced away, wistful. "Mortals don't live forever, Aud."

For the first time, Aud felt a twinge of sorrow for Vidar and his Midgard lover. "Of course." Then she ventured to say, "I'll still be here when you return."

He shook his head, irritated. "I can't think for a moment about my return," he said. "As to who will be here and who won't, it matters little to me. I would rather that you were somewhere else and happy."

Chastened, she put aside her mending and pulled on her cloak. "I'll go for the wolfsbane now," she said.

He didn't reply and she slipped out into the cold evening alone.

Vidar, long used to the suppleness of forever, now felt the pressure of time's passing. There was so much to do. He intended to sit up all night preparing to destroy Odin's seeing-

water, but fell asleep by the fire long after midnight's shadows had lain themselves across the cold grass outside. He
slept too long and had to wait until the following dawn to
make his trip to Valaskjálf.

All was quiet within the great hall when Vidar arrived,
the evening's revelry having given way to the stupor of
drunkards. The weather was mild, the sky still starlit, and the
sea unfolded and withdrew in its ponderous rhythm far
below. Pausing outside his father's home, Vidar was overcome by a tide of melancholy so heavy and deep that it stole
his breath. To be with Victoria, to enclose that soft body in
his arms, to live a life next to her and listen every day to her
tender voice and the warm rhythm of her breathing . . . It
seemed that he couldn't move, seized by the ache of longing, but he had to move, he had to ensure the monster inside
the hulking black building wouldn't discover them.

He unpacked Arvak's saddlebags and drew out a chicken
carcass.

"Arvak, go wait under Odin's window," he said, giving
the horse a pat on the flanks.

As Arvak walked off, Vidar set out for the dog kennel, a
rickety wooden outbuilding in a dirt pit at the northwest
edge of the compound. Odin's fourteen dogs were empty-
eyed beasts, intent only on the pursuit of flesh. Odin kept
them hungry to make them more vicious killers. Any one of
them would happily snap Vidar's hand off at the wrist if he
weren't careful.

Vidar approached the kennel and peered through the
chained gap between the gates at a mass of tangled bodies,
flanks rising and falling in sleep, limbs twitching. Only
Odin could command them, so if Vidar introduced chaos
into the pit, Odin would be compelled to leave his chamber.

He made a low whistling sound under his breath. An instant later, two dogs bounded toward him, snapping and snarling. Vidar took a step back, even though a heavy twisting chain held the gates firm. He pulled out his hunting knife and dangled the chicken between the gates. One of the dogs leaped up to snap at it, setting the chains rattling loudly. Vidar plunged the knife into its throat. Blood spurted.

Instantly, the other twelve dogs were awake, scenting the blood and desperate to find its source. Vidar stood back and watched for a few seconds as they descended on the injured dog and began to tear it to pieces. A din of howling and yelping and barking rose up into the crisp night air, and Vidar sprinted away from the pit and around to Odin's window.

He listened, catching his breath. Movement inside, Odin's low voice grumbling, then the sounds of doors opening and closing. Odin's horn, close by, then disappearing into the distance.

Sagging against the wall, Vidar prepared himself for the next stage of his plan. As long as the dogs still barked he was safe. He eyed the shutter in the window, high up on the wall.

"Arvak, you must hold very still," Vidar said, grabbing his tools and climbing onto the horse's back. "Closer to the wall now, that's it. Now, forgive me . . ." Gently, he rose to a standing position, his feet braced against the saddle. Arvak whickered softly. "I know it's uncomfortable, old friend. I'll try to be quick."

Using his chisel, he removed the nails that held the shutter in place. The opening created was too small for him to crawl through, so he took his saw and widened the window. In his baggage he had a new shutter, purpose-designed to fit the new space, which he would fix before he left so that Odin would never know he had been there.

Arvak shifted in discomfort, and he had to place his hands on the wall to steady himself. "Just a few moments longer, Arvak," he muttered, and the swell of the sea and the cold breeze swallowed his voice. The dogs barked on. He removed the final piece of wood and placed his hands firmly into the opening. He eased himself forward, half-in and half-out of the window as he checked beneath him. A trunk overflowing with furs. He could have asked for a bigger place to land, but not a softer one. He fell forward, landing awkwardly on his shoulder, then stood and took a few moments to scan the room in the dying firelight. Every corner was crammed with riches: furs, gleaming bronze and gold, barrels of wine, glittering bejewelled weapons, oak trunks full of trinkets. Which one was the seeing-water in? His mother had described a crystal bottle. He supposed the best way to find it was just to open trunks and start looking.

A sound from the bed made his heart stop. He snapped his head around to see a woman lying there, almost buried beneath the covers, in a deep drunken sleep. Vidar had never seen her before and assumed she must be one of his father's servants. He didn't know how long he could rely upon her to sleep, but he had to be very quiet.

He began to search. Long minutes passed without any luck. He dropped a bag of dried flowers on the floor by accident and bent to pick them up. At the same time he saw a small flat trunk underneath Odin's bed, and knew instantly that this must be where his father kept his most important and treasured possessions. How to draw out the trunk without waking the woman in the bed?

Carefully and quietly.

He lay on his stomach on the floor and closed his fingers over one of the silver handles and pulled gently. The bed was low; the trunk bumped softly against the wooden frame. Vidar held his breath. The trunk slid out. He opened it and saw the crystal bottle.

"What are you doing?"

Vidar jolted upright, one hand on the bottle. The woman sat up in bed, naked, her hair tumbling around her shoulders.

"Vali?" she asked in a blurry voice.

Of course, this woman had never seen him before and mistook him for his brother.

"Yes," he replied quickly. "Odin asked me to find his finest wine." He held up the bottle.

"Where is he?"

"A problem with the dogs. He'll be back soon. Go to sleep."

She muttered something and fell back onto the blankets, lapsing once again into drunken sleep. Vidar emptied the seeing-water into a flask, then returned the bottle. He checked that he had everything and scrambled back out the window.

"Just once more, Arvak, I promise you," he said, tucking the bottle into a saddlebag and standing to screw the new shutter into place.

The barking was easing off. Vidar finished his work and urged Arvak off toward the cliffs.

"To the beach," he said, guiding Arvak toward the long slope down to the grey sand.

The sky was growing pale as they cantered along the beach, but the sun had not yet broken over the edge of the world. The grey water pulsed a rhythm and petrels swept by overhead.

He reined Arvak in and sat for a moment gazing out to sea. He was so close . . . as soon as Aud had finished the poison, he could take care of Sjáfjord and be gone. Vidar felt as though his heart were permanently in his throat, waiting for something to go wrong. The sun glowed over the horizon and Vidar turned and began to make his way home toward Gammaldal. He paused near the crest of the cliff and glanced back toward Valaskjálf, in time to see a tall figure on a black horse arriving near the stables. Loki, probably coming for supplies. Fortunate that he hadn't arrived ten minutes earlier and seen what Vidar was doing. Perhaps luck was on his side after all.

Aud needed to travel a long way into the woods to find nightshade for her poison, past the stream and the whispers of the wood wights, to the very place where she had first asked Vidar about Midgard. She lingered there a while, mindful that she didn't want to see Vidar return from Valaskjálf. It was growing too painful to witness his desperate passion for another. She wondered if he had slept at all since his return. He looked worn and hungry to her, as though something were eating him from within. The poison was brewing and every time he asked her if there was any chance it was ready yet, she had to tell him "no" and watch the muscles in his body contract with anxiety. He accepted her answer, but grudgingly, leaving her feeling as if it was her fault that poisons—magical poisons at that—took so long to brew.

Aud stopped at a flat, mossy rock on a slope and sat, looking up at the dreary sky. The air smelled moist and green. If only Vidar loved her. If only Loki hadn't so much power over both of them. If only she had never let Helgi ride Steypr. A finger of sunlight prised through the clouds and lit up the leaves. Two of her problems, she had to accept, were beyond her control, but one of them perhaps she could still do something about. Loki. Things had ended so badly the other night. Perhaps if she stopped by to see Loki, she could sweeten him again, make sure he behaved himself. He had told her he liked her, after all.

She picked herself up and, tucking herbs into her bag, wound down the path toward Loki's.

Thin, drooping branches crowded around his house as though trying to claim it. She fought off a pale vine and knocked. A swirl of wind picked up leaves and scattered them across the front path. No answer. She pushed the door open but found the house empty. Then she heard hoofbeats and went outside to wait for him.

"Aud," he said, smiling, "I wasn't expecting you." He was dressed all in black, a gold thread woven around the edge of his sleeves.

"I've had trouble getting away," she said, encouraged by his smile. "You seem happy."

He dismounted and kissed the top of her head. "I'm in a fine mood," he said. "I've done the most hilarious thing this morning."

"What is it?" Aud said, and though she still wore her smile, she felt uneasy. Loki's grin was too wide and his pale eyes were glittering wildly.

"It's so funny, I know you'll love it," he said. A sudden gust gathered leaves from his roof, showering them over Aud and Loki. "I've been out visiting the family. Vidar annoyed me so much the other day, all pious and in love with his mortal woman."

Aud's heart turned to ice. "Loki, what did you do?"

"What do you think?" he said, the smile disappearing. "I told Odin everything."

Twenty-Nine

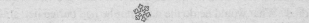

Vidar waded into the water at Sjáfjord while Aud waited on the sun-dappled slope nearby. The poison was ready. At nightfall he would be on his way to Midgard, ready to begin a lifetime with Victoria. He wouldn't see these valleys and woods for many long years.

He stilled himself and waited for the water to do the same. It seemed such a simple thing that he wanted: neither riches nor honor, nor glory in battle. Just love, just one mortal lifetime.

The water became like dark glass around his ribs; he drew the runes and waited.

A vision formed of Victoria, her pale skin and hair; she was talking to two men; she looked anxious. He tried to grasp her words as they hushed and murmured in his ears but he could make out little. He studied her face and thought about what the years would do to it. Yes, she would grow old, and he did not mind. He would love her still, and not an instant of doubt accompanied that thought. Yet, he was haunted by what she had said: *there's a romance in growing old together, Vidar.*

If only he could. If only he could swap an eternity as the son and savior of Odin for a mortal lifetime as the lover of Victoria, with the possibility of children and a warm home for them all. The second seemed to him the richer choice by far, for what would he do when Victoria had grown old and died? What would he do the day after he had buried her, still in his young, immortal body? Return to Asgard and go on?

Vidar closed his eyes a moment and collected his thoughts. It wasn't wise to fret about the future when the present was already fraught with worry. He opened the flask with the poison in it and poured it into the fjord.

The image in front of him clouded over. The poison was working.

The glassy black water began to bubble and froth. From the measureless depths an eddy of anger swirled upward. Vidar realized too late that he was a dangerous distance from the bank.

"Vidar, get out of the water!" Aud cried.

Vidar turned and began to wade toward the grass. The water sucked at his legs and boiled around him. He lost his footing, fell under.

Bitter water filled his mouth. He struggled upward. Around him the water was wild with blurred colors and images, all the things that had been seen in Sjáfjord over the centuries, blending and boiling together. He shot up, broke the surface and began to swim. A rushing sounded in his ears. From the deepest fissures in the fjord, an angry roar was gathering intensity. The furious current threatened to suck him down. Aud was shouting and waving at the edge of the water. He struggled, moved forward a few feet, then was pulled back. Aud's hand was extended toward him, her other hand braced against a rock. His fingers brushed hers. The current caught his cloak and sucked it from his shoulders. He propelled himself forward, caught her wrist.

"I've got you!" she called.

He heaved forward, got the top half of his body over the rock and climbed from the water to sit back and watch. A whirlpool spun behind him. He watched his cloak disappear into it, dragged into the measureless depths. Death had been close; did he fear it? He tested himself, imagining in detail the sour gush of water into his lungs, the black pressure of the fjord on top of him, squeezing out the light. No, he did not fear death. He feared a separation from Victoria far more. He caught his breath.

Aud clutched his arm. A long groan eased out of the water. It began to still.

"Thank you, Aud," he said, panting.

"I thought I'd lost you."

The fjord settled. Its black surface was clouded and dim. Aud glanced over her shoulder, and the sun gleamed in her auburn hair and he realized he would miss her.

She turned back and saw him looking at her, and smiled. "What?" she asked.

"I leave for Midgard at first dark. I will miss you, Aud."

She glanced away, trying to hide a smile. "You'll forget me soon enough," she said, climbing to her feet.

"Wait, Aud," he said, gently taking her wrist, "sit by me a while. I have things I want to say."

Aud reluctantly sat beside him, her knees curled up to her chest protectively.

"Am I really so frightening?" Vidar asked.

She took a deep breath and glanced around her. Then,

seeming to settle on a decision, she met his gaze and said, "I have heard that you were a fearsome warrior in your day, Vidar," she said, "but nobody warned me to protect my heart from your kindness."

"I never sought to hurt you," he said.

"Yet you have," she said quietly.

"For that I am sorry. Have you given thought to what you will do once I'm gone?"

She shrugged. "Can't I stay at Gammaldal?"

"You'd be welcome to, but I fear that an envoy from Valaskjálf will eventually come; and then you won't be safe." He leaned back on his elbows in the grass. A bird hopped close to the water and drank from it, as though nothing had changed. "I have cousins in the north, beyond Idavíd. They aren't very well known to me, but I believe they may be good people if you go to them."

"I'll go to Loki," she said.

"Is that what you want?"

Her cheeks flushed and he realized he'd angered her. "No, Vidar, it's not *what I want*. I want to return to Vanaheim. I want to be with my son. I want . . ." She trailed off, her eyes glazed with tears.

"Aud?"

"I want you to love me, Vidar," she said softly. "You don't. I can't go home. I can't be with Helgi. I made my choice and am prepared to suffer the punishment, so please don't torture me any longer with these concerns for my future, which I can tell are just afterthoughts to you."

Chastened, Vidar bowed his head. His hair dripped onto the rock. "I'm sorry, Aud. You aren't an afterthought."

"But I'm not as important as her."

"I love her."

"Why?"

Ordinarily he would be silenced by such a question, but Aud had opened her heart to him and there could be little harm now in him doing likewise. "She is precious, she is mortal. Her heart beats faster than ours, and her skin is softer, and she arouses in me the tenderest, most passionate, most unrelenting feelings."

Aud's mouth tightened. "I can only wish you happiness then."

"Happiness will be ours for only a short time. Aud, I am doomed to watch her grow old and die. I would exchange anything I had of value to grow old and die beside her." He stopped, uncomfortable with having spoken too much.

"But fate would have it otherwise," Aud said, her eyes drawn to the west.

"Yes."

"We are all slaves," she said, her gaze far away.

"I will leave Arvak in your good care," he said gently. "If you treat him well, he'll always be faithful."

She didn't respond.

He touched her shoulder. "Aud? Are you listening?"

She turned and her dark eyes were serious as they met his. "Vidar, if you could ask the Norns for anything, what would it be?"

His body tensed. "What do you mean?"

"Would you be mortal? Disavow your Aesir blood and be a mortal man, to grow toothless and old and stiff in the joints?"

"To be with Victoria? To father children with her?"

"Yes. Would you?"

"I would."

"Then come with me. I'll show you where they live."

He felt excited and frightened all at once. "Aud, are you sure? Helgi?"

"I'm no longer his guardian, Vidar. Helgi is not my child to mind, to fret over, to keep well and happy. I accept that now."

"Is it not your last pleasure to see him?"

"It has not been a pleasure for a long time."

He took both her hands in his and his mind was too overwhelmed for his tongue to form words of gratitude. Finally, he whispered, "Then, Aud, I will accept your offer and be in your debt until the world's end."

"Come, then," she said, climbing to her feet. "Anything is possible now."

Aud led him so far into the dark beneath the World Tree that he feared she would lose them both in the passageways, but as he was framing a gracious way to express his doubts, a faint glow emerged around the next bend.

Aud held a finger to her lips and took his hand. She led him silently around the rocky outcrop and into the grotto where the Norns lived.

There was a moment of peace as he watched them work, their fingers flying over the glittering rainbow threads. Then one of them glanced up and suddenly everything was in confusion.

"Aud! What have you done?"

"I knew we couldn't trust her."

"This is your fault."

"No, it's your fault!"

"She'll never see that brooch again."

"Sisters! Sisters!" Aud cried, hands aloft as she tried to calm them. "Sisters, I am sorry. Let me explain."

They huffed and muttered, but quieted.

"Sisters," Aud continued, "I am sorry. I don't expect your forgiveness. I'm a wretched creature, but I could no longer stand to see Helgi and be separated from him. I'm prepared to end our appointments."

"This is your fault, Skuld," Verda muttered.

"I knew no good would come of what you told her."

"You should think before you speak."

"Sisters, listen to me, please. I have brought Vidar to you because he wishes to make a request. Whether you fulfill it or not is your decision. I haven't told another soul where you live, and you can move on as soon as we are gone. Vidar is dear to me, and I saw it in my power to help him. I . . ." Aud faltered and Vidar stepped forward.

"I love a mortal woman," he said. Their dim faces were unsurprised in the gloom, watching him by the almost light of the rainbow threads. "I wish to be mortal with her."

"You wish to be mortal!" Urd squawked. "You wish to die?"

Vidar hesitated, a fraction of a moment, then gathered his courage. "I do. At a life's end, as an old man, by my lover's side."

"That will change everything," Skuld said. "You are marked out for other things by your family."

"I have a surfeit of brothers who could take the yoke as well as me, and probably relish it. Give my fate to Vali."

"Or Thor," Aud interjected, glancing meaningfully at Urd. "He would always be grateful to the sister who promoted his glory."

"I am prepared to make a payment, as Aud has," he said, rushing into the thoughtful silence that Aud's comment had aroused in Urd.

"Have you a thousand years to give us?" Skuld said, taking her hands off the thread and pointing a long bony finger at him.

"He can serve his thousand years first," Urd suggested.

"No, no," Vidar said. "I have to be with Victoria now. Tonight." He was growing concerned. It would become dark soon. He had hoped to get away the instant the sun fell behind the world. But the Norns clearly wouldn't be rushed.

"His father's the problem," Urd said knowingly. "After last time—"

"His father is right to be worried if he's standing here telling us he wants to be mortal."

Vidar turned to Aud, and whispered, "How long will it take them to decide?"

She shrugged. "Seconds, hours, it's all the same to them."

"Why can't you stand up to your father?" Verda asked accusingly, her eye fixed on him.

"My father won't listen to reason," Vidar said. "My father thinks with his sword."

"Grant him the wish, I don't care," said Skuld.

"Give his fate to Thor," Urd said. "He might be grateful enough to visit."

"Oh, you are a ninny, Urd. Thor wouldn't be interested in a wizened old fool like you," Verda reprimanded.

"Sisters, please," Aud said. "Vidar hopes to return to Midgard tonight."

"We won't be rushed!"

"We need an hour to decide!"

Vidar slid to the ground and rested his back against the wall. The chill of earth and stone seeped into his body, making him shiver. It would stay dark for many hours. He still had time to cross the bridge. A new fate gleamed up ahead of him, an ordinary, happy fate. "I'll wait, sisters," he said. "What's an hour? I'll lose more than that if you make me mortal."

The hour turned into two as the sisters bickered among themselves in low voices. Aud sat beside him, her eyes fixed on the floor of the cave. She looked young and vulnerable, a childlike confusion coloring her expression. Vidar wished he felt something more than pity for her. He wished he ached for her. He reached out and squeezed her hand. "Thank you, Aud," he whispered.

She offered him a weak smile and a shrug. He wanted to say he was sorry. Instead, he remained silent.

"We have it!" the Norns chorused.

Vidar sprang to his feet. "What have you decided?"

Skuld's fingers were pulling thread up from the floor. "I'm finding it now."

"What do you mean?"

"We've decided to grant your request, Vidar," Verda said.

Vidar's heart lurched in his chest.

"Here it is," Skuld said, her fingertips twitching over an inch of the thread. She looped it over her fingertip and pulled out a small knife. "This may hurt a little," she said, and snapped the blade into the thread.

Vidar felt a jerk inside him, but no pain.

"What was that?"

"That," Skuld said, holding out her palm, "is a little piece of fate. Yours and Victoria's." She held three inches of thread, still pulsing with rainbow colors. "It's connected to all the other things you are fated to do, together and apart, ordinary and extraordinary. And it's enough to change everything."

"For everything will change, Vidar," Urd said. "You are used to your immortal blood. You could walk all day and night now, but only a few hours as a mortal."

"Your joints will ache."

"Your stomach will be at the mercy of whatever food you eat."

"You will grow forgetful."

Vidar, poised on the moment of destiny's turning, grew impatient. "I welcome it all," he said. "Victoria and I must be together, at any cost."

"Take this," Skuld said.

He moved forward and she dropped the thread onto his palm.

"You see that the colors still beat in it," Verda said. "That means possibilities are still in play. Once your new fate is decided, it will turn black."

"What am I to do with it?" Vidar asked.

"Keep it safe," Urd said. "Take it to your father."

"My father? I have to see my father?"

Skuld took up the explanation. "My sisters and I are concerned. We believe you are afraid of your father."

Vidar drew himself to his full height in indignation. "I am not afraid of my father. I am afraid of what he will do to those I love."

Urd tittered. "Oh, he's afraid."

"If you are not afraid," Skuld said forcefully, "then it will be no trouble to take this thread to him."

Vidar bit down on his pride. "What must I do?"

"You must take this thread to him and declare your intention to be mortal. The change of fate will happen upon that moment."

"My father will be angry. He will still go after Victoria."

All three sisters were shaking their heads.

"No, no," said Verda. "Thor will have gathered your fate."

"Odin won't care. You'll be the least-favored of his sons."

"He'll let you go. He'll forget you."

Vidar looked at the thread, so fine and delicate in his rough palm.

"Now listen, Vidar, for this is important," Skuld said. "We will not ask for your thousand years, as you are giving up far more than that in becoming mortal. However, should you misuse the thread, one thousand years is instantly forfeit."

"You are *only* to ask for mortality to be with Victoria."

"Don't you dare change any other aspect of your fate."

"You will not like the punishment."

Vidar was only half-listening, gazing at the thread and trying to slow the rhythm of his blood. "Anything is possible," he said.

"Vidar," Skuld warned, closing his fingers over the thread, "the thread will turn black when your fate is decided. Or if either of you dies."

Vidar's head snapped up. "What do you mean?"

"Death is the end of fate's possibilities," Urd said, almost absently, as she resumed her work.

"When fate is no longer in play, it no longer has color," Verda added, picking up her loom.

"Yes, but why do you tell me this?"

Skuld fixed her pale eyes on him in the dark. "Vidar," she said, "do you know where your father is?"

Vidar's blood chilled in an instant. "My father . . ." With sudden terror, he turned to run back through the labyrinth.

"Wait, Vidar!" Aud called. "You need me to help you find the way!"

He found it by instinct, retracing their steps until fresh air beckoned ahead. He emerged into the first shadows of evening. Black clouds were eating the stars from the east and thunder growled and shuddered down on the hills and valleys.

"No. Oh, no."

Aud burst from the tree behind him, panting. "Vidar? What's wrong?"

The wind howled in the enormous branches above them, the screech of an ancient goddess wronged. Vidar whistled for Arvak.

"Odin," Vidar managed to gasp, handing the thread to Aud who slipped it into her apron. He whistled again. Arvak appeared from the shadows. Vidar searched his pack, hoping until it hurt that this was just an ordinary storm. His hand closed over the flask of seeing-water he had stolen from Odin's chamber.

"Help me, Aud," he said, handing her the flask. The note of despair in his voice set his own nerves loose. "Pour some of this water into my hands."

She handed the flask back, taking charge. "No, your hands will shake too much." She cupped her own hands in front of him. "Go on."

He poured the seeing-water and Aud held perfectly still while he drew the runes.

"Quickly, Vidar," she said. "It runs between my fingers."

Vidar peered close in the dark. Bifrost. Heimdall. Odin on Sleipnir, galloping to the edge of the cliff. He turned, plunged a spear between the two pillars of the Bridge.

"Close it!" he bellowed, though it was little more than a whisper to Vidar's ears.

Heimdall said something that Vidar couldn't hear.

"I said close it!" Odin roared. He turned his back and urged Sleipnir on. "Do not open the bridge under any circumstances. No man shall cross until I return with the woman's head."

Thirty

❄   ❄

[Midgard]

❄

I had never felt fear before. I knew that now. At exam time in my university days, unable to sleep or eat in anticipation of that hushed moment when I flipped the paper over to see what horrors awaited me, that wasn't fear. The time I'd been sitting in an empty carriage on the Circle line in the early morning, when a drunken skinhead had lurched on board and threatened to kill me unless I gave him my purse, that wasn't fear. Perhaps those occasions had been worry, concern, anxiety, but fear was something different.

When I realized that Odin was on his way, fear split open the world around me and let in a bright, sizzling heat. My body felt so vulnerable and helpless that I half expected it to collapse to the observation deck like a straw doll.

I locked the door behind me and took a moment to still my heart and admit some order to my head.

Was it possible, even a little, that this was an aberrant but explicable weather phenomenon? Time grew elastic as I leaned against the back of a chair watching the readouts blinking and bleating in front of me. Skepticism had so long been my default setting that the idea of sounding the lock-down alarm seemed at first preposterous.

The women and children, hanged and burned, like ghastly dolls.

The image came back to me. If Odin was responsible for this storm and sought to repeat history, then other people were in danger too. My skepticism would be no comfort to me if I hesitated too long.

I pressed the lockdown alarm and the siren began to pulse throughout the station and out over the cabins. I pressed my face against the glass and could see lights coming on in windows, wondering what I had started, and whether Vidar would come to help us.

One of the computers beeped and I turned to see the urgent e-notification flashing. I opened it. It was from the Institute, but in Norwegian. I typed "translate" and sent it back. Twenty seconds later it was there again. *Check your readings, Kirkja.*

Presuming they meant the high temperature, I typed, *Readings accurate.*

The white letters flashed onto the screen: *Storm cell size? Bomb system?*

I flicked my eyes to the radar, and my heart jolted. A storm, two hundred and fifty kilometers across, was approaching from the northeast.

"Dear God," I muttered, fingers on the keyboard ready to reply. Then a brilliant flash and a mighty crack temporarily disabled two of my senses. When I opened my eyes, all the computers were resetting, flashing notification that the cable was down. Lightning had struck the satellite dish.

"What the hell is going on?" Magnus roared, dashing up the stairs.

"It's a bomb cyclone," I said, arms helplessly flapping at my sides. "Two-fifty across. It's going to knock us out."

Magnus threw open the door to the observation deck and gazed anxiously at the sky.

Josef and Alex burst in.

"What is it? How big is it?" Alex panted, heading straight for the radar PC.

"They're all out," I said. "Lightning hit the satellite."

The others were gathering. Gunnar dived under the desk trying to restore the computer lines. Magnus put on his best calm voice and told everyone to listen. The lockdown alarm continued to pulse.

"It appears we're in the path of a bomb weather system approaching from the northeast. I don't want anybody to panic, as we're sheltered on that side by the forest and this building is designed to withstand extreme weather. But lightning has taken out our satellite dish and—"

Another flash and a crack. Maryanne yelped with fear. Darkness descended and the siren abruptly cut off. My heart contracted and I began to tremble uncontrollably.

"What happened?"

"Somebody get a flashlight."

A beam of white appeared in the dark and lit up our anxious faces. Gordon strode out to the deck and shined the flashlight down on the generator shed. "It's been hit," he said.

I ran to his side and peered down. The shed was blasted and black, a gaping hole in the roof. "Oh, God," I gasped, forcing breath in and out of my lungs.

"Our generator as well?" Josef said, bewildered.

"I'll go," Frida said, pulling on a raincoat. "I'll get the backup running."

"No!" I cried. "Nobody can leave."

The hysteria in my voice alarmed Maryanne, who touched my hand with icy fingers. "What is it?" she asked.

Magnus peered at me suspiciously. "Victoria?"

"Magnus, can I talk to you?" I said, eyeing Maryanne's trembling face. "In private."

Magnus indicated that everyone else should go inside and slid the door closed behind us. The wind was gathering in power, rushing through the treetops and rattling over the observation deck. The air was thick with humidity and the smell of approaching rain.

"What is this all about?" he asked angrily.

"I sounded the lockdown alarm because I saw someone."

"Someone? Who?"

"A stranger. A man." I reached up to measure his imagined height. "With an axe. I don't want to panic everyone, but I think we're in extreme danger and need to stay locked down."

Magnus ran his hand over his face and dislodged his glasses. "I can't believe this," he said. "First the satellite, then the generator. Now a murderer?" He straightened the frames and squeezed my upper arm. "We have to keep our wits, Victoria. Be an example for Maryanne."

I nodded, my throat too dry to speak.

"Where did you see him and where did he go?"

"I saw him near the instrument enclosure, but then he disappeared back toward the fjord," I lied. "He's big and has a beard and looks really mean."

"How on earth did he get to the island?" Magnus muttered to himself. "Come on, inside. We have work to do to secure the station."

Seven faces waited anxiously for us by the light of a

waterproof flashlight. Magnus held his hands up. "I want you all to be calm. It appears that there is someone on the island with us."

Maryanne slumped into the sofa, her face white. A general murmur passed around the room, drowned out by a roll of thunder.

"Given that we don't know who he is or what he intends, Victoria sounded the lockdown alarm."

"Can't we go out and look for him?" Carsten suggested.

"He may be armed and nobody here is qualified to be a hero. We're scientists. We will do the rational thing. We are going into lockdown, then we will sit in here and wait out the storm." Lightning flashed, momentarily drowning the room in thin blue light. "When daylight comes, we can reassess the situation. Until then, everybody stays inside. Now, let's get to work."

A weird semicalm followed as we made ourselves busy. The black panic that had inhabited me began to withdraw as I concentrated on small tasks: finding kerosene lamps, opening up the linen store for blankets and pillows, helping roll down the aluminum shutters that would protect the windows from the force of the storm, taking charge of arming the rec hall door. The wind's roar intensified and the pines were howling beyond our cocoon of metal and carpet. The violent bang of thunder occasionally shuddered down on us, or lightning would flicker under the cracks of the shutters, but Magnus's plea for us to remain rational was working. We got on with it, and half an hour later we were locked down and hiding in Kirkja Station.

I made an effort to convince myself that the storm was coincidental and not the work of vengeful Norse gods. Physical processes were usually responsible, no matter how extreme the weather. In this latitude, at this time of year, a strong thermal contrast between air masses could develop an intense weather system within hours. Yes, the knocking out of our electricity and communications seemed deliberate, but both were metal and targets for lightning.

The fear continued to bubble underneath. However, until the storm had passed, until morning had come, there wasn't another thing I could do. For the moment, I was safe.

I took refuge for a few silent moments in the female toilets, splashing my face and leaning my sad, tired head against the mirror. My skin looked pale in the glow of the kerosene lamp, which rested on the bench. Where was Vidar? I was helpless. I could do so little here in the mortal world. I needed him to save me, to save all of us, if Odin was determined to repeat history. I had no other resources to draw on.

I slumped to the floor, pressing my hands into the cool tiles and letting helpless tears run down my face. I yearned for him, but I also yearned for life and light and safety. I didn't want to die, but to live without him seemed empty.

The door banged open, making my blood jump. It was only Maryanne. She registered that I was crying and began to cry too.

"Oh, Vicky, what's happening?" she pleaded, sinking to her knees next to me and clutching at my hands with damp fingers.

"It's all right, Maryanne," I said. "We're safe in here."

"How did somebody get on the island? It's not a real man, is it? It's a ghost or a demon."

I hesitated too long before answering and her face crumpled.

"I should have gone months ago. When you first arrived.

That's when it all started happening. I'd only heard the ghosts once or twice before then, but something in you triggered it off." Her words tumbled over each other. "Now it's too late. They're angry with us. He's going to kill us, isn't he? The demon? Is there more than one? You'd tell me, wouldn't you?"

A gust buffeted the building, shaking the walls. The shriek of the wind in the trees was unearthly, like one of Maryanne's demons wailing for revenge.

"Maryanne, hush," I said firmly. "I'm frightened too. But we're safe in here, and if you can stay calm until the storm has passed and daylight comes—"

"Then what? You know what comes after daylight? More night. More shadows for them to hide in and wait for us."

My stomach hollowed. She was right. Odin wouldn't simply disappear once the sun had risen, nor lose interest once a day or two had passed. He would hunt me until he found me and killed me.

"We might be able to get the satellite fixed and call for help," I managed.

My fear ignited hers and she fell into helpless weeping.

"Come on, Maryanne," I said, pulling myself to my feet and offering her a hand. "You must pull yourself together."

"I don't want to die," she sobbed.

I reached down and helped her up. "You won't."

"What if he tries to get in?"

"He can't," I said forcefully. "Let me take you to find Magnus. He'll make you feel better."

I left Maryanne with Magnus and Gordon, and went in search of Gunnar. Alex and Josef had dossed down on the floor of the control room; Carsten and Frida had unlocked the old tearoom and were attempting to make hot cocoa with tap water. Gunnar had colonized a space under the stairs, filled it with blankets and pillows, and was reading a book by the light of a torch.

"Just like being a kid again," he said as I slid down beside him.

"You'd better preserve the battery. Might be a while before we get the power back on," I said, switching off his torch. The only light came from between the stairs, which formed bars of shadow across us. "Gunnar, can I ask you something? A hypothetical? Would you sacrifice yourself for the good of others?"

"That's a tricky one. Do you mean would I die for a cause?"

"No, much more mundane. If people . . . friends of yours, were in danger . . ." I trailed off, unsure how to finish the question without giving away too much.

"Vicky?" he said.

"It doesn't matter. It's a stupid question."

"I think that good people know the right thing to do at the right time," he said. "Does that answer your stupid question?"

"Maybe," I said.

"What's this all about, Vicky?"

Hail had started pounding the roof, as though stones were being hurled down on us. "I'm frightened."

"There's no safer place to be in a storm than locked inside a weather station."

"It's not just the storm. Remember the missionaries? The extreme heat?"

"Yes."

"It was thirty-two degrees before the storm started."

"But there hasn't been a frost. And the high temperature

probably had something to do with the thermal movement."
He smiled at me. "Vicky, I had no idea that stuff had worked
its way so far into your imagination."

"It seems so real," I said, but my voice was drowned out
by thunder.

"It's just a storm, Vicky," he said.

"And an axe-murderer."

His voice dropped to a whisper. "Did you really see an
armed man?"

"Gunnar . . ." I turned on my side to examine his face in
the dark. "No. But I'm almost certain he's out there, and it's
too great a risk not to lock down."

"Is it the man you wanted to smuggle off the island?" he
asked.

"No."

"But he's got something to do with him?"

"Yes." I held a finger to his mouth. "Don't ask any more
questions. I can't answer them."

"Yes, you can. You can tell me anything. I won't judge
you."

His gentle assurances disarmed me. I closed my eyes and
said, "It's such a mess, Gunnar. I don't know where to start."

"At the beginning."

I weighed up my story in my mind, and tried to draw
from it the important threads and separate them from the supernatural details which would have Gunnar thinking I'd
lost my mind.

"I've met someone, Gunnar," I said. "His name is Vidar
and he's been here on the island. I can't tell you how he ar-
rives and leaves, but he's trying to escape from his family."

I opened my eyes and Gunnar's gaze was locked on mine.

"His father is here," I said. "At least, I'm almost certain

he is. I've seen the signs . . ." I laughed self-consciously. "It's all a bit cryptic, isn't it?"

"You're in love with him, aren't you?" Gunnar said. "I can make sense of a lot of things you've said and done lately if it's love."

"Yes," I said. "It's love. I'm sorry."

"Why are you sorry?"

"I know that you . . . you know . . ."

Gunnar sat up and hugged his knees. "It's all right. I don't love you, Victoria," he said. "I thought it might be possible one day, that's all. I've not known you that long, and I'll miss you sorely when I go, but you haven't broken my heart."

"I'm glad." I knew he was lying.

"Are you sure you can trust him? Vidar, I mean."

"Oh, yes."

"Your plan was to help him get off the island."

"Yes, and take him where his family can't find him anymore."

"Are they really so bad?"

"His father is insane and violent. We're all in danger." I dropped my gaze. "But it's me he wants."

Suddenly, a bright torch beam was shined into my face from between the stairs.

"Is that right?" Magnus said. "Victoria, perhaps you'd better come out of there and explain yourself."

Maryanne hovered by Magnus's shoulder, glaring at me as though I'd betrayed her. I crawled out from under the stairs and opened my mouth to explain, but found no words for it. Gunnar was beside me. He reached for my hand, but I gently pushed it away. The others had gathered on the staircase to listen.

"You *know* this person?" Magnus demanded. "There's a violent, insane man with an axe on the island with us, and you *know* him?"

"I don't know him," I blurted. "I know *about* him."

"I heard you tell Gunnar you were going to smuggle him off the island."

"No, that was somebody else."

Maryanne's voice rose to a shriek. "She said the demon wants her, not us. We're safe if she leaves."

Magnus's voice took on an exasperated tone. "Maryanne, for the love of God, will you calm down. There's no demon, and I'm not going to put Victoria outside in the storm. I just want to—"

His words were abruptly cut short by a frantic banging on the main door. Everyone froze, my knees shook.

"What was that?" Maryanne gasped.

"A branch hitting the door?" Carsten suggested.

The banging again, then a hideous bellow, half-animal half-human.

"What the hell?"

"It's him," I breathed, clutching at Gunnar's sleeve, fear hot in my stomach.

Then, rhythmically and violently, a *thud-thud-thud* against the door.

"He's trying to get in."

Magnus shook his head. "It's just a branch, Carsten's right."

"Magnus, didn't you hear the—"

"It's a branch!" Magnus screamed, and his face flushed deep red.

"There's somebody out there." Josef raced down the stairs and across the floor to the door.

"Don't open it!" I screamed.

"Of course I'm not going to open it," Josef said. "And neither can he get it open. It's double-reinforced iron. I'm just going to take a look." He indicated the spyhole in the door, then turned to peer through it. "There's nothing there," he said.

The relief in the room was palpable.

I hurried to the door and pushed Josef aside, pressing my eye to the spyhole. I saw a mad fish-eye view of the world outside, the swinging trees and the cabins all silent and drenched on the slab. My heart began to slow.

Then, glass smashing around the other side of the building. The office.

Maryanne screamed, "He's going to kill us."

"Stop it, Maryanne, stop it," Magnus shouted. "He can break the windows, but the shutters will keep him out. The entire admin building is secured."

A howl from the broken window. I peered around the corner, saw three meaty fingers hooked around the shutter, blood dripping from them.

"*Láttu konuna fara út!*" he shouted. He shook the shutter, it rattled but didn't budge.

"What is he saying?" Alex asked over the din.

"Send out the woman," Gunnar translated.

"Then send her out!" Maryanne shrieked.

"We're not sending Vicky outside to confront a madman," Josef said.

"Victoria, do you know this man?" Magnus demanded. "What have you done? Are we in danger? Why is he here?"

"Listen!" Alex said sharply.

We grew quiet and listened. The shutter rattled furiously. Behind it, nothing.

"The rain's stopped," Josef said.

The rattling ceased abruptly, a weird silence. Not only had the rain stopped, but the wind had died down and the thunder and lightning had ceased.

"That's not possible," Gordon said.

"Upstairs," Josef said. "The observation deck."

"Don't open any doors," Maryanne called.

"I'm not going to open the door," Josef said irritably as he clattered up the stairs, Alex and Frida on his tail. "I'm going to pull the shutter."

Smash.

Another window in the office. I jumped. My teeth hurt.

"Oh, God, oh, God," I said.

"It's all right, Vicky," Gunnar said. "Magnus is right. We're safe in here."

The rattling started again, the incomprehensible shouting. I looked at Gunnar and he seemed very young and vulnerable.

"Magnus, you have to see this," Josef called from upstairs.

Magnus and the others left; I followed, then paused at the top of the stairs.

Josef and Alex had manually rolled up the shutters on the glass doors to the observation deck. Above us, the clouds were dissolving. I could see stars.

"This is insane," Gordon said. "The storm is melting into the sky."

"I've never seen anything like it," Magnus gasped.

Frida's nose was pressed against the glass. "What is

that?" she asked. "Like a white shadow creeping across the grass."

My shoulders tightened.

Magnus shielded his eyes and stared for a long time before turning and saying what I knew he would say. "It's frost."

I folded my arms around my middle. "This can't be happening," I said, but nobody heard me, so baffled were they with the weather. I stole down the stairs, where the smashing and shouting continued. My stomach felt like water. I unlocked the door to the rec hall carefully, lifted the bar and slipped out.

The rec hall was cold and empty, and very silent without the fridges and freezers running. I stopped for a moment to gather my courage. Maryanne was right. Odin wanted me and, hopefully, once he got me, he would leave the others alone. I still held out hope that Vidar wasn't far behind him, but I couldn't allow Odin to beat down the door and slaughter everyone.

But to be so brave was almost impossible. I hesitated in the galley for nearly two minutes, then decided I had to move *then*, immediately. I steeled myself and opened the door to the outside world to meet my fate.

Thirty-One

The whole world had begun to freeze. The chill shimmered over me as I stood, peering into the darkness. The ground was carpeted with frost and the raindrops on branches had solidified to silver. Silence upon silence, so eerie after the bang and clatter of the storm. Then, the faint groan and creak of the ice contracting.

A shadow at the main entrance. Odin.

Electricity shot to my heart and I started to run toward the forest. Gunnar had called it a good place to hide, and Vidar had proven it. Perhaps I could elude him long enough for Vidar to arrive. My heart thundered in my ears, but I could hear the monster behind me, roaring in his strange ancient language. I had a hundred feet on him and plunged into the dark of the trees before he could catch up. I pressed myself against a tree trunk and tried to stop my body from trembling to pieces.

It simply isn't possible to escape him.

The searing realization nearly knocked me to my knees. In that instant, waiting for him to find me, I didn't know whether to run, to hide, or to give up. I hated every option, and I could hear his footfalls drawing closer.

A cold hand clamped around my ankle and I gasped, then was pulled to the forest floor. I found myself staring at Skripi. He dragged me behind a fallen log, finger to his lips to indicate I should be silent. My hands were cut by broken twigs and my clothes were soaked and freezing. Violent shudders shook me. Odin drew closer. I shrank back against Skripi and wished he was more than a scrawny wood wight. My pulse pounded in my head. He moved into sight, a bare three feet away, huge and powerful as a bear, his features hidden in shadow.

Then he walked right past us.

Skripi leaned against my ear. "Don't move," he whispered. I didn't. I was perfectly still for two whole minutes, and would gladly have remained still for two hours, but Skripi eventually roused me, and said, "We're safe for now."

"How did he not see us?" I whispered.

"His left eye," Skripi said. "It's missing. If you stay on his left, he can't see you. We must be very quiet. I'm taking you back to my hole."

I didn't want to risk Odin's hearing us by asking for clarification. I just rose to my feet and followed him.

"No, no!" Skripi hissed, turning on me. "You are too loud. He will hear."

I thought about Vidar teaching me to move silently in the woods. *Your feet have to be as sensitive as your hands.* Although he had warned me against removing my shoes, I couldn't see any other way to be as silent as Skripi demanded. I stopped and slipped out of them. With one in each hand, I began to walk.

The cold was excruciating, but I could feel every twig

and pebble beneath me and negotiated my way over them quietly.

Skripi and I crept through the trees like two ghosts, while the frost spread its wintry fingers over everything. The stillness remained unbroken, as though the forest held its breath. My feet ached from the cold and were bruised on sharp pebbles. At any instant I expected Odin to burst from the trees, axe raised over his head to split me in two. The night took on a surreal cast, as though I were watching myself in a movie. It was 4:00 A.M., with frost and a monster chasing me. Skripi turned and pressed his finger to his lips, and I felt so removed from reality that I nearly laughed.

"This way," he whispered, indicating a hole at the base of a tree trunk.

"What?"

"My hole," he said.

The tree was tall and broad, and two of its roots spread apart four feet before disappearing into the soil. The gap between them was black and empty.

"We're going in there?" I asked.

"Shush. Follow me." He crouched and disappeared into the hole. The scent of smoke tickled my nostrils. My feet throbbed. Skripi's head popped out again. "Come on, Victoria. There isn't time to wonder."

I knelt and poked my head into the hole. It led into a tunnel. Skripi was scurrying ahead of me. I followed him on all fours. There was light down there, and smoke drifted toward me. The tunnel opened out into a sort of room about four feet high and ten feet wide. I sat back on my haunches and looked around me.

Skripi's home was a subterranean cave, not tall enough to stand in, but certainly large enough to hide in. The floor was covered in mats woven from pine needles and animal fur, warm and soft. The walls were stone, but hung with more mats. The room was circular and pots, pans, sticks and stones were piled up against the walls. It looked like a cross between a medieval kitchen and an animal's den. Skripi threw a log on the fire and it flared to life. Smoke began to fill the cave and I coughed.

"The smoke disappears slowly," he said, kneeling next to me and pushing me onto my back. "Put your feet near the fire, Victoria. Poor things." He clicked his tongue. "Your right foot is all scratched up. I'll fix it for you." He disappeared off down another tunnel and returned a few moments later with a pot of sweet-smelling ointment. He sat near my feet and rubbed it into my skin.

I propped myself up on my elbows. The coldness was withdrawing from my body and the ointment was numbing the pain in my feet.

"Thank you," I said, because I didn't know what else to say and manners always prevail in the strangest of circumstances.

"Thank *you*," Skripi said. "You killed my sister."

The battle with the hag seemed so long ago that I wondered momentarily if I had dreamed it. "I guess I did," I said, and once more experienced the odd sensation of swinging out of my body to watch myself from afar. "I feel weird," I said, pressing my hand to my forehead.

"Lie back," Skripi said.

I did as he said and stared at the roof of the cave while he massaged my feet. Over and over, I tried to make sense of what had happened to me that evening. The hag, the storm, Odin at the door, hiding in the forest. I replayed it and replayed it in a loop, afraid that if I stopped thinking of it I would lose my connection to reality forever and be cut adrift into madness.

Skripi's hands left my feet and he came to sit near my head. "You are safe for now, Victoria. What is making you so pale and fearful?"

"I wish there was an ointment for what's happening in here," I said, tapping my forehead, unable to steady my voice. "I've seen things that I never thought I'd see."

"You're frightened."

"Well, obviously."

"It's more than Odin being here that frightens you. It's the thought of Odin being anywhere, of him existing at all."

I couldn't answer. Instead I sat up and stared at the fire. I took sidelong glances at Skripi, trying to make his odd face and features more familiar. "How certain are you that Odin won't find us here? Won't he smell the smoke?"

"Odin has no skills in tracking or in staying quiet. He has always relied upon force and the wits of others."

"Can he sense us? You know, the prickle you told me about?"

Skripi shook his head.

"Are you sure? If the hag could call up to him, surely he must be able to zero in on us somehow."

Skripi crawled over to the other side of the cave and began searching in a sack made of leather. "Would you like something to eat?"

"Why are you changing the subject?"

He held up two pieces of dried meat. "Dried fish or dried rabbit?"

The thought of either turned my stomach. "Skripi, why don't you answer me?"

He dropped the pieces of meat by his sides and his oily

eyes became round and pitiful. "Don't be angry with me, Victoria. It was only a little lie."

"Lie? What lie?"

"The hag. My sister. She couldn't . . ."

Confused as I was, it took me nearly thirty seconds to catch on. "She couldn't what? You mean she couldn't . . . she couldn't have contacted Odin to tell him about me and Vidar?"

Skripi hung his head in shame.

Anger flared. "Then why the hell did you tell me that? I risked my life to suck her breath out!"

Skripi put his hands up in front of him, his spindly fingers reminding me of the rune on the stone around my neck. "I had to, Victoria. I couldn't kill her, because she only appeared inside the building and I couldn't get in. And you've protected your own kind by killing her."

I sagged across my own knees. "Don't pretend you care about my 'own kind.' You did it for yourself. You told me you can't go home until they're both dead."

Skripi crawled across the floor toward me. "It's true, but if you'd ever seen Idavíd, even once, you'd know why." He sat beside me. "You can still trust me to keep you safe, Victoria."

"But for how long? I can't hide in this hole forever. Is there any chance at all that he'll give up and go home?"

Skripi's eyes grew sad. "Odin has no mercy in his blood."

"I was afraid of that."

"But Vidar will come." Skripi's voice dropped to a gentle whisper. "This is all about Vidar, isn't it? All the horror and the pain. To give yourself to him?"

I sighed. "Yes."

"And if it works? If he overcomes his father?"

"We'll be together," I said, superstitious now about naming my dearest wish.

"That would make you happy?"

"For the rest of my life."

"Returning to Idavíd would make me just as happy," he said. "You see?"

I met his gaze for the first time, without flinching. "I see, Skripi."

"Lay your head in my lap, Victoria. I can take away your worry and you can sleep."

"I doubt that I'll sleep," I said, resting my head in his lap anyway.

"Close your eyes. I'll tell you stories of Idavíd."

I closed my eyes. He had a strange smell about him. Not unpleasant, like the smell of wet fur on a beloved pet.

"Imagine you are a bird," he said. "The air is full beneath your wings and you slice through the sky like the edge of the moon cuts the night. You look below you and see a green so wild and deep that it makes your heart ache. Mist hangs still around the treetops and collects in the valleys and you dart down through it and into the trees. The shadows are long and dark, and only a little sun breaks through to make patterns on the ground."

Miraculously, my anxiety was easing, as though Skripi's words were medicine to my mind.

"Inside the wood is the bustle and thrum of life, of my kind making their homes among the trees, of our children playing in the long grass and running down to the lake to swim where the sunshine can find them. So imagine now that you are a fish, and you slip into the water with a flash of your silver tail. Beneath the surface are graceful drifts of weeds pulsing in the watery sunlight and schools of fish darting around in patterns. The water is cool and clear. Come out of the water and walk on four feet; be a squirrel and climb high up in a tree because winter is coming and the sky is grey; snow pitches down and ice hangs on the branches but the pines stay green, so even the glittering white carpet of the cold season can't hide the wild color."

He stopped for a moment, then dropped his voice to a whisper. "But there is more. Magic lives in Idavíd. Imagine yourself in your own body, standing between the trees on a mild spring day. If you close your eyes and hold your breath . . . do you feel it? The pulse of magic throbbing between the trees. Spiders spin their webs and catch the energy on the silver threads. The forest is alive with it. And we are right there at the center of Asgard, right in the heart of the land, and the Aesir don't know about the magic because they have never stopped for a moment to close their eyes and hold their breath."

For a long time I waited for him to speak again, listening to the crack and pop of the fire. He stroked my hair, and said, "Sleep, Victoria. Vidar will be here soon, I know."

Vidar. Thought of him drew a smile to my face and I slept.

It seemed I slept for a long time, and I woke ravenously hungry and with a bursting bladder.

"What time is it?" I asked, sitting up groggily. "I'm hungry."

"It's late afternoon," Skripi said. "I'm making you food."

"I need to . . . you know . . ."

"You'll have to go up to the forest. Be very careful."

The fear crept back into my body. I pulled out the

runestone around my neck to show him. "Is this any use to me out there?"

"*Eolh* is little protection against Odin."

"Then it's useless?"

"Almost." He shrugged. "Odin is mighty."

I hesitated.

"Go on," he said. "Quickly."

I crawled back up the tunnel until I saw daylight ahead of me, paused near the opening and peered out.

The world had turned white. Frost laced the undergrowth and the trees were encased in silver-white like frozen giants. The sun glinted off the ice and frost, making diamonds. It stole my breath, I had never seen anything so beautiful and so terrifying.

I listened for Odin, but heard only the sea, faint and far away, and the gentle creak of the ice. I quickly climbed out and relieved myself, then hurried back down into Skripi's hole.

He put a bowl of soup in front of me, but the shiny floating black things in it drove away my appetite.

"You told me you were hungry," Skripi said, sitting cross-legged next to me.

"I was."

"Try to eat something."

I tasted the soup bravely and tried not to think about what was happening above ground. What if Odin became so annoyed at not finding me that he went back to the station? Would the doors hold him off forever?

"This is such a mess." I sighed. "I can't see a way out of it."

"Let us wait. Vidar will come for you. He's a powerful man with the blood of giants."

"Really?"

"So the stories tell us. He will save his father from the jaws of Fenrir." Skripi smiled, his face creasing into uncanny shadows in the firelight. "There is another story about Vidar. About how he renounced his family for the love of a mortal woman."

I smiled too. "I can't believe it's me," I said. "I don't believe in anything. Or, at least, I didn't. And all along—"

"Once you've known a great love and lost it, it's easier to condemn happiness than it is to believe it will come again." He cast his eyes downward. "That's what my siblings did. When we were first sent here, they swore they didn't want to return home, but I never gave up hope. And now, thanks to you, I'm a little closer to my dream."

"Well, I'm not beheading the draugr for you," I muttered.

"No. But Vidar is coming."

I couldn't help but smile. "Ah, I see. All this concern isn't just for me."

"I do care, Victoria," he protested earnestly. "We help each other."

"Yes, we do. Thank you. And thank you for the soup. It's delicious. Just don't tell me what's in it."

I lay down on the soft floor in front of the fire after our meal, and Skripi sang me songs of Idavíd and I thought about the future, waiting for me just beyond this trial. If Vidar came, I could be safe. Somehow, maybe, we'd be together. An ache of longing overcame me, curled up like a forest creature underground, a longing for something that I had known and then lost. Slipping away and slipping away from me.

Hours passed, Skripi didn't tire of singing. Then,

abruptly, he stopped. His head cricked to the side, like a bird listening for something.

"What is it?" I asked. My tired heart wanted to race but hadn't the energy.

"I felt a shiver."

"Odin?"

"No. A shiver in the night. Bifrost has opened."

I started upright. "Vidar?"

"I hope so."

I pulled on my anorak.

"No, Victoria. We can't go out. We'll wait here for Vidar to find us."

"I have to see him."

"But Odin—"

"I have to see him before he does something foolish." Such as agree to go home with Odin and never see me again.

"Victoria, it's not safe."

"I don't want to lose him!" I cried, turning on Skripi. "You don't have to come with me. I'll be careful. I'll stay on Odin's left, I'll move silently. Vidar will be looking for me, I know it."

Skripi touched my hand and I felt that unearthly calmness emanating from him. "I won't stop you," he said. "May good things come to you. And should you and Vidar have a chance to speak, ask him about the draugr."

"I will. May good things also come to you."

I crawled up the tunnel and emerged into the early evening. Lights from far away filtered through the trees. The electricity was back on at Kirkja. This knowledge gave me confidence. Yes, Isleif and his followers had succumbed to Odin's power, but this was the twenty-first century.

I climbed to my feet, looking right and left, watching the

fog of my breath disappear into the dark. My bare feet were frozen, but I couldn't be quiet any other way. Which direction? Vidar usually camped near the northeast. I took two steps. A noise behind me stopped my heart. Before I could turn, a massive meaty hand had clapped onto my shoulder and wrenched me around.

I found myself, for the first time, face-to-face with Odin.

Thirty-Two

[Asgard]

Vidar watched the water run between Aud's fingers. He was numb with shock.

"I'm sorry, Vidar," Aud said.

"It can't be."

Aud tried to touch his hand but he flinched away.

"It can't be!" he screamed to the stormy sky. Already, as Odin left Asgard, the clouds were drawing away, the branches of the tree began to calm, but in Vidar's blood the storm continued.

"I'm going after him," he said.

"You can't. He's closed the bridge."

"I'll make Heimdall open it."

"How? Reason with him? It's too late, Vidar."

"It's not too late," he roared, turning on her. "Where is the thread?"

Aud pulled it from her apron and held it out on her palm. "Here."

"You see, the colors still shine. Fate is not decided. She is not dead."

"Stop to think, Vidar. Heimdall is a mighty warrior, used to fighting off giants who want to cross Bifrost. Even if you picked up a sword, you couldn't defeat him. Victoria is easy prey. Odin will find her and it will be over."

"Don't say that! Victoria is intelligent and resourceful. She knows the signs, she'll be on her guard. It's not like the first time, when they only had a church to hide in. Their buildings are made of metal and stone; they have locks that no key can open. She'll wait for me, she needs me."

Aud shook her head; the clouds dashed and dappled over the moon to illuminate her pitying face. "Vidar! The bridge is closed, Odin is in Midgard, Heimdall is undefeatable. You must accept it."

Vidar's eyes drew downward to the tangled roots. Down there, a thousand years ago, he had buried his sword in the tree with a violence known only to those who disavow a hated part of themselves.

"I am sorry, Vidar," Aud said.

And deep in the fens of Jotunheim, Jarnvidja was raising a wolf named Mánagarm with teeth and claws that were certain death to Aesir.

He turned to her and grasped her upper arms. "Aud, I accept nothing. Will you help me?"

She looked surprised, perhaps even frightened. "Yes, of course. But I think—"

"She'll be safe until I get there, I know it. I have to circle a little way around the tree. Wait here and mind the thread for me. It may take me half an hour."

Aud looked puzzled, but nodded and waited.

Vidar began to move around the huge trunk, eyes flicking over the knots and roots to find a familiar mark. Aud was right. He would never defeat Heimdall with his own

swordsmanship, especially as it had been a thousand years
since he had felt the weight of Hjarta-bítr in his hand, but if
the troll-wife could be bullied into giving him just one of
those poisonous teeth, he would be formidably equipped to
force the bridge open. Fleetingly, he felt a shiver of guilt.
For love, he had sworn away from violence, but this night he
had more fears than hopes. The bark of the tree was rough
beneath his palms as he traced his fingers over its swollen
curves. Aud disappeared behind him. The tree had changed
and grown in the last thousand years. The roots were a
snake's nest of confusion. He peered into the shadows.

To kill would not be necessary; to persuade with threats
would. There would not be time for him to win Jarnvidja
over with his story, as he had won Hel over all those years
ago. Although he believed Victoria would be safe in the
short term, locked in that steel box, Odin's anger would in-
tensify the longer he was frustrated in finding her. He was a
powerful man, and cunning when sober. The journey to Jotunheim and back would cost Vidar most of the night. He
crouched and leaned into a gap in the roots. He remembered
a curious knot in the wood, like an old woman's face, but in
this half moonlight all the knots and twists of the tree were
grotesque faces.

Then the clouds parted on clear sky and the moon's full
brilliance frowned down. He saw the glimmer of steel. He
dived on it. His hands closed over the crosspiece and, with a
mighty heave, he drew it from the flesh of the tree. Friction,
a blockage, then a *clang* as it came free, still gleaming. The
faint glow of red radiated from it in the dark.

He hurried back to Aud, holding the sword in front of
him.

"I have never seen you bear anything but hunting weapons," she said.

"I am a desperate man," he replied, sliding it into his belt. "Where is the thread? Do the colors still shine?"

She held out his dark cloak, flipping up the lower corner for him to see. "I have sewn it into your cloak so that you don't lose it. You see, the light of possibility is still in it. I fear if you do battle with Heimdall, it will turn black and neither you nor your mortal lover will be around to talk of your love."

"I'm not going to Heimdall. Not yet. I'm going to Jotunheim."

"Jotunheim? Now?"

"I have no time to explain. I will not be your master before this night is over, but I ask for one last service from you. Wait at the top of the ridge with Arvak." He pointed up the wide, steep stairs. "I will return before first light and I need him to be rested for the journey to Valaskjálf."

"You'll never make it in time," she said, then seemed to realize that her pessimism was unwelcome. "I'm sorry, Vidar. I will take Arvak up to the ridge immediately, and we will wait there for you until your return."

Vidar pulled on his cloak, the feeling of invisibility a familiar one. Desperation lit his muscles and spine, and he began to run, to bleed into the darkness, on a frantic journey to the outlands.

Aud led Arvak up the steep stairs in the moonlight, then encouraged him to lie down in the long grass to wait for his master. She sat next to him, her back resting against his as he drew the deep regular breaths of sleep. She shrank under her cloak against the cold and gazed out at the high branches of the World Tree and beyond it to the plains that marked the border of Vanaheim.

Vidar would lose his love, of that she was sure. It was her fault, and he would find that out. Somebody would tell him: Loki, Odin, perhaps even Aud herself. So she retained no hope that he would come to love her once Victoria was lost. She worked on shutting down that part of her heart; there was no future for her and Vidar. Whatever happened on this night, she would need a new place to live. It would probably be Loki's house.

Beyond the flat grasslands lay still fjords and gentle hills. If she closed her eyes, she could imagine the long reeds at the water's edge moving quietly under the impetus of the breeze, the moonlight's silver glow, and grey shadows shifting over empty spaces. Somewhere, her son was sleeping, warm and curled around himself, lashes long on his cheek. The starlight that saturated her skin also glimmered above the house where he lay, and for an instant Aud felt a jolt of connectedness to him, as though sharing the same sky was equivalent to holding him. The instant passed and she dared not open her eyes for seeing how alone she was in the world.

Arvak's rhythmic breathing and warm hide soothed her tired body and brain, and she fell at length into a light doze. The sound of hooves approaching from the east roused her, and she stood to see the shape of horse and rider emerging from the dark.

Loki.

"I thought I might find you here," he said, drawing to a halt beside her.

"How?"

"I waited at Gammaldal for hours. Then I guessed that if you and Vidar were somewhere together, your guilt must have persuaded you to take him to the Norns. Is that where he is now?"

"I won't tell you another thing."

"I'm right, aren't I?" he said, dismounting and setting Heror to wander. "You hated yourself for telling Odin and had to make it all better."

"I didn't tell Odin!" she shouted. "You did."

"I was just the messenger," he said, hand over his heart.

"You have ruined everything for Vidar. Odin has closed Bifrost and gone after the woman."

Loki's face twisted into a sneer and he threw his hands apart expansively. "What do I care? What do I care for a mortal woman or for Vidar's heart? I care no more for them than I would care for a worm I see eaten by a bird. Life isn't fair, Aud. Why should Vidar be the one who gets the better of it?"

Aud trembled in front of him, hearing sense in his words but unable to reconcile what she had done. "I hate that it's my fault!" she cried. "He's so unhappy."

Loki shrugged.

She slid to the ground again. "He will despise me. I have to leave Gammaldal."

"Are you asking me to take you in?"

She looked up at him, steeling herself for what she must do. "I can't go back to Valaskjálf. Vidar says he has other relatives in the north."

"Come to me, Aud. I'll take care of you—until I get bored with you, which will happen very quickly if you continue pining for Vidar."

Aud shook her head. "I won't pine for him. I have yearned for too many things that aren't mine to possess. I

will live out my sentence in acceptance and submission if
you take me in."

Loki crouched next to her and touched her hair. His voice
was cruel. "Acceptance and submission will suit you, Aud,"
he said. Then his voice grew tender. "The moonlight suits
you too." He stood and gazed down into the valley. "I'd better go and see those hags before the night is over. I expect
you've warned them."

"No," she said, "but they were very angry about my
bringing Vidar. They'll be on the move before long."

He whistled for his horse. "Heror," he said, patting the
horse's nose, "you head home without me. I'll come back on
foot."

Aud watched as Heror galloped off into the distance. She
turned to see Loki looking at her.

"You're not going to stop me?" he said.

"No. I doubt that I could. What will you ask them for?"

He rubbed his chin. "Hmm, I'm not certain. I haven't had
long enough to think of a good favor, and now I'm so
rushed, I hope I don't do something rash." He laughed, then
pushed Aud with his toe. "Where have you hidden your
sense of humor?"

"I don't care what you ask them for," she said, leaning
her head against Arvak. She meant it; what happened next
hardly mattered.

"You should," he said, turning away from her and moving toward the stairs.

"What do you mean?" she asked, but he didn't answer
and she was left to wonder and to wait for Vidar throughout
the long night.

*   *   *

The sprint across the valley made his legs ache, the water of the bay was freezing, the swim gouged his lungs and made his shoulders burn, but Vidar did not slow. He called on every drop of his giant's blood to give him the strength to continue. The big muscles in his thighs begged him to pause when he climbed out of the water, but instead he pushed himself up the slope and started running again. The cloak woven from Heimdall's cloth was dark around his shoulders. From time to time he would pull up the corner to check that the rainbow colors still glowed in the thread of fate. On each occasion, the fear that he would see it turn black urged him on, as fast as he could go.

The cloak disguised him from the predators in the woods, and he turned off the track toward the marshy ground where Jarnvidja made her home. Given he was already dripping and cold from the long swim, the boggy ground didn't bother him. Sedge scratched at his legs and the moon reflected in puddles and gullies of water. He sniffed the air. Smoke from the west. He pushed on. Cold and tired and lungs bursting and despair in his heart, he pushed on.

Jarnvidja's home beckoned in the distance. A wolf howled, sending a shiver up his spine. He paused a moment to catch his breath, ankle deep in a pool of muddy water. He advanced more slowly, gathering his thoughts, allowing his muscles to restore themselves. The hilt of his sword waited beneath his frightened fingers. His hand closed over it and drew: lighter than he remembered. The house was made of mud, the roof of turf, behind it a mudbrick enclosure. The smell of animals was strong and hot in his nostrils. His blood thundered past his ears as he threw back the cloak and pushed open the door.

A round, hunched woman blinked up at him from the

fire. One of her eyes was greatly smaller than the other, milky and half-lidded. A filthy scarf covered her hair. She lifted her nose and sniffed the air, an expression of contempt crossing her mouth. "Aesir," she said.

He raised the point of his sword and pressed it against her chin. "I won't hurt you if you give me what I want," he said urgently.

"What do you want?" she asked, her eyes narrowing to slits.

"First, I want you to call your wolves and pen them where they can't hurt me."

"And after that?"

"I will tell you in my own time," he said, dropping the point of the sword and pulling her to her feet. "Now hurry."

Despite her appearance of age and feebleness, she moved quickly and easily, and Vidar told himself to be wary. He stood at her shoulder, sword at the ready, as she lit a lantern at the door of the house. She opened her mouth and howled, a long series of notes and yelps. Her voice echoed out over the fens and touched the trees in the distance. Dark shadows began to slink toward them.

"Come," she said to him, "I'll take them to the enclosure."

One by one the wolves came, and she spoke to them in a strange, guttural half language of words and dog sounds. The lamplight reflected in puddles. The wolves eyed him suspiciously, but followed her orders as she ushered them into the pen. When the last was through she moved to drop the bolt.

"Wait," he said, "which one is Mánagarm?"

Jarnvidja turned her face to him and growled low in her throat. "Who told you of Mánagarm?"

Vidar touched the point of his sword to the soft flesh at her side. "Bring her out." Jarnvidja emitted another strange noise and one of the wolves split off from the pack and came toward her. She was grey and black, hunched in the shoulders, with a long, heavy tail. She looked no more dangerous than the others, but Vidar kept his distance anyway.

"Bring her inside and chain her," Vidar said, stepping back. "I'll instruct you what to do next."

Jarnvidja shot the bolt and guided Mánagarm ahead of them into the house. By the firelight, she fetched a chain and chained the animal by her back leg to a carved pillar. Mánagarm seemed too placid to be the fearsome wolf his mother had told him about and Vidar grew suspicious.

"Is this really the mighty Mánagarm?" Vidar asked.

"It is."

"With teeth and claws deadly to Aesir?"

"Yes. Because Aesir are pitiless scum and are less trouble when dead."

Vidar didn't respond to her insult. "She looks no different from the others."

"Look a little closer, Vidar. First, the others are all female. This one is my *son*."

Vidar allowed himself a little smile for not spotting the obvious difference. "I see."

"Second, if you give me an object that belongs to your family, I will show you what my son is capable of."

Vidar reached into his pack and found the carving he'd packed as a present for Victoria. He flung it to the dirt floor at Jarnvidja's feet. "Go on."

She spoke to the wolf, who lifted a paw and brought it down on the object. One of his claws scratched the wood lightly, and the carving suddenly blew into pieces. Vidar ducked as a flying splinter flew past his face.

"So you see," Jarnvidja said, "that Mánagarm is indeed mighty against Aesir, though I expect you now wish to kill him."

"No, you misunderstand me. I mean no greater harm. I only want one of his teeth."

Jarnvidja grew pale. "No, no," she said, shaking her head. "We cannot anger him so."

"That is why he's chained."

Her voice became plaintive. "Then let me go to the fens and gather herbs for a sleeping medicine. We can't pull his tooth while he is conscious."

"There isn't time," he said. "You are his mother. He will allow you to do it." Vidar lifted the sword again, pointed it at her heart. "You cannot refuse, troll-wife."

She locked eyes with him in the dim room, while the wolf waited at her feet. "So I cannot," she said at last, "but I must warn you that anger makes him grow."

Vidar tasted a hint of unease. He dropped his voice. "I need one tooth, then I will leave you and your wolves alone forever."

"He doesn't look different from the girls, but they eat chickens and he eats anger."

"Just the tooth, Jarnvidja."

"I give him a little every day, tell him stories about your father and brothers, even some about you. He thrives on it, it keeps him alive. But too much anger and—"

"Enough!" Vidar cried. He was tired, and brutally aware that the night was slipping away. "I don't care if he's ten feet tall tomorrow, for I leave this place tonight. Get me a tooth, and wrap it safely in something of yours, and I will leave you be."

Jarnvidja crouched forward, speaking in a low, comforting voice to the wolf. She pulled a ribbon from her apron and encouraged the wolf to open his mouth. Vidar kept his sword steady on her back. The wolf snarled, the snarl grew into a yelp, into a howl. Vidar took a step back. A splatter of blood hit the floor and Jarnvidja fell backward, holding the tooth aloft.

Vidar could hear nothing over the hideous howling. The animal snapped its jaws and shook its head right and left. Mánagarm tilted back his head and Vidar could see the bloody gap where the tooth had been. His jaws opened wide, his body shuddered and, easy as taking a breath, he swelled, becoming three inches taller in seconds. A fierce yellow light crept into his eyes and he shook at his chain angrily. Outside, the other wolves had started to bark and howl.

Vidar was so amazed by this sight that his notice was momentarily diverted from Jarnvidja. Movement from the corner of his eye jolted him back to attention. Too late he saw that she clutched the bloody tooth in her hand, ready to strike him with it. A white-hot urgency gripped him. Without a moment's shadow to think, he brought up his sword and thrust it between her ribs.

A gasp. His or hers, he did not know.

He pulled the sword out, was horrified by the slide and the friction, once so familiar to him. Blood began to flow. She dropped the tooth and clutched the wound. Mánagarm's growling abruptly stopped.

"Fool," she wheezed. "You set in motion your family's fate."

She fell to the ground with a thump, dead.

Vidar turned. Mánagarm stared at Jarnvidja, looking for all the world like the son she had claimed him for, bewildered at his mother's death. He turned his eyes to Vidar and howled.

Vidar untied the scarf from Jarnvidja's head. She was almost bald beneath but for some wispy white hairs. Using the scarf, he carefully picked up the tooth and wrapped it, then tied it into the corner of his cloak. The howling intensified. He glanced over his shoulder to see that the monster was growing again. Jarnvidja's words echoed in his head and a cold sense of dread overcame him.

He turned and ran, leaving Mánagarm to strain against the metal cuff, which would pinch him and make him angrier, make him larger, and pinch him all the more. No energy could be expended thinking about the future, nor about the vow to himself he had broken. There was only the energy to run, on and on into the night, racing the sunrise.

He hit the water in the dark, swam until his muscles felt they would explode, pushing himself as fast as he could go. He refused to look up, as though the sky would stay dark as long as he wasn't watching it, but when he dragged himself to shore, the deeper shades were giving way to blue in the distant east.

"It's not morning," he called to the indifferent sky, stumbling forward and falling to his knees in hopelessness, as the first beam of orange sun hit the shadowy branches of the World Tree.

Thirty-Three

A ud waited for him at the top of the three hundred and
thirty-three stairs. He collapsed on the grass and stared
up at the dawn sky.

"I didn't make it," he said, hopeless and despondent.

"The night will come again," she said, fetching him the
water flask. "Do you have what you need to force Heimdall
to open the bridge?"

Vidar sat up and took a long draught of the water. "I do,
but I fear Victoria may not still be alive by evening." He
struggled to his feet. "I must go to Valaskjálf and wait near
Bifrost. The moment that the sun falls behind the world
I'll—"

Aud's hand was on his shoulder. "Don't be a fool. You
need to rest. You can do nothing during daylight, so return
with me to Gammaldal. Eat, sleep and prepare yourself."

"I won't sleep, Aud," he said, "not while there's a chance
this thread will turn black when my eyes aren't upon it."

"Well, eat and prepare yourself." She whistled for Arvak,
who was sniffing in the grass a few yards away. "You told

me that Victoria is locked behind metal and stone. She will
be safe until tonight. You look as if you might drop dead if
you don't rest."

Vidar felt fatigue seep into every muscle and bone. "Yes,
yes, I must rest," he conceded, "and I must think about how
to use this new weapon. You will help me, Aud?"

"Of course," she said. "Now come. Back to Gammaldal."

He lay, almost catatonic, by the fire for two hours, while
Aud made him a meal, found him fresh clothes and hung his
cloak to dry. Every ten minutes or so, he would ask her to
check if the thread were still colored, which it was. Each
time, he took comfort that Victoria was still safe, but ago-
nized over the fear and bewilderment she must be feeling.

"Something went wrong," he said to Aud as she sat across
from him and broke the bread. "Odin found out."

Aud didn't meet his gaze. "It matters little where he
found out. Now that he knows, we have to deal with it."

"You didn't tell anyone, did you, Aud?"

She shook her head and handed him a cup of wine. "I said
nothing."

Vidar swallowed the wine dispiritedly, thinking about the
previous night in the woods of Jotunheim. How easy it had
been to pick up a weapon and kill. How natural. As though
it were in his blood.

"I despise myself," he said, slumping forward.

"Why, Vidar?"

"I killed the troll-wife."

A half instant of silence alerted him to Aud's surprise.
"You did what you had to do," she said evenly.

"I swore I'd never kill again. After last time."

"It's true, then?" she asked. "That you killed Odin's servants out of spite?"

He put his face in his hands. "Not spite. I killed them because they were there in front of me, Aud. That is the person I used to be."

A long silence drew out between them and the fire crackled in the quiet room.

"But you are different now," she said softly.

Vidar looked up. Her dark eyes were fixed on his, patient and tender.

"I thought I was," he said. "But last night—"

"You were desperate. You were mad with anxiety, and tiredness, and—"

"I killed her. It was instinctive, born into me." A shudder seized him. "I cannot escape my family."

"If you get to Midgard tonight, you can change all that."

"And if I don't? Let me ask you something, Aud. I killed Jarnvidja for a tooth from the wolf Mánagarm, poisonous only to Aesir. His anger made him grow and it will continue to do so. I left him chained up, there in the hut in the fens. The troll-wife said to me before she died that I had set in motion my family's fate. What do you think she meant?"

Aud considered for a few moments, her eyebrows drawn down.

"Vidar," she said. "What is the name of the wolf that the stories of men say will swallow Odin at Ragnarok? The one you are fated to save him from?"

"Fenrir," Vidar said.

"The fen-dweller," Aud said, nodding. "Then it's him?"

"Grown to monstrous size. He will lurk in the fens for thousands of years, then finally break his bonds and unleash the evil from Jotunheim."

"It's too far distant for you to consider," she said. "Think of the present, think of tonight." She came to crouch next to him and touched his cheek. "Don't despise yourself, Vidar. A man's character is not decided in one act, nor is it necessarily decided in his past. In each moment, you can be a good man, a kind man. You have been kind to me."

Vidar felt tears prick his eyes and quickly turned away from Aud. "Thank you, Aud," he said, forcing his voice to be smooth. "I have rested long enough and now I must be active again." He pulled himself to his feet, tested his aching muscles by taking his weight first on one leg, then the other. "I need to make a weapon that will turn Heimdall's blood to ice when he sees it." He handed her his cloak. "Aud, you are Vanir. I can't touch the tooth for fear of death. Could you unwrap it and help me to set it in the end of a spear?"

"Of course," Aud said warily, peeling back the scarf to reveal the tooth.

Vidar fetched his hunting spear. "We'll need to bind it tightly," he said, then a loud crack echoed around the room. The spear had broken. "What happened?" he said.

"As soon as the tooth touched it, it split," Aud said.

"Because it belongs to me," Vidar replied, nodding. "Of course."

"What will you do?"

"Go outside and cut a new branch."

"The trees are Asgard trees, they belong to the Aesir," she said. "The same thing will happen."

"Then what can I build a weapon from? I can't hold the tooth in my hand."

"My loom," Aud said, indicating where it stood in the corner. "It was made in Vanaheim. Take off the crossbeam. We can glue the tooth into the hollow at the end. It may not look like a fearsome weapon, but it will serve the purpose."

Under Vidar's instruction, Aud dismantled the loom and

set the tooth in the end of the crossbeam. It looked ridiculous, too short and thick for a spear, the tooth set off center and the glue congealed around the end, but there wasn't a more powerful weapon in Asgard at that moment, and the afternoon shadows were drawing long. The hope had started to beat in his heart again, the morning's despair evaporating into the cool sky.

"Will you come with me to Valaskjálf?" Vidar asked as he pulled on his shoes and cloak. "I might need your Vanir hands if the tooth comes loose, and you can bring Arvak home once I've gone."

She forced a smile. "Do you really need me?" she asked hopefully.

He stood straight and met her gaze. "Your company would help me, to steady my hands and remember my breath," he said softly, "and I would like a last fond memory of Asgard to take with me."

"Then I will come."

All the way to Valaskjálf, snuggled against Vidar's back on Arvak, Aud allowed herself one last sweet fantasy. He loved her and belonged in her arms, the late-afternoon sun and the waving fields of spring flowers blessed their union, and they were heading to the beach to make love on the warm sand. As the woods deepened and the shadows dimmed, reality was upon her once more and this time she bowed to it.

Vidar was going to Midgard to become mortal and love a woman named Victoria. Aud was to return to Loki and make the best of things with him, until he grew tired of her. After that? It didn't pay to think of it, but she was through with struggling against life and fate. Once Vidar was gone, she intended to turn her heart to stone until her exile in Asgard was over.

"We will wait here," Vidar said, pulling Arvak up.

The hump of Valaskjálf's back was just visible through the trees, the sea roared, and one of Bifrost's pillars caught the sun. Vidar dismounted and checked the corner of his cloak for the hundredth time. He helped Aud down and she sat on the forest floor. Low beams of sun shot through the trees, deepening, by contrast, the shadows that circled them. She watched as Vidar unpacked Arvak, his strong hands working and his shoulders moving against the material of his clothes. Then he leaned against the horse's neck and patted him vigorously.

"I will miss you, old friend," he whispered, and Aud had to look away. It seemed too vulnerable a moment to watch.

Vidar sat with her. He was pale, and his hands trembled.

"Are you frightened?" Aud asked.

"Yes, of course."

Aud glanced toward the pillar. The sun's stain was fading from it. "Will Heimdall come out? If the bridge is closed?"

"If not, I'll go in and get him."

The shadows drew longer; the night insects in the forest began to chirp. Aud's heart quickened. She had only minutes left. He stood, readying himself.

"Vidar," she said, swallowing hard. "I know your mind is on other things . . ."

He tilted his head to consider her. "What is it, Aud?"

"Is it hard to leave, Vidar? Is it hard to leave home, and immortality, and everything you have ever known?"

His eyes grew sad. "Yes. And no."

"I loved you, Vidar."

"I know. I am sorry."

Aud slid her arms around him. "Hold me, just one moment. It is all the comfort I will have for a thousand years."

He embraced her, and said, "I'm not equal to such a responsibility. You must try to find comfort in other places when I'm gone."

She stepped back, alone again, a solitary soul inhabiting a solitary body in an empty space far from home. "Farewell, my own, my true love," she said, and tears brimmed and ran down her face.

"Good-bye, Aud." He turned and pulled up the hood of his cloak, and melted into the shadows.

Heimdall sat with his back against the northern pillar, picking his teeth with a fingernail. Vidar watched him from the rim of the trees, then pulled the edge of his cloak to his lips and kissed the bright thread.

"Soon, Victoria," he said, gathering resolve. The fresh sea air was salty in his nostrils as he strode from the forest, and the water's draw and pull echoed off the cliffs and gusted up toward him. He was nearly upon Heimdall before he slipped out of his cloak and made his presence known.

Heimdall scrambled to his feet, surprised. "Vidar! Where did you come from?"

"Open Bifrost," Vidar said. The wind off the sea caught his cloak and sent it flapping behind him.

Heimdall laughed. "Certainly. Shall I carry you down to Midgard on my shoulders, too?"

"It isn't a joke."

"It should be. Odin ordered the bridge closed. You see his spear?" Heimdall indicated the spear, buried halfway into the ground at the exact midpoint between the pillars.

Vidar strode to the spear and drew it from the ground. He

snapped it over his knee and threw the pieces over the cliff. He turned and called, "Can you see how little I care for Odin's orders?"

Heimdall approached, still smiling through his beard. "It hardly matters what you think of Odin's orders, because only I can open the bridge."

"Open it and I will spare your life."

Heimdall pulled himself to his full height and puffed up his chest. "I kill giants, puppy. Now run along back to Gammaldal and live like a gelding until you can be of some use to your family."

"You are not my family," Vidar snarled. "I disavowed you long ago. I go to Midgard to be cut free from you all, finally, and I vow tonight that nothing will stop me. I will be with Victoria."

Heimdall shrugged. "If you wait long enough, Odin will be back with her head. Is that not enough to keep you warm at night? It's said that you wouldn't know how to use the other parts." He began to walk away and Vidar watched him for a few moments, summoning his bravado. Just past the northern pillar, Vidar grasped Heimdall's shoulder and turned him around.

"I possess the most powerful weapon in Asgard," Vidar declared over the roar of the ocean below, "and I will use it on you if you do not open the bridge."

Heimdall's eyebrows twitched momentarily, but soon the bluster had returned to his voice. "Is that right? Well, let me see this mighty weapon and the negotiations can continue."

Carefully, mindful not to let the tooth touch anything he owned, Vidar drew the crossbeam from his belt.

Heimdall doubled over with laughter. "The stories about

you are true, then! You have become more woman than man. You threaten me with a loom. Oh, I quake, I quiver!"

"You see what it does to the land of the Aesir," Vidar said, and he turned the rod so the tooth pointed downward and drove it hard into the ground.

A shudder moved underneath them, as though miles below the soil a mighty giant had awoken and stretched. Vidar saw Heimdall's shoulders hunch in fear. Where the tooth had entered the ground, a crack appeared and began to widen. As it did, a dreadful roar emerged from the fissure: Asgard crying in pain. The crack ran farther to the north and Vidar realized that his demonstration would have more serious consequences than he'd imagined. He jumped over the fissure to the stable side of the cliff, and Heimdall did the same. The scar opened and a huge chunk of the cliff face dropped and crumbled, sending rocks and dirt tumbling into the sea below.

When the dust had cleared and the roar had ceased, Vidar turned to Heimdall. He was still staring at the broken cliff face.

"Will you do as I say?" Vidar asked.

"What is that weapon?"

"Will you open the bridge?"

"Odin ordered it closed."

"I will kill you, Heimdall," Vidar said, and suddenly knew it wasn't an empty threat. The certainty turned his stomach over, dragged back the tide of self-hatred. If Victoria was murdered, his family would pay, all of them. Heimdall first, but then every other swine and whore in Valaskjálf, then he would wait by Bifrost for Odin to return and plunge the wolf's tooth deep into his father's heart.

Heimdall licked his lips. "If you kill me, I can't open the bridge and the woman is dead anyway."

"But at least I get to kill you."

Heimdall tried a smile. "Your eyes unnerve me, Vidar. Are you still sane?"

"Open it. Let me cross."

Heimdall hesitated a moment and Vidar raised the crossbeam.

"Yes, yes," Heimdall said, "but don't bring that weapon back into our world."

"Once I am gone, Heimdall, I will never return."

Heimdall strode to the northern pillar and touched it with his palm, then jogged to the southern pillar and did the same. A hum began to buzz on the air and a glimmer of rainbow light licked over the pillars before silence and darkness returned.

"It's open," Heimdall called, and his voice was nearly whipped away on the wind.

The sea roared below and the wind gusted over the cliff. Vidar collected his cloak and stepped up to the edge between the pillars, and gingerly put out his toe. Light flared beneath it. He turned. Heimdall stood, a still, white statue passive in the distance. Below him, his father waited. Victoria waited.

With a deep breath, he stepped onto the bridge of colored lights.

Aud did not want to wallow in memories and imaginings. She left Arvak outside the house at Gammaldal while she went inside to pack. She kicked over the fire and searched through her things. The loom was useless without a crossbeam; Loki would have to steal a new one for her. Clothes, a basket of dyed wool, her sewing box. She paused near the dying fire and saw a half-finished carving Vidar had been working on.

Her fingers reached for it without her brain's consent. She sat and gazed at it in the grey shadows as the room grew cold and dark and empty. Although she wanted very much to take it with her, she resisted. It was over. There was no energy left in her for yearning, only submission.

Aud placed the carving on the table and collected her thoughts. A few favorite pots and pans, and the rest she left for the dust and the years. Outside, she opened the gates to set the farm animals free, then she packed Arvak and climbed onto his back.

"Well, Arvak, we belong to Loki now," she said, urging him forward. "We must make the journey to whichever fate awaits us."

Arvak seemed to know which way to go.

Thirty-Four

[Midgard]

I screamed. Odin laughed and it turned into a snarl. He was easily six and a half feet tall, and as solid as a side of beef. His clothes were filthy and stank of alcohol, and his beard was overgrown and stained and unkempt. His arms were bare except for spiraling gold arm rings, jammed on so tight that the skin puffed out in the gaps. A round helmet was pushed down on his wild yellow hair; a metal piece rested on his nose between his eyes. One eye was pale blue and fixed on me, the other was an empty socket, which I instinctively avoided looking at. An axe and a club hung on a belt across his hips. His bared teeth were crooked and yellow, and spittle hung in his beard. He looked like a man who would eat babies, and all this registered on me in the split second it took him to reach for his axe. I struggled against him, but he shook me and I fell down. He towered over me and shouted.

"Kona, hvers vegna blótuthu fjölskyldu minni?"

"I don't know what you're saying," I replied, hands defensively over my head, wriggling backward.

"Tjádu thig fyrir mér áthr en thú deyr!" His voice was harsh and loud, and echoed and cracked in the frozen forest around me.

He raised the axe and I scrabbled away from the blow and pulled myself to my feet. His axe hit the tree behind me and he took a second to free the blade. I ran as fast as I could. My bare feet gripped the icy ground, giving me an advantage, because he slipped and had to steady himself before following me. I dived behind a row of bushes on his left and willed my heart and breath to be still. I could hear him approaching, but Skripi had said he couldn't see with that left eye. So I shrank back into the leaves and waited.

He drew into sight and I held my breath. He walked past me and ten feet farther up the path and I let my breath go again. He turned.

Now I wasn't on his left, I was on his right, and his good eye had discovered me. Strangely, I found that I couldn't move. Or didn't want to move . . . or . . . something. In studying his gaze, I had connected with the dark void under his helmet where his left eye should have been, and I was like a rabbit in headlights.

I thought I saw, within that black space, a swirling sickly light.

I thought I saw a great emptiness connected to the icy reaches of the universe.

I thought I saw the full weight of my own mortality, dragging me inexorably toward it.

The sound of branches cracking roused me. No, the sound had made Odin break his gaze and I was set free from its hold. I kept my head down and ran. I pelted through the trees, away from Odin, heading back toward the station, tripping, skidding, stumbling, but moving as fast as I could. Still he drew closer. I could hear his panting and smell his sweat and knew that I would run out of energy long before he would.

He had the edge of my anorak and then it slipped from his hand. He was big and clumsy, I was small and desperate.

I ran.

I burst through the trees and found myself in the clearing.

He dived and caught me around the feet, bringing me crashing to the ground. And so it was all going to happen again.

I kicked at him, got a little way from him, toward the anvil-shaped rock, but then realized I didn't want to go there, not again. It had already been painted with my blood. In my moment of hesitation he flipped me flat on my back, then sat on my ankles and raised his axe. I flung one hand out to try to struggle into a sitting position. My fingers brushed the head of a soil thermometer that Magnus had inserted into the ground. I yanked it from the earth and sat up, plunging it into Odin's empty socket.

He screamed and fell backward, dropping his axe. I didn't wait to see if he would get up. People do that in movies and end up dead. I got to my feet, snatched up the axe and kept running, wondering when my legs and lungs were going to give out. The clatter of metal on stone alerted me to the fact that he'd got the thermometer out of his eye. His screams and bellows echoed through the forest like the sounds of a monster being tortured. I almost didn't hear the other voice, faint and far away.

"Victoria!"

It was Vidar. "Here, here!" I called.

His voice was closer this time. "I'm coming, I'm coming."

"Quickly, Vidar." I stopped and looked around. Odin was nowhere in sight but I could hear footsteps all around me and didn't know to whom they belonged. So I stood perfectly still and hoped Vidar would get to me first.

Pounding feet, running through the trees. I raised the axe, knowing I was pitiably unable to wield it. If this was Odin, I was just going to have to stand there and take what was coming.

A shadow emerged from my left and I collapsed to my knees.

It was Vidar.

Vidar threw a cloak over us both and crouched on the ground next to me, his arms around me.

"Victoria," he gasped, covering my face in desperate kisses, "I've found you."

"He's right behind me."

"He can't find us under this cloak. Come with me, we'll find a safe place to hide where we can talk."

He helped me to my feet and I leaned on him heavily. The cloak was made of some weird dark material that seemed to bleed into the shadows of the forest; I almost couldn't see us. Vidar led me to the beach. The frost hadn't held on the sand and my feet sank into the fine grains gratefully. The wind was cold, but the sand was soft and Vidar laid me down and stretched out next to me, making sure the cloak covered us from view.

"He won't look for us out here," Vidar said. "He'll run around in the trees for a long time before he'll think of heading for open space."

"I thought I might never see you again."

"I thought the same."

Vidar's face was close to mine. I touched it lovingly. "What happened?"

"I'm not certain, but I'm here now, and I have something to show you." He wriggled so his left hand was loose and showed me his index finger. Around it, he had tied a piece of colored thread. It glowed gently in the dark.

"What is it?" I asked.

"It's our fate. I have to confront Odin to change it. One of my brothers will become my father's protector, and he won't care where I go or what I do."

"So we can be together?" I said, hope swelling in my heart.

"Yes. More than that, we can have children, and grow old together, and be buried next to each other. I'm going to become mortal."

On top of the fear and the fatigue, his words undid me and I began to sob. "No. It's too much."

He smiled; his dark eyes were so dear to me. "It's too late. That's the bargain I made. If I misuse this thread, I'm sentenced to a thousand years in servitude." He dropped his lips to my cheek. "You're stuck with me, Victoria. For life."

The tide surged in my chest. I brought my tears under control. "Why, Vidar? Why me?"

"Because the stars wished it to be so," he murmured against my skin.

He kissed me, his tongue gently touched mine, and I felt a shiver of longing and fear.

"Vidar, we have too much to lose," I said. "We're vulnerable."

His warm fingers were in my hair. "I'll protect you, Victoria. Whatever happens."

"So what do we do next?"

"I have to find Odin. Nothing can change until I have spoken to him."

I realized that his voice no longer sounded confident. "You don't want to speak to him, do you?"

He tried to smile, but failed. "Victoria, would you think me less of a man if I told you I'm afraid of my father?"

I gazed at him a moment and realized that he was anxious about my answer.

"Of course not," I said. "He's a monster."

This time he did smile, though only weakly. "Let's not waste another moment," he said. "You stay by me. We'll find him together."

Vidar's fingers were like a vise holding my hand as we made our way back through the trees.

"Don't leave my side," he said. "He'll want to get you away from me. Stay by me."

"I will," I said, checking that Odin's axe was tucked firmly into the waistband of my jeans.

"He'll be angry. He'll shout and wave his club about. Don't be afraid."

"I won't."

He caught his breath. "Can you hear that?"

I strained my ears. "No."

"Somebody coming toward us."

"Odin?"

"Not heavy enough."

I looked around, thought I could make out a light approaching between the trees. A moment later, Gunnar appeared, wielding a kerosene lamp and his fake Viking sword.

"Gunnar!" I gasped.

"Victoria! You're safe!"

Vidar stepped forward. "Nobody is safe. Odin walks the forest. You must return to your metal box."

Gunnar's expression was one of utter bewilderment. "Who?"

"Gunnar, you have to go back to Kirkja. Right away. There's nothing you can do here."

He was looking Vidar up and down, registering the details of his dress. "What's going on?"

"Go, Gunnar. I'll explain it all in the morning, I promise you."

Footsteps in the undergrowth.

"Go!" Vidar hissed. "Go now."

Gunnar turned and Odin hulked out of the trees at the same moment. Vidar shouted something in his own language, but Odin raised his club and ran at Gunnar.

Gunnar dropped his sword and lamp and started to run. Vidar took off after him. I snatched up the lamp and followed in his wake. Branches whipped me and the cold bit my feet. Moments before, I'd been certain about what would happen next. Now chaos had been reintroduced. The light bobbed ahead of me. I kept my eyes on Vidar's back and ran as fast as I could. Still he drew away from me, and I had to redouble my efforts not to lose sight of him.

Up ahead somebody cried out in pain. Gunnar. I wanted to scream. The trees thinned. We were approaching the lake. I burst from the trees to see Gunnar's body lying twisted and insensible over a rock near the edge of the water. Odin stood over him with his club raised. Vidar, suddenly aware that he had created too big a gap between us, was coming back up the slope for me. Gunnar was easy prey.

I didn't think, I just pulled the axe and threw it. It

bounced off a branch and landed on the forest floor, at least ten feet from Odin.

He turned and snarled at me. Vidar stepped between us.

Odin began to bellow, not words, just a horrible insensible shouting that echoed around the forest. The lake was covered in wide shards of ice, and cracks appeared in them as Odin's shout went on and on.

I couldn't leave Gunnar lying there. What if he was dying? I slipped out from behind Vidar and ran down the slope to him. Vidar saw me, moved to cover me, putting himself once again between his father and me. The shouting went on, just as Vidar had predicted. It was a terrifying noise, but I tried to block it out. I set the lamp on the ground next to Gunnar and felt for a pulse at his throat. He was still alive. I pulled the rune off my neck and wrapped it around his wrist. Despite Skripi's lack of faith, I had to believe the rune might be some protection for him.

Odin's shouting had turned into words now, more of that strange guttural language they spoke. Vidar tried to reply but Odin roared over the top of him. I glanced over my shoulder. Vidar, dark-haired and gentle-voiced, smaller than his father yet bravely holding his ground. Odin, wild and fair-haired, shouting him down over and over again. Vidar raised his hand. I saw the gleaming colors of the thread.

Odin howled. Then abruptly stopped.

The thread still glowed. What had caused his silence?

I noticed he was gazing over my shoulder. And smiling.

Vidar turned. Called out, "Victoria!"

Seaweed and pale fingers around my waist. I screamed. The draugr threw me in the lake. Ice-cold. My breath stopped. I tried to call for Vidar, but sour freezing water rushed into my mouth. A confused set of images: weeds and eyes and the lamplight watery in the quiet lake. I pushed upward, away from the draugr's clutching hands. I hit ice. I tried again. More ice. I was trapped. My lungs grew solid.

That's all I remember.

A wide, black gap exists in my memory at that point, as if I lost myself for a short time, but then light and sound and life rushed back on me, and I opened my eyes somewhere very bright and very warm.

"I've done this before," I said, and noticed that my throat wasn't sore, as it had been the first time I had been under with the draugr.

I was in bed in my cabin. Carsten was nearby, and Gunnar too.

"She's conscious."

"Where's Vidar?" I asked.

"Victoria, you've had an accident. What can you remember?"

"Where's Vidar?" I asked again, growing desperate. I sat up and tried to throw off the bedspread. "What's going on?"

"Rest, Victoria," Carsten said.

"I don't want to rest. I'm fine."

"You shouldn't be," he huffed. "You should be brain-dead. You were under the ice for four minutes."

"She's perfectly well," Gunnar said. "I told you."

"Stop talking about me like I'm not here!" I shouted. "Where is Vidar?"

Gunnar said a quiet word to Carsten, who nodded and left. I waited, horrified at the possibilities. It was daylight outside.

"Vidar's gone, Vicky. I'm sorry."

I couldn't make sense of what Gunnar meant by gone.

"Is he coming back? What did he say?"

Gunnar shook his head. He had a graze on his forehead. "He's not coming back."

"How do you know?"

"He spoke to me before he left. You have to let me tell you what happened."

I slumped back on the bed. "How can he be gone?"

"You were dying, Victoria. He did something . . . I don't understand all of it."

I began to cry, suspecting what had happened. "Just tell me."

"The draugr took you under the ice. I came to. I saw you go under. Vidar dived in, couldn't find you. The big fellow . . . Odin?"

"That's his name."

"He was laughing. They were speaking Old Norse . . . I couldn't make it all out. But I think he said, 'She's dead by now. It's over.' Vidar dragged you out of the water and you were blue." Gunnar glanced away, a puzzled expression on his brow.

"Go on."

"That's when the thing came out of the water."

"The draugr?"

"Maybe I imagined it. I'd had a blow to the head."

"What did it look like?"

"Just like the stories say. A bloated man-monster, covered in weed. He was crawling along the ground like one of those lungfish." Gunnar tried to imitate the movement with his hand. "He was coming for me. There was an axe on the ground, and I picked it up and . . ." He looked up and smiled weakly. "This is all crazy."

"I know."

"I remembered that you're supposed to cut off a draugr's head. I flailed out, his head came clean off. Then it wasn't a draugr at all, just a pile of pondweed and you still lay dying in Vidar's lap, not breathing, pulse growing weaker.

"Odin left, he shouted some insults at all of us. Vidar was bent over you, trying to breathe life back into you. He was getting more and more frantic, calling your name. And then . . . I don't really understand what happened. He held up his hand and said something in his own language. Something about you, and about living and old age. There was a flash of color on his hand, and then it dimmed. You breathed. He laid you down in the mud and buried his face in his hands and cried."

I felt my heart drop into my stomach.

"He gave me this." Gunnar felt in his pocket and pulled out an animal's tooth. I took it from him. "He said to use it if Odin came back, that he had to go and that you'd understand why. He said to tell you to get away from the island and that he loved you forever."

I stared at Gunnar. Vidar had used his one chance to change fate to keep me alive. And that meant that we weren't going to be together after all. A wave of despair and yearning crashed over me. It also meant he had to serve the punishment.

A thousand years.

"I'll be dead before he can come back," I said.

"Vicky, I don't understand. Who were those people?"

"You know. You've read about them."

He stood up and ran his hands through his hair. "It's my fault, isn't it? If I'd never turned up, like an idiot . . ."

I looked at him. He was right. In a sense.

"Can you forgive me, Victoria?"

Or was it really Gunnar's fault? Or my fault for not warning him what was really going on? Or Vidar's fault for wanting too much, as those in love always do? Or Magnus's fault for bringing me to the island in the first place?

I saw the blame vanish backward into a long chain of cause and effect. Events that had seemed so casual, decisions I had made so carelessly, had actually been carving my future in stone. It seemed searingly important that I make the right decision in that moment.

"Victoria?"

"I can forgive you, Gunnar," I said, "if you'll take me to the other side of the world with you."

Thirty-Five

[Asgard]

As Vidar approached Gammaldal, two black shadows in the night sky circled him. Hugin and Munin, his father's ravens. Odin would never again let Vidar out of his sight; once was an accident but twice was a pattern, and Odin was afraid of his own fate. Vidar picked up a stone and cast it into the sky. It clipped one of the birds on the wingtip, but neither of them slowed.

Bad enough to see Heimdall's smug face at his return to Bifrost. Or to hear the taunts of his assembled brothers who had come down from Valaskjálf on Odin's urging. How he despised them. If the Norns went through with it, made him spend a thousand years in the company of his family's enemies, it would not be such a bad thing.

His blood was hot and his brain was hotter. He had to find Aud, make her take him back to the Norns. He could not accept this fate. To be apart from Victoria after all he had suffered . . . it was impossible. The Norns would have to be forced to fix things. He would do the service in Vanaheim, even if he had to do it as an old man once Victoria was gone. They had to let him go back to Midgard and be with her. Watching her breathe again, on the shore of the lake, had been an agony. He couldn't stay to kiss her lips and tell her he loved her, for fear that the Norns would take back their favor if he lingered too long.

The house waited in the dark. No smell of smoke rose. He pushed open the door. The room was in darkness, the fire had been kicked over. Aud was gone.

A moment of emptiness shivered over him. Alone.

Then a shadow moved in the dark. A woman, cloaked in black, emerged from an alcove between pillars. She pushed back her cowl.

Vidar peered into the dark. "Verda?" he asked.

"Skuld," she corrected him. "You made your deal with me."

"Why are you here?"

"My sisters felt we hadn't been clear enough in our negotiations. None of us expected you to return to Asgard."

"Things went badly for me." Vidar dropped to his knees and touched the hem of her skirt. "I beg you to give me another chance. You see, I've kept the thread." He held out his hand, the black thread still tied around his finger.

"There will be no other chances, Vidar," Skuld said, drawing a deep breath. The darkness moved over her face eerily. Vidar sat back on the floor. "My sisters and I have moved our residence, much deeper inside the World Tree, and we don't intend to make any more bargains with anyone. Least of all you." She crouched in front of him and tilted his chin upward so he had to meet her gaze. "I am very disappointed. We gave you great power and you misused it."

"She was dying."

"You will pay the price."

Vidar dropped his head and let the hopelessness claim him. "She is lost to me, then?"

"A second time. Have you wondered, Vidar, whether you are not meant to be together?"

"I know we are. I feel it like . . ." He wanted to say the Midgard word "electricity," but found no counterpart in his own tongue. "Clearer than lightning, hotter than the sun."

Skuld rose and sat on a bench. "Sit with me, Vidar."

He did as she asked. His joints felt stiff and his heart felt tired.

"You made a bargain with us, Vidar," she said. "If you don't adhere to the terms of the deal, I have to take back what I've done. Victoria will die."

He set his teeth. "I know. I'll take the punishment."

"How do you feel about the punishment?" she said, and a cruel smile touched her lips.

"I do not relish being a servant to the Vanir, but I hope to find some pity and good work to fill my time."

She laughed. "You're not going to Vanaheim," she said. "What made you think that?"

Vidar was puzzled, hopeful even. "What do you mean? I believed I would receive the same punishment as Aud—service to my family's enemies."

"Yes, the same punishment as Aud," Skuld said. "A thousand years of service to the Aesir."

His blood turned to ice. "What?"

"Surely you knew you'd be drawn back to them eventually?" She stood and pulled the cowl back over her head. "Pack your things, Vidar," she said. "You leave immediately for Valaskjálf."

Aud stirred and wondered why she was awake. The sun wasn't up, she was warm. She turned over.

Loki was not in bed next to her. Outside she heard the whinny of a horse.

She closed her eyes and tried to slip back into sleep, but curiosity kept her awake. What was he doing outside with the horses? Especially Arvak, who was hers to keep.

She pulled a blanket around her and cracked open the door.

"Good, you're awake," he said. "We have to leave soon." He was tightening Arvak's saddle, and leading a rope between him and Heror.

"Leave? Where are we going?" She fought the disappointment. If half a warm night in Loki's bed was all she was destined to receive, then she would take it gratefully and ask no further questions.

"I'm taking you somewhere. Somewhere you've never traveled to before."

"Why?"

"Because it's time. You can't stay here with me, I like living alone."

"But where am I going?"

He turned to her, wringing his hands and fluttering his eyelashes. "Where am I going?" he mocked. "What will happen to me?" He gave her a push. "Go on, inside. Get dressed. Timing is everything."

Aud dutifully returned to the house and pulled on warm clothes. Each time her mind turned to worrying thoughts and protests, she shut it down. How many years, she wondered, until that shutting-down became a natural reflex? How many before it became irreversible? Loki knew she had to stay in service to the Aesir, so she was either heading north to the cousins Vidar had mentioned past Idavíd, or east to Valaskjálf.

"I'm ready," she said, emerging from the house.

"Come here," he said, dragging her toward him and pulling out a scarf. "I must tie this over your eyes."

"Why?"

"Because I am your master," he said, tightening the knot. It caught a strand of her hair, but she didn't cry out.

He kissed her lips gently. "You are in the dark now, Aud. You must trust me. Let me help you onto Arvak's back."

Blindfolded, she found her way into the saddle and leaned forward to clutch Arvak's mane. "May all the stars have pity on us," she said to him quietly, and he whickered in response.

Loki made an urgent noise and they were away, galloping toward an unknown location.

As the hours passed, and Aud grew more adept at shutting down the unhappy part of her mind and its endless protests, Loki sang her songs and told her bawdy stories, although she didn't smile or laugh. She clutched Arvak for life and comfort, and wondered how much longer she would be blind to the world around her.

The sun came up. She felt the warm glow and saw through the blindfold that the light had changed. Definitely not heading east, the sun was behind her. Which meant they were heading west, and now she was completely confused because they had been riding for hours and . . .

"Loki," she gasped, gripped by panic, "don't tell me you've led me to Vanaheim."

"And what if I had?" he said.

"I'm not allowed back here. The old fate will be restored and Helgi will die."

"I couldn't let that happen," he said, adopting the mocking voice again. "Now sit still. I told you, we're going somewhere you've never traveled to before."

Accept, accept. She drew a deep breath and relaxed in the saddle. Time passed. At length, they drew to a halt and she heard Loki dismount and approach.

"Are you ready?" he said.

"I am," she replied.

He helped her down and unpicked the knot in the scarf. "Look, Aud. See where we are?"

The blindfold fell away from her eyes and she was standing in the apple orchard near her home in Vanaheim. Her heart filled with air.

"No, no, Loki!" she cried.

"Shush, girl. Listen," he said sternly, "those hags owed me, you remember. I told you I'd bring you somewhere you'd never traveled to before."

When she turned puzzled eyes to him, he leaned close and said, "Aud, it's the past."

"The . . . ?"

And then she heard it. In the distance. Helgi crying because he'd woken up alone.

The sound she made echoed loudly in her ears: a gasp, a sob, a whimper.

"Go, then," Loki said. "I'll untie Arvak. You see, I'm not so bad, am I?"

But she barely heard him, because she was running, running so hard that her knees shuddered under her weight and her blood sizzled with heat and longing. She burst into the house and there he was, three years old, huddled by the bed.

"Helgi, my darling Helgi," she cried, and the alarm and surprise in her voice made him cry harder. She clung to him and he soaked her shoulder in tears and the world stuck in her throat.

"Mama, Mama," he said, "you were gone for so long."

"I know, my darling," she replied, pressing him tight against her, "but I'll never be so foolish again."

Thirty-Six

[Midgard]

Wellington is right at the bottom of the north island of New Zealand. It's beautiful here in late summer, and it's a long, long way from Othinsey, from Bifrost, and from Odin himself. A long way from Vidar, too, I know. But I'm a practical girl—in the last life, in this one, and in any more to come.

Gunnar pulled every string he could to get me a job here. In the end, all the Meteorological Service could offer me was sixteen hours a week hosing out the hydrogen chamber and mopping up the storeroom. I'd prefer to be busier. The empty hours get inside me, hollow me out. Gunnar keeps me occupied: if he's not making jokes about how ridiculous I look in waterproof overalls, he's leaving his clothes and books all over the little flat we share, for me to pick up.

But we're not lovers. Gunnar would like it very much if we were, and I am so very fond of him. But I've known a love infinitely greater, a love potent enough to eat the sun. I know that that love is gone and cannot return for a thousand years. I know a thousand years is longer than I can imagine, that it takes me beyond the horrors of old age and death and decay and the wide nothing after it. I know all this, and yet I save my heart.

I often dream of Vidar, when I'm burrowed down in sleep. We're together, his hands on my hands, on my body. His eyes are dark and serious, and he says to me that he will be mine forever. No matter what happens, he will make certain that we are together, and that I'm not to be afraid of death, or silence, or his father. That he'll find me and bring me back to him. I die a little when I wake, and lie there a long time, empty and nauseous, and wonder if it's just a dream. Then I rise and check in the little box under my bed: a wolf's tooth, a rune, two wooden carvings and a shard of a thousand-year-old axe blade. Proof that impossible things happen.

Why shouldn't impossible things happen, after all? We travel through our weary lives with an illusion of secure places and choices, because to acknowledge otherwise would make living unbearable. But the elements are still in play, all the time, a collection of glowing rainbow colors that fall into black precisely when we don't expect them to. There was a time, not so long ago, when I thought I could explain everything. Yet it never occurred to me that I couldn't explain even the basics. Life, love, fate.

What I do know are these things. Love is mighty. Souls, once they touch, always save an imprint of one another. The sun rises and sets on my world and on his.

I wait and I hope. Foolish hope. It's all I can do.

Epilogue

[Seven Years Later]

Vidar's fingers worked expertly, fitting the gate into the lintel. He ignored the occasional snarl of Odin's dogs; they were annoyed to be tied up so long while Vidar mended the gate. It was dusk, and they were keen to be free, to be hunting in the woods. Vidar took his time, testing the latch and adjusting the hinge. Hoofbeats from the edge of the forest barely registered. Visitors were always coming and going from Valaskjálf. Such visits had little to do with Vidar, who had spent the last seven years in service to his family. The drunken fools had barely noticed the signs that Vidar had noticed: a dark cloud gathering in the west, the distant howling echoes that traveled on the wind, the boiling seas and the long, harsh winters. A thousand years might yet pass before the long twilight that signaled the end, but it was coming. Without doubt, it was coming.

Vidar stood back, realizing that the hoofbeats had not thundered down the path to the stables. He looked around. A chestnut stallion. Two hooded figures on his back, one adult and one child.

He peered into the semidark. "Arvak?"

Vidar dropped his tools and began toward the hem of the forest, where the two riders sat motionless. The dogs began to howl, realizing that their freedom was still suspended. Vidar checked around him nervously. Nobody watching. In the shadow of a mighty spruce, he stopped and reached a hand for the horse's nose.

"Dear old friend," he said, surprised to find himself so choked on emotion. He had thought his heart hardened to stone.

The first rider pushed back her hood. It was Aud, her body ripened by womanhood and happiness, with the elaborate tattoos around her eyebrows that indicated her full initiation into the Vanir magic. She was a seidhr princess now, the most powerful of her family.

"Vidar," she said slowly, smiling. She turned to the boy behind her. "This is my son, Helgi." She glanced around, nervous. "Join us in the woods. I would talk to you without the eyes or ears of Valaskjálf to witness."

Vidar followed her into the trees, puzzled. Night deepened overhead, and the shadows in the forest pooled to black. She dismounted at a small clearing overgrown with tiny saplings. Vidar sat on a flat rock while she helped Helgi down. His hood fell back to reveal a solemn-faced blond boy, who stood protectively close to his mother.

"How did you find each other?" Vidar asked.

Aud shook loose her long, dark hair. "Fate, it seems, is not so immutable as I had thought."

A barb of pain to his heart. Fate had treated him cruelly.

"I'll be quick, Vidar, because I know that your family will miss you if I keep you too long. You are well?"

"As well as I could be. Given my situation."

"Good. Good." She smiled, and an unaccountable glint of excitement came to her eye. "These last seven years, I have thought of you every day. Not because I love you. Those feelings have long since grown cold. I have thought of you, because I played a part in the awful mess . . ." She trailed off and wouldn't meet his eye. "I have borne a burden of guilt. All my magic, all my hard work in seidhr training, has tended toward one thing."

Vidar waited, expectant, puzzled. In the distance, the dogs barked on.

"Rescuing you, Vidar."

He shook his head. "I can't be rescued. I'm bound by fate."

"Listen now. Have you seen your brother Thor in the last few days?"

"No. He went riding. Hunting, I think."

"I know where he is." She smiled again, as though she could barely keep inside some delicious secret. "He's with the Norns."

His confusion made him unaccountably irritated. "Aud?"

She grasped his hand in her cool fingers. "Urd loved Thor. I always remember her speaking of him, so fondly, so tenderly. Seven years ago, the Norns hid themselves from me. I knew if I wanted to deal with them, I had to have the right bait. Two days past, I put Thor under an enchantment—he thinks he loves Urd—and I set him to wander in the World Tree, following him secretly." She giggled. "You should have heard him: drunken love songs echoed through the roots for days. Finally, Urd caught him. And when she did, I caught her."

Vidar's heart was starting to speed.

"I made a deal, that if she would grant me one change of

fate, I would leave Thor under the enchantment for as long as it would last. If she refused, I would remove the enchantment immediately. By that stage, he had taken her spindly hand and was pressing his lips into it fervently. She agreed."

"What fate have you changed?" he asked, trying to still his blood, which pounded so fast past his ears that he couldn't hear the sounds of the twilit forest around him.

"You know, Vidar. We tried it once before." She reached into her cloak and pulled out a length of colored thread. Stepping forward, she began to wind it around his wrist.

He stared at it, hot with anticipation.

"You will be a man, Vidar. The moment you step onto Bifrost. You will be mortal, you will grow old, you will die. Your fate has gone to Vali. By the time Odin notices you're gone, the new destinies will be in place and he'll remember you only as the son who disappointed him greatly, who he is proud not to miss." She tied a knot in the thread. "But the enchantment on Thor will not last forever. My magic is not yet that strong. I hope, for your sake, that it may last a mortal lifetime. But you must live your life with Victoria, knowing that it could all end at any moment." She patted his wrist and her dark eyes met his. "And in that lesson, lies the real truth about being mortal."

Vidar felt tears prick his eyes. That morning, there had only been the crushing weight of fate upon him. Now, a path had been opened, unexpectedly, sweetly.

Aud handed him Arvak's reins. "I wish you luck, Vidar. She is a long way from Odin's Island. But you found her once before, in the depths of Niflheim. I'm sure you will find her again."

Vidar finally regained his ability to speak. "I haven't words to thank you, Aud."

"There is no need for them, Vidar. I treated you badly. This is restitution." She turned to her son. "Helgi, as we discussed?"

Helgi nodded and Aud tousled the boy's hair. "My son, it seems, has enough elvish magic from his father's side to make us quite an unstoppable pair. Give us five minutes to go ahead and distract Heimdall. Then go, and don't look back."

They raised their hoods and scampered off. Vidar's hands trembled as he adjusted Arvak's stirrups. He realized he was panicking; if Heimdall would not let him pass, this new promise would be broken. He didn't know if his tired heart could endure that again.

Vidar mounted Arvak, leaning forward to pat his neck. "I'm glad to have you with me, old friend." He turned the horse toward Bifrost.

Thundering down the path, he saw the tall pillars. At the north pillar, two hooded figures stood next to a statue. No, it wasn't a statue, it was Heimdall, frozen. Aud gestured that he should move, and quickly.

"Go, Arvak. Forward."

The ground shuddered beneath him, the colors on the thread around his wrist glowed. The air seemed to tremble around him, the sweet weight of mortality pressing itself into his immortal flesh. The cliffs edge loomed ahead, the night sky opened.

With a flash of hot colors, the ground dropped away and the stars exploded at Arvak's hooves. The thread turned black, and Vidar was on his journey.

About the Author

Kim Wilkins was born in London and grew up at the seaside in Queensland. She has degrees in English Literature and Creative Writing, and has won four Aurealis awards for fantasy and horror. Her books are also published in the UK, U.S., and Europe. Kim lives in Brisbane with her partner, her son, and two spoiled black cats.

You can write to her at mail@kimwilkins.com, or find more information at www.kimwilkins.com.

More
Kim Wilkins!

Please turn the page
for a preview of

The Autumn Castle

now available

from Warner Books.

*P*lease don't make me remember, please don't make me remember. Inevitable, however. Christine had known from the moment the man had glanced at her business card, his eyebrows shooting up.

"Starlight. That's an unusual surname."

"Mm-hm."

"You're not any relation to Alfa and Finn Starlight? The seventies pop stars?"

Pop stars! Her parents had considered themselves musicians, poets, artists. "Yeah, I'm their daughter." Amazingly, her voice came out smooth, almost casual. She didn't need this today; she was already feeling unaccountably melancholy.

"Oh. Oh, I'm so . . ."

"Sorry?"

"Yes. Yes, I'm very sorry."

Because he knew, as most people did, that Alfa and Finn Starlight had died in a horrific car accident from which their teenage daughter had been the only survivor. Suddenly there was no point in resisting anymore: she was back there. The English Bookshop on Ludwigkirchplatz, its long shelves and neat carpet squares, spun down to nothing in her perception; it was all blood and metal and ground glass and every horror that those evil, stubborn thirty-five seconds of consciousness had forced her to witness.

"I'm sorry too," she said. Her lower back twinged in sympathy with the remembrance. She wouldn't meet the man's gaze, trying to discourage him. He was pale and clean-shaven, had a South African accent, and was clearly battling with his impulses. On the one hand, he was aware it was rude—maybe even distressing for her—to keep asking about the accident; on the other hand, he was talking with a real-life survivor of a famous and tragic legend. Christine was used to this four seconds of struggle: enthusiasm versus compassion. Compassion never won.

"When was that again? 1988?" he asked.

"1989," Christine replied. "November."

"Yes, of course. My sister cried for days. She'd always had a crush on Finn."

"I think a lot of women did."

"He was a good-looking man, and your mother was beautiful too."

Christine smiled in spite of herself, wondering if the man was now pondering how such stunning parents had managed to produce such an ordinary-looking child.

"One thing I've always wanted to know," he said, leaning forward.

Christine braced herself. Why couldn't she ever tell these people to leave her alone? Why had she never developed that self-preserving streak of aggression that would shut down his questions, lock up her memories. "Yes?"

"You were in a coma for eight weeks after the accident."

"Yes."

"The kid who ran you off the road didn't stop."

"No."

"And there were no witnesses."

"That's right."

"Then how did they find him and convict him?"

Yes, her back was definitely twinging now, a horrid legacy of the accident, the reason November 1989 was never really consigned to the past, to that cold night and that long tunnel. Her doctor back home would tell her that these twinges were psychosomatic, triggered by the memory. She had no idea what the word for "psychosomatic" was in German, and the doctor she had seen twice since her arrival in Berlin two months ago was happy to prescribe painkillers without too much strained bilingual conversation.

"I was conscious for about half a minute directly after the accident," she explained. "The kid who hit us stopped a second, then took off. I got his license plate, I wrote it on the dash."

"Really?" He was excited now, privy to some new juicy fact about the thirteen-year-old story. Many details had been withheld from the press because the driver of the other car was a juvenile. The law had protected him from the barrage of media scrutiny, while Christine had suffered the full weight of the world's glare.

"I'm surprised you could collect yourself to find a pen, under the circumstances," he continued. "It must have been traumatic."

Oh, yes. Her father crushed to death; her mother decapitated. Christine smiled a tight smile; time to finish this conversation. "If you phone at the end of the week, we should be able to give you an estimated due date for that book. It's a rare import, so it could take a number of months."

He hesitated. Clearly, he had a lot of other questions. Chief among them might be why the heir to the Starlight fortune was working as a shop assistant in an English-language bookshop in Berlin.

"All right, then," the man said. "I'll see you when I come to pick it up."

Christine nodded, silently vowing to make sure she was out back checking invoices when he returned.

He headed for the door, his footsteps light and carefree, and not weighed down with thirteen years of chronic pain, thirteen years of nightmares about tunnels and blood, thirteen years of resigned suffering. A brittle anger rose on her lips.

"By the way," she called.

He turned.

"I didn't have a pen," she said.

"Pardon?"

Had he forgotten already? Was that how much her misery meant to anybody else? "In the car, after the accident," she said. "You were right, I was too traumatized to find a pen."

His face took on a puzzled aspect. "Then how . . . ?"

Christine held up her right index finger. "My mother's blood," she said. "Have a nice day."

— from the Memoirs of Mandy Z.

Once upon a time, a Miraculous Child was born. That night was the last of April—Walpurgis Night—on the summit of the Brocken in the Harz Mountains. It has long been thought that the devil holds court on the Brocken on such a night, but I am not a devil (for that Miraculous Child, dear reader, was me); I am the only son of the thirteenth generation of a special family. In the dim, distant past, my ancestors bred with faeries, bringing our family line infinite good fortune, but making a terrible mess of our gene pool.

My name is Immanuel Zweigler, but I am known as Mandy Z. I am an artist, renowned; I am wealthy beyond your wildest dreams, and always have been, for my family has money in obscure bank accounts in sinister places the world over. I am color-blind, truly color-blind. I see only black and white and gray, but if you wore a particularly vibrant color, perhaps a little of its warmth would seep into my field of vision and be rendered the palest sepia. But I have an extraordinary sense of smell, and an extraordinary sense of touch. That is why I like to sculpt.

You may wonder why someone so miraculous has waited until the age of forty-eight to commence his memoir. Simply, it had never occurred to me to do so, but then the British journalist came to interview me. He was a genial man. We had a good conversation and then I left him with the view from my west windows while I went upstairs to fetch a photograph— I always insist on providing my own photographs to be published with interviews. I was rummaging in the drawer of my desk in my sculpture room, a room I prefer to keep private, when I heard the British journalist clear his throat behind me.

"You should not have followed me in here," I said.

"This is extraordinary," he replied, advancing toward my latest sculpture.

Ah, the beautiful thing, so white and gleaming with gorgeous curves and ghastly crevices.

"It's called the Bone Wife," I told him as he ran his fingers over her hips (she only exists below the waist at present). I was amused because he didn't know what he was touching.

"Are you going to finish her?" he asked, gesturing to where her face would be.

"Oh yes. Though some would say she is the perfect woman just as she is."

He didn't laugh at my joke. "What medium are you using?"

"Bones."

His fingers jumped off as though scalded. "Not human bones?"

I smiled and shook my head. "Of course not."

So he returned to his examination, confident that these were the bones of unfortunate sheep and pigs, and then I gave him his photos and asked him to leave. I sat for a long time looking at my Bone Wife, and mused about my continued disappointment in how I am represented by the world's media, and about how so much of what I do can never be made public. I wanted to read about a version of myself that I recognized, even if I had to write it with my own pen; and that's when I decided upon a memoir. I decided to celebrate me. Miraculous me.

Not human bones?

No. The thought is as repulsive to me as it was to the British journalist. As is the thought of animal bones; I bear no grudge against our four-legged companions. Not human bones, not animal bones. A rarer medium: faery bones. The bones of faeries I have killed.

Because, you see, I have a measureless loathing for faeries. And I am the Faery Hunter.